BLOOD, MUD AND CORPSES

A ROYAL ZOMBIE CORPS STORY

C. M. HARALD

HARVEY & HARVEY PUBLISHING LTD

INVITATION TO MAILING LIST

*J*OIN THE *C M Harald mailing list and download a free copy of the Royal Zombie Corps prequel, 'On Discovering A Zombie', the collected letters of Dr Oliver Hudson. Find out what happens in the 1980s story 'Point Zero'.*

See the back of this book for details of how to subscribe.

CONTENTS

PART 1 - BLOOD, MUD & CORPSES

1

CONSCRIPTION

"The war was not going well for the Allies. The Somme was a disaster. Casualty rates were horrific for both sides; one advancing into a hail of machine gun bullets, the other crushed under the weight of artillery. The Battle of Arras was meant to be the turning point in the war. Stories, rumours even, of strange events existed. Stories circulated among us Tommies, of a phantom battalion battering through a hail of machine gun fire, falling upon the Germans with unheard of rage. They called them tigers."

Oliver Gill. Captain in the 1st Battalion, Somerset Light Infantry. Interviewed post-war for an unpublished research paper on the Battle of Arras, 1917.

"Without the timely intervention of novel forms of warfare, the conflict would have been drawn out and become costlier in lives. The extensive contributions of the new branches of the military, most notably, the Royal Tank Corps, the Royal Air Force, and the Royal Zombie Corps, made a significant impact on the duration of the war and contributed to the successful conclusion of the endeavour."

British Government White Paper on the post-war re-organisation of the Armed Forces, July 1919.

'STAND TO ATTENTION!' SPITTLE flew from the barked order, missing Alfie Marsh as he further straightened his already rigid body. His adjustment was better, but still did not satisfy the drill instructor. It did not matter how hard Alfie tried. The new uniform was a size too big and even if it fit, Alfie would still have appeared scruffy wearing it. He had always possessed this unique talent.

Corporal Simpson walked around the recruit, singling Marsh out from the rest of the squad for that particular, personal attention that only a drill instructor could give. This was nothing new. It had happened a dozen times since Alfie arrived a week ago, the only recruit on the receiving end.

'Boots are disgusting,' the corporal snapped, scuffing the marred surface with his heel. 'I should be able to see my face in them.' It did not matter how many hours Alfie spent polishing the boots, he could not achieve the same mirrored surface as his companions. On the one occasion he was successful, the shiny shoes were then splashed in a muddy puddle as he exited the barrack block.

'Shoulders back, chest out,' the corporal snarled. Alfie braced even further in response to the command before the corporal addressed the wider squad. 'Useless, all of you. You're meant to terrify Kaiser Bill, not make him die of laughter.'

After a range of insults, the drill session continued. Hours were spent marching around the parade ground in perfect order; dressing left and dressing right; forming fours and about turning. More than once, their errors brought the complaint of 'Bloody conscripts' from the instructor.

With a resigned air, the recruits counted off the minutes until a quarter past four, watching the clock on the north side of the parade ground. Week after week of drill, spit and polish lay behind them, an unchanging routine designed to instil discipline and uniformity while increasing stamina. At least they got better at the drills, turning from civilians into soldiers, even if Corporal Simpson would not acknowledge the progress.

Not one of them had volunteered for military service. They were the first wave of conscripts to be called up after January 1916, introducing compulsory military service. Britain was running short of soldiers, much of the regular army destroyed in the brutal battles of 1914 and 1915, with the rest being brought back to Britain to train replacements, or scattered across the volunteer army now in the field to provide the patriotic enthusiasts with some experience. The volunteer army answered General Kitchener's, and Britain's, call in 1914 and early 1915 with great enthusiasm. These patriotic men, rushed through training, had been in combat for the last year.

'Bloody Army,' Joshua Wells muttered when he thought the corporal was out of earshot. 'Should have volunteered for the Navy when I 'ad the chance.'

'Rum, bum and concertina, eh?' Alfie quipped back the old saying about the Royal Navy, teasing his companion.

'Silence in the ranks!' The corporal bellowed.

Unlike his brother James, Alfie Marsh did not volunteer when the war began. His brother was now fighting somewhere in Belgium. James Marsh was among those who joined in the period after the declaration of war when enthusiastic young men rushed to sign on for a quick and glorious battle. With many friends, they rushed to Canterbury to join up; training together and now serving alongside each other in the 12th (Eastern) Division. While the 'Pals' battalions were popular, the conscripts Alfie now joined alongside were from mixed areas, ensuring no one community would have to shoulder too many casualties from the conflict. Widespread rumours suggested whole towns were losing their young men as Kitchener's Army full of 'Pals' battalions took to the field.

The drill ended on time. The recruits were dismissed, and except for those assigned to fatigue or work parties, they could spend their time polishing their boots and preparing their kit for inspection the next morning. A subdued air emanated from them as they wandered off to their evening of preparation. The work may differ from the exercise of the day, but it was still tiring and tedious.

Marsh found himself assigned to fatigues again. He had lost track of the reason, as he spent most of his spare time receiving one punishment or another. Perhaps his bed was not correctly made or his frugal possessions not stowed away; maybe it was because of a drill mistake, or because the crease on his trousers was not correct? His instructors took glee in pointing out his many failures as a soldier. On this occasion, the punishment was laps of the parade ground carrying a full sandbag on his shoulders. The sand got everywhere, stinking of extinguished cigarette butts. Alfie knew that after this punishment, it would take him hours to clean his kit, but it would have to be ready for the morning.

After a few weeks of drill, the training changed, becoming more interesting for the recruits. By this point, Alfie could almost match the expectations about his appearance and kit, with much help from Joshua Wells. Wells was a slight young man, the same age as Alfie, from London. A more capable recruit, Wells had taken Alfie under his wing, alongside smuggling extra cigarettes to the rest of the squad. These cigarettes were sourced from the central stores and then sold on for more than the going rate. Plenty of men were ready to pay the higher price, as the weekly tobacco ration, while generous, was not enough for some. Wells would also acquire small quantities of contraband alcohol, but carefully, not allowing his fellow trainees to get drunk.

Finally, the recruits got away from the parade ground, with a few field exercises on the agenda. The first night exercise was a disaster, with Wells preventing Marsh from wandering off on his own while the squad paused for a break on their march. Alfie disappeared into the woods to relieve himself, but became disoriented in the dark and fell into a drainage ditch. Wells had tracked down his shouts for help and brought him back to the road. They both received a long dressing down from the instructor, who added an extra two miles to the route as a punishment. This sanction did not go down well with the rest of the squad, and for the next few days, Marsh experienced unexplained tampering with his kit just before inspection; always something different, such as a muddy handprint on his sheet or a scuff on a boot. After a while, the punishments from the squad eased off as Marsh rose to the challenge, improving his soldiering. However, he was never good enough for the instructors.

'Run towards Fritz, stick it in 'im, twist, thrust again and pull it out,' barked the instructor, his voice projecting across the assembled ranks while he walked up and down. 'Direction, strength and quickness, all while you is overexcited. It is no walk in the park. This here bayonet,' he said, holding up the rifle with bayonet attached to the end, 'gives you a reach of five feet. Aim it at Fritz's throat, and when you see an opportunity, lunge forward with it.' He mimed the action for the trainees.

'Now Fritz is going to do everything in 'is power to stop you skewering him with this here toothpick. You may have to make a feint to get him to open up.' Again, the movement was demonstrated. 'Or you may need to knock his weapon out of the way if he is hiding behind it.' There followed another mime.

'Now this is life and death for you lads; be quick and use your wits. But, mark my words, your assault will fail if the surrounding men do not know how to use their bayonets. So we practise, and we will practise a lot.' The ranks moaned as they became aware they would be drilled through the many actions without mercy until each was second nature.

'Davies. Why would you use a feint?' The instructor asked, breaking up the moans.

'To get him to open up so I can stab him, Sergeant,' Davies said. The tall trainee stood at the front right of the rank.

'Correct, boy,' the instructor said. He chuckled with good humour. 'Now we are going to start off with a few short dashes, and then I'll give you lot some lethal weapons to play with.'

'But Sarge,' Davies complained, 'When are we going to learn to shoot?'

'The enemy is hiding in great big 'oles in the ground. Shooting will do nothing to him, boy. It is only by chasing them out of them damn 'oles that we'll win this war.' The rest of the recruits breathed easy. They had been expecting an outburst from the Sergeant. Despite all the spit and polish, and 'silence in the ranks', they discovered questions were the encouraged method for learning bayonet drill, a clear contrast to all their other training so far. The sergeant explained how the British Army valued the use of the bayonet. With a thorough understanding of its usage, the weapon would be lethal, something simple rote learning of a few positions from an authorised instruction manual could not achieve.

The bayonet drill proceeded with a startling efficiency over the following days. Each session was brief and engaging, with the steps explained and practised. The training made an excellent contrast to the physical exercise and dull drill which filled the rest of their time. Bayonet practice grew in popularity as the recruits showed their passion and initiative by making attacks on the straw-filled sacks. At first, Alfie was disturbed that the targets were stuffed with the wood from broken up crates to simulate the resistance of bone, but he soon appreciated this as much as the other trainees.

'Stab it you great lazy bastard, don't tickle it!' the sergeant shouted at Davies, who held back when thrusting the blade-tipped rifle at a sack.

'I am, Sarge,' Davies snarled, hitting the sack so hard straw and pieces of wood fell from the hole he tore in the stomach area.

'Your turn, Marsh,' the sergeant pushed Alfie forward.

Marsh ran yelling at the sack; his rifle thrust out at the imagined enemy throat. As he got close, he stabbed at the throat, thrusting and withdrawing, just as he had practiced.

'Not bad, Marsh,' the sergeant said prematurely. The bayonet stuck in a piece of wood. Marsh tugged, but the blade did not come out.

'Put some muscle into it!' the instructor shouted. However, as he struggled, Marsh could not release the bayonet, despite twisting the rifle one way and the other.

'Want some help, Alfie?' Wells laughed, as Marsh tried raising a foot to the sack so he could get more leverage.

'Give it to me,' the sergeant snatched the rifle out of Marsh's hands. With little effort, he pulled the bayonet free. 'Practice lad, that's all it takes.'

'Can't march, can't keep his kit clean, can't stab the enemy. What use is he?' a voice from the back of the squad called to widespread laughter.

'He'll be our bullet shield. There's no other point to him,' Taff Morgan said. Occasionally the short Welshman helped Alfie with his kit, and at other times ridiculed him. Morgan had never publicly criticised him before, but the comment represented the growing view of the group of trainees.

A week after the incident with the lodged bayonet, the recruits visited the rifle range for the first time. Alongside the river estuary, the site was desolate and windy. Low clouds threatened rain. As trainees, they already knew the basics of maintaining and cleaning their Lee Enfield rifles. Using training rifles, they could strip, clean and reassemble, as well as load, with their eyes closed. Marsh found the most challenging part was loading the ammunition onto the clips used to insert the rounds through the breech and into the magazine. Each round overlapped the base of the previous cartridge, alternating above and below, otherwise they would jam in the magazine when the bolt cycled them into the breech, a situation no soldier wished to deal with while in combat. While using the dummy rounds, he had jammed his training rifle several times, and on one occasion he had forced the rounds into the magazine with such strength he broke the spring, another lethal problem in battle.

Laying on the worn grass of the range, he worked the bolt with speed and confidence, aiming downrange, firing. He was not up to the speed and accuracy of the pre-war regular soldier, but he could see the target had a close grouping of rounds. On either side of him, his peers grew in confidence. Marsh again worked the bolt. It jammed solid, refusing to shift backwards or forwards. Marsh knew, yet again, he must have lined the rounds up incorrectly on the clip. He raised his hand to summon help. Over walked Corporal Simpson.

'What have you bloody well done this time, Marshy? You is bloody useless.' The firing on either side slackened as everyone stopped to listen. They all knew Marsh was going to receive another dressing down for his latest failure as a soldier, and Corporal Simpson would be delighted to deliver it.

'My gun's jammed, Corporal.'

'Gun!' The entire range heard the corporal shout, 'It ain't a bloody gun! That's what the Navy has on their great big bloody ships. Guns! This is a rifle, and you will treat it with respect!'

Marsh ignored the anger, holding up the butt of the rifle so the corporal could take the weapon without risk. With rough efficiency, Simpson went about working the bolt free, ejecting the jammed round.

'Here, make sure you load the bloody thing correctly next time,' Simpson said, handing the rifle back, all the time the barrel was pointing downrange.

'Thanks, corporal,' Marsh said under his breath.

Marsh received extra duties, this time stripping and reassembling his rifle. At least this punishment might make him a better soldier, unlike some fatigues he had been detailed to in the past.

Wells sat alongside him on a trestle bench, sharing the same punishment. Being a poor shot, he had also experienced the corporal's ire.

'Let me help you with that,' Joshua said, taking the clip and showing Alfie how to load the rounds the correct way. He patiently helped, not for the first time.

'Do you think we'll do alright when we go out there?' Alfie asked, showing the fear which penetrated to the depths of his soul. Everyone around him seemed so sure of themselves.

'We should do fine, why not?' Joshua replied, smiling as he did so.

'It's just we don't seem to be much use. You can't shoot, and I can't do anything without some corporal tearing me to rags.' Alfie cycled the bolt a few times, ejecting the cartridges without a jam.

'Kaiser Bill doesn't have an army of corporals, thank God. He just has lads like us, just as fucked up, I should think.'

'So you reckon we'll be fine when we go into action?' Alfie asked, stopping after loading a clip into his rifle.

'That's the point of all this training, isn't it? They get us to where we can function, even when everything around us is going to hell.' Joshua waggled a fresh clip of practice ammunition to emphasise his point. He then closed his eyes, picked up an empty clip and fed the rounds into it, demonstrating the second nature of the skill. Alfie chuckled as Joshua's hand roamed the table, grasping for a cartridge which had escaped him in his blindness.

'Weapons drill is one thing, but if my life is going to depend on highly polished boots, I'm stuffed.'

'We'll get by, and I'm sure the mud will soon see off any problems with your boots.'

Towards the end of their training, in late July, an unexpected letter arrived. The training platoon had just completed a night exercise when the mail call brought Marsh a message from his family. Both his parents and older brother communicated with him in this way, but this reply was far quicker than expected. While some trainees in the platoon did not receive regular post, shorn from their families and previous lives, Alfie was not among them.

He sat back on his bunk, opening the envelope, anticipating the latest news from home. The envelope had been written by his mother. Alfie experienced a moment of concern as his brother was deployed on the Western Front, and rumours were spreading about the new offensive on the Somme and vast numbers of casualties. The newspapers had been obtuse about these losses, a worrying sign. Recent arrivals at the training camp had brought news of a flood of telegrams in their communities, announcing the missing and the dead. Training was sped up, and the entire squad suspected a growing need for urgent replacements.

'Dearest son,' his mother opened. 'It is with great sadness that I write to inform you of the death of your brother, James.'

Alfie's eyes welled up; the worst had happened. He paused before reading on. He did not know how much time passed before he looked at the letter again. The familiarity of his mother's handwriting provided no comfort. His brother had died a hero, not on the Somme, but during an attack in Belgium during the early part of July. His mother wrote of a letter received from his commanding officer. James had been taking part in an assault. Unharmed during the attack, showing great bravery, he had gone back out into no man's land to rescue a wounded friend. He had been killed by a sniper, cleanly and without suffering. His commanding officer was recommending him for a medal.

Alfie could not take it in. Re-reading the letter several times, the words struggled to penetrate his reality. His ever-present big brother James, whom Alfie had idolised as a child, was no more, dead in a muddy field. No more would he be able to play football with him, fight over the slightest thing, or receive his excellent counsel.

'What's up, Alfie?' Taff Morgan asked, having noticed Marsh had been pondering the letter for a long time.

'My brother, he's dead. Belgium,' Alfie spat the sparse words, words which meant something tangible now he had said them aloud.

'Bugger!' Taff spat, leaving his own letters to sit at the end of Marsh's bunk.

'They're putting him forward for a medal. A sniper got him.'

'Damn.'

Alfie crumpled, and the tears began. He did not reveal how his mother was reminded him the family hopes were now carried by him. His family expected him to go out and take revenge against the evil Fritz.

It might not be the done thing, but Taff still knew how to respond as Marsh broke down. He held him through the worst of it.

The next morning was a grey one for Alfie, despite the sunshine. All his thoughts were of his deceased brother. As the platoon drilled, Alfie let his mind wander over the example his brother had set for him. James had been good at everything, not in a way which left Alfie jealous, but in a quietly competent way. Alfie knew James proved the model soldier, reaching the highest standards while passing through training in his 'Pals' battalion. Every step, James had been the perfect soldier, nothing like the misfit his younger brother was proving to be.

Even months into training, Alfie still failed to fit the mould of the regimented soldier, well presented, competent in all his tasks. How could he live up to the expectations of his family when he could not even meet the basic expectations of his country? How would he achieve revenge upon an enemy which resisted the best the British Empire could throw at it? Alfie worried he would let his mates down, putting them at risk, knowing he would struggle to survive the maelstrom. He would fail to avenge his brother and fail his family.

'Marsh! You're out of step!' Corporal Simpson shouted in a voice which echoed back from the buildings surrounding the parade ground.

Alfie checked his step, falling back in time with the rest of the squad. His mind restarted the loop which had been playing all morning.

At lunch, after drill, Alfie sat with Joshua Wells. He knew the regimented exercise gave him too much time to think. He picked at his food. The canteen had made a stew with dubious meat, followed up with spotted dick pudding. One good thing about training was the generous food. You could go up for more if you were still hungry. You did not care about the origin of the meat in the stew; hunger being the best sauce. For some recruits, this was the first time their bellies had been full. They had been hungry as civilians despite the successful health reforms of David Lloyd George and the Liberal Governments in the lead up to the war. They were in better condition than the two in five British recruits unfit for service before the Boer War. The government had examined the health of the working man, finding general ill health was caused by poverty. The Liberals had set about creating a massive program of health insurance for workers, free health care for children, and a program to replace unsanitary housing.

'I had no expectations from my family. Well, there was an expectation I would fit in,' Wells said, having just demolished his dessert. 'My parents escaped the pogroms in Russia and came to England, so they wanted me to grow up to become a good Englishman, but other than that, there were no expectations. I suppose it was because anything that happened to me was going to be better than what happened to them as Russian Jews.'

'My family didn't have any expectations for me either,' Marsh replied. Being a middle child, his older brother James had all the family expectations placed upon him, such as taking on the family trade, continuing the family name, and striking out into the world. Alfie had been expected to do well, but was never the focus of family attention, receiving the cast-off clothes while coming second in attention and support from his parents.

'I trade this and that, finding things that were hard to find. You know what I mean? A bit of a fixer of issues,' Joshua explained. 'You have to use your wits to survive in the poorer parts of London.'

'Well, you always seem to have a stash of chocolate and cigarettes.'

'It pays to get to know the quartermaster, especially if you can help him out from time to time. You wouldn't believe how easy it is for things to disappear from the stores,' Wells boasted. 'Even the quartermaster is at it.'

'That's got to be the only way you can manage the roaring trade you do,' Alfie said, smiling to show he meant no ill. Plenty of people would make a big deal out of it, some who would go as far as linking Wells' skills to his heritage.

'Well, if you ever need anything, you know whom to ask. My career path is why I didn't volunteer for this war; I had a good scam going with this well-off widow. Between the two of us, we was well off.'

'So, do you have anything that's going to help us survive this war, then?' Alfie asked, 'What do you have that can help us with that? I'm a useless soldier, but I want to do my family proud.'

'Nothing much. We just keep working hard, doing the best we can, making sure we duck at the right time. I've not got any magic tricks up my sleeve.'

'But I've been doing the best I can, and I'm still useless.' The despair again threatened to overwhelm him.

'I'll help you with what I can. After all, I've been helping you with your kit for ages and the others will help, especially Taff and Davies. If we all stick together, we'll increase our chances of surviving this war.'

'I suppose so. Watch each other's backs and look out for each other.'

'Well, that's how it works in the rougher parts of London, so I don't see why it'd be much different in the Army. Oh, and one other excellent piece of advice, never volunteer for anything. That's the sort of behaviour that'll get you killed,' Wells said, grinning.

'I thought volunteering would be the best chance for me to prove myself, though.'

'No, it's the best way for you to end up as worm food. Brave soldiers do not get to grow old, you know,' Wells explained. With how the war was progressing, he suspected no soldiers would survive long enough to grow old.

That night, Alfie lay in bed, unable to sleep, mulling over his worries. His body was hardening because of all the exercise. He no longer fell straight asleep each evening, exhausted by the training. He thought over the expectations thrust upon him by the weight of the letters received from his family. In their patriotic fervour, they expected him to make the family proud by his brave exploits upon the battlefield. His parents may have had in mind some patriotic and heroic endeavour such as those circulated by the London Illustrated News in which the chiselled hero would overwhelm the inferior Hun, rescuing helpless Belgian civilians, pure jingoistic propaganda.

Yet, Alfie knew his extra family responsibilities were far greater than a simple vendetta against the enemy. The good name of his family mattered, but there was more than that. He would now be expected to continue the family line, something Alfie had not considered. He would be expected to marry and produce children. The thought of children of his own, and the responsibility such fragile young lives would bring, was not something he considered compatible with war. For Alfie, marriage had been a consideration, especially with some girls he had spent time with before being conscripted, but it would be foolish to set about creating a family during a war, when he would be away at the frontline for months on end. The point was moot, anyway. He was not inclined to marry at present, and knew no woman he would wish to partner with. The whole idea of family was something he would place to one side until the end of the war, assuming he survived.

The worst issue forcing its way into his thoughts was the absence of his brother, James. They had been great friends, James always looking out for his brother, rescuing him from fist-fights that had gone wrong. Alfie may not be the best soldier in the world, but he held his own in a scrap. While he had been on the receiving end of a few beatings, they had toughened him up. Alfie had been proud when James had volunteered for the Army. He had joined among the first wave of recruits, responding to the patriotic call of General Kitchener. James had joined with many from the community, enough to create a Pals battalion recruited from among their neighbours. Although Alfie had been old enough to join, he had held back, believing the risking of one son more than enough to maintain the family reputation.

Several reasons existed for Alfie's failure to be taken in by the patriotic fervour that had washed over the country in August 1914. He knew there was more to the war than a simplistic clash of heroic Allies against the militaristic Prussians who had invaded defenceless Belgium. Alfie knew about the traditional tactics employed by armies of all nations and wondered how they would stand up to the vicious new weapons of the twentieth century. He had no desire to take part in this experiment. The machine gun was already causing havoc with the neat rows of soldiers all the nations insisted on fielding. The French were still not even using camouflage colours. At least Britain had dealt with that issue during the Khaki Election, another response to the failures of the Boer War. Artillery also put him off volunteering. The War Office had dragged its heels, eventually issuing large numbers of helmets to protect heads from shrapnel. Alfie knew the one he now possessed might be a lifesaver. If only they had been handed out at the start of the war, when troops entered combat with cloth caps. Soft caps had proved an even greater disadvantage when the warfare descended below the surface of the ground, into the trenches, where head wounds occurred with greater frequency.

The enormous casualties of 1914 and early 1915 did not surprise Alfie, and justified his avoidance of the Army. The recent casualties now being reported from the Somme were no great surprise. At this rate, the nation would burn through its manpower, chewed up by modern industrialised warfare.

Alfie opened the footlocker at the bottom of his bed and took out the cloth and polish. He peered at his boots. They seemed fine to him, but he knew they would not pass inspection in the morning. He needed to survive modern warfare, and the army had him cleaning his boots with spit and polish. He placed the cloth and polish on the floor and lay back on his bed.

Despite his disapproval of an ill-planned war, Alfie had still completed work beneficial to the war effort. He had worked the land, helping ensure there was enough food for the population, or less of a gap to be filled by imports. However, as only a mere farm labourer, when conscription began, his occupation was not protected, leaving him no option but service. At least the Army gave him a chance to be outside, even if that meant going to the trenches. He could not conceive what it would be like, locked up in one of those sardine cans the Navy called warships. Also, being in the Army, he was more likely to find action compared to the 'stay at home' Navy. The Navy was supposed to be the pride of the Empire, each dreadnought costing over a million pounds, but it had yet to engage in any decisive combat with the enemy. In the Army, he would make a difference, if he could ever learn to soldier.

While Alfie had worked on the farm, he had grown strong and built his stamina. This advantage had not been enough for the Army, but it meant in this respect he struggled less than his urban counterparts. He also missed the excellent food fed to farmworkers. However, conscription was an opportunity for him, one Alfie needed to make the best of. As he sat considering his boots, he decided he would not just survive combat, but do his family proud. Such goals did not mean he would throw himself at the enemy, or volunteer as Wells had cautioned against, but he would do his best to dish out to Fritz more than he received. Alfie resolved to throw himself into his training with renewed vigour. The Army knew what they were doing. He would not let them down. He would stick with his friends so they would all stand the best chance of surviving and taking the battle to the enemy.

Alfie picked up his boots and, for the first time, put his heart and soul into polishing them to the highly reflective surface his instructors demanded.

2

FRANCE

Q "As the founder of the Experimental Battalions, you can discuss the questions regarding the ethics your form of warfare has raised in some quarters. I ask, did, or do you, experiment with live volunteers?"

A "The morality of using the reanimate dead was something we discussed in quite some detail. Several experiments were undertaken, including with live volunteers, to create new tigers under our command."

Q "So, in the language of the popular Press, you allowed living soldiers to volunteer to become 'zombies'?"

A "Yes, this was the case. These men were an insignificant source of tigers and only allowed during our initial research. Following events, such as those which occurred in London, there were plentiful sources elsewhere. However, unlike the popular Press, we must recall there was no end in sight, nor a ready supply of tigers. We had stumbled upon a new war-winning weapon and were exploring how best to use it. Considering the contribution of the tigers to the outcome of the war, the 'sensationalist' stories of Fleet Street are little more than base rabble-rousing."

Q "You have been compared to Dr Frankenstein by some sections of the Press. Do you consider these descriptions apt?"

A "Dr Frankenstein and his creation are works of fiction. As a doctor of medicine, I can confirm that the tigers are not like the monsters of Frankenstein, and do not inhabit the pages of books in libraries. Tigers shortened the war with a consequential reduction in the number of casualties on both sides."

Questioning of Brigadier Oliver Hudson, Commanding Officer, Royal Zombie Corps. Transcript committee of closed session On the Conduct of the War Committee, House of Lords Select Committee, 21st August 1919.

L ATE IN THE SUMMER of 1916, the recruits shipped out to their new units. It came as a surprise to Marsh and his friends, who were expecting a traditional deployment pattern. Few among them were sent to receive additional specialised training, something now reserved for soldiers too young for overseas service. Because of the significant numbers of new soldiers conscription had made available, traditional deployment patterns were changing. Upon completing basic training with the home battalion of the regiment they had joined, a soldier would be deployed to the overseas battalion. However, the vast number of casualties caused by the industrialised warfare in Western Europe and the Dardanelles, especially with the ongoing Somme offensive, meant this old system could no longer adequately supply the vast numbers of replacements the front lines demanded. Some soldiers joined newly created formations following the completion of their basic training, and the unit would continue to work up for some time in Britain before deployment overseas. Other soldiers were sent as piecemeal replacements for frontline units pulled away from the battlefields. These units were expected to recover in reserve, or on quiet sectors of the front. In many cases, replacements were sent to infantry depots while they awaited the summons to their new unit.

Most of the members of Marsh's training platoon were sent to the infantry depots. Having escaped the rigidity of the training camp, they soon found themselves on a troop train to Richborough, travelling across the Kent countryside to the busy wartime harbour. Expanding under the watchful eye of the Royal Engineers, unlike other Channel ports, Richborough specialised in the shipment of bulky goods and equipment overseas.

'Where do you think they're sending us?' Taff asked, swaying as the train clattered over a set of misaligned points.

'If it's away from this overcrowded carriage, I'll be happy,' Ted Simmonds said. 'It can't be worse than being stuck here with you smelly buggers.' The third class carriage was hot, the sun beating through the windows into the overcrowded carriage.

'We'll be out in the fresh air soon enough,' Alfie said. 'Crossing the Channel, and I doubt it'll be on a train ferry. I heard they've not yet built the docks for them at Richborough.'

'I thought the place was supposed to be secret?' Simmonds asked, 'How do you know what's going on? Are you some sort of master spy now?'

'Me?' Alfie snorted. 'Josh is our spy. He overheard a bunch of officers chatting about it. Apparently, they're using barges at the moment, and we'll be catching one of those, not a ferry. All the other ports are jam-packed, and they can't fit us in.'

As if summoned by the mention of his name, Wells entered the far end of the carriage. A smile on his face suggested his latest mission had been fruitful.

'Just shifted a whole carton of cigarettes to some Scots in the next carriage, and look what they gave me,' Wells said as soon as he reached the group. He revealed the bottle of whiskey, opening it with no further delay. Taking a quick swig for himself, Wells passed the bottle around his friends.

'What if we get caught?' Taff asked.

'Just because your family are teetotallers, doesn't mean you need to jump at your own shadow. Do you see anyone who cares around here?' Wells said. Taff took an extra long swig when the bottle came to him, his friends approving his disregard for family tradition.

'So we're all going to the same depot in north France?' Marsh asked.

'Aye, bet that means Belgium'll be where we end up then,' Davies said, putting out his hand for the bottle.

'At least we get to stay away from the bloody Somme,' Simmonds said, just loud enough to be heard. He did not wish to tempt fate with the idea.

'It'll all be peace and quiet then, unless we end up at Wipers,' Morgan suggested. Ypres, a vital area of the front in Belgium, was only marginally better than the vast bloodbath taking place on the Somme, a situation that would reverse as soon as the autumn rains turned Flanders into mud.

'That's no way to think of it,' Wells said. 'We'll have plenty of opportunities to live well and comfortable wherever we go, as long as I'm around.'

'What? Even if we're up to our necks in the mud?' Morgan asked. 'We ain't able to float like the Navy.'

'We're not the Navy, that's right. But wherever we go, we're going to sock it to the Germans,' Marsh said. His patriotic proposal raised cheers from his increasingly intoxicated friends. The bottle continued to pass among them, increasing their merriment. They were not the only group of soldiers on the train responding in this way. Far from it, most were enjoying the camaraderie and supplies of alcohol, finding it useful to cover up their nerves. Few men were sober when the train arrived at the destination.

They disembarked at Richborough and boarded a small troopship which plied the route between England and the continent. To their surprise, they found a functional little ship, not the barge they had expected, the single funnel puffing out dirty black coal smoke. Porters rushed about, loading boxes of supplies aboard, everything from ammunition to cases of corned beef. Bulky supplies were being loaded onto barges, and every bit of space was used.

Marsh leaned over the railing. The murky river water gently lapped against the hull. His thoughts dwelt on the coming challenges, his mind clouded by the alcohol consumed on the train.

'Want a smoke?' Wells offered a cigarette from a crumpled packet, which Marsh lit, inhaling with enjoyment before blowing the smoke far over the side of the ship.

'It's bloody bleak here,' Wells said. 'Is this what we're fighting for?'

'What? Do you want the White Cliffs of Dover, a military band and a horde of fawning young ladies?' The sarcasm was apparent in Marsh's response.

'Why, yes. I wouldn't mind if the King himself came to wave me off as well,' Wells said getting into the spirit, the alcohol helping to lubricate his humour.

They talked for a while, suggesting outrageous ways their country could wave them off. The troopship slipped its moorings and travelled down the partially dredged river, heading to the open sea beyond the sand dunes. Both riverbanks displayed indications of rapid construction, with the Royal Engineers radially expanding the port facilities. The sunlight sparkled off the waves lapping the shore as the river bank gave way to the beach at high tide, and then the sea. In a few hours, they would disembark at a northern French port, a train no doubt ready to transport them to a replacements depot.

'I wonder if we'll ever see poor old Blighty again?' Marsh asked as they watched Broadstairs and Ramsgate pass to port.

'Of course,' Wells said. 'If for no reason other than I've got to spend all the money I've been making while ripping off the supplies.' He grinned and offered Marsh another cigarette. 'Besides, we're sticking together, so you'll be back at the same time as me.'

The troopship landed its cargo at Boulogne, one of the main harbours in northern France. Alongside many other soldiers, Marsh and his compatriots awaited their turn to disembark the ship via the narrow gangplank. Incredible feats of organisation ensured there was no waiting and they were hurried to the neighbouring train station, embarking on another train journey. This trip was mercifully short. Their destination was the third station along the line, the small fishing town of Étaples.

As they disembarked from the train, a fierce sergeant greeted them, forming all the soldiers into ranks while a corporal walked up and down calling names and places they were assigned to. Two of the soldiers Marsh had trained with were detailed off elsewhere, but Davies, Morgan, Simmonds, Marsh and Wells were all sent to the same pickup point. Most of the other soldiers from the train joined them. Lined up in ranks, the men marched to the Infantry Base Depot on the edge of the ancient town. The depot was overused and worn, with standardised huts and widespread use of tents. Marsh and his fellows were directed to a tent on arrival, one already billeting a couple of men.

'You can have those beds over at that end. This is my end,' a private said, yawning as he stretched on his bed.

'Thanks,' said Wells. 'Smoke?' He offered the ice-breaking cigarette from an open packet.

'I smoke.' The soldier sat up to take the offered cigarette. A packet of England's Glory matches materialised in his hands, and he lit the cigarette before lying back on his bunk.

It took them a short time to unpack their kit. The new arrivals soon establishing their new tent-mate was a member of the regular pre-war army who somehow survived the chaotic early stage of the war. Most of the pre-war professional army had been destroyed at the battles of Mons, Le Cateau, Aisne, and First Ypres. As Wells plied their new friend with cigarettes, Daniel Scott opened up. His regiment was based in Madras, India, before the war and had only returned to Europe after being drawn into the Dardanelles Campaign.

'We shipped out to Gallipoli. It was a total farce. It couldn't have been worse organised. The trenches were right on the cliffs overlooking the beaches,' Scott said. He fidgeted with his cigarette as he recounted the conditions, unaware of the slight tremor in his hand. 'Illness was rife. We couldn't keep things clean for fear we'd be shot by a sniper. I came down with a severe case of dysentery and was evacuated to a hospital ship. While I was getting better, the regiment pulled out of Sulva Bay, and we got taken to Egypt to recover, guarding the Canal. Join the British Army and see the sodding world.'

'What's it like under fire?' Taff Morgan asked what everyone wondered. This was the first time they had a veteran in front of them who did not outrank them.

'It's bloody awful when the other lot gets going. 'Whizz-bangs, machine guns and the rest. Johnny Turk even had great big darts they dropped out of planes. You can't hear yourself think, and some lads just went to pieces,' Scott said, aware of the attentive audience around his bunk. 'You keep low in the trenches and just hope that if you're going to get hit, it's clean and quick. You don't want to evacuate with a bloody awful wound. At Gallipoli, the beaches took constant fire, and you probably won't survive an evacuation. Clean and quick is the way. You're either dead and don't have time to know it, or you've got a decent chance of a Blighty.'

Several of them nodded, knowingly. A Blighty wound would send you back to Britain, the million-to-one injury that would not cripple for life but would prevent a return to frontline service. A Blighty was the only injury men hoped for.

'Are the Turks good soldiers?' Davies asked.

'They beat us, you know?' Scott gazed intently at Davies. He understood the raw recruits would either learn from his hard-won experience or die in short order. 'Mehmet is sturdy. He's badly equipped, but he fought tooth and nail to kick us out. Even the ANZACs were impressed, and they don't seem to respect anyone. I'll tell you what was worse though, the great big bloody flies. Great stonking bastards, buzzing around all the time. They'd crawl all over your face when you sat still for more than a second. You knew where they'd come from and why they were there as well, and there was sod all you could do about them.'

'So why are you here, then? I thought this place was only for us new lads,' Taff asked, wondering why such an experienced soldier was separated from his regiment.

'I caught some splinters on the Somme in early July. Was lucky, really lucky. Most of the lads didn't make it. Sheer bloody stupidity that attack.' The new recruits were surprised at the venom, having been subjected to endless civilian propaganda about the war effort. 'There wasn't much left of my unit, so I got sent here once I recovered, and like you lot, I'll end up filling whatever gaps come up rather than returning to my unit.'

'Must be tough getting split up after being with one bunch of lads so long,' Wells said, handing over a small flask he had concealed in a breast pocket.

'You could say so. Anyway, there was no-one left that I knew, hardly anyone from the original battalion.' Scott said, taking the flask and swigging from it. 'Best off, moving on now.'

The routine at Étaples followed a similar pattern to the last weeks of training. Marsh was relieved to find an exciting diversion from the hours of drill instruction, watching aircraft being ferried across the Channel. These flew the short distance over water, first successfully attempted by Louis Blériot seven years earlier. The planes landed at nearby grass strips, ready for ferrying to their new units. Alfie was fascinated with the incredible invention and had been since learning of the first powered flight by the Wright brothers. The idea of being free, soaring like a bird, appealed to him, never more so than when he stood in the muggy heat of the drill field. It would be cooler that high up, with all the air rushing by the fast-moving aircraft. Perhaps he should volunteer for the Royal Flying Corps, if the opportunity present itself, although they would be unlikely to give a simple soldier, a flying post. He knew they preferred officer applications from the infantry instead.

Étaples was not just about drill and the repetition of lessons already learnt. The depot was a finishing school for the newly trained infantry. Alongside the spit and polish of the parade ground, there was additional military training on operating in the field. With the sprinkling of veteran soldiers returning to the fight, the recruits could learn, first-hand, the tactics and skills necessary for survival on the modern battlefield.

'You did what?' Taff said, so surprised he let go of his gas mask. He recovered the bulky shroud from the ground.

'We'd piss on a handkerchief, or any other rag you could get your hands on, put it across your mouth and then breathe through that. The chemicals in your piss would stop the worst of the gas,' Scott said, smiling at the disgusted faces of his bunkmates. The group practiced gas drills, having been assigned to the same training platoon at Étaples. Most of the men were recently arrived soldiers, fresh from their basic training in England.

'Mind you, it doesn't work with some of the newer gases. They contact your skin, from what I've overheard from the officers. You don't even need to breathe the gas for it to kill you.'

'Bloody hell,' several voices muttered.

'I don't think either side has used these new toys yet, but that's the buzz now,' Scott said to the mortified soldiers around him.

Taff pulled his bulky new mask over his head, the big round lenses making him appear like some creature from a Jules Verne novel. He took his time tying off the straps and tightening the material around his neck, achieving an airtight seal.

'I can't see anything in this bloody thing,' Morgan said, his voice just audible. The two lenses were lopsided, preventing him from using both his eyes at the same time.

'And we can barely hear you, Taff,' Wells said. 'Perhaps you should wear that bleedin' thing whenever you sing.'

Morgan lurched comically across the grass attempting to grab Wells, who jumped out of the way. Part-blinded, the Welshman could not find his quarry, who kept hiding behind him.

'Lads, once you've got one of these things on your head, you can't see much,' Scott said, waving his empty canvas mask at the end of an outstretched arm. 'You need to work together as a team. Fritz will be right in the gas cloud, trying to catch you struggling with your mask, if you have one, of course. He'll use your panic and fear, but you can bet he'll be wearing his mask. Then he'll hunt you down, one by one, working in small groups.' Everyone in earshot recognised the sharing of hard-won wisdom. In recognition of his experience, Scott had gained his corporal stripes a few days after they arrived at Étaples. The stripes made no difference to the surrounding soldiers. Scott already possessed their respect.

'We pair up. You make sure your mate is wearing his mask, help solve any problems he has putting it on. Then you work together at all times, one on the right, one on the left. You can't look everywhere in these things, so you take the sector in front of you, let the lads off to your sides deal with what's in front of them. Make sure you stick close together so that you can hear each other. And if your mate cops it, or wasn't there to begin with, find someone else to support. Hell, make a small group if you need to.'

The training sergeants left the small group alone to run the training by themselves, instead concentrating on squads not in possession of an experienced soldier. Most of the training staff had no frontline experience, much to the general resentment of the veterans who rotated through the camp. The desk-bound, rear-line soldiers more than made up for their lack of combat experience with self-belief in their ability to drive the soldiers on towards the enemy. Informed by the details in the updated training manuals, these non-commissioned officers whiled away the war in the comfort and safety of a French port. They had already earned the nickname of 'Canaries' because of their ability to sense and avoid danger. No doubt a witty miner had begun the trend, with the small yellow birds a recent addition to coal mines, alerting the miners to the build-up of dangerous gases. The sergeant in charge of the current drills knew an experienced veteran when he saw one, and unlike many of his Canary peers, felt no need to intervene.

The tension in the camp was noticeable. An incident had occurred prior to Marsh and his squads' arrival, at the end of August, when a stubborn Canary had turned off the hot water while some ANZACs were showering. To fool around with Australians and New Zealanders guaranteed an outburst of verbal abuse, and these ANZACs had a fair number of Gallipoli veterans among their number. These experienced men recognised many of the Canaries for what they were. Before the British sergeant knew what he had let himself in for, an Australian private had unleashed a torrent of abuse. The private was arrested and resisted being taken to the prison compound. Several of his mates stepped in to help free him. Four of the men were court-martialled and sentenced to death, including the vocal private.

The incident had caused a great deal of disgust among the enlisted soldiery in the camp, and many of the commissioned men in the nearby officer's field. Three of the guilty men had their sentences commuted, being members of the Australian forces, which forbade the death sentence for their troops. However, one private, an Australian in the New Zealand Expeditionary Force, did not have his sentence commuted, as New Zealand's army still retained the death sentence. There had been a great uproar among the assembled troops. Now the masses awaited the execution of the punishment with fury. Of course, the Canaries felt vindicated by this treatment of the troops and the confirmation of their own importance, even if it had little bearing upon the skills they actually possessed.

'Right lads, let's suit up as quick as we can. Get yourself into pairs and be ready to defend yourselves once you're masked up,' Scott instructed. He knew keeping busy would train the inexperienced soldiers, while the activity would keep prying busybodies away.

Wells and Marsh paired off, as they often did when allowed to choose who they were going to work with. As Scott shouted, 'Gas, gas, gas, gas, gas!' they hurried into their masks, tying the cords so the canvas became airtight around their necks. Once ready, they faced their corporal, looking outwards at slight angles from each other, maintaining a good defensive watch.

'Wells!' Marsh gave a muffled shout. 'On your left.'

He spotted Taff Morgan sneaking up on them. Taff had not put on his mask, instead attempting to catch the rest of the squad blindsided. Wells turned to face the stalking Welshman, who gave up on the alert targets, preferring to rugby tackle to the ground a figure which was probably Ted Simmonds. Neither Simmonds, nor his partner Davies, had their masks on correctly. As a result, the pair were not ready to protect each other, instead; they were still adjusting their masks. The rest of the squad laughed at the lesson and Simmonds, his mask thrown to the ground, chased Morgan, seeking revenge.

'Here, Alfie, you may be rubbish at the spit and polish, but you're sure quick at spotting trouble,' Scott said, standing next to Marsh to watch the entertainment. 'Maybe there's a real soldier in you somewhere.'

Marsh's chest swelled with pride at the compliment from the combat veteran. Perhaps he would achieve his promise to avenge his brother and uphold the family name.

As the days wore on, Marsh found the fake trenches to be the most engaging part of their advanced training. Several lines of trenches had been dug to simulate conditions in the front lines. Barbed wire hung everywhere, although the soldiers could see little as they moved up the zig-zagging communications line to the secondary trench.

'Too much grass around here,' Scott complained, risking a quick glance over the parapet. Even though there was no simulated enemy fire, his caution delivered an important lesson to those who saw him.

'What's wrong with that, Corporal?' Wells asked, eager to learn more.

'The shell churn obliterates everything. I was in a woods one time, well it was a woods at one point, but a few days later the shelling had turned it into a cratered mud-hole full of matchsticks.'

'If there's that much shelling, how will we survive?' Wells grimaced at the image Scott had painted in his mind.

'You keep low. Don't stick your head out of the trench. You'll hear any shells that are coming close, by the whistle,' Scott said, pausing, then pointing upward. 'If the whistle keeps getting louder, you hug the ground and pray.'

'So why don't we build deep bunkers like the Germans? Surely those things would keep us safer from the shelling?' this time, Simmonds asked the question.

'Well, the Brass think you'll get too comfy; it'll sap your "offensive spirit" and you'll pass the war brewing tea in comfort.' Scott unslung his rifle. His movements were jerky. He was not amused by the ideas promoted by the General Staff who ran the conflict from the safety of chateaus in the rear of the line. 'You realise, there would be a lot less dead blokes on our side if the Brass had to live in the trenches. They'd be sure to dig deeper then.'

Today, as usual, the Canaries kept clear of Corporal Scott, aware he was a combat veteran who would not tolerate their strictly academic knowledge of the war. As a result, Scott continued to pass on his hard-won lessons and battle-tested opinions. None of the Canaries would have dared criticise the General Staff. None of the Canaries would dare challenge the battle-hardened corporal. Besides, the wiser Canaries could see Scott was developing his squad.

'Right lads, this second line trench is as far as we're going forward today. This down here is the fire step,' Scott said, showing the raised wooden boards on the trench wall facing the imaginary enemy lines. 'Climb up and have a see, lads. Just remember in the real thing, you peak for too long, and a Hun sniper will take your face off.'

The squad clambered up onto the fire step, placing their rifles along the top of the parapet in front of them, pointing at the imaginary enemy as they peered over the top.

'I can't see,' Taff whined.

'Open your eyes,' Marsh retorted, a fraction of a second ahead of several laughs.

'I'm too bloody short, you idiot.' The Welshman jumped up and down on the fire step in the hope he would see over the top.

'We'll have to get you a box to stand on then,' Wells said, generating more laughter.

'Being short's a bonus, don't you know? I'll be able to hide behind Marsh's great hulking arse. He's such a piss-poor soldier, he'll only be any good as a bullet shield.' Taff leaned against Marsh as if seeking the physical protection of his body, almost knocking them both off the fire step.

Taff yelped as Marsh kicked him in the ankle.

'Right,' Corporal Scott interjected before the horseplay got out of hand. 'The difference between this second line and the next is that the front line's a complete mess from the shelling. Also, Fritz will have a better chance of taking a shot at you when you're in the front line. When we're in action, we'll only spend a short time in each line because the Brass will rotate us out to keep us fresh. Perhaps the only time we'll be in the front line will be when we're going over the top.'

The silence was uneasy. The squad all wanting to ask the same question, yet worried about how it would be perceived.

'What's it like going over the top, Corp?' Wells asked on behalf of them all.

'It's bloody awful. We all line up along a stretch trench and wait for our artillery to stop. Then when the officers blow their whistles, we climb up our ladders and pray the Germans aren't yet out of their deep bunkers, 'cause if they are, they're already pointing their machine guns at us.'

Everyone listened as Scott leaned against the trench wall. Several men sat on the fire step, facing him. 'Doctrine says we move towards the enemy at a steady pace. The ground is often so churned up and scattered with wire, you can't run. The biggest danger is the machine guns. They dish out death, and they're hard to avoid. Fritz has them positioned, so there are two or three supporting each other and his wire will funnel you into a trap; so you get shot from the front and both sides. Just do your best and keep your head down. It's like walking into iron rain. When you get close to the enemy, lob a grenade or two. Neither side is keen on taking machine gunners prisoner, so be ready with your bayonet and don't expect them to surrender.'

'It must be hell,' Simmonds observed.

'Aye, it's bloody hell. You'll be terrified and any man who tells you they're not scared is bloody well lying or mad.'

'There must be a better way to deal with them?' Marsh asked. 'There's got to be something cleverer than walking into the enemy guns.'

'Well, if you figure it out, make sure you tell the Brass about it. Maybe we'll be in Berlin by Christmas then.' Scott grinned at the futile idea. 'Digging the Hun out with artillery, that's all we can hope for. We started the fight thinking we'd have a quick war of movement. Everyone said we'd be in Berlin by Christmas. That's last Christmas, not the one before, you know. But we hadn't banked on the machine gun and how we'd have to dig in to avoid bullets.'

The orders to move out arrived after dark. The squad was going forward as reinforcements to a quiet sector in Belgium, with the entire squad remaining intact rather than dispersing individuals across several units. This news had a positive effect on the men as they had spent their time training together, and had grown in confidence with the addition of Scott to their number. Now they would be kept together when moving into the line. Only one of them, the experienced soldier, realised the reason for this change of policy. Scott cleaned his rifle to help calm his nerves. He knew the sheer number of losses experienced by frontline units was why they were not being sent off as individual replacements.

3

OVER THE TOP

"We observed the first cases in 1916. Occasional reports emerged of animate corpses in the trenches.
These reports were rare enough to be dismissed as
the desperate hallucinations of stressed soldiers. More
enlightened medical practitioners considered the reports symptomatic of 'shell shock', an early attempt
to diagnose what we today know as Post-traumat-
ic stress disorder. Unlike the Germans and French,
the British General Staff did not dismiss these cases,
possibly because of suspicions regarding the validity
of 'shell shock' as a medical condition. The British,
therefore, adapted to the emergence of the zombie on
the battlefield."

Milton Davies, A History of Zombies and Warfare,
(London, 2016)

MARSH EXPECTED TO BE deployed to a quiet sector in Belgium, near the coast. He was surprised when their orders were superseded, having been about to leave Étaples for a calm sector. Their newest orders instead directed them to join a unit deployed in Flanders. They travelled by train, the only evidence of war being the large numbers of men in uniform, the occasional plane and the large numbers of motorised trucks running looping routes from the railway stations to the depots nearer the frontline. Yet, as they got closer to Flanders, the evidence of warfare grew. A few scars marred the fields, the occasional bomb crater or burnt-out aeroplane wreck. There were large numbers of airfields, supply dumps and camps of all sizes, an area where the Allied armies had built-up their forces.

Their new unit was being held in reserve, and their new platoon rapidly absorbed the replacements. The platoon had been mauled a few days earlier. Marsh, and his squad, were not the only replacements in the company, the whole transplanted intact from a replacement depot. Few veterans remained from the original platoon, and those few experienced soldiers were all like Daniel Scott: hollow-eyes and drawn-faces, shocked by their experiences. Wells got the story out of one of the original complement of their adoptive regiment for a couple of bottles of red wine he had liberated from Étaples.

'It was sheer bloody murder. The ground was soft, as it often is around here. We couldn't get up enough speed to cross no man's land, and we failed to surprise the enemy. Fritz was waiting for us. Our barrage stopped, and they came out of their dugouts with machine guns. Sheer bloody slaughter,' the veteran, Tom Matthews, said, taking a swig from the wine bottle. Despite his shaking hands, he got the bottle to his lips without spilling the wine. 'We broke and fell back on our lines. Hardly anyone survived. It was a massacre. We were supposed to take out this blockhouse, but we didn't get close, barely out of our own lines.' His voice trailed away, and he filled the silence with another swig from the bottle.

'Looks like we'll be bringing the regiment up to strength,' Scott said. The patterns were obvious to his experienced eye, and he waved at the many replacements milling around.

'Well, you won't have long to wait, Corporal,' Matthews said, finding his voice again. 'That blockhouse is still in enemy hands and there ain't no-one else around here to take it. I overheard the Commanding Officer saying we'd be attacking as soon as you lot arrived.'

'Corp, aren't we going to get any rest?' Davies asked, feigning tiredness in his movements.

'It doesn't sound like it. Check your kit, lads. We're going to be busy soon enough. Make sure everything's in working order.'

The new arrivals did not have to wait long for an officer to lay claim to them. Lieutenant Sellers, acting commanding officer of D Company, explained they were joining the under-strength company. Even with all the replacements, there were not enough men, so Sellers split the soldiers into two makeshift platoons. Scott's replacement squad was made up to full strength and Sellers was satisfied he had been sent someone with a bit of experience in Scott, even if the other replacements were green. The old hand, Matthews, found himself assigned to Scott's squad and set about checking his kit with a passion bordering on religious fervour, knowing full well what awaited him.

'What do we do with our packs when we attack?' Davies asked while the squad and platoon leaders took part in an impromptu conference behind a hedge.

'I ain't lugging it into battle,' Marsh said. 'It's far too cumbersome.'

'Any excuse to leave behind your boot polish, eh?' Taff Morgan said.

'You can talk. If you don't take your pack with you, you'll need something else to stand on or you won't be able to see over the top of the trench.'

'Whatever we do, I'm not leaving this carton of cigarettes. Some bastard'll nick them,' Wells said, tearing up the outer packaging. He set about stuffing individual packets of cigarettes and other items into his various pockets and pouches. He even removed ammunition to make more room for his contraband.

'I'll put money on us leaving our packs here,' Matthews said. 'Then when we've finished, we'll come back and pick them up. Well, some of us will.'

The under-strength company moved out, combat ready, leaving behind anything which may hinder them in the task ahead. Dusk fell as they made their way forward to the trench system, and the darkness was total by the time they entered the rearmost trench. Marsh was surprised by the quietness of the front lines. He had expected there to be the overwhelming noise of battle. Occasional gunshots broke the silence, and an explosion rumbled in the distance. 'Corp, I thought it would be noisier than this,' Marsh said when he caught Scott's attention.

'It's often quiet. The only time things get busy is when there's an attack. Otherwise, we leave Fritz to his business, and he leaves us to ours,' Scott said, his voice a little above a whisper. 'They'll have extra ears in no man's land, listening for the possibility of an attack or any other movement. When we get closer to the reserve trench, we'll get told to keep the noise down.'

The prophetic words came true as they left the third line trench, entering a zig-zagging communication trench leading to the reserve line. A grim sergeant reminded them to keep the noise down. Marsh recognised the soldier, realising he saw him when they set off hours ago. Marsh suspected it must now be the middle of the night. He did not bother to check his watch. He could not see the hands in the darkness, for there was no luminous paint on them. A flare lit the sky in the distance. Marsh wondered what the land around the trenches looked like, but was not curious enough to risk raising his head and getting shot. Despite the dry weather, there was still mud everywhere. The low-lying land was always saturated with water. His imagination filled in the gaps for now.

The communication trench was well built. Duckboards on the floor were made from ammunition crates, keeping the passing men out of the muddy water. The sides of the trench were shorn up with wood and steel poles. Sandbags topped the parapet on both sides of the communication trench to ensure the enemy could neither see nor fire along any extended stretch. The constant zigging and zagging of the trench ensured no substantial length of the trench was subject to enfilading fire, even though the communication trench led towards the front line. The sheer number of dugouts surprised Marsh, as did the short spurs along the trench. It would be easy to get lost among the heavy mortars, aid stations, and toilets. There was even a rest area, complete with humorous signs such as "No Man's Land Theatre" and "The Mud Cabaret." On successfully reading the signs in the darkness, Marsh glanced at his watch, hopeful he could make out the time, but the light was still poor.

The column arrived in the reserve trench, where they rested for the few hours before dawn. The tired men made themselves as comfortable as they could, leaning against the walls of the trench, with many of the veterans going to sleep. Among the newer soldiers, few slept, suffering from an overload of adrenaline, being so close to the enemy. An atmosphere of excitement and fear prevailed.

'Taff, do you want a cigarette?' Wells asked, offering a newly opened packet.

'I can't pay you back, mate,' Morgan said, shaking his head.

'Pay me back by watching our backs when we go over the top.' Wells shook the packet. A cigarette slid loose.

'Look at your boots, Taff,' Marsh said. He laughed, pleased to notice the levelling effect of the mud clinging to the boots. 'They're just as messy as mine. Does that mean I'm now as good a soldier as you?'

'Never. You'll never be as good as me. You can't march,' Morgan said, quickly enough for Marsh to suspect his friend had readied the response in advance.

'Fat lot of use marching about around here,' Matthews said, his groggy voice coming from under a pile of clothes in a corner.

'I thought you was asleep, Tom,' Marsh said. He realised not all the veterans slept well, despite appearances. He did not want to dwell on what this discovery might mean.

'It's hard to sleep with you lot all talking such nonsense. Seeing how I'm awake listening, you'd better give me one of those fags.' Wells handed over the cigarette, a hand emerging from the bundle of clothing to receive one. Matthews was intent on staying in his warm cocoon.

'Is it right that I can't get a wink? Is it normal? I'm shattered,' Simmonds asked. Like most of the others, he held a cigarette in one hand, nursing a warm enamel mug of tea in his other hand.

'Is it the first time in action for you lot?' Matthews asked. He lit the cigarette. In the brief flash of light, his hands and face were visible, the rest of him remained hidden under the discarded clothing.

'Yes.'

Matthews drew on the cigarette, the tip glowing red. He appeared to consider his response. 'It's not like you'd expect. You join up, getting into uniform and thinking all the girls are going to swoon over you; you think you'll give Kaiser Bill a bloody nose, but it ain't like that. I'm sure your Corporal has told you all about it. He's seen action.' His face glowed red again as he drew on the cigarette.

'Scott did. He taught us what he could, none of that spit and polish bollocks. Everything was useful stuff, how to survive,' Marsh said.

'I hope you all paid attention because most of the stuff which happens out here has never made it into any training manual.' Matthews drew again on the cigarette as the soldiers sat waiting for him to dispense his wisdom. 'You'll feel every emotion from fear to euphoria over the next few hours.'

'I'm not scared,' Davies said with a bravado which did not match his internal turmoil.

'You'll piss your pants as soon as you meet a German,' Morgan said.

'No, save that piss in case Fritz has any gas around,' Wells said, reminding everyone of Scott's lessons about emergency gas masks.

'Well, at least I'll make a good show of myself. Someone like Marsh, he's a misfit. How will he survive?' Morgan asked, boasting while putting Marsh down.

'Survival ain't about spit and polish. It's about luck and good sense. A good soldier in a war isn't the same as a good soldier on the parade ground,' Scott said, surprising them all. He had arrived quietly, making far less noise than they expected, his meeting with the company sergeant now concluded.

'Maybe you lads are not scared now, but you soon will be. Or more likely, some of you're just full of it,' Matthews said, fixing Morgan and Davies with a glare. 'Any man going over the top is terrified, a liar, or a madman.'

No-one dared contradict Matthews. Alfie wondered what Scott thought, but the corporal just nodded his head in agreement. Matthews coughed and threw off his cape. 'There're plenty of madmen around here, believe me, but most of them are the senior officers behind the lines.'

'Keep low. Move fast. Don't run in a straight line. That's pretty much all you can do,' Scott said, reminding them of his earlier lessons. 'But I'll add to that. If you come under heavy fire, get into a hole and then skip forward from hole to hole whenever you can. Don't follow some glory-hunting officer who'll keep you out in the open. He'll be dead within minutes, and so will you.'

'Holes, Corporal?' Davies asked, not sure what the experienced man meant.

'Bloody great enormous shell holes,' Marsh interrupted, to a few chuckles. Clearly, their misfit had been learning.

'That's right, Alfie. There's shell holes everywhere out there, barbed wire as well. The artillery should take the wire out before we advance,' Scott said, allowing Matthews time for a sarcastic laugh. Scott grinned, rather than issue a reprimand. 'Let's just say the wire will still be there, so make your way around it. Don't get tangled up in it, as you'll be a sitting duck. Run like hell. Don't reload or muck around with anything.'

'Don't reload? It'll only take me a second to reload,' Davies said, having still not learned to be quiet.

'That'll be a dozen machine gun bullets hitting you in that second,' Scott said. He winked at Matthews, knowing that hearing it from two veterans would reinforce the lesson. 'Keep moving. Matthews, tell 'em what to do when they hit the enemy trenches and blockhouse.'

'Jump in the 'ole and stab anything that's not wearing a British uniform. Don't waste time reloading if you can see a Boche, just charge him down and skewer him with your bayonet. If you think there's an enemy around a zig-zag, then chuck a grenade first, wait for it to pop, and then charge around the corner, sticking anything still moving with your bayonet,' Matthews said. His hand shook as he scratched his chin, leaving a smear of mud. 'Now the blockhouse will be the problem. We can't charge it down, as it'll have all the approach routes covered. So, the best way to get there is along their own trenches. It'll have a back door or something we can lob a grenade, or two, through. Have I missed anything, Corp?'

Dawn found the squad deployed to the right of the platoon, itself on the right flank of the company. As was routine, the morning stand to, saw them ready to receive a dawn attack from the Germans. They drew their bayonets and stood alongside one another in silence, ready to mount the parapet and defend the trench. In the hours before dawn, they had been moved up from the support line. The front line was overcrowded with nervous soldiers from the many units gathering for the assault. The tension of being so close to the enemy was fraying many nerves, with Morgan and Simmonds exchanging punches before

Corporal Scott pinned Morgan against the trench wall to stop him from pursuing the defensive Simmonds. Matthews went quiet again, no doubt recalling his previous experiences of combat.

In another hour, the attack would begin. Flashes behind them announced the commencement of the artillery barrage, the explosives intended to break the wire and pummel the German defences. As the shells whistled overhead, on their way to the German lines, the troops stood down from their position on the fire step and the rum ration was issued early for the day. Marsh and Wells sat in silence, nursing their small rations of rum. The alcohol was not enough for them to get tipsy on, but at least it helped distract them from the constant crash, thud, and vibration of the artillery barrage.

'They got the rum here without losing any of it,' Scott said. He sounded surprised. 'The number of times the stuff never makes it to the lines, you'd be surprised.'

'No hot food, mind,' Wells complained. 'Although I suppose it's difficult getting it up here. I should imagine any smoke from cooking fires would draw artillery strikes.'

'You don't get much hot food in the front line. You're right about fires, so by the time the food has been carried forward, it's almost always cold. Besides, it'll take too much organisation to feed everyone this morning,' Matthews said, breaking his silence for the first time since he explained how the attack would go ahead.

The advance was small in scope, aimed at dislodging a blockhouse at the centre of a small salient in the lines. Only two battalions were to be used in the assault, with the first wave seizing the German front-line trench and neutralising the blockhouse. The second wave was reinforcements to fight off the expected German counter-attack. The squad already knew their part in this action. Scott had prepared them well. They were to swing around from the right, enter the German trenches, secure them, and attack the blockhouse from the rear.

'Why does the time pass so bloody slowly?' Marsh said, fidgeting with his webbing.

'What? Are you desperate to get out there?' Simmonds asked. He also fidgeted, but with his empty canteen.

'Well, if Marsh goes first, at least we can all hide behind him. He's only useful as a bullet shield,' Morgan said, joking as usual.

'Why hide behind someone Taff, you're so short they'll not see you,' Wells said, dodging as Morgan threw himself across the trench, attempting a good-humoured attack, but missing as Wells twisted out of the way.

'As long as you give me a leg-up out of this here hole in the ground, I'll be fine. Otherwise, I'll be stuck down here, and they'll shoot me for desertion.'

Ten minutes before the attack began, orders came down from the officers for a final kit check and for the men to ready themselves. Scott wandered up and down, checking his squad was prepared for action. He was pleased to note all appeared as it should. Some desk-bound colonel would have thrown a fit at the state of the soldiers, their uniforms covered in dirt, but what mattered was the ready weapons and equipment.

Five minutes before the attack was due, the order to fix bayonets was passed along the line. The long steel blades clicked onto the end of each rifle, the sound of the steel just audible over the continued noise of the barrage. Each soldier now possessed a much-extended reach, tipped with a lethal blade. Groups of men gathered around the bottom of the trench ladders, propped along the sides of the trench, pre-positioned for the advancing troops to climb over the parapet.

Scott, at the top of their ladder, sneaked a glance over the parapet into the no man's land beyond. 'It won't be long now. As soon as the artillery stops, we'll listen for the whistle, and then off we go.' Scott said, loud enough for those gathered below.

The guns fell silent. The last shells completed their overhead journeys, exploding along the German lines. After the last shell exploded, a deafening silence descended. The men braced themselves. Davies and Simmonds went white; Morgan was ticking, his face twitching; the two veterans, Scott and Matthews, appeared determined, yet both shook. Marsh realised he too was shaking, standing first at the ladder with his hands on the rungs, ready to scale the trench wall. Wells stood behind him, and Marsh could only guess how terrified his friend was.

After what seemed an eternity, the whistles blew all along the line and Marsh felt an urgent push from Wells behind him. Marsh fumbled his way up the ladder, disconnected from his body, which seemed to move without conscious thought. As he cleared the parapet, he almost stopped, shocked at the sight before him. Wells continued pushing from behind, moving him on. The scene was unearthly, a cratered waste of soil, muddy craters and torn up land, while a pall of smoke hung over the German lines. Sticks of wood attached to strands of barbed wire stood everywhere, and what appeared to be bodies, lay in no man's land. Marsh could barely make out the enemy trench, but a raised line, their reverse parapet, was just visible over one hundred yards away. Before he moved again, he wondered if friendly shells had been landing close to him.

He made off at a trot, seeing the first winking light from the low-ly-ing blockhouse to the left. This was followed by the rat-a-tat sound of a well-managed machine gun, firing in short bursts to conserve ammunition and ensure accuracy. Even further to the left, another machine gun started up. The voices in front of him were shouting in German. The noise of his own blood rushed through his ears as he ran around an uncut clump of barbed wire. He almost lost his footing as he slipped on the loose and uneven ground. He held his rifle ready to shoot, but found no targets, although a few single winks of light appeared along the enemy parapet as the German riflemen reached their defensive positions and opened fire.

Marsh did not look to either side. He had no time to see what was happening. Yet, he could hear his squad mates advancing alongside him. Somewhere behind, Taff was swearing, a constant stream of profanity as if enough words would create him a bullet-proof shield. Screams came from his left, and he knew the machine gun bullets were tearing into the advancing troops. The enemy also responded to the main body of the advance with mortars, causing a series of small explosions.

A nearby explosion forced Marsh to drop to the ground, scrambling into a large water-logged shell hole. Within seconds, he was joined by the rest of the squad, all following Scott's pre-battle advice. The group was miraculously intact, although Taff Morgan had changed the focus of his swearing to how he had bloodied his hand on an errant strand of barbed wire. They all fit into the crater; their feet wet from the pool of water at the centre.

'We can't go back out there,' Wells said above the noise, several bullets cracking overhead to underline his point.

'If we stay here, their big guns will get us,' Matthews said. He moved off across the crater to the side nearest the enemy.

'You're right, Tom,' Scott said, joining Matthews to peek over the edge of the shell hole. Satisfied, he issued commands. 'Davies and Morgan, you're going to get up to the edge, here, and lay down some covering fire. Aim low over the enemy trench right ahead of us. I doubt there'll be anything to hit, but it'll keep their heads down. Everyone else, we get out and charge the remaining distance.'

No questions came from the battle-stunned inexperienced men. Scott pointed at Davies and Morgan. 'When you two have emptied your rifles, reload and then follow the rest of us. Everyone, be clear on this. When we're in their trench, use whatever you can to fight, even your shovels. We'll head along the trench towards the blockhouse as fast as we can. I'll cover our rear with a few grenades. Questions?' Scott asked, taking the time to look at each one of them. There were no questions.

Scott checked his safety was off and they positioned themselves along the edge of the crater. At Scott's nod, Davies and Morgan leapt to the top of the crater and began shooting. Their fire was not aimed, but quick and would keep the defender's heads down. Without pausing, the rest of the men leapt out of the shell hole. Someone screamed in terror, not pain, as they sprinted the short distance to the German trench. Scott paused and threw a grenade along the enemy trench to deter any relief attempts from that direction.

In seconds, Marsh entered the German position. He jumped over the parapet and fell into the trench, landing awkwardly, but not injuring himself. In a moment of heightened awareness, time almost paused, and he realised he was shouting, screaming even. A German soldier turned to face him. Marsh's rifle pointed at the defender, and he fired a single shot, hitting the German in the shoulder, the impact propelling him into the trench wall. Without conscious thought, Marsh closed on the wounded man, charging the enemy with his bayonet leading the way. As the German slid down the fire step, Marsh thrust the bayonet into his chest. The grate of bone on the blade travelled along the length of the rifle. His training kicked in and he followed the bayonet drill taught to him in calmer circumstances. The German was dead by the time Marsh withdrew the bayonet.

In the chaos, there was insufficient time to reload. Too much was happening, a blur of action and desperate fighting. Marsh set off, running to the end of the zig in the trench. Within a few seconds, his senses restored themselves, and he realised the rest of his squad was defeating the defending Germans who occupied this stretch of the trench. His only conscious thought was to wonder why so few Germans manned their line, compared to the number of men the British always seemed to pack into their own defensive positions. Stopping short of the bend in the trench, Marsh went down on one knee, working the bolt on his rifle to reload, and then pointing the weapon so he could shoot any reinforcements emerging from around the corner. He noted how much the bloodied bayonet at the end of the long rifle shook. Wells placed one hand on his shoulder and then leaned round, throwing a grenade beyond the bend in the trench.

A crump, and a scream, announced the detonation of the grenade, with the squad advancing into the next length of the trench, shooting and stabbing as they went. Again, Marsh noted a few Germans defended the trench. He also realised the terror of entering the German trench had receded and he could fully engage in conscious thought again. In less than a minute, the next stretch of the trench had been cleared. Marsh was positioned to attack around the next zag in the line when three Germans ran around the corner, their own bayonets ready. Marsh shot, taking one down; however, the other two men were upon him in an instant. He parried one thrust from the pair of enemy bayonets with the wood of his rifle, but the second German slammed Marsh's weapon against the trench wall, forcing the Englishman to drop the rifle. Marsh grabbed at a piece of wood lying next to him, using it to stop the next thrust from the Germans, the enemy bayonet getting stuck. The wood was torn from Marsh's hands. Before panic could set in, one assailant dropped with a loud bang. Wells rushed by, chasing the remaining German back around the corner.

Well aware of how close he had come to death, Marsh picked up his rifle. He was not prepared to let his saviour get too far ahead of him, even though the ringing in his ears threw him off balance. The debt he now owed Wells may soon need repaying.

This next stretch of the trench was connected to the blockhouse, deserted apart from the man Wells pursued. The German slipped, and Wells caught him in no time, stabbing with his bayoneted rifle, no quarter given.

Scott caught up with them, having seen his two men advance around the bend. The corporal did not pause, arming two grenades as he ran up to the blockhouse. He dropped the explosives through an undefended open gun slit, which should have protected the blockhouse from just such an assault. As Marsh and Wells caught up, there was the muffled crumps of the grenades exploding followed by a shriek. The machine gun, facing across the barren contested land, ceased firing at the same instant. Smoke drifted out of the firing slit into the trench. Wells gave another grenade to Scott, who pulled the pin and threw it as best he could through the firing slit. Straight after the grenade exploded, Wells kicked down the door at the back of the blockhouse and ran inside.

'All dead!' came the muffled shout from inside, before anyone else could enter the fortification.

Marsh watched the action behind him. His squad had caught up and were barricading the route behind them so there would be no swift counterattack along the stretch of trench they had just cleared. From the other side of the blockhouse, the remaining Germans surrendered to the rest of the platoon, aware they would not hold off the attackers without the fortified machine gun post.

The British company had taken the objective, and a quick count led Alfie to conclude his friends had come through unscathed, excepting bruises and minor cuts from the hand-to-hand fighting. Such good fortune was not experienced by the rest of the company. The machine gun had extracted a bitter price. Several walking wounded helped secure the trench, and there were far fewer soldiers than had left their starting position. The cries of injured men could be heard from all around, the dead remained silent.

More British soldiers jumped over the parapet, the forgotten follow-up wave, surprising the survivors of the first wave.

'Time to pull back, lads,' a sergeant from among the reinforcements shouted. He had somehow landed on both feet without the slightest effort, his hard-won experience showing in every movement.

'Why, Sarge? We've knocked out the blockhouse,' Scott asked.

'Cause there's been a change of plans. Further up the line, the attack didn't go so well. The Krauts are readying a counterattack. We're here to cover your arses while you get out. We'll also set a demolition charge, so the bunker doesn't become a problem again. After that, the sergeant shrugged in resignation. 'We'll pull back too. Now, can we get on with our work?'

The sergeant and his troops took over the trench, posting look-outs and readying the satchel charges on the walls of the bunker. Scott gathered his squad, the men demoralised as the news of the withdrawal sunk in. Soon the company would be back to their start point.

4

RESCUE

"Global pandemics remain an ever present threat.
Two emerged from the trenches of the Great War."
Hudson, O, 'One Hell of a War: The Memoirs of
Brigadier Oliver Hudson,' (1934, London)

'RIGHT LADS, GATHER ROUND,' Scott instructed his squad. 'We'll cross the field as quickly as we can. Once we're in our trenches, get ready to give covering fire in case Fritz counterattacks, but be careful not to shoot any of our lads when they pull back after us. If we're quick enough, we can get back to our own lines before the Germans can respond. Oh, and keep low, 'cause if you've not been listening, he's still lobbing the odd mortar around.'

'Not again. Bloody hell,' Simmonds complained. 'We've already crossed no man's land once, and now we've going to do it again, and this time showing our bloody arses.'

'Yes, but without a bloody great machine gun shooting at you this time,' Wells said, a grin plastered across his face. 'Scott and I put paid to that.'

'Ready then?' Scott said. 'Let's go.'

'Alfie, what's wrong with you?' Wells asked, noticing Marsh standing still rather than climbing the parapet like the rest of the squad.

'I thought I was a bloody goner until you saved my bacon,' Marsh said in a quiet voice, his hands shaking. 'I'm not sure I'm ready to go out there again, not yet.' The adrenaline of the assault had worn off, and Marsh was less than confident he could work his legs properly, let alone climb out of the trench.

'You ain't dead yet and I saw how you took them on with that piece of wood.' Wells slung his rifle and offered a hand. 'Look, I'll help you out and across to our trenches.'

Wells took hold of Marsh, letting the exhausted man lean on him. They walked to a crumbled part of the trench wall, where it was not so steep. Within a minute they were exposed again, in the open, heading back to friendly lines alongside the survivors of their company. An itch began between Marsh's shoulder blades, almost as if the enemy had their sights lined up on him. He was totally unprotected. The battlefield was much quieter than during their advance. He recovered his strength as the fresh danger released more adrenaline into his system. Marsh pushed away from Wells so they would present smaller targets to any eagle-eyed German sniper.

There was a growing noise, like a freight train arriving. Without conscious thought, Marsh dived into a nearby crater, immediately followed by Wells. Whatever was about to land was much bigger than a mortar bomb. A loud crash sounded, louder than anything he had experienced before. The shock travelled right through his body as the blast lifted him from the ground. He landed, followed by lumps of mud and stones. His ears rang again, the acrid scent of explosives burning his nostrils. Wells was also prostrate on the ground, his face vacant, the same as Marsh.

There began a nightmare of explosions as the Germans launched their counterattack, bombarding their former trench, the British lines and the ground in between. Marsh and Wells scraped themselves into the wall of the crater, relying on the myth which spoke of shell holes never getting hit a second time. The oozing mud, a little way below the lip of the crater, sucked at their feet. During wetter weather, the mud would have dragged them down and consumed them.

In a quieter moment between explosions, Marsh contemplated the contents of the shell hole. The crater was a decent size and appeared to have been created by the explosive force of a large piece of artillery. In places, the rim of the crater was uneven, where later explosions had created their own smaller craters. Strands of barbed wire ran down one side. There were a couple of corpses, one bloated and wearing a British uniform, the other merely a skeletal hand sticking out of the mud. At the centre of the crater stood a pool of water that stank beyond belief. A faint miasma hovered over the surface, rippling with the shock waves of nearby explosions. A fragment of a brick wall lay on its side. Perhaps there had once been a building here, Marsh wondered. Eventually, he noticed a pair of legs behind the bricks, moving, not dead. Someone else shared their refuge with them.

Marsh worked his way around the central pool, crouching, hoping to avoid any errant shell splinters from the barrage. Wells watched him, but did not move, readying his rifle in case the other soldier posed a threat.

'Wells! He's one of ours,' Marsh said once he identified the uniform. Wells moved around to join him, wary of the dangers.

They did not recognise the soldier. The man could not talk and struggled to regain his feet, having seen his rescuers. Marsh did not recognise the unit insignia, rather he was distracted by the badly dented helmet the man wore. He had been hit on the head. Maybe a glancing blow had knocked him down, his helmet saving his life.

'Argh,' the soldier said, hands reaching towards them in supplication.

'Are you all right, mate?' Marsh asked, wondering if the head wound may be worse than he suspected. He had heard tell of wounded men removing their damaged helmets to find the metal had been holding their skull together.

'Argh,' the soldier replied as he continued to stagger towards Wells.

'You better sit down, mate. You're concussed,' Marsh said, concerned he was not getting any response.

The injured soldier leapt on Wells, pushing him down the crater wall toward the pool in the centre. From on top of Wells, the soldier's teeth snapped at his rescuer's face, his hands clawed at Wells' uniform, all the while making wordless sounds.

'Help, Alfie, get him off me!' Wells panicked and hit the wounded man in the ribs. 'He's trying to bite my bloody face off.'

Marsh tried to pull the assailant off his friend, but the soldier possessed great strength and Marsh could not shift him.

'Stop him! Use your gun.' The snapping teeth almost closed on Wells' cheek.

Marsh raised the butt end of his rifle. 'Stop!' he shouted, slamming the butt down hard onto the side of the soldier's head, just below the rim of the askew helmet. The soldier fell to the side. Wells scrambled out from beneath the unconscious man.

'What the hell is going on? He was trying to bite my face off,' Wells said, face white, his whole body trembling. He wiped his hands across his face and then checked them for blood.

'I don't think he got you,' Marsh said, as Wells found no injuries.

The wounded soldier sat up. He gazed at Marsh, stunned, not unconscious. A red mark was forming across the side of his face where the rifle butt had made contact. Other than this visible mark, he seemed unaffected. He just sat still, making noises like before, and snapping his jaw.

'Look, Alfie! What the fuck is that?' Wells almost screamed.

'What?' Marsh asked, amazed the man had shrugged off the impact of his rifle butt. He had been about to ask the injured man what was going on.

'His chest. He's got a great big bloody hole in his chest.' Wells scrabbled away, grasping for his rifle. Once he had it in his hands, he pointed the weapon at the wounded man.

'Cover me,' Marsh said. This was incredible. He wanted to know what was happening. The man was badly injured. They needed to get him back for medical aid, as soon as possible. Marsh moved towards the injured soldier, his hand outstretched before him.

'Don't touch him, he'll bite you,' Wells said, aiming along his rifle, his shaking hands defeating his attempt.

'Come on, lad,' Marsh said in a soothing voice. 'What's your name?'

'Argh,' the soldier said, gazing at him, the eyes showing little sign of consciousness and no sign of the violence which had just occurred.

'You look like you're hurt bad. Let me check you out.' Marsh placed his hand on the soldier's shoulder. The man did not resist. 'You're cold. How long have you been out here?'

'Argh,' the soldier said, turning to Wells. He sniffed, and snapped his teeth together.

'Calm down now. Wells won't hurt you.' Marsh checked over his shoulder to make certain his terrified friend was no threat. 'Now let's have a glimpse at that wound.'

The chest wound was terrible. A fragment of shrapnel had carved a chunk out of the soldier's chest. The wound penetrated deeply and appeared as if it might go as far as the heart. The soldier did not flinch as Marsh probed the wound.

'How the hell are you still alive? This must hurt like hell?'

'Argh.'

'I don't like this, Alfie. It's not right,' Wells said, gripping his rifle tighter.

'We can't just leave him here. He's badly injured,' Marsh replied, tearing the wounded man's tunic so he could get better access to the wound. He placed a large bandage across the gaping wound, tying it off around the soldier's chest. 'Put your arm around my neck, and we'll get you out of here.'

Marsh lifted the wounded soldier, and they staggered up the side of the crater. Wells kept a careful watch, both for the enemy and on the injured soldier.

The German shelling had reduced. Now seemed as good a time as any to make a break for their own lines. No-one was in sight, nor was there any gunfire.

'Let's get out of here while we still can. They've stopped shelling,' Marsh said.

The remaining trip across no man's land was hard work. The soldier said nothing, groaning from time to time. He was in considerable pain. While quite mobile, one of his legs did not work correctly. Marsh thought he was one incredibly lucky chap to have lasted for so long, but could not imagine how he would survive much longer with such a severe injury. Once the pain set in, it would be impossible for the man to survive. Obviously, the shock of such a traumatic injury was keeping the pain at bay, a small mercy. Marsh redoubled his efforts, and they climbed back into their own trench, having drawn no enemy fire in the few heart-rending minutes it had taken them to cross the disputed land.

'Stretcher bearer!' Marsh called. Two medical orderlies attended to the casualty, lying him on a stretcher.

'Jesus! How did you survive?' an orderly asked the casualty.

'Argh,' the soldier replied.

'I think he's in shock. He's said nothing, but keeps snapping at my friend here,' Marsh said. The injured soldier snapped his teeth at the nearest orderly, but did not move in any other way. 'Just like that. It's like he's lost the ability to talk.'

'We'll come with you,' Wells said. 'Let me just let an NCO know.' Wells ran off to find a sergeant from their battalion.

The casualty clearing station was a brick-lined, half-buried bunker just behind the third line of trenches. Unlike the trenches, which were made with temporary use and limited comfort in mind, the casualty clearing station was designed for greater survivability. Half dug into the ground and then topped over with concrete and earth, here the injured would be safe from anything but a direct hit. The aid post was far safer than the first aid station the orderlies had bypassed in the second trench. The two men claimed the injury was too life-threatening to waste time there.

The room they were waiting in was full of moaning casualties. Wells stayed by the entrance to the long hall, not wanting to be surrounded by such pain and suffering. Marsh stayed with the soldier they brought in. The man was still in shock, but Marsh found his name on his identification disc, "J. Gibson". Marsh continued to talk to the injured man while they waited for the doctor to arrive for the initial assessment. The conversation was one-way. Shocked, Gibson could not find any words in response. Their wait drew out. The clearing station was overworked following the recent action, and every case in the room was significant. The injured waited on stretchers, experiencing varying degrees of agony, ready to be taken outside to the tented operating theatre.

Many of the wounded came from the two battalions involved in the attack. From what Marsh could discover, there had been heavy casualties during both the attack and the German counterattack. Marsh and his squad had been fortunate to make it into the enemy trench with so little harm to themselves. Wells had tried to find out what happened to the rest of their squad, but discovered little. While still in the trenches, Wells had discovered Scott was alive, and the battalion was being pulled out of the line to recover. Wells had been ordered to head back to the assembly point after they dropped off the casualty.

'Come on, Marsh,' Wells called from the doorway. 'We've got to be going, otherwise we'll get reported as deserters.'

'Five more minutes. Doctor's due soon.'

'They promised that ages ago, things are too busy. They aren't going to make it round in time.'

'Excuse me,' a voice behind Wells said. Wells moved aside for a doctor wearing a blood-soaked uniform and operating gown. 'Things are busy, but your lad is next on my list.'

'Ain't my lad, Sir,' Wells said. 'We found him in a shell hole. Tried to bite me, he did.'

'I see. He did not achieve his aim then?' the doctor asked, sparing the shortest glance to check Wells' condition. He knelt next to the patient, checking his condition. 'The stretcher-bearers mentioned him to me. They've instructions to look out for cases like his.' The doctor took the patient's wrist to check his pulse. 'So what's your name, then?'

'Argh,' said the patient.

'Gibson, Sir. That's what his tag says,' Marsh said.

'I see. So you don't know the casualty. Now let's see this wound of yours, Gibson,' he said. The doctor let go of the patient's wrist and checked the bandaged chest wound. He stood up and clapped his hands. 'Right, you two, either end of the stretcher please, we'll take him out to the tent.'

Wells and Marsh carried Gibson out to the operating tent. The inside of the heavy canvas was splashed with blood, with sawdust on the floors to soak up the spills of bodily fluids. The air carried the scent of blood and other less pleasant substances. An orderly cleared up the mess made by a previous patient.

'So he's not given you any trouble then?' the doctor asked.

'Not really, Sir, other than attacking Josh here when we first found him,' Marsh said, stepping back from the operating table.

'It's unusual for them to be this calm. We must investigate this a little further,' the doctor said, turned to address the busy orderly. 'Jones, make sure you get the details of these two men when we've finished in here.'

'Sir, are you going to save him?' Wells asked.

'Well, it depends what you mean by save,' the doctor said, pulling a Webley pistol from a satchel hanging on the back of the chair.

Before Wells or Marsh could do or say anything, the doctor crossed the short distance to the operating table. He fired a single round into Gibson's head. The back and side of Gibson's head exploded as the shot tore a path through his brain. The bullet had been aimed so the bullet exited the head at an angle, entering the ground on the other side of the operating table, followed by ejected brain matter. What was left of Gibson's face gazed at the ceiling of the tent. His features were still. A small hole in his temple smoked from the heat of the weapon's discharge.

'Sir! What the hell are you doing?' Marsh screamed, staggering and holding his hands to his head.

'Orderly!' The doctor called for an assistant, who then stood between the two men and the doctor. 'He was already dead.'

'What, Sir? He was alive. We all saw him,' Marsh said.

'Dead, I say, and not in the usual sense.'

'But, he was walking and—' Marsh stopped talking when Wells placed his hand on his friend's arm.

'I knew it. Something wasn't quite right. I said it, didn't I? He was a bloody golem, not really alive,' Wells said to his friend. 'Let's listen to the man and find out what's going on.'

'Sage advice and an interesting, but incorrect comparison, young man,' the doctor countered, wiping some imaginary blood from the end of the pistol before returning it to the satchel.

'What do you mean, Sir? Who the hell are you?' Marsh asked.

'I am indeed a doctor. My name is Colonel Hudson. And, your friend, Gibson, was undead,' the officer replied.

'You've already said he was dead, Sir. What do you mean, undead? Why was he moving and everything?'

'The body was reanimated. We don't know why yet, but we have received several reports of these events. Indeed, I have some small experience myself. It was unusual your friend did not attack everyone within reach.'

'Attack?'

'Yes, attack, literally trying to bite and claw the flesh off the living,' Hudson said, waving his hands.

'But he tried to attack me,' Wells interrupted. 'He was biting and clawing until Marsh here hit him with his rifle butt.'

'Yes, what you describe would be normal behaviour, comparable to our own observations.' Hudson ran his hand across his mouth as he thought. 'What we have not yet seen is one of these undead behaving in a restrained fashion. On the rare occasions these creatures make it back to an aid station, it is usually because they are horrifically injured, too injured to attack anyone, and, of course, too injured to survive if they were actually alive. Gibson here would pretty well fit into this categorisation.'

'Is this a German secret weapon? Where have they come from?' Marsh asked.

'I'm not really allowed to tell you, and if it were not for the extreme unusualness of this specific case, I would not say any more,' Hudson said. He peered at both of them, weighing up the need for security, before continuing. 'We don't yet know. They may be a new enemy weapon, they may not. We have found animate corpses in both British and German uniforms, and some have been positively identified by individuals who knew them in life. What I can tell you is it only seems to be linked to a few locations. A few troops in the line have reported repeatedly shooting soldiers who continued attacking them. But of course, in time of war, the human body can perform many feats of bravery and foolishness.'

'We've not heard anything about this, Sir,' Wells said. 'Surely if there are other incidents like this, word would get around?'

'It's wartime, young man. Rumours are easily suppressed or trans-formed into myths. Besides, this has only begun recently. Mostly we have explained it away as a mania brought on by exposure to the violence of the front line. In fact, this was the explanation I intended to give you.'

'Surely people are getting hurt by these things, killed even?' Wells asked.

'Who can tell on the battlefield? You get bitten by a soldier. Well, that happens in hand-to-hand fighting as well. Being bitten usually carries no further risk that the actual harm of the bite and the subsequent risk of infection. The human mouth is a sewer of bacteria. Mind you,' Hudson said, examining them carefully, interested to see how they would respond to the next piece of information. 'Those who get bitten by the likes of our friend here, are often repeatedly bitten, and there's not much of them left afterwards.'

'You mean the bastard was trying to eat me?' Wells's voice rose as the colour drained from his face.

'That would appear to be the case. Yet, observations suggest more of these creatures can be created because of their bite, with some form of infection passed onward,' the doctor said, hurrying on before Wells could interrupt again. 'But the question is, why did he not eat you? How did you get one of these things all the way back here, intact? So far, the only reliable way to stop these creatures in the wild is a bullet through the brain.'

Wells and Marsh exchanged blank looks, neither able to assimilate what was being said. They were terrified at having come so close to such a fearsome predator.

'Now young man, I must ask you what else you did or said? I want to know about anything you may have left out. I really must insist on this. After all, anything you recall may be for the good of the war effort.'

Doctor Hudson interrogated the two soldiers for quite some time. It seemed he was a colonel with an assignment to investigate such peculiar happenings. He had only been using his surgical skills to help at the aid station because of the additional casualties caused by the attack. Now the doctor had something relevant to his assignment, he discarded his emergency medical role. Other than repeating what had happened, Marsh and Wells could not shed any further light on the puzzle of the animate corpse. During the conversation, the medical officer explained some French West African troops had coined the word 'zombie' upon encountering one creature. Not only did the Colonel explain these colonial troops seemed to have a word for the phenomena, but the creatures already had a place in Western thinking. He explained how, across the centuries, influential thinkers, people such as Descartes and Huxley, had investigated consciousness. These new creatures seemed to fit within Descartes' concept of the ghost within the machine, just with a different purpose to the spirit Descartes investigated.

Most of the logic went over the heads of the two conscript soldiers, and of course, none of these avenues of investigation revealed anything useful to Hudson. However, the zombie Marsh and Wells had brought in was the most interesting case so far. Hudson would pull some strings to further investigate what had occurred. The exquisite corpse, now before him, was a perfect specimen for further study. With luck, Hudson hoped to discover the source of the reanimation. The contributions of Marsh and Wells, bringing this zombie in, could prove important.

Eventually, Hudson allowed the two soldiers to return to their unit, promising he would contact them again with additional questions. In the meantime, they were sworn to silence, forbidden from divulging information about the unnatural nature of the casualty. The Colonel provided them with a pass. Without it, the military police would pick them up as deserters.

Short of a major German offensive, the two soldiers would get some rest time before the army called upon their services again.

5

THE VILLAGE

"Outbreaks of the syndrome among the civilian population are to be purged with maximum efficiency."
British Trench Standing Order from late 1917.

H IS RIFLE TURNED INTO mud every time he tried to use it as the Germans kept coming at him. The weapon ran out of bullets, jamming each time he attempted to reload. The only weapon he had at hand was a wooden plank, which riddled with rot either splintered on the unstoppable Germans or could not be wielded with enough force to cause any harm.

Marsh awoke from the dream, sweating. He took a deep breath, remembering where he was and what had happened. On reflection, it was strange he had a nightmare about the incident fighting the German in the trench, rather than a dream of the genuine horror of Private Gibson. A zombie, the doctor had said, animated or reanimated dead attacking humans. How could this be? Had mankind gone too far with technology, some eccentric scientist releasing a horrific plague amidst the desperation of a brutal war? Would this indeed be the war which would end all wars, with humanity literally consuming itself?

As Alfie thought through the events of the previous day, he wondered why the Colonel had been so interested in him. The zombie Gibson had not attacked, at least not after the initial assault on Wells. Marsh had hit Gibson on the head with his rifle butt, yet Hudson had discounted this as the reason the zombie stopped attacking. Hudson had explained the creature did not suffer injuries in the same way as humans, and an impact on the head was not enough to incapacitate or change its behaviour. Injuries, such as losing limbs, which may have caused the death of a human, proved mere inconveniences to a zombie. It would continue attacking until the brain was destroyed.

The Colonel had sworn them to secrecy, and upon being reunited with their squad, Marsh and Wells had omitted the details of what occurred when they met Hudson. They kept close to the truth, leaving out Gibson's death and his attempt to eat Wells. The curt note from the Colonel had fulfilled the needs of their commanding officer, even if their story had not satisfied their squad mates.

Wells was just as disturbed, if not more so than Marsh. After all, Wells suffered the assault, not Marsh. Alfie wondered how his friend was doing. He suspected Wells slept poorly as well.

The squad gathered, just as intact as they had been when they last visited a German trench together. Each man relayed their own stories of escape, many of them fortunate, blessed with an element of luck. Wells and Marsh continued to edit their own story. Davies and Matthews had escaped together, straight back into their own trench. Morgan, Simmonds and Scott each spent varying amounts of time pinned down in shell holes during the artillery barrage, which heralded the German counter-attack.

Examining the clearing, while drinking a mug of tea sweetened with condensed milk, Marsh could see how much the battalion had suffered. Already under-strength before the attack, the force now comprised just over one hundred men. This number was just enough to fill one functional company. The squads comprising their platoon had taken the least casualties. Another platoon, which had assaulted the blockhouse from the left, was decimated by the full wrath of the machine gun.

'NCO's, five minutes!' a corporal shouted from the edge of the field.

'That's it then,' Corporal Scott said, getting up and tipping the remains of his tea on the grass.

'Maybe the war's over and they're sending us home,' Morgan said, mumbling over his own hot mug, not in the slightest bit optimistic.

'Nah Taff, we'll be taking up the Kaiser's personal invitation to march through the centre of Berlin before we go home,' Simmonds said, brightening up at the opportunity to expand upon Morgan's sarcasm.

'You're both wrong,' Wells said, joining in on the act. 'They're about to be told that I'm now the quarter-master general. Then they'll be going to get me my coach and horse plus a whole wagon of beer.'

When the laughter stopped, Marsh raised the issue which had been playing upon his mind. 'When we were in that trench, I thought I'd bought it,' Marsh said. They listened with solemn faces, each replaying their own worst memories. 'I mean, there were two of them, and they disarmed me. I was left hitting them with a plank of wood.'

'Aye, and you won, didn't you? Otherwise, you wouldn't be here,' Matthews said. 'So don't dwell on it. You survived.'

'But I shouldn't have got into that kind of position in the first place,' Marsh said, not processing what Matthews had just said. 'I couldn't defend myself. I'm not cut out to be a soldier.'

'And that's why we buddy up, isn't it?' Matthews poured the dregs from his mug onto the grass. 'Wells stepped in and did what your buddy should do. We look out for each other, and by doing so, we each have a better chance of surviving.'

'But am I a liability? I wasn't cut out for training and I seem no better here.' Marsh glared at Taff, who was readying a flippant response. 'And none of your shit, Taff.'

'No-one's cut out for this war. It grinds men up. There's nothing you can do if fate has dealt you a duff hand. The good, the bad, we all go the same way,' Simmonds said. 'See the rest of the battalion. We got lucky and attacked a soft spot. The rest of them had to charge machine guns.'

The survivors were ragged, tired if not exhausted. As the NCOs attended their meeting, the men of the battalion sat around their stoves in depleted groups. Most of the men sat quietly, a few talked. Many of them displayed visible injuries, glancing hits from shrapnel and cuts from the barbed wire. A few soldiers showed evidence of mental illness, with uncontrollable shakes among the most obvious indications. Very few of the men looked capable of further military action, a depleted battalion further bled and exhausted by a brief, and partially successful, action. The blockhouse may have been knocked out, but the Germans still possessed the trench. The fortifications would soon be rebuilt.

'Move out in ten minutes!' Corporal Scott called as he walked back to his squad. A spring was visible in his step. He was also no longer a corporal. Fresh sergeant stripes were pinned on his sleeve.

'What're those, mate?' Taff asked, among the first to notice Scott's good news. He pointed at his own sleeve.

'I've been temporarily bumped up to sergeant. I'll be taking the platoon role. Wells, you're the best out of this rabble, and you're enough of a criminal to be a corporal. Catch!' Scott said, throwing a set of old corporal stripes at Wells. Wells caught them.

'But Sarge, what about Matthews?' Wells asked, a tentative smile on his face. He wanted the promotion, but worried about offending Matthews.

'It's fine Wells, I mean Corporal Wells. The Sarge here knows I ain't no leader, you are,' Matthews said, walking over and offering his hand to the new corporal.

Matthews was just the first. Wells was soon surrounded by his friends offering their congratulations.

'We're moving out of the line,' Scott said, a malevolent smile choking off some cheers. 'It's not a rest, though, lads. We're needed in a little village just south-east of here, some sort of civil disturbance.'

'Corporal Wells, and Marsh, come with me,' Scott ordered, emphasising the new rank. Scott walked off, knowing they would follow.

'The Commanding Officer has received a curious message about the two of you. It's come down from division. Would you care to tell me what dirty tricks you've been up to?' Scott asked, giving the two friends the chance to implicate themselves in the sort of criminal behaviour which was never far from Wells.

'Well, you see. Something kind of happened during the last attack—'

'And we've been ordered not to tell anyone about it, Sarge.' Wells said, interrupting before Marsh went too far.

'I see, well, the orders from on high have asked that you two be present when we enter the village. It was explained we should listen to any wisdom you should offer while we are there. It was also suggested that Wells lead the squad and is tasked with keeping Marsh safe. I don't care for all this nonsense, so it's a good job I agree you're the best man to lead the squad, Josh.' Scott let the words hang in the air. 'Would either of you care to tell me what the hell makes you two so important?'

'Er, Sarge, we were ordered not to talk,' Wells said, repeating his instructions. 'We can give you advice, but our orders were explicit on what we could not say.'

'Whoever ordered you, are they here? Bollocks, they ain't. Are they big? Are they about to shove their massive size ten boot up your arse?' Scott said with menace.

'No Sarge,' Wells said, gulping. He then stayed silent hoping Scott would not follow through on the threat.

'Sarge, I'll give you some general pointers, so we all stay safe,' Marsh said.

'Be careful, Alfie. Don't cross the line,' Wells said. He paled under Scott's glare. The veteran was a natural sergeant.

'Don't trust anyone we find there. Keep them at a distance. If we have to shoot anyone, only aim for the head. Don't ask me why, I can't tell you,' Marsh said, stopping to think for a moment. 'Oh, and if it looks like things are under control, don't shoot.'

'Alfie? What's that last bit about?' Wells asked. 'Don't you mean shoot, regardless?'

'Trust me,' Marsh said. 'Think about it.'

'Well, if you two comedians will not give me a straight answer, I'll have to follow your suggestions. I'm sure the CO adores this lack of clarity. Perhaps he'll be able to get more out of you.' Scott said. He walked off to spread the advice to the rest of the unit, muttering about 'the fine mess' his men had got themselves into.

'What a great start to life as a corporal,' Wells said, complaining.

'I've got news for you. It only gets better. They'll not give you a pay-rise for months as it's a battlefield promotion,' Marsh said, knowing Wells would make good the difference with a couple of his illicit deals.

'There's always a bloody silver lining with you, isn't there?'

The small village comprised less than two dozen buildings, running along the sides of the road. A couple of farm buildings, the typical small farms found in the area, were set further back from the road. A copse of trees on the other side of the village presented a natural boundary, marking the end of the settlement. The village was silent, lifeless. Being far enough behind the front line, only a partial evacuation would have been the most attempted, so the village should not have been deserted.

The under-strength battalion broke from the road and entered a loose skirmish formation as it entered the edge of the village. Wells' squad was kept in the centre of the line, held in reserve so Wells and Marsh could deploy according to need. The officers and NCOs remained suspicious about the naming of the two soldiers in the orders. Quite a few questions had been posed, and several threats issued, but neither soldier gave away more than they had already revealed.

'It's quiet,' Morgan said, stating the obvious. He shifted his grip on his rifle so he could respond to any sudden threats.

'What do you expect? This is a tiny little village. More sheep than villagers here,' Sergeant Scott said.

'At least we're well behind the front line,' Morgan said. 'There'll not be many pesky Hun machine guns around here.'

'Keep on your toes, men,' the Captain said. He led the under-strength battalion. 'Wells, take your squad into the centre of the village and check this place out. We'll stand ready, here at the edge.'

The village remained untouched by the war in any discernible way, the front line having not passed through the area. Fields had not been ploughed by artillery, the buildings all stood intact, and no marauding soldiers liberated supplies or were billeted upon the locals. The squad moved into the village, rifles ready, each man staying close to whatever cover offered itself. They were greeted by an unnatural silence, no human noises, no animals, not even birds.

'It's like a ghost town,' Wells said to Marsh. They sheltered behind a water trough at the entrance to the village. 'Taff, Davies, check that building on the left,' Wells ordered.

The two men ran up to the first building, a small single floor home. They peaked in the front windows before opening the unlocked door and charging in. Within a minute, they returned to the street.

'Clear, Corporal,' Davies called. They had only received minimal training in house-to-house fighting before their deployment, but had worked out some basic tactics on the way to the village.

'Next building then,' Well said, waving his fingers in a circle above his head.

The squad proceeded towards the centre of the village, checking each building one by one. The rest of their diminished platoon joined the task, speeding up the process. No villagers were visible. The silence was unnatural, and rather than becoming casual in their searches, the men grew tense. Something was not right.

Only a few buildings remained in their search, including the village bakery and the small church. As they closed on the remaining buildings, the combat strength of the entire battalion, all one hundred soldiers, deployed across the road behind Wells' squad, ready to deal with any trouble.

'Smells like something died in there!' Taff Morgan roared before opening the door to the old church.

'Stop!' Marsh shouted, but it was too late.

'What the fuck!' Morgan backed away from the open doorway, so surprised he almost dropped his rifle. His foot slipped on a cobblestone and he went down on one knee before rising and running from the doorway.

An inhuman, animal noise came from the open doorway, and within seconds, the villagers appeared. The soldiers had not been told what to expect, despite the guarded guidance given by Wells and Marsh. In a moment, Marsh realised this secrecy was a mistake. These men needed to know what they faced, and maintaining security was not a good enough excuse. He knew he was right as he observed panicked glances spread among the soldiers as the civilians exited the church, running towards them. The villagers moved with great awkwardness, some shuffled, some ran, many limped. Several appeared to possess horrific wounds, chunks missing from the flesh, exposed bones visible on unsteady limbs. One teenage girl, beautiful in the flush of youth, was missing part of her face, the jawbone exposed.

'Shit!' shouted the battalion Lewis gunner, firing an uncontrolled burst into the growing crowd. The recoil kicked the machine gun up in his hands, many of the bullets missing, flying above the villagers' heads before burying themselves in the stonework above the doorway. However, a few of the panicked shots found their mark, and five villagers dropped to the ground as the bullets smacked into their torsos. Rifle fire joined in from all around as other soldiers responded to the horrific vision emerging from the sanctified building. The volume of fire grew as the terrified riflemen watched the villagers, floored by the first machine gun volley, rising from their slumber.

The Lewis gunner exhausted his ammunition and set about changing his ammunition disc. Before he completed the attachment of the new magazine, the first villagers were upon him. They knocked him to the floor, tearing and biting as the man screamed in agony. The crescendo of rifle fire reached a peak as the creatures closed upon soldiers trained for trench warfare, not for the unnatural combat they now faced. Widespread trepidation spread as the soldiers realised a few villagers were staying down when hit by the heavy rifle bullets. Instead, they arose and continued their attacks.

Marsh watched as one middle-aged woman charged down a rifleman. Three times the soldier shot her, three times she fell to the ground, and three times she got back up again. After the first impact, she limped, but that did not sufficiently slow her. The bullets seemed to do no damage at all. The soldier drew his bayonet, trying to fix it to the end of his rifle, but he was too late. She smashed into the man, tearing and clawing, her teeth snapping at his face.

Marsh recovered his wits and fired, aiming at the head of his target. A single shot and the villager dropped, not rising again. He had been so busy watching the horror playing out around him; he had forgotten to remind the soldiers of the one critical piece of advice he had been given for dealing with these creatures. 'Aim for the heads!' Marsh shouted above the noise, but to no avail.

The Lewis gunner had been left by the horde. His crumpled and partially consumed form arose, immense damage having been done to his exposed hands, face and neck. Blood still poured from a neck wound, damaged neck ligaments leaving his head lopsided as he turned to face a soldier outside the bakery. The soldier panicked and shot at the horrifying visage which had been his compatriot. In seconds, the Lewis gunner fell upon the rifleman, biting and tearing.

'We've got to get out of here!' Wells was close enough Marsh could hear him over all the noise. 'We're being overrun by these things.'

'Zombies, that's what the Colonel called them,' Marsh said as he loaded a fresh clip of ammunition into his magazine. He was surprised he did not fumble the clip, jamming the rounds in the breech. He realised his control was down to the relentless training he had undergone.

'Fall back to the edge of the village! Fall back!' their captain shouted. Several sergeants and corporals echoed him.

A rout began, not an organised withdrawal. The under-strength unit was now reduced to half the size it was before the church doors opened. Several soldiers, overwhelmed by the villagers, were rising to join the ranks of the zombies. The devastation was not one-sided. There were zombies which no longer moved, having been on the receiving end of severe head injuries during the melee.

His rifle clicked on an empty breech once more, and Marsh looked up while reloading his rifle. Five bore down upon him and Wells. Wells, rifle up, was missing the heads of his targets as often as hitting them. Two of the zombies dropped to the ground. The remaining three leapt at Marsh. He used his rifle as a barrier to keep them from biting. He had not even had time to fit his bayonet, not that it would have been much use as it was effective against flesh and organs rather than a bony skull. The three creatures pushed Marsh to the ground, one on top held back from his face by the rifle Marsh held protectively across his own chest. An odour of rot came from the snapping mouth. In a moment of abstract lucidity, Marsh realised the villager was not breathing. The corpse was cold, an animated death, just as Colonel Hudson had described it. Out of the corner of his eye, he could see Wells' rifle butt coming down upon the head of one of their three remaining assailants.

'Stop! Stop!' Marsh shouted in the desperate frustration of the struggle. He used all his strength to push the zombie off him. The zombie stopped struggling. It relaxed and Marsh pushed it aside. The creature fell away and did not attack him further.

'What did you do?' Wells asked, rifle pointed at the two zombies on the ground by Marsh. Both still moved, but no longer attacked. 'Why aren't they attacking? What's happening?'

'I don't know,' Marsh replied. 'Look over there. They are still attacking.'

The two villagers stood up but still did not move to attack either Marsh or Wells. They snapped the air, as if sensing prey nearby, aware of the proximity of the living, but not with sufficient clarity to attack.

'You shouted stop, and they stopped. Isn't that what happened?' Wells scratched at his nose as an idea formed. 'Tell these two to move over there,' Wells said, pointing to a doorway.

'Go there,' Marsh said to the zombies, pointing at the doorway. The two villagers shuffled over without complaint, teeth snapping, their senses drawn to the living.

'We're on to something here.' Turning to the zombies, Wells said, 'Sit down and stay.' The villagers ignored him. Wells looked at Marsh encouraging him to try.

'Sit down. Stay there,' Marsh commanded. The zombies sat down and did not move from the spot.

'Bloody hell! Let's see if we can get the rest of this lot under control,' Wells said. He still did not trust the compliance of their recent assailants. His rifle continued to cover the passive zombies.

The remains of the battalion had formed an old-fashioned infantry square. The formation was ideal for holding off attackers from different sides, but was no longer part of modern military training. An 'old hand' among them had come up with the idea in a moment of desperation. The battalion was about to be wiped out, down to less than forty soldiers. Over one hundred villagers and former infantrymen faced them, all reanimated as zombies. Three sides of the square underwent constant attack. While the soldiers had adjusted to the idea of shooting the zombies in the head, such accuracy required control under pressure. Close-quarters fighting was what they had been trained for, but a bayonet was not as effective as it was against ordinary flesh and blood. They were now engaged in a close-quarters fight they could not win.

'Josh, cover me. I'm going to get close enough for my voice to be heard,' Marsh said, before running up behind the line of zombies attacking one side of the square. He ducked low, hoping he would not be hit by stray bullets, or worse, mistaken for an assailant.

'Sit down!' Marsh shouted as loud as he could.

All the zombies within earshot sat down. They ceased their attacks, even though Marsh had not told them to. The unexpected change did not stop the soldiers from taking advantage of the new situation, shooting each zombie in the head. Marsh ran into the centre of the square, issuing the same commands to the zombies assailing the two other sides of the position. The zombies ceased attacking and sat down. The remaining soldiers did not hesitate.

'What the hell is going on, Marsh?' Scott said, after shooting an old Frenchman at point blank range. He considered shooting Marsh next, but seemed to change his mind as the Captain joined them. 'And don't give me none of your "I can't tell you, Sarge" bullshit.'

'They're called zombies by the French. Division reported small numbers in our sector of the line, and they've got a Colonel Hudson of the Medical Corps working on it. Wells and I came across a fellow in the middle of no man's land and took him back for medical aid. It turned out he was a zombie, and that's when we met Hudson, who swore us to secrecy.'

'Well, if you had told us what we were up against, and that you can do something about them, we would not have suffered so many casualties,' the Captain said, spitting on the ground in disgust.

'Sir, Alfie didn't know,' Wells said. He had seen Scott's anger and then the grimace the Captain had shown. If he did not intervene, there was a risk one of them would put a bullet in Marsh.

'Didn't know what, Corporal?'

'Know these creatures would do what he told them. I was there when we took one to the aid station.'

'Yes, Sir. It's something I didn't know about,' Marsh said. 'Now I think about it, it makes sense. The guy we took back to the aid station, he did what I told him. He even stopped trying to attack Wells when I said so.'

'I bet that's why the Colonel took a special interest in us then,' Wells said, piecing together the pieces. 'He was suspicious about why the zombie behaved so passively. He must have suspected one of us did something to it.'

'We did nothing.'

'But, Marsh, you did something. You didn't hit it or anything, but you told it to stop, so it stopped. Just now you told them to stop, and they did.'

'Well, it's a shame we've killed the lot of them then,' Scott said with something of a sarcastic tone. 'If you can order these things around, I'm sure the Brass would have loved to have you sending them at the Krauts.'

The Captain nodded his agreement with Scott's assessment.

'Maybe we can still do it,' Wells volunteered, aware the immediate danger had passed.

'What do you mean, Corporal?' the Captain asked.

'Before we came over here, we were cornered. Alfie told a couple of zombies to stay, and they did. I bet they're still there now.' Wells nodded his head to indicate where he had left the zombies unattended. 'We kind of forgot about them during all the excitement.'

'Go fetch them, Marsh,' the Captain ordered. 'Wells, go with him. And Scott, make sure our lads hold their fire but stay alert. We don't want another scrap like the last one.'

The two men ran over to where they had left the two zombies, skipping the corpses of soldier and civilian alike. Scott commanded the rest of the troops to stand ready, reminding them to hold their fire. Several complaints were made, but the threat of a 'boot up yer arse' was sufficient as one of the lesser consequences for disobedience. Marsh was relieved Scott was ramming home the instructions. He did not want to get shot by his own side, especially now the fight in the village was over. At least Marsh hoped the struggle was over. There could be other zombies hidden in places not yet searched.

'Coming out!' Wells shouted, readying the survivors.

'Stand and walk into the open,' Marsh commanded the two zombies, which were where they had been left.

At Marsh's command, the villagers stood and walked into the middle of the street. Other words, such as 'stop' worked on the villagers, and Marsh was thrilled as the creatures responded. The moving corpses made no aggressive move towards either Wells or Marsh, but they still snapped the air, making noises like groans. With a series of precise instructions, Marsh moved the two villagers, so they stood before the wary troops. The business end of several rifles tracked each zombie, the operators ready for the slightest provocation. With a flash of inspiration, Marsh ordered the zombies to lie face-down on the ground, a position which would put the soldiers at ease.

'My God, man!' the Captain exclaimed. 'They're under your control. I wouldn't have believed it if I'd not seen it with my own eyes. Not that I'd have believed anything we've seen in this village. But at least we're safe now, what with these things doing as you tell them. Think of the possibilities? I thought these beasts were unstoppable and worse than the Hun to deal with. Imagine what a platoon of these would do to the enemy.'

'So we'll not get eaten then?' Taff Morgan said, sounding disappointed. He had a few scratches across his face from a close fought hand-to-hand combat with an unpleasant old lady.

'No, we'll not be eaten. But not just that,' the Captain said, answering Morgan's question as if it were serious. 'These beings are almost invincible. Machine guns and rifles hardly harm them. Other than a direct hit, artillery will not be effective either. If they are dead, then gas will not harm them either. But, best of all, they are following instructions. This could be the decisive weapon we've been searching for, something to win us the war.'

'Aren't you getting a bit ahead of yourself, Sir?' Marsh asked. 'We've only two zombies, and who knows how many we'll need, or be able to control.'

'Well, I'm sure the chaps with the prominent foreheads and big brains can figure that out for us. Also, we had an entire village full here. You saw what happened when they took out our men, some of our own rose and joined the villagers.'

6

A PLAN

"I possess positive evidence of a variation in the syndrome. This variance has been demonstrated through an ability to control the reanimated. The implications for the war effort are significant."

Undated correspondence from Col O. Hudson to an unnamed recipient. This letter is part of a collection of documents obtained by Milton Davies, published as an appendix in Milton Davies, A History of Zombies and Warfare, (London, 2016)

THE RAGGED REMAINS OF the battalion made camp a long way from any other units. Too few people remained for them to be called a battalion and anyone without combat experience, passing close enough, would suspect they were a much smaller formation. A veteran of the trenches would mistake them for a unit torn apart by the brutality of trench warfare. No passerby would guess the true reason the battalion self-isolated itself.

Before leaving the village, Marsh searched for more of the undead, but no more functioning zombies were discovered. Plenty of evidence existed of villagers and British soldiers who had turned into zombies, but were destroyed in the last fight. No other living survivors were discovered either. The entire population of the village had been destroyed by the outbreak and the successful British suppression mission. They eliminated the unrecognised threat to the British rear areas, even if it proved a costly exercise for the unit involved.

Before they exited the village, the two zombies were bound and gagged. The soldiers were wary of their captives, guards who knew what their charges were capable of. The prisoners were secured, restrained in a canvas tent, while the remains of the battalion licked their wounds. Including the walking wounded from the earlier combat against the Germans, most of whom returned to them in dribs and drabs during the evening, there were only seventy-two effectives in the unit. This was not even enough soldiers to form a company. In due course, the battalion would either be broken up, to provide replacements for other units, or withdrawn from the line for a lengthy period of rebuilding. Of course, the battalion had been under strength when Marsh joined. Yet, even in a much depleted state, they had been thrown first into an assault, and then into a policing operation worse than any combat.

Among Marsh's friends, only Simmonds suffered severe injuries from the zombies. Their luck had held both through the combat with the Germans, and then in the brutal fight in the village. Simmonds, much to his annoyance, was sent off to the aid station. Sent off was a bit of a misnomer, as Colonel Hudson arrived with an aid station as soon as they made camp, so Simmonds only suffered the inconvenience of a short walk. The aid station was sited in the middle of the small battalion encampment. Hudson examined every single soldier who had engaged the zombies. Those who were bitten and scratched, such as Simmonds, were detained for further observation. Rumours spread about their encampment being surrounded by other detachments, primed to open fire should zombies take over the aid station and surrounding tents. Such a scorched earth policy would have worried the survivors more if they had not been so exhausted.

Hudson was in good humour, and this went a long way to reassure the survivors. In the doctor, they recognised a man who knew about the zombies. He would not be present if there was a significant risk. The tired soldiers were also amused as Hudson clapped his hands with delight when Marsh showed his unprecedented control over the two captive zombies. The captives even cooperated when Hudson took tissue samples from them. Hudson made Marsh's head spin with his avalanche of questions, trying to piece together what was going on. Some questions seemed relevant, but other enquiries about Marsh's relationship with his parents seemed less so. Perhaps Hudson was a student of Freud, Marsh wondered at one point.

For the first time, every soldier in his vicinity seemed focused on Marsh, looking up to him with respect in their eyes. This was a novel experience. Used to the tolerance of other soldiers, their contempt at worst, he was unused to receiving their respect. His colleagues might be suspicious, as there were unnatural things occurring, and several were shaken to their core by the unexpected changes to their world-view; however, compared to the alternative of being torn apart by a ravaging horde, Marsh had become a talisman. The experience proved much better than being a person to be wary of, or even feared for his incompetence.

Other units stayed away from the camp, but Marsh still heard the popular rumours of how the battalion had been deployed against civilians and an entire village ended up dead. However, stories about zombies were quashed, and prying individuals remained at a safe distance.

Marsh kept playing the events of the day over in his mind. The sheer horror, coupled with the pace of change, set him on edge. The power he seemed to possess over the zombies astounded him. He could not believe it. His mind wandered to the impact these zombies might have upon the war. He could see how small groups of zombies could drive the Germans out of their trenches, taking out impregnable fortifications which held up entire divisions. Of course, the enemy might consider similar uses of these creatures, and he despaired at the thought of countering such a move.

Colonel Hudson sought out Marsh. Once Hudson had completed his examinations of the wounded, it was clear he wanted the junior soldier's opinion. Taking Marsh aside, he had explained his theory. Marsh would have been honoured to be consulted, but his perceptions of himself were already overwhelmed by his unexpected new status among his peers.

'You see; these creatures appear to be mindless in their pursuit of living flesh to consume. They attack in a rage and are hard to stop, except for you, of course, there is something going on which allows you control,' Hudson said, walking around the tent, puffing on a cigar. He had allowed Marsh to sit, an unexpected experience for someone of Marsh's lowly rank. 'From the samples I took from our mutual friend, Gibson, I confirmed the existence of a bacterial component to these animate dead. It could be a bacterium which energises and animates the dead, while cutting the element of personality and social restraint their higher brain functions provide.'

Hudson waited until Marsh nodded his head before continuing. 'Your two new animated samples have allowed me to confirm this. I have discovered the involvement of a bacterial process and we are now testing the groundwater in the area as the bacteria appear to be as comfortable in water as in the host. We are also tracking down food supplies which may have been contaminated and shared between our victims. As a method of transmission, tainted food is unlikely, but it cannot be ruled out. For now, the General Staff accept my recommendation to extend the civilian exclusion zone behind the front lines so no further unfortunate incidents occur involving the local population.'

'I don't know why, but those who are bitten seem to turn into zombies once they have died. It does not seem to happen to individuals who survive an attack. Perhaps something in our immune system inhibits the bacteria, preventing a takeover while the victim is still alive? Perhaps even you have been infected with the same bacteria, allowing you to communicate with them? Now, let me write that idea down before I forget it.' Hudson walked over to the desk, scrabbling among the refuse for a pencil before scribbling the idea down on a sheet of paper. 'Have you noticed how those dead civilians respond to your orders? You're speaking to them in English, a language which they possessed no understanding of while alive. Some things you say to them are too complicated to be words picked up by chance. This suggests you are communicating on some other level which they understand; maybe telepathy or the utilisation of an undeveloped part of the brain? Again, these are things I must explore. I wonder if we can get anyone else here to command these zombies? I know some of the boys have tried, with no luck so far. Getting back to my previous point on bacteria, we may use this to create new zombies and use them as weapons.'

'But, sir,' Marsh objected, a ripple of horror crossing his face. 'We can't create new zombies. It would be criminal. You may get the odd volunteer, especially among the seriously wounded, but you can't deliberately infect people.'

'There you are wrong, young man. It would be no more criminal than the use of poison gas. Some would also argue no less criminal than deploying machine guns. Have you ever considered the fighter pilot? Should he survive flight school, he has a minimal chance of surviving six weeks of combat before he falls from the sky in his blazing coffin; you know they don't even give pilots parachutes to use? We are even developing another weapon where men are encased in metal to cross the battlefield; while choking on the fumes of the engine used to propel them. You also forget the Royal Navy is blockading Germany into starvation. In this war, we have to think the unthinkable. People are making hard choices, taking risks and dying as a result.'

'My goodness, Sir. Are you saying the ends justify the means? That it would be correct for us to create zombies, if doing so shortens the war?'

'I will not argue the intricacies of consequentialism with you, young man. You want to do that, find a chaplain. However, anything that shortens the war and reduces the burden will be an improvement on the current bloody stalemate. Did you know that during the first three days of the Somme, we lost over forty thousand men?' Hudson dropped the horrifying bombshell of the total British casualties, losses which had been concealed, even from the enlisted men on the front line.

'It couldn't have been that many, Sir?' Marsh said. He hoped the Colonel was exaggerating. The numbers were beyond belief, even for someone with his limited experience of fighting in the trenches.

'What if, for a fraction of that cost, we could break through the German lines just by turning a few thousand troops into zombies? These would be zombies under our control, although in a less than perfect situation, this would still be a course of action worth following, even if we possessed no control. Imagine, a new Battle of the Somme won with a handful of animated corpses, tens of thousands of deaths averted.'

'What if the Germans are thinking the same way? What if they've got zombies, too?' Marsh asked, a whole range of horrifying scenarios running through his mind.

'All the more reason for us to rush ahead with our development of the zombie as a war-winning weapon. They caught us out with poison gas, the U-Boat and the forward-firing interrupter gun on fighter aircraft. We can't have them catch us out on this. At the moment, you are the most prized asset in our entire Empire, the only person we know of who can control zombies.'

'You can't mean that, Sir.' Marsh said, the blood rushing from his face as he understood the significance of Hudson's words.

'Well, until we can find someone else who can control these zombies the way you can, you are unique. We know how to create more zombies, and failing all else, we'll recruit them from the German front line. However, we don't know how to create another one of you.'

'So how will we go about solving that problem, Sir? It sounds as if you've already thought through the issue.'

'Much as I'd love to vivisect you, I would kill the goose which laid the golden egg,' Hudson said, chuckling at the loud gulp which emanated from Marsh as the younger soldier processed what vivisection meant. 'First, we need to establish methods of transmission. We will examine whether animals can receive the infection either through injection with the bacteria or from the zombies themselves. I will also see if I can find a few desperate volunteers in the casualty clearing stations, men who have no hope but still wish to strike a final blow against the enemy. However, I do not conceive how we can find more of you, nor how we can recreate your unique skills.'

'Sir, maybe the zombies can find others that can lead them? Perhaps if I took one zombie, crated it and located it near large numbers of troops who took turns to shout instructions, we'd find more people like me. We'd keep the ruse secret, but be able to observe any reaction from the zombie to instructions. If the zombie reacts, we'll have found a new handler.'

'I like the idea. It's better than the options I was considering. Now the easiest places to undertake this would be in the infantry depots on the coast,' Hudson said, running with the idea. 'There will be plenty of men redeploying after a stint on the front lines. You'd have to watch out for spies so you'll need security, but such a plan would give you the access you'd need to large numbers of soldiers. Perhaps I could arrange a letter from the General Staff to ease your way. If the Staff were to change the training regime in the depots to include a section on command, perhaps on shouting orders, you would have an easy way to identify potential men to control our zombies.'

A silence formed as the two men thought through the idea.

'Hmm, Marsh, I think we have a plan coming together.' Hudson scratched at the stubble on his chin. 'Away with you then, and not a word to anyone else. I will think about this tonight and draft your orders tomorrow.'

PART 2 - TIGERS ON THE WESTERN FRONT

7

RECRUITING

'From the initial deployment of tigers, it was not clear
if they would be the decisive war-winning weapon we
hoped for.'

Hudson, O, 'One Hell of a War: The Memoirs of
Brigadier Oliver Hudson' (1934, London)

F OLLOWING THE ACTION IN the village, new orders arrived for
the battalion. The formation was being taken out of the line
to investigate the 'interesting circumstances' of the animate corpses.
Although the orders were signed by the General Staff, many of the
men suspected Colonel Hudson had written them. Marsh knew for
certain the Colonel was behind them, and despite being a lowly soldier, Hudson had consulted him on several points. A few replacement troops were expected, and widespread testing of soldiers was
beginning. Hudson hoped potential handlers would be found for the
zombies.

Of far greater importance to Marsh, Wells sourced several fresh eggs and a slab of bacon, which left Marsh satisfied after a tasty breakfast. It did not take a genius to deduce an officer's mess nearby was missing breakfast, but none of them experienced the slightest trace of guilt.

Another resourceful member of the battalion found a few goats from somewhere, and Hudson was engaging with experiments on the animals. As part of the investigations into Marsh's newfound skills, he also underwent a significant number of tests.

'Morning Sarge, come to use me as a pincushion as well?' Marsh asked Scott, already annoyed by all the needles being stuck in him during a goat-less experiment.

'Stand to attention when an officer enters the room,' Scott said, but the grin on his face showed he was joking about standing to attention, but not about an officer entering the tent.

'Congratulations, Sir.' Marsh shook Scott's hand while patting him on the back. He was careful not to shake loose the needles stuck in his arm.

'I've been made up to acting lieutenant. No pay rise, but a battlefield commission,' Scott said, delighted to be promoted to rank far beyond which he would have believed possible in his pre-war army career.

'We must have taken more of a beating than I thought if they've commissioned you.' Marsh smiled from ear to ear, delighted for his friend.

'We must have taken more of a beating than I thought, Sir,' Scott said, emphasising his new title before continuing. 'This was all your doing, what with the zombie situation. When Colonel Hudson wants something, he gets it. He wanted our battalion, and he needs officers to help run it. He's our new commanding officer now.'

'I thought he was just a medic, not a fire-eating combat officer.'

'It seems he's a bit more than he appears. The battalion has even been renamed. We're now the 1st Experimental Battalion, and we seem to be priority on everything but new pairs of hands. Clearly, there's an advantage to having a colonel running an outfit of this size, rather than a major or lieutenant colonel. I'll even have an officer's uniform by tomorrow. But that's not the half of it.'

'There's more? We've only been here a short time, and everything's changing again,' Alfie said, raising an eyebrow and adding a cheeky, 'Sir.'

'Wells is being made up to sergeant, and you're going to be corporal.' Scott removed a pair of stripes from his pocket and handed them to Marsh. 'Congratulations.'

'You'll have your own squad. Wells will be the platoon sergeant, and I'll be your officer. You can pick your own lance corporal.'

'Are you sure I'm ready for it?' Marsh asked, well aware his reputation as a soldier left a lot to be desired. He had scraped through training, and so far, survived combat through luck and teamwork.

'You are joking, aren't you? You're the only person here who can control these beasts. I'm surprised you're not being promoted higher than corporal.' Like the other remaining soldiers in the battalion, Scott had Marsh to thank for saving him. When the unit was almost overrun while attending to a civil disturbance. The General Staff had omitted to inform them in advance the disorder was caused by zombies, not that the soldiers would have believed such creatures existed. Yet, Marsh and Wells were already familiar with zombies, having met one in the front lines, Marsh unexpectedly controlling the creature. This drew him to the attention of more important people.

'So am I.'

'You may be rubbish at the spit and polish, but you've survived the Germans once, and the zombies twice. In my book, that makes you perfect for running something.'

'I want Tom as lance corporal. He knows what he's doing. He's a veteran and doesn't want the job, so he'll do it well and not take any crap off the others,' Marsh said. They both knew he would have to undertake a great deal of persuading to convince Matthews to take the role.

'He's a good choice, but you'll have to work on him. If he wanted a promotion, he'd have taken one a while back,' Scott said, presenting a massive grin. 'Now Corporal, the Old Man wants to see you. Let's get those stripes stitched on double-quick, shall we?'

'Ah, Lieutenant Scott and Corporal Marsh. I was just considering you, Corporal,' Colonel Hudson said. Hudson had a dead goat on his desk. He wore surgical clothes and was in the middle of a dissection, his writing desk standing in for the lack of an operating table. Marsh did not want to know why the Colonel had thought about him while dissecting the animal.

'Scott, can you wait outside, please? The Corporal and I have some scientific matters to discuss.'

'Marsh, I would offer to shake your hand but...' Hudson waved his gloved, bloodied hands in the air as Scott took his leave. 'Now, have a look through that microscope over there. Yes, the one on top of the chest.'

Marsh peered through the lens. He had never used a microscope before, and while he knew what to do, he struggled to get his eyes lined up correctly. Feeling a bit of an idiot, he closed one eye.

'Well, what do you see, man?'

'Little things moving around in a liquid, Sir,' Marsh said, doubting himself. He was neither certain of what he could see nor why the Colonel would require his opinion.

'Bacteria!' Hudson proclaimed, almost jumping with enthusiasm. 'These are the very bacteria we find in the zombies. They have no natural business infesting a corpse, so I suspect these are the animating principles of the creatures. We have found them in our zombies, but this sample was in the blood of this here goat. But does this goat arise to savage me?'

'No, Sir.' Humouring officers was always wise, especially if you did not understand what they were talking about. His mind wandered to Scott. Now Scott was one of that other breed, would it mean he would need humouring as well? Marsh experienced a denseness in his stomach at the thought.

'Rhetorical question, Corporal. Of course, the goat is not acting in such a way. I am therefore going to hypothesise the animal cannot be reanimated. So far, only humans seem to be reanimated by these bacteria. Still, I will need to test a variety of other creatures to establish the universality of my theory.' Hudson caught Marsh's attention, a shiver running through Marsh at the apparent joy he noted in the officer's demeanour, unsure if he identified pleasure at the working hypothesis or the future dissections.

'I'll also have to investigate if eating this infected animal flesh corrupts a human. Potentially, our cooking processes neutralise the bacteria. Now that will be a fascinating investigation,' the Colonel said, his face went blank as he contemplated this avenue of research. 'Nevertheless, we must turn our attention to your mission.'

'Mission, Sir?'

'Yes, you suggested it yourself yesterday. It's damn useful to have someone like you around, someone who can work hands-on with the zombies. It removes a lot of the guesswork from my own investigations.' Hudson said, humming to himself as he removed his gloves, cleaning his hands on a filthy rag. Once clean, he picked up a cardboard folder from among the papers chaotically covering a chair. The chair was doing service as a substitute desk while the desk was used for dissections. 'These here are your orders, along with the passes and letters, to ensure you receive the full cooperation you need. Included is even a letter from General Haig himself, should you find your other authorisations do not persuade others to the importance of your work. Please do not use Haig's letter unless you absolutely must. It will draw more attention to you than is politic. It's far better you keep a low profile.'

Marsh took the folder. A letter from the head of the British Expeditionary Force in France, Marsh wondered, given to a simple bloody soldier. This whole zombie business was being taken seriously if General Haig was being kept informed. He wanted to take out the letter and read it, but the Colonel was already talking again.

'Of course, you may not reveal the nature of our special project to anyone. The details are classified as "Most Secret", and you'll find the letter from General Haig is red printed, so any staff officer will recognise it is from him by that alone. Now, just to clarify how secret this project is, I report directly to General Haig. His chief of staff knows we are working on something experimental, but not what it is. So, the details of our work are only known by one man outside of our encampment, the General himself. Any leaks will be dealt with harshly, and this will be explained to each individual before they leave this camp. Secrecy is vital. In the meantime, we have military police forming a perimeter around our position to prevent contact with the outside.'

Marsh knew the military police had done a poor job of stopping Wells from liberating breakfast from a neighbouring unit. He would not notify Hudson of the breach.

'Now, from this point onward, our cover story is we work with exotic animals. We're searching for combat applications on the battlefield. With our immense commitments in India, it will surprise no one we would seek to leverage opportunities offered by the sub-continent. Therefore, we will use the cover name of 'tiger' to describe our charges. To everyone, except those directly involved, research into unusual animals will be our purpose. This cover also has the added side benefit of giving us the excuse to bring in large quantities of livestock for experimentation, and I'm sure some of the meat will find its way into the mess pots as a bonus.'

'Tigers it is then, Sir,' Marsh said. It seemed a plausible cover, but he was no expert in such subterfuges.

'As you visit the infantry depots, you will maintain the illusion of caring for a captive animal. Everyone will assume we have a man-eater, and they would not be wrong. Because of the experimental nature of our work, the tiger must not be revealed to anyone other than the team of handlers. Be very firm with any busybodies who should cross your path. I'm sure there will be some old India hands who would like a nostalgic nosey at an exotic pet from India.'

'Now you will travel with your squad. There's no sense in splitting you boys up. I'll attach a newly arrived Staff Sergeant to keep you organised and make certain Lieutenant Scott accompanies you. These two will run interference with the busybodies and will be briefed on your orders and the permissions therein. You job is to focus on the core aspects of the venture, identifying and recruiting men who can control our special beasts, assuming we are correct in our supposition about control. On issues relating to our tigers, you will have my authority to act as you see fit, reporting to me,' Hudson said. A mischievous grin flashed on his face. No doubt the man was considering how a lowly corporal could abuse such authority. 'Of course, on all other issues, you will follow the normal chain of command through your non-commissioned and commissioned officers. I allow you this discretion because there is no-one better qualified for this task than you.'

'Your primary aim is to seek other servicemen who can control the tigers. I will continue experiments here with volunteers, but we must find other natural handlers if we are to make any use of the tigers as a weapon.'

'Are there questions, Marsh?' The Colonel ended the interview by scrutinising a severed piece of goat.

'When do I get going, Sir?' Marsh asked.

'Right away. Godspeed,' Hudson said, dismissing Marsh.

Marsh left as quickly as possible. He did not like the sounds he left behind as the Colonel returned to his grisly work. Marsh soon found Lieutenant Scott. The newly minted officer was hovering by the

Colonel's tent, confused by his new elevated status, and if not by his rank, then by the radical challenge to his understanding of the afterlife.

'I've got our orders, Sir,' Marsh said.

'Yes, the Colonel briefed me earlier. It should be a fun tour. Étaples will be our first stop, I believe,' Scott said, grimacing. 'I never thought I'd end up back there, but at least we won't be running around like the other poor sods. Perhaps someone will recognise me? I can't wait to see the look on the faces of some of those Canaries. Those bastards are a right miserable lot, and they'll be even more miserable when they discover I'm now an officer.' Scott rubbed his hands together. 'Oh, I shouldn't talk like that in front of you nowadays. We'll also meet up with the new Staff Sergeant when we get there. Bit of a fire-eater apparently, Simpson or something.'

'Who, Sir?' Marsh's blood ran cold. Simpson was a common enough name. The one he knew from training had been a corporal, not a sergeant. Yet, Simpson had left an indelible mark on Marsh's psyche, his contempt for Marsh crystal clear, especially the trainee's inability to function in a spit and polish army.

'William Simpson. I don't know a lot about him, other than he's up for the Military Medal after taking out a machine gun nest. His last unit was wiped out in the attempt, but he still persevered.'

'Sounds like a proper hero,' Marsh said. It did not sound like the William Simpson he suffered under during training, a man who had not seen combat in this brutal war. Hopefully, this was just a case of a commonplace name. The Simpson he knew was not the type to be flexible enough to survive battle, wedded as he was to his Victorian ideas of soldiery.

'Get the squad ready. We'll leave for the railhead in an hour. I'll make sure the transport for our pet is ready,' Scott said, dismissing Marsh.

For once, Marsh managed a half-decent salute.

The return journey to Étaples was far more comfortable than their first journey to the front had been. For a start, there was no fearful anticipation of the unknowns of combat on the front line. The train was not crowded, and they had an entire carriage to themselves. At one end of the carriage was a large, locked mail compartment. Inside was a sturdy animal crate, almost completely sealed from the outside world.

'We're going to find some girls when we get to Eat Apples,' Morgan said, using the slang for Étaples. Variations of this theme had occupied him for most of the journey. Now, as the train sat waiting in some sidings for the line to clear, the idea was wearing thin with the others.

'What girls? You've been to Étaples, and there were no girls, not a single one,' Simmonds said. He had rejoined the squad just before they departed with their special crate. Despite being bitten by a zombie in the village, Simmonds had not turned into one himself. They were all relieved, as somehow their little band had survived going over the top, and the policing action in the village. Being bitten was not enough to turn you into a zombie, something of a reassurance for them all.

'There must be some women? Those bloody Canaries must have them hidden away?' Morgan complained, hoping to keep his dream alive. 'They've got every other luxury there. Why'd they not have girls too?'

'Canaries don't like girls, everyone knows. That's why there's no girls there. They only like themselves, don't you know?'

'What about the fishing town?' Morgan asked. 'There must be plenty of girls there.'

'If there's any of them there, the officers will have already got them all for themselves,' Simmonds said. 'Even the fishwives I 'spect.'

'I'd let you know, lads,' Scott said, laughing. Because of the unusual nature of their mission, he was travelling in the same compartment as squad rather than sitting in a separate carriage for officers. He was enjoying himself. 'But I've got to nursemaid you lot instead, so no trips to town for me.'

The journey passed slowly. At one point, the train was seriously de-layed. Rumours of sabotage and aerial bombing circulated, commu-nicated from the outside world via Wells. Wells successfully liberated several bottles of wine, claiming he purchased them with an exchange of cigarettes. The rest of the journey passed with great cheer, and any further delay went unnoticed. The sheer volume of traffic moving toward the front lines was impressive. Train after train of soldiers, supplies, and heavy equipment such as artillery flowed by in an un-ending procession.

The train arrived at the railhead, rain pouring down from the dark sky. The remnants of the alcohol in their bodies provided little insulation. As the travellers unloaded their cargo onto a wheeled wagon, the new staff sergeant introduced himself.

'Staff Sergeant Simpson reporting for duty, Sir. Thought I'd meet you here so I could lend a hand,' Simpson said, his loud voice emanating from a body held stiffly at attention. The new arrival topped his mar-tial display by firing off a crisp salute to Scott.

'Welcome, Simpson. Go grab a corner of the crate, and we'll bring you up to speed later.'

'Yes, Sir.' Simpson accepted the dismissal and took care to place his kit in a place sheltered from the rain.

As they manoeuvred the animal crate out of the carriage, Marsh got a good look at the face of the new arrival. His heart sank. At least he had been prepared for the possibility the new sergeant was someone he already knew. He was close enough to elbow Taff Morgan and indicate with his eyes where to look.

'Dear God Almighty!' Morgan shouted, almost upending the crate as he let go of the pole.

'Taff! Get a grip,' Wells shouted, unaware of the reason for Morgan's exclamation. Morgan continued staring at Simpson. 'Taff!'

'S-Simpson,' Morgan said. He would have spat on the ground, instead stuttering over the name. He pointed at the new arrival, as if seeing a ghost.

Every man present turned to glare at Simpson, the crate rocking on the poles. Simpson eyeballed each man, his face turning grim as he noticed the stripes adorning Wells and Marsh. Simpson was about to launch into a tirade, but a growl from the crate drew everyone back to the task at hand. With haste, the team loaded the cargo onto the back of the wagon, following it aboard, squeezing in under the canvas cover to stay out of the pouring rain.

'What the hell are you doing here?' Wells asked Simpson, disgust clear in every word.

'I could ask the same of you,' Simpson said with equal venom.

'He's the new staff sergeant,' Marsh said. 'The Old Man mentioned it earlier, although what are the chances? I didn't think it would be the same Simpson.'

'You knew? You could have warned us,' Morgan said, glaring across the narrow space.

'Well, it's you rabble again. Intact as well. How did you lot escape the front lines?' Simpson asked, an accusatory tone in his voice. He suspected something untoward had occurred.

'How did you escape England?' Davies snapped back. Simpson had so far avoided active service on the Continent.

'Escape England, Sergeant. Some of you still don't have a clue how to speak to your superiors,' Simpson said, glaring at Davies, who flinched as if a punch had been thrown his way. 'I was sent out to see action, at last. However, it appears the Powers-That-Be think I'll be better used nurse-maiding you lot again.'

'Feed him to the bloody tiger,' Morgan muttered under his breath. Everyone heard.

'What's that Morgan? What are you muttering about?' Simpson asked. 'You lot need to shape up. You've spent five minutes in the trenches and you no longer look like soldiers.' Despite the rain, Simpson's uniform was immaculate.

'Spit and polish don't stop bullets, Sarge,' Marsh said, emboldened by his friends.

'The expert himself speaks,' Simpson said, a tone of distaste in his voice. 'Alfie Marsh. Good God, somehow you've even been promoted. Perhaps you weren't the complete wash-out you appeared to be. And

Joshua Wells, you've made sergeant. Where did you rustle up those stripes from? Did you steal them?'

'The war takes all types, Sergeant,' Marsh replied, not sure how to respond to such hostility.

'So what do you know about our tigers?' Wells asked their old drill instructor. He was going to enjoy explaining the secret project.

'Boots aren't shiny enough,' Simpson said. He scuffed the sole of his boot across Marsh's poorly polished boots, daring his victim to react.

They had been at Étaples for a week, yet Simpson still insisted on parading them every morning. The new arrival had set himself the mission of forcing the detachment to meet his own high standards of appearance. This, he argued, was because the troops passing through the depot needed to see actual soldiers who had seen action while setting a good example. Simpson even insisted on a small amount of daily drill, something approved by the long-term resident Canaries. Simpson soon made himself a reputation envied by the camp non-commissioned officers who were tasked with drilling and moulding the troops passing through the replacement depot. Lieutenant Scott stayed away, letting Simpson get on with his project, knowing it was best to keep the detachment busy, so they did not get into trouble during their idle time. Besides, if Simpson got his way on this issue, it was one less complaint Scott would have to listen to from the Sergeant.

The troops were dismissed from parade and joined Wells, who had excused himself from drilling in order to engage in some foraging. He had liberated some chocolate from the supplies department for a selection of battlefield mementoes. The souvenirs were not from the battlefields, but the supply staff could not tell. Meanwhile, Simpson had gone to file some paperwork, so there was no need to worry about sharing the spoils with him or suffer the atmosphere he emitted.

'How many more days will it take here?' Simmonds asked, bored by their return to the routine of Étaples.

'A couple more days to get through the rest of the camp,' Marsh said. 'Some new arrivals got in last night, and we'll need to check them. Once they're done, there'll be no point hanging around waiting for more. We'd be better off moving on somewhere else.'

'Then what?' Davies asked.

'We move on to the next bloody camp. We keep on hunting until we find what we're looking for, or get redeployed,' Simmonds said.

'At least we'll be away from this dump. The other depots have to be better,' Davies said. 'You didn't hear about mutinies in them.' He referred to the incident in the summer between the ANZAC troops and the Canaries who trained the soldiers who passed through the camp.

'But we've not found anyone yet. Surely, we should have found some-one who has some sort of control over the tigers?' Davies asked, dispir-ited by their lack of success.

'That means this 'ere Marsh is an endangered species,' Wells quipped. 'He's one of a kind, so we better not break him.'

'Don't let Simpson catch you saying that. He'll shout "Hallelujah, there's only one Alfie Marsh in this here spit and polish army" and then hark on about Queen Victoria's time and General Gordon,' Morgan said to some laughter.

'Seriously, if I'm the only one who can handle the tigers, we'll never turn them into a useful weapon. It's all very well having a few of them running around the battlefield, but we need hundreds to make a difference, if not more,' Marsh said.

'But how do you control them?' Simmonds asked around a mouthful of bartered chocolate. This was a common question.

'I've absolutely no bloody idea,' Marsh said, unsure how many times he had given the same answer.

'And how did the foreign ones in the village understand you when you was talking English?' Morgan asked.

'Same way we understand you, Welshman. We don't,' Simmonds teased, earning a punch from Morgan.

'I don't know how it worked in the shell-hole,' Marsh explained before going into the same details he had already shared with the Colonel. 'I don't need to see them. The experiments Colonel Hudson conducted show that. I don't think they need to hear me either, and it doesn't matter which language they used to speak, they still understand me. The Colonel said it might be some kind of spiritualism, or subliminal consciousness. He kept talking about this bloke, William James, and the idea of spirituality. Also, he thinks it may be connected with Hinduism. The word he kept using was telepathy.'

'If Hindus are involved, there're some Indian soldiers here. We might want to try them?' Matthews suggested.

'You know only some Indians are Hindu, don't you?' Wells asked. He had been sitting, listening in silence, but now the matter of religion had come up, he joined in. 'Maybe there's something to the idea of your control being in the mind. I was there when those tigers set about you in the village, likewise when you stopped Gibson from eating me in the shell-hole. The things just stopped on your command. They didn't seem to have heard anything. They didn't think about it, the reaction was so quick. Perhaps you fired your thoughts straight into their minds?'

'Hudson tried to get me to use just my mind to control the tigers back at the camp, but I couldn't seem to get them to do what I wanted. It almost seemed like they knew I was talking to them, but they couldn't quite hear what I said.'

'Perhaps you need some more practice?' Wells suggested. 'Not using words works when you are stressed. We've got a tiger here. You should spend some time trying to send it your thoughts.'

'That would be a better use of my time, much better than polishing my boots.'

'Aye, and you could tell it to eat Simpson and do us all a huge favour,' Morgan said, too widespread agreement.

'Pass me more chocolate,' Simmonds said, unwrapping the bar, after it was handed to him.

'Simpson doesn't like the tigers,' Wells explained. 'When Scott told him about them, he went apoplectic. He near enough accused Scott of lying about unnatural beasts. He even suggested the tigers were an unfair weapon, at least until Scott pointed out poison gas and machine guns. In fact, Marsh, he may dislike the tigers more than he dislikes you.'

Scott had briefed Simpson on the detailed operations of the 1st Experimental Battalion. The new arrival did not believe what he was told, at least until he was introduced to a zombie. The shocks continued for Simpson, especially when he discovered how Marsh, a useless soldier by his standards, possessed such control over the creatures. Scott explained how their encounters with zombies had shown not only Marsh's unique skill but also the potential combat use of tigers.

'That fits. He's not checked on our pet again and always keeps clear when we do the experiments to find other handlers,' Davies said, around a piece of chocolate stuffed into his mouth.

'He'll have to get used to having them around. If this idea takes off, we'll be the people doing all the work,' Marsh explained.

'Left turn!' the young recruit shouted. Fresh from England, having only completed his training within the last few weeks, the boy did not even comprehend these seconds could determine his future. If the hidden zombie responded, he would end up in an experimental unit. If not, he would end up in almost any unit, having been sent to the infantry depot.

'No,' Marsh said. He glanced through the slit into the animal cage, seeking any sign of response to the orders of the men outside. Davies, who was standing in the entrance to the tent, gave a subtle shake of his head, passing on the judgement to Wells, who continued to audition the men outside.

'Sorry lad,' Wells said. 'You aren't ready yet.' He called to the next soldier in line, 'Next.'

As planned, their project took up a corner of the parade ground. Their cover was the acquisition of men with exceptional command voices for accelerated promotion and training. The open secret was their work involved animals. The animal crate containing the tiger was concealed in a canvas tent, supervised by Marsh. Soldiers paraded in front of the tent, with their backs to the shelter. Wells put them through their paces before asking each man to demonstrate his best command voice. From their experiments in Belgium, they knew Marsh could command the tigers from this distance and in these conditions.

'About turn!' the next soldier shouted. A moment later, Davies shook his head again. Wells moved on to the second rank of soldiers. They had already screened thousands this way, further reinforcing the growing belief in the uniqueness of Marsh's ability.

'Next!' Wells shouted.

'Right turn!' the next soldier barked. Davies did not shake his head.

'Carry on, private, give another command,' Wells said, in the absence of any response from the tent.

'About face!' This time, Davies nodded.

'What's your name, private?' Wells asked.

'Bill. Rose, I-I mean William Rose, Sergeant,' the private said. Sweat broke out on his forehead at the sudden interest.

'Fall out and wait at the tent behind you. We'll talk again,' Wells said.

Rose left the parade formation of soldiers. He bit his lip, drawing blood, while making his way to stand by the tent. Rose knew this sergeant was searching for command potential and had been so fussy. He was very surprised to have been selected and did not notice the startled look a corporal gave him from the entrance to the tent.

The rest of the afternoon passed with the discovery of one other person able to influence the captive tiger. The successful detection of two potential zombie handlers caused significant celebration. After several days searching with no success, in one afternoon, two people had been discovered who could control the tigers. Marsh was delighted he was no longer alone. Morgan was grinning smugly, as the second person had been discovered from among a group of Indian soldiers awaiting redeployment following their recovery from minor injuries.

'I told you to check out the Indians, didn't I?' Morgan gloated.

'Yes, and I told you Indians aren't all Hindus, too. The man we picked out was a follower of Muhammad,' Wells said with an even bigger grin.

'Marsh, are you going to train these new handlers?'

'I wouldn't know where to begin. I barely understand it myself. Colonel Hudson has some theories, and he'll work with them as soon as they reach him. We've still got some searching to do,' Marsh replied. 'We've got to find more men to make this project work, but at least we now know I'm not the only one.'

'So, they'll not be staying with us then?' Morgan pulled an unhappy face, disappointed at not being able to show off in front of the new recruits.

'They'll go back to our camp. Scott has signed their travel warrants. They'll be off tomorrow,' Wells said. 'We'll carry on around the depots.'

There were several groans of disappointment.

8

FIRST COMBAT

Who would have believed such creatures existed? I should not have believed it possible, but for my own experiences. Yet, we have been able to exploit this situation and providence appears to be smiling upon our endeavours. As I described in my last letter, I believe we know how to use these creatures to break the stalemate on the Western Front. As I write, late into the night, my men are advancing into battle. Within a few scant hours, I will know if we possess a war-winning weapon.

Undated correspondence from Col O. Hudson to an unnamed recipient. This letter is part of a collection of documents obtained by Milton Davies, published as an appendix in Milton Davies, A History of Zombies and Warfare, (London, 2016)

T HE END OF 1916 was approaching by the time Scott's squad returned to the battalion camp in Belgium. They had travelled around nine British infantry depots, recruiting thirty-two handlers from the tens of thousands of soldiers they encountered. The handlers took all forms, not just Indians, but ANZACs, men from all over the British Isles, Canadians and even a single Belgian who had used his dual nationality to join the British army rather than the tiny Belgium counterpart. All were enlisted men. The recruiting squad could not investigate options from among the officer pool. Officers were reserved for the exclusive recruiting attention of the Royal Flying Corps.

The war had progressed little during this time, with no end in sight. Deadlock reigned across the battlefields. Exhausted, the armies disengaged, digging deeply into the ground, unable to advance, but unwilling to concede territory. Soldiers questioned how much longer the conflict would last. The Battle of the Somme had ground to a bloody halt in November and few sustained advances had been made since. Casualty rates on the Somme remained an open secret. The stalled offensive, along with a growing realisation the Royal Navy failed to break the Germans at Jutland, did not bode well for the future. Even the slaughter at Verdun between the French and the Germans was reaching an indecisive end, despite a year of fighting. Yet France had recovered much of the territory Germany had taken earlier in the campaign.

The encampment of the 1st Experimental Battalion was now further behind the lines and experiencing considerable growth. The first thing which struck Marsh, as he returned to the new base, was the improved security. Three fences surrounded the encampment, patrolled by Military Police. A great deal of signage warned potential intruders of the risk they would encounter dangerous animals. Colonel Hudson had spun out the cover of experimental animal combat uses, and later Marsh heard a wolf howling. Upon investigation, he discovered a range of animals obtained from zoos. These were sited along boundaries for the nosey, potential spies, or aerial spotters to draw the conclusions Hudson wanted them to reach. Temporary barracks and administration buildings sat on the outside of a secure inner area of the camp. In this secured inner area, the actual work was undertaken with the tigers, where they were held and research was conducted. This was all done safely away from the non-handlers. The non-specialist parts of the battalion stayed away, knowing little more than the myths fed to them by the men present when the first tigers had been captured.

A further thing which struck Marsh was the small number of soldiers present in the encampment. Very few fighting soldiers were visible, with the most visual specialism being the Military Police. Actual combat soldiers within the Battalion were rare. When Marsh later spoke to Colonel Hudson, he found the unit had not been brought up to normal infantry battalion strength. It had been kept in a weakened state with the intention of those few soldiers present, providing battlefield security for the handlers and their charges. A full-strength battalion was not needed.

The last weeks of 1916 descended into a routine of tactical planning and the sharing of skills and knowledge the different handlers were developing through trial and error. Few tigers were available for the work at hand. Besides the two Marsh had captured, a small number were delivered from the front. Colonel Hudson was still having trouble establishing the mode of transmission to the initial patients and his experiments at creating additional zombies were stalling. If you died because of being bitten, there was some chance of turning into a zombie. The Colonel estimated someone in these circumstances had a seventy-five per cent chance of reanimation, but this figure was speculative.

Hudson's research led him to suspect those men returning from the front line were most at risk. Whether they were infected with the bacteria close to, or at the moment of death, there was a positive correlation with the creation of zombies. Suspicions remained regarding this bacterium not having been delivered by the zombies, but being present on surfaces or in a liquid. Regardless, the evidence confirmed a minimal geographical dispersal of cases. In the British sectors, this amounted to a ten-mile stretch of the line. The French had grudgingly confirmed cases in their sectors. Unfortunately, some examples from the front resulted from secondary infections. These individuals often arrived in small groups, having been killed by the zombie they sought to capture. Clearly, there was a threat to the front-line soldier from these untamed creatures. Rumours existed, which the Colonel refused to deny, of deliberately inflicted cases whereby the Colonel may have administered the bacteria to terminally wounded casualties. A joke circulated through the barracks, about how the army would soon replace firing squads with eternal conscription as a zombie.

Few tigers were available. Minus those spent because of experimentation, there were fifty tigers. Spread among the thirty-two handlers recruited, thirty-three when Marsh was counted, there was a great deal of slack in the system.

Even caring for zombies had proven a subject of trial and error. The original zombies had shown little evidence of degradation, with minimal rotting noted. These zombies were fed animals, but it was unclear by what process they extracted energy from the flesh. Their food seemed to pass through their digestive system in an unprocessed form. For all intents and purposes, the tigers were dead. They possessed none of the functions found in a living human. Zombies did not breathe, they did not digest, their hair and nails did not grow. They possessed neither the urges, nor emotions, of a human being, just one overriding drive to consume the living. Nothing about the creatures suggested they were still alive, except in one respect, on the bacterial level, there was some life. Namely, the very bacteria which animated them, and colonies of the naturally corruptive bacteria found in human bodies. The corruptive bacteria seemed to make little progress against the reanimating strain or the possessed flesh.

Once the first handlers arrived, actual experimentation with controlling the zombies started. These first handlers arrived after recruitment in the camps, long before Marsh returned from his mission. Several handlers were already proving more effective than others, with the distance of command being a key factor. Some handlers could only control zombies with direct line-of-sight, while a tiny number used merely a thought. With practice, most handlers proved able to improve their abilities, and with extra tigers being made available for training, a few handlers found they could control large numbers of zombies as long as the instructions remained simple. In a minimal number of cases, handlers showed the ability to control considerable numbers of tigers with significant precision.

Then, of course, there were accidents. The accident everyone guarded against was exposure to an attack by a tiger. Unfortunately, some troops became complacent around the passive zombies, letting their guard down. Only a single accident was needed to put an end to this laxness, the ranks of the tigers swollen by a further five animated corpses. Other men were more fortunate, becoming victims of bites and scratches, but not significant injury leading to reanimation. Even when under command, the tigers sometimes snapped and scratched at nearby humans without the special ability.

Casualties also occurred among the tigers. This happened when the surrounding humans became scared, or on occasions when a handler lost control. Once, a handler slipped and banged their head on a large stone. Upon losing consciousness, the two tigers under their control became independent and charged the unconscious handler. The handler did not survive the attack and did not reanimate. However, the two tigers had not escaped the attentions of the terrified security squad accompanying the handler. Thus, the thirty-three handlers had become thirty-two. Yet even with diminishing numbers, Colonel Hudson did not sanction a further recruitment drive as he wanted to focus upon developing tactics.

Some strategies were worked out and trialled in the controlled conditions of the camp. Most of the thinking was devoted to the offensive applications of the new weapon. A ratio of around ten tigers to each handler was reckoned to be the nucleus of an effective combat group. Each group would be accompanied by a rifle squad of five troops. Utilising careful movement across the battlefield, the humans could stay alive behind the tigers, the undead drawing enemy fire.

The tigers themselves did not need to be as careful as the living on the battlefield, with only sustained machine gun fire, and direct hits from shelling, a problem. Some troops, such as Marsh and his squad, experimented with even faster movement, with small teams moving from cover to cover. Marsh applied this pace to both zombies and humans, hoping to close on the enemy trenches. From there, they would launch an assault led by the zombies in the role of shock troopers, followed by the rest of the squad. While under a fierce attack, the enemy should collapse, and the objective would be secured.

Marsh was supported in his experiments by an emerging ability to control at least fifty tigers at one time, a number only limited by those tigers available to the unit. This phenomenal skill was far beyond any yet shown by anyone else in the battalion. Yet Marsh knew he would be restricted in combat with far fewer zombies under his control than he could manage. While this was an expediency based upon resources, it would allow him to bring newly created zombies under his influence. This would further swell the ranks of the unit while preventing reanimated corpses from becoming a problem for the follow-on forces and his own security squad. Despite the experimental work by a few handlers, most teams in the battalion pursued the standard infantry approach of moving toward the enemy with minimal distraction. If such strategies were good for barely trained citizen soldiers, they were considered good enough for undead rabble.

The battlefield survival ability of the zombies led to the development of another assault technique. Several tigers were spent in attempts to prove this method. This tactic was arrived upon by accident, when a volunteer machine gun team experienced great distress during a live-fire experiment. They thought they had destroyed a zombie, only to find they had shot it in half, the top half continuing to advance upon them. The team fled in terror as the half corpse mounted their sandbag; the handler having to call the zombie off to prevent friendly casualties. Thus, a second tactic had formed around the idea of saturating a target with large numbers of tigers. Fortified positions were vulnerable to coordinated attacks, and could be approached from several directions by dozens of tigers. Eventually, the tigers would overwhelm the objective. Even if damaged by defensive fire, nothing short of a headshot would prevent their victory. Unfortunately, this approach proved impossible as things stood. Not enough tigers were available to deploy in overwhelming numbers.

Regardless of the tactics available, there now existed a potential method for breaking the stalemate on the Western Front. This standstill, enforced by the horrific defensive power of the machine gun and modern artillery, saw the traditional offensive tools of cavalry and massed infantry neutralised. Colonel Hudson had sold General Haig, commander of the British Expeditionary Force in France, on the idea the tigers could function as a breakthrough weapon. They could smash the enemy front line with conventional infantry and cavalry arms exploiting the gap. Haig had been animated and talked about the use of a combination of arms, including the new 'tank' weapon which was being developed and first experienced action in late summer at Deville Wood. However, Hudson suspected that just like the 'tank', and the improved high explosive shell before it, Haig would deploy the tigers too soon and in insufficient numbers to force a significant breakthrough.

The new concepts needed combat testing. Late in December 1916, the battalion moved up through the lines for their first attack since reforming as an experimental unit. The attack was to take place in a small and quiet sector of the German front line, held by some Bavarian troops. The primary aim was to test the tiger tactics in a combat environment, with the view of expanding to a larger scale at the earliest potential opportunity. This trial would be conducted by assaulting a small forward trench and machine gun post with tigers. Regular troops would provide a second wave to secure the objective once the enemy was forced to withdraw. Secondary experiments existed, notably the acquisition of additional tigers through combat recruitment, and testing the survivability of the existing reanimated corpses.

While moving into position, the tigers were transported in individual windowless cages. If anyone questioned this, the handlers would spin out the exotic animal cover story the battalion continued to operate under. Several times Marsh contemplated how true this was, despite the misleading intention of the cover story. Reaching the rearmost reserve trench, the cargoes were unloaded from the light railway with handlers taking direct control of their charges. As planned, each handler controlled ten tigers, every group supported by a rifle squad acting as both protection for the handler, but also to police the tigers should the handler be incapacitated. The soldiers knew the danger: should a handler lose control of his charges, no quarter could be given. The men in Marsh's team knew their individual roles.

The communications trenches were cleared of regular soldiers to avoid any panicked encounters and maintain secrecy. Each rifle squad, bringing up the front and rear of their special team, also kept other troops away. Marsh's team arrived at a former supply dump in the second line, and the unit gathered under camouflaged canvas, ready for their last move into the forward trench. With so few tigers, only five combat groups were available, along with additional reserve handlers and riflemen. Marsh kept his zombies quiet, their unnatural movements continuing to spook the accompanying humans, despite months of exposure to their charges.

The time dragged out as they awaited a short preparatory artillery barrage planned for a little while after dawn. Under cover of the artillery, the unit was to move into the front line, ready to launch their assault. Marsh's stomach twisted, his fear of combat rising in his awareness. The horror of his single experience of the trenches still tormented his sleep, and now spilled over into his waking mind. The faces of the German men waiting ready to kill him appeared in his mind as he waited for the appointed time. Betraying similar concerns, Lieutenant Scott checked on his men with the quiet nervousness of a veteran readying to return to the fight. Marsh found it hard to concentrate, and his rational fears seemed to influence his undead charges, who snapped the air with increasing frustration at the length of the wait.

'Marsh, you look a mess,' Simpson said. He was on his own pre-battle rounds. He looked Marsh up and down. 'You're barely able to control yourself, let alone face the enemy.' Simpson grabbed at a piece of Marsh's webbing and attempted to straighten it. Marsh shrugged him off, and the tigers grew even more agitated.

'I've been in action before Sarge, I know what to expect,' Marsh said, hoping the other man did not spot the tremulous tone.

'Well, you need to make sure you don't let us down. We can't have you embarrassing us. It's bad enough you look the way you do.'

'I'll be fine Sarge, I've got my combat group backing me. I know how to use these creatures, too.' He could tell Simpson was not convinced, so he added, 'I'm the only person who's used a tiger in action.'

'Well, make sure you don't mess up today,' Simpson said, walking away, ensuring he got the last word.

'Bastard!' Morgan sneezed the word into his hand as Simpson went by. The sergeant choose to ignore the comment.

'He's just edgy like the rest of us, Taff,' Marsh said, excusing the sergeant's attitude.

'No, he's not Alfie. He has no heart, and he has no soul. Don't defend him,' Morgan said. 'He's always on your case. He can't accept a soldier can be good without joining the spit and polish brigade.' Morgan spat to show what he thought of the sergeant and his attitude.

'Taff's right. We're all on edge,' Davies agreed. He pulled his bayonet out, sharpening it for the third time that night. 'We all know what going over the top is like, but we ain't taking it out on each other like he does. Bloody useless instructor and now a bloody useless sergeant.'

'But don't forget, he got a gong with his last mob,' Simmonds said. 'He must be useful for something.'

'Army's full of shits like him,' Matthews interrupted, speaking from experience. 'Get over it and move on, or you'll go mad. I saw enough of them when we were training at the start of the war, all those regulars telling us what to do. I reckon he's a glory hunter, so he'll buy a plot soon enough.'

'Or he'll get everyone killed in his search for glory,' Morgan said.

'You lot look cheerful. Who died?' Wells asked as he arrived. He possessed an air of smugness, which suggested he had been foraging rather than completing his own pre-combat checks.

'Simpson,' Marsh said, rolling his eyes. In the pre-dawn light, Wells could see the gesture, but had already picked up the meaning from Marsh's tone.

'Helpful as always, I presume. Did he criticise your sewing this time?' Wells said, pointing to the new corporal stripes on Marsh's arm. 'You've earnt those. You're the best handler we've got, and the Colonel knows it. Show that fucking idiot, Simpson, what you can do.'

'And you lot,' Wells said, addressing the rest of the team. Their chuckling ending. 'Make sure Marsh gets through this alive, otherwise I'll come down to hell to kick your immortal arses.'

9

THE ATTACK

Our men were terrified. I debriefed several, gaining their trust through the usual methods of reasonable care and shared acquaintance. One junior officer used the word 'valkyries' to describe this new British weapon. This was despite the male gender of the assailants. His description fits with the reported phenomenon the French have been calling 'zombies'. The effectiveness of this new weapon is how it strikes fear into the hearts of the defender. Witnessing their peers being torn asunder completely undermines the morale of the defender. We must deploy defensive measures at the earliest opportunity to dispel the spreading of mythic stories about the powers of these so-called 'valkyries' or 'zombies'.

Fragment from a report on the first British deployment of Tigers on the Western Front. Colonel Nicolai, German Military Intelligence. Undated, but believed to have been written during late 1916. The report was found among fire damaged German archives in 1963.

T HE BARRAGE COMMENCED SHORTLY after dawn, timed so the Bavarians would be exposed, lining their trenches, waiting to receive a dawn attack. The Colonel had proposed this timing to catch the enemy out, although such thinking was commonplace in military circles.

Despite it being the second time the men in Marsh's combat group were in action, the sound of the shells travelling overhead still set their teeth on edge. Davies pulled out his sharpened bayonet, testing it upon the remains of a wooden ammunition crate. He decided it was still too blunt and began his routine of sharpening it again. Marsh passed around cigarettes. He almost dropped the packet, his hands shook so much. Matthews found a semi-comfortable part of the fire step to sit on and discretely sipped from a small flask. Morgan and Simmonds were busy playing cards.

Marsh looked around at the other combat groups and wondered why he only had a four-man squad supporting him. The rest had at least five men besides the handler and their charges. While he contemplated, Wells returned.

'I thought I'd join you, Alfie,' Wells said, grinning. 'I deliberately kept you short-handed so I would have an excuse to come along for the action.'

'It'll be just like the old times then,' Marsh said, offering his friend a cigarette. They both knew the old times he spoke of amounted to a single occasion.

'Just like the old times. Oh, and by the way, you're still in charge of this combat group. Just 'cause I've got the stripes doesn't mean I'm going to be deciding anything. You've got the tigers, so we do what you do and go where you go.'

'Five minutes until the off,' Lieutenant Scott walked off to his position on their left. He stood next to a trench ladder, eyes glued to his timepiece. He also intended to fight alongside Marsh.

The shelling stopped, and the tigers became even more restless, picking up the scent of fear around them. Scott raised his whistle to his lips, eyes still on his watch. He blew at the same time as another officer further to the left of the assault group also blew his whistle.

'Up and forward,' Marsh said, commanding his animated corpses to rise. A group of zombies climbed up a cattle ramp prepared for this purpose. The tigers could handle ladders. Experiments showed they could, but most handlers could not communicate sophisticated enough instructions for them to follow. The humans climbed out of the trenches using the usual assault ladders. As Marsh stepped over the sandbagged parapet, he perceived a long line of zombies spreading from their trench exit points. Commanding his charges forward, Marsh rushed towards a crater a few yards ahead of him, ducking as he ran. The depression would provide him with some protection to advance from. The rest of the squad, along with the additional sergeant and officer, spread out around him, also moving from cover to cover, ready to protect him from either the enemy or out-of-control tigers.

By the time the Bavarians manned their parapet, the fastest tigers from Marsh's combat group were closing on the enemy position, far ahead of the living members of the assault force. The machine gun post opened fire. Two zombies fell, knocked down by the kinetic energy of the bullets, only for them to rise and resume their charge toward the enemy. The machine gun was set up to shoot at a low level across no man's land, intended to hit knees and body mass, not the vulnerable heads of the zombies. Yet, either there was a lucky shot, or a skilled marksman among the enemy. Another two zombies fell in quick succession. This time, their skulls exploding as bullets smashed through them.

The shooting was all one-sided. None of the advancing men were firing on the enemy trenches. The living attackers happily let the dead draw the full weight of the enemy's defensive fire. As he advanced, Marsh ran from crater to crater, keeping as low a profile as possible. He also zig-zagged to present a more challenging target. No bullets came near him. The enemy continued to concentrate their fire on the rapidly advancing zombies.

Marsh nearly missed the first of his tigers reaching the enemy trench. As loud as he could, Marsh shouted the order to attack before running down the steep side of a crater and losing his line of sight. The first panicked screams emerged from the German trenches. Without losing his footing, Marsh sprinted up the other side, loose earth clinging at his boots. He ran around an undamaged length of wire, his small team of guards matching his pace.

Upon arriving at the enemy trench, a wave of horror passed over Marsh. He got his first glimpse of the chaos and destruction as he climbed over the parapet. Two of the enemy were down on the floor, one with his Stahlhelm helmet torn off, his neck broken by the impact of a tiger landing on him. The other soldier had bite marks all over his neck and face. His hands were also badly bitten as he sought to defend himself against the overwhelming strength of an attacking zombie. Even as Marsh watched, the dead Bavarian reanimated, the bacteria working life back into the broken body. Further along the trench, four zombies assaulted two more soldiers, including one wearing a traditional Pickelhaube helmet.

'Ich ergebe mich!' the Pickelhaube wearing soldier shouted at Marsh and his armed escort.

'Leave them be!' Marsh shouted the order, but was too late to save one Bavarian as his arm was torn into by the teeth of two tigers.

The squad took custody of the last intact enemy soldier while Marsh assembled the new zombies reanimating along the trench. An enemy machine gun, further along the line, ceased firing, overrun by another combat group. The attack had been a success, and Marsh still had control of eight of his original ten tigers. Two of the surviving zombies were badly damaged by the machine guns. Three new zombie recruits were also added to Marsh's group of zombies, proving combat conditions were the best recruiting grounds for the new unit.

Eager to secure the trench, Marsh moved along the wooden boards, taking time to check the possibility enemies would not come around the bend at the far end of the trench. He missed the bunker entrance hidden behind some crates. He also missed the soldier who emerged, bayonet held in hand, determined to avenge his fellows while driven half-mad with fear from the cruel zombie assault. The man rushed Marsh, they fell to the ground, the Bavarian on top, forcing his bayonet at Marsh's chest. Despite his surprise, Marsh grabbed his attacker by the wrists, yet the Bavarian's weight drove the knife point into Marsh's battledress. In a moment of pure terror, Marsh knew he could not win. With bloodshot eyes, the man appeared crazed by what he had seen, his long droopy moustache damp with the morning dew. A timeless moment occurred as they looked into each other's eyes. There was a moment of peace. Marsh prepared to surrender to the inevitable, to give up. Without warning, the Bavarian was lifted off Marsh, held high in the air by a rampaging tiger. The terrified enemy was dashed to the ground, a swarm of zombies diving on him. Within seconds, the undead had shredded their victim's flesh and were gnawing on his limbs. One tiger punched at the stomach, pulling away strips of clothing, piercing the taut flesh with torn nails. The creature gorged itself on the spilt contents.

Marsh rose as he saw the horrors. The zombies, his zombies, had swarmed an enemy to save him. The Bavarian had died horrifically. No, in a terrible moment, Marsh realised the man was still conscious. He was being eaten alive. The tigers had picked up on Marsh's distress, guided in by the terror of their handler. He knew he could control the tigers with words, and sometimes with thoughts. Yet this time, he had not cried out, nor had he thought out instructions or orders. Instead, the undead had responded to the situation, acting to protect him. It seemed as if the zombies extended his mind, tools which could be set upon a problem without deliberate thought.

As Marsh gathered himself, the tigers killed their victim, consuming their prey beyond the point of reanimation. If sizeable parts of a corpse were needed intact for reanimation, there was little left of this man. Marsh wondered if reanimation would still occur. The brain was as yet undamaged. The tigers put his rumination beyond doubt when one smashed the skull of the Bavarian soldier and began consuming the victim's brain.

With the trench cleared, shouts and screams came from further down the line. Marsh could not spot any targets for his tigers and so spread his charges along the line to prevent them from being wiped out by a lucky artillery hit. His security squad kept their distance, and it took a while for Marsh to realise why. They were horrified at what had happened to the man who had ambushed Marsh. They had no desire to provoke the wrath of the undead.

'We're falling back. The second wave has already been called off,' Lieutenant Scott said, moving along the trench, his pistol drawn. He stopped when he reached Marsh. 'Get your team ready and get going. Those idiots, up the line, thought they were playing on the Somme and marched their bloody tigers over the field. They didn't have enough left to overrun the enemy.'

'What, they didn't use the terrain to get in close like we did?' Marsh asked, wondering when he had lost track of Scott during the chaos of the advance.

'No, bloody Simpson was with them and demanded standard doctrine be followed.'

'Nothing standard about using tigers,' Marsh said, half surprised Simpson had overruled the handlers.

'Sergeant Wells!' Marsh called. His friend was wary as he came closer. 'Can you organise covering fire if we need it? We'll retreat using whatever cover we can find. You come after us as soon as we've cleared the first lot of wire.'

'Can do, Alfie,' Wells replied. 'Lieutenant, will you be coming with us?'

'Wouldn't miss it for the world,' Scott replied, swapping his pistol for a rifle the enemy had discarded. He checked the action and sighted down the barrel before loading some rounds he recovered from a nearby corpse.

Marsh brought his tigers out of the trench and hastened them around the first clump of wire into no man's land. The rifle squad pulled back, having not needed to fire upon the enemy, but bringing their prisoner with them. Even the enemy artillery had not fired yet. All was quiet.

His tigers mostly kept up, although two were falling behind, having been damaged in the lower limbs. He would have to look these two over in case the damage led to further problems. Zombies did not heal. Marsh had some ideas about how he could repair them. A glance up the line revealed another combat team pulling back, although they possessed far fewer tigers. His group of tigers were more valuable than he first thought, so he eased them from shell-hole to shell-hole to help protect them in case the enemy opened fire.

The occasional crack of a bullet passed overhead as the enemy fired optimistic shots from their reserve lines, but these were of little of significance. Marsh knew further attention would come from the front line as soon as the enemy seized back their trench. They were likely working their way forward via the undefended communications trenches connecting each trench line. He was wrong. The picture changed as mortar rounds began landing in no man's land. The enemy counter-attack was underway.

Marsh paused behind the remains of a stone wall. He thought it may once have been a small building, although the shattered wall now stood only a few feet high. He watched as the security squad weaved their way across the mutilated terrain he had traversed, mortar rounds exploding around them. One second, all his friends were running, the next, a mortar round hit Simmonds. Mud, metal and body parts flew in different directions as Simmonds ceased to exist. Marsh screamed his name, but no-one heard over the noise of battle. Simmonds had disappeared in the blink of an eye.

As Marsh looked through tear-filled eyes, Colonel Hudson mounted the enemy parapet before breaking into a run across no man's land. Hudson was the last to leave the now deserted enemy trench, ensuring his men got out first. Marsh watched as the Colonel leapt over a strand of wire, his athleticism belying his age. The mortars continued to fall in rapid succession, one landing close to the Colonel, who was blown off his feet. Marsh dug his nails into his hands, terrified he would have to watch another man die. Without conscious thought from Marsh, the tigers left their shell holes and raced back to the Colonel. The medical man regained his footing and staggered back towards the enemy lines, stunned by the blast.

'Fucking hell, Marsh. Have you lost control of them?' Wells shouted, levelling his rifle to shoot at the backs of the tigers as they tore past him, advancing in leaps and bounds on the Colonel. The creatures were travelling far faster than they had at any point in the battle. Their speed was superhuman, even those damaged in the combat. Wells fired, missing his target and letting out a stream of swear words.

'Don't shoot!' Marsh shouted, a glimmer of hope formed within him. He knew what the tigers were doing. 'They're trying to help him.'

'What?' Wells called back, reloading and taking aim again.

'Think! The trench, they moved to defend me when I got scared,' he said, his voice clear during a lull in the mortaring. Wells lowered his rifle, looking incredulous as the thought took hold. 'I got scared again. I think they're protecting him for me.'

'That's one hell of a chance to take. If you're wrong—' Wells again raised his rifle and aimed, checking his fire while hoping Marsh was correct, ready if he was not. At this distance, Wells knew his chances of a hit on a moving target were minimal. Knowing he needed to hit the head of the zombie, he almost gave up in despair.

The first tiger reached the Colonel, bundling into him, almost like a rugby tackle. Instead of falling to the ground, the zombie rose, demonstrating immense strength by throwing the Colonel across his shoulder. Turning on the spot, the reanimated corpse headed toward the Allied lines, several other tigers falling in behind it. They were using their bodies to prevent any Bavarians from getting a clear shot at the Colonel. The tigers, which did not join in, also headed back towards the Allied trenches at their original pace, apparently satisfied with their efforts to protect the Colonel.

'Let's go!' Marsh shouted to Wells above the noise of another incoming barrage of mortar rounds.

Knowing there was nothing else he could do, Marsh left his cover and hurried back to friendly lines. Within seconds Marsh, his tigers, the Colonel and the protection squad, arrived in the forward British trench. Without waiting for further orders, Marsh moved everyone into the communications trench and back to the reserve lines so they did not spook the follow-on troops, who were still positioned in the forward trench. The tigers and their accompanying living soldiers were no longer needed. The assault had failed and the follow-on troops were readying to repel an expected enemy counterattack.

'What the hell went wrong?' Marsh asked when Wells pushed his way through the crowded communication trench so they could talk.

'Simmonds is gone,' Wells said, the exertion of combat masking some of the emotion.

'I saw it happen. There's nothing left of him. Bloody Simpson and his messing around with our tactics. We'd have won otherwise, and Simmonds would still be here.'

'What about the Old Man?' Wells asked, also surprised by the unexpected behaviour of the tigers.

'He's just stunned and peppered with a few bomb splinters. Mind, he's half scared to death by his close encounter with our tigers. He'll be fine, but he'll be off to the medics. You know, I didn't realise he would come forward with us. I thought he was just a medical man running an experiment.'

'You think he'd miss the chance to see all he's put in place? He's staked his reputation on us.' Wells removed his helmet and ran his fingers through his hair now they were away from the falling mortar bombs. His fingers came away dripping with sweat. 'That was a close one.'

'Closer than you realise,' Marsh said, running his fingers along the neat bayonet cut in his battledress. He reached inside his clothing and wiggled his fingers out through the hole.

'Marsh, you worthless piece of shit!' the shout travelled along the reserve trench. If there had been enemy listening posts out in no man's land, they would have heard every single word and identified the British positions from the noise. Even if the enemy were not English speakers, they would have recognised the tone of voice and been thankful it was not directed at them.

'Where are you, you worthless excuse for a soldier?' Simpson bellowed, coming closer. The sergeant was heading their way, intent on expending his frustrations on Marsh.

'What do you think the idiot wants this time?' Davies asked.

'Probably to know who left the kettle on,' Morgan said, before becoming silent as he remembered Simmonds was not there to laugh at the joke.

'If we ignore him, he might go away,' Davies said. He lit a new cigarette from the glowing stub of an exhausted cigarette, knowing his optimism was misplaced.

'There you are,' Simpson snapped, steaming around the bend in the trench. Marsh, Davies, and Morgan leaned against the trench walls, their tigers secured long ago. 'Stand to attention when I address you.'

The three did not respond, showing no sign of paying attention to the sergeant. Their lack of reaction further irritated Simpson. His rage grew.

'What the hell were you doing out there?' Simpson demanded. His face was going red with anger and an arm flapped vaguely in the direction of the enemy trenches.

'What do you mean, Sarge?' Marsh asked, pushing himself away from the trench wall and putting his hands on his hips, attempting to stand his ground.

'You bloody well know what I mean, man. Sending all those zombies after the Colonel. Is it not bad enough we use these vile beings? You want to make it worse and set them on our own side?'

'But the CO is safe, Sarge. My tigers got him out,' Marsh said. He could not see what Simpson was getting at. Was the man seeking any excuse to attack him?

'It's unnatural. That's what it is. The Colonel would have made it back fine, but no, terrify everyone with those zombies chasing after him in an unauthorised manoeuvre.'

'It worked, Sarge. He's safe.'

'Only by some superb fortune. I saw you hide away back there, terrified. You lost control of your tigers, and they went back to kill him,' Simpson said, sneering the accusation. 'You panicked, and they attacked. It was pure luck you got them back under control before any damage was done.'

Marsh glared at Simpson but did not answer. Something truthful struggled to rise to the surface in what Simpson said, but the sergeant would never understand Marsh appeared able to control the tigers on an instinctive level.

'If it's not enough for you to use your tigers in an unauthorised way, there's also your actual attack. You should not operate your zombies in that way. You are expected to follow standard infantry doctrine, advancing upon the enemy en masse,' Simpson said, getting right up in Marsh's face. His breath stank, and he used his physical bulk to intimidate.

'No Sarge, we were to try out new tactics, not use the old ones. That was the whole point of today. Tigers aren't infantry, you know,' Marsh said. He was fed up with the bullying of the sergeant. He did not know if it was the experience of the attack, but he was not prepared to back down.

'I can bloody well see that, can't I?' Simpson asked, sarcasm lacing his tone. 'Who gave you permission to experiment?'

'The Colonel and Lieutenant Scott, on account of we've new weapons and we need to learn how to use them.'

'Well, in the future, you do things the way I tell you. I don't care if General Haig or Christ Himself tells you otherwise. I'm in charge, and you do what I bloody well say. Is that clear?'

Marsh nodded, but did not trust himself to speak. He knew he would not pay the slightest bit of attention to the sergeant. Simpson took the silence as agreement.

'You're a bloody worthless soldier. I should have sent you off to the cookhouse when I first saw you. Peeling spuds is all you're good for. It's a miracle we've found any other use for you in this war.'

Simpson stormed off. Marsh breathed a sigh of relief once the sergeant rounded a bend in the trench. He leaned back against the trench wall, unsure if the encounter was a greater emotional drain than the intense combat they had just been through. He wanted to rage; he wanted to cry; he wanted to stop reliving Simmond's death. Fortunately, he was struck dumb.

'What does he know?' Davies asked, now Simpson was safely out of earshot. 'He's probably just jealous he messed up, and you didn't. If he'd not cocked up, we'd have held the line, and Simmonds would still be bloody here.'

'Well, I know who got it right out there. I'm sure the Old Man will see things the same way,' Morgan said, reassuring a silent Marsh.

10

RESISTANCE

'It is with considerable concern I feel the need to voice
my opinions to the War Office. General Haig has dismissed my valid objections without due consideration
of their merits. To pursue the use of this new weapon
is contrary to my conscience as an upstanding Chris-
tian.'

Extract from a letter sent to the War Office in January
1917 by a Corps commander in Belgium (name with-
held for publication). Published by On the Conduct
of the War Committee, House of Lords Select Committee, 1919.

T HE NEXT TIME MARSH clashed with Simpson was a week later.
Colonel Hudson was busy measuring the accumulated combat
damage to the zombies. Hudson had been both grateful and delighted
by Marsh's intervention on the battlefield. The Colonel, other than a
few scrapes, had been stunned by the explosion and had Marsh not

intervened, he would have wandered no man's land aimlessly while under fire. The discovery of another facet of the ability of some handlers had been worth the danger, in the Colonel's opinion. Ignoring the post-battle order from Simpson to cease innovation, Marsh had discussed several new ideas with the Colonel. Not least among these was the use of some sort of body armour, or at the least, head armour to protect the tigers from lethal shots.

The debacle of the general attack, which Simpson had been at the root of, had reduced the number of re-animate dead available to them. While the assault had made over a dozen new zombies, twenty-three of the original number had been lost to enemy action, and a further five were of no further use, being humanely disposed of on the battlefield. In this sense, the attack was a failure. However, Marsh's localised success, with careful battlefield movement, led to the Colonel adopting the tactic as the default approach for the unit. Likewise, the Colonel was impressed by the use of zombies to rescue him and was playing with ideas whereby zombies could clear casualties from a battlefield. Such a plan would be far too revolutionary for the Royal Medical Corps, but it could bear fruit if ever sufficient numbers of zombies and handlers were available. As yet unexplained, there remained the matter of the instinctive command Marsh possessed over the zombies and how this seemed to be communicated by mere thought alone. No other handler had yet showed such affinity with the reanimated dead.

Simpson, therefore, was aggrieved as he watched the soldier he considered incompetent, being feted as successful in this new form of warfare. Simpson took his opportunity when Scott and Wells were visiting the front lines in the company of other handlers, investigating possible zombie sightings intent on capturing the undead. Without his friends around Marsh to protect him, Simpson vented his anger. The latest form involved Marsh peeling potatoes ready for the cooks in the evening. Simpson had previously tasked him with many menial activities, including cleaning the toilets and extra guard duty. The most obvious occasions of bullying happened when there was no-one else around to challenge Simpson. However, even when witnesses were present, subtle bullying still occurred. When his friends suggested revenge against the sergeant, Marsh dismissed the whole idea as foolish. It never occurred to Simpson that Marsh would raise the issue with the Colonel. Likewise, it never occurred to Marsh to take advantage of his privileged access to the Colonel.

Marsh was unhappy. He spent his time thinking about his abilities as a soldier and the challenge of making his family proud. These things he could not easily reconcile. He was not sure how his family would respond to the knowledge he had unexplained and specialised skills with the tigers. He was quite certain his family would not approve of zombies. Once the creatures became common knowledge, he suspected many people would be horrified. He knew his family would suffer from trepidations: his heroic brother being used as a zombie had the option been available when he died. He would be a stain on the memory of the dead. After all, the zombies were the children, brothers, husbands and fathers of people back home, not manufactured weapons of warfare.

To be reanimated as a tiger was a horror Marsh would not wish upon anyone. But then, the needs of the war were paramount, and he was convinced they could get the tiger concept to work, saving lives in the long run. Even though the zombies ruthlessly dealt death, he knew their use was necessary, just as killing in war was essential to achieve their ultimate goals.

Marsh still doubted his capability as a soldier. Unusual and useful, yes, but capable? Marsh knew he did not fit the mould of a typical soldier. Not only was it about his non-combat deficiencies, especially the ones pointed out by Simpson, but also how Alfie got himself into trouble on his limited visits to the battlefield. One such instance occurred when the Bavarian had taken him by surprise in the last attack, or the hand-to-hand bayonet fight he had ended up in during his first action. Yet, each time he had got himself into trouble during the last attack, his skill with the zombies had helped him out of the situation, even helping him to save others.

The second problem was the development of a more effective use of the tigers on the front line. Marsh had a few ideas he wanted to develop. He had already brought the concept of head and body armour to Colonel Hudson. When he had inspected the tigers following the last attack, he had found sustained machine gun fire had done a great deal of damage. The flesh had been torn away by bullets, and impacts with obstacles. Most of the zombies continued to function perfectly well with such damage, as did those new zombies recruited from among the enemy ranks. In the worst cases, limbs had been damaged beyond the point of repair, with these zombies having to be put down. Few surviving tigers had taken any damage to the head, but he knew from the reports of the action, those shot in the brain fell instantly. Clearly, there were grounds to protect critical joints and heads, improving the battlefield survivability of the already tough zombies. Prisoner interrogation had also shown the enemy was still working out how to address the zombie threat. The Germans were terrified by the tigers, fearful of becoming zombies themselves. However, any head protection for the tigers could counter-productively reduce the element of fear the enemy experienced, further highlighting a weakness they could exploit. Any head protection might also further limit the ability of the tigers to function aggressively by restricting their movements, senses, or attack methods.

One of the key concepts Marsh intended to propose to the Colonel was the removal of artillery barrages before any attack. Marsh was confident in his ability to move the tigers close enough to the enemy trench prior to an assault, allowing the element of surprise to overcome the defenders. By moving the tigers quickly and quietly, using the carnage of no man's land to conceal them, they could close on an enemy position, remaining undetected. This would ensure the maximum shock value while also reducing the opportunity for the enemy to organise return fire. By sending the follow-up troops straight after the assault team launched, there would be little chance of the enemy keeping, or recovering, a trench. Such surprise assaults could be followed up with an immediate attack on the enemy reserve trenches, creating the potential of a much sought after breakthrough. His entire approach would make extended and expensive artillery barrages redundant. The enemy would have no warning of a tiger assault.

'Got you peelin' spuds again, has he, Alfie,' Wells asked. Marsh almost removed a fingertip on the sharp knife. His friend had crept up on him while he daydreamed.

'Josh, you're back! Pull up a stool and give me a hand,' Marsh gestured to a spare ammunition box which would serve as a stool. Several sacks of spuds waited to be peeled for the cooks. 'What's that you're hiding?'

'Oh, this?' Wells turned to reveal a large and unusual gun, half concealed on his back. He put down a large canvas sack he was carrying on his other shoulder. 'This is a Chauchat—'

'A chau-what?' Marsh interrupted, perplexed by the name.

'A Chauchat. It's French, a beauty. It's a machine gun small enough to be fired by one soldier. I thought it would be useful seeing how I'm not a great shot. So I got myself one. Perhaps if I can put enough bullets out there, I'll hit something.'

'Nice. Where'd you pick it up?'

'You really don't want to know.' Wells sat down and lit a cigarette instead of helping his friend with the potatoes, then laid the gun across his lap. 'It's a light piece of kit, so it'll be useful in a trench and it carries twenty rounds, which it can fire off pretty damn quick. Makes it ideal for storming a trench or taking the head off a zombie. But there's no fussy reloading after every shot. You get twenty shots before you have to mess around with reloading. It's smooth and quick.'

'But the magazine is open.' Marsh wondered if his friend already recognised the obvious problem with the weapon. Alfie was rather proud he noticed the weakness, despite his general competence as a soldier. 'You'll get mud in it, and the whole thing will jam up.'

'Well, the Frenchie who gave it to me pointed that out. You know, as we're not likely to be rolling around in the trenches for weeks on end, I thought it would be fine. Besides, he told me if you grease the cartridges and only put nineteen into the magazine, it's less likely to jam. Also, you only fire short bursts of three of four shots to avoid the barrel overheating. It goes off target if you fire too many bullets at a time,' Wells said. He thought for a moment before passing the weapon over for Alfie to inspect. 'And it will stop dead anything it hits, so it's perfect for what we're up to.'

'Blimey, it's light.' Marsh had expected something much heavier. He surveyed the weapon, the potatoes forgotten. 'You can't stick a bayonet on the end.'

'It won't need a bayonet when it can spit out three or four rounds in the same time it would take you to skewer someone. Plus, I'd not need to get so close.'

'I like the idea, heavy firepower, full-sized bullets which will have more stopping power, and multiple shots which will be ideal in a trench or when trying to deal with a rogue zombie. Maybe we should have one in each squad, or some other weapon like it. It would give real firepower to support the tigers when they advance, much more than our simple protection squad can put out.'

'And it protects us against the tigers should any handler get taken out,' Wells said, addressing the primary concern among the protection squads. 'I've got us some other goodies, as well. Perhaps we should try them out. If there's any you like, you could suggest it to the Colonel?'

'Oh, what else have you got?' Marsh's curiosity was piqued by the unusual weapon. He placed the Chauchat on the floor.

'Well, it turns out this particular Frenchie had a fair bit of trench fighting experience. The bloke fought at Verdun for most of the last year. So I made some trades for some other kit he said was useful for trench raids.' Wells opened the canvas sack and rummaged around. He withdrew an enormous blade.

'What the bloody hell is that?'

'A machete.' Wells said, drawing the large knife from the sheaf. The blade was flat and more than a foot long. 'It comes from the colonies and I've seen things like this called cutlasses by some blokes back home. Some of the more charming gentlemen around the docks carry them. I never thought of using one myself, but it'll hack right through a limb if it's kept sharp. It's perfect for taking on the enemy or for dealing with any unruly tigers, especially as tigers won't drop when you skewer them with a bayonet.'

Marsh took the blade, measuring the heft, and attempting a few chopping motions. The blade chopped clean through a potato he placed on top of a discarded ammunition crate.

'Careful,' Wells said as he watched Marsh pull the blade from the top panel of the crate. With minimal effort, he had almost chopped all the way through.

Marsh handed back the machete, which Wells sheathed and placed back in his sack. Next, Wells withdrew a thin, but long, dagger. 'This here is a stiletto. The blade's strong enough to punch through light armour, which is what medieval knights used to use it for. It's useful in the trenches, but you'll need to be close to use it. Frenchie suggested we use it for quiet work like taking out sentries during trench raids, as well as hand-to-hand fighting when you can slip it by someone's defence.'

Marsh took the stiletto and balanced it on the side of his hand. 'Very nice. That's a seriously sharp point. You know, you could use it as a weapon of last resort for any out-of-control zombie. It's long and sharp enough to pierce a skull and it'd go right into the brain.'

'Exactly, one destroyed zombie. The other thing Frenchie suggested was using any trench shovels we'd got to hand. Of course, we already know that from our own trench experiences, but again, it's a sharpish blade if you swing it hard enough. It can shovel through mud, so it'll go through flesh.' Wells had unclipped his entrenching tool and was running his fingers along the digging edge.

'I suppose you could always sharpen it?' Marsh said, surprised his friend was carrying a shovel. Wells often discarded it as surplus weight at the first opportunity and had lost several to date.

'Of course. There's one more thing in my bag of tricks.' Wells reattached his entrenching tool to his webbing and again theatrically opened the top of his canvas sack. 'This, my friend,' he said, revealing the firearm, 'is a Winchester 1901 repeating shotgun. It's lever action, so easy and quick to reload and it takes 10-gauge smokeless cartridges.

I've got plenty of them off Frenchie as well.' Wells handed Marsh the shotgun and a couple of boxes of cartridges.

'Perfect! It's perfect for fighting in trenches. That and your Chauchat will give us lots of stopping power to use where we need it.' Marsh worked the lever-action on the shotgun. 'I thought we weren't allowed shotguns in the trenches because of the lead or something?'

'I heard the Germans think the weapons are cruel, so we're not allowed them because of some gentleman's agreement. But then, they're saying the same about zombies as well. Leave it to the Colonel to sort out. He may even get hold of some of those new pump-action shotguns. They're even quicker to use than this lever-action gun,' Wells said, handing over another case of shotgun cartridges. 'You take the shotgun, it'll give you better close up protection and you can worry about running the tigers while we worry about protecting you.' He watched as Marsh loaded the weapon, giving the instructions, 'Five cartridges in the mag and two in the lever.'

'Both times we went over the top. This beauty would have been handy. I could have found a use for it,' Marsh said, thinking about the close scrapes he had experienced. On both occasions, he had been let down by the precision and size of the modern battlefield rifle. The shotgun would give him a much better close-range weapon, and being shorter than a bayonet-tipped rifle, it would be much easier to wield in close-quarters combat. Unfortunately, it did not have a bayoneted tip, but a single shotgun blast should do the job just as well.

'So I've got a stiletto for each of us, but only one machete for now. I thought I'd give the machete to Davies. He's a tall lad, so will have a good reach and it'll give him something other than his bayonet to keep sharp when he gets nervous.' Wells grinned when he mentioned

Davies' tick. 'Tell him to keep close to you, and he'll be able to use it to help keep things under control should anything go wrong.'

'Good idea, but make sure he keeps his rifle. He still fancies himself as a decent shot, even if he's never proven it. Anyhow, he'll only need the machete for the close-quarters stuff.'

'Agreed. I'll keep the Chauchat myself,' Wells said, stroking the weapon with a lover's touch. 'That'll give me an excuse to always accompany your team, especially as you're a man down without Simmonds.'

'Why don't you get someone to work up some kind of stick, or club, like we've seen other units using?' Marsh asked, referring to the improvised clubs used by both sides in trench warfare. 'Then we'll each have something else for close-quarters combat.' Marsh paused, deep in thought, before adding, 'We'd also be able to use them as part of a silent attack. I've been thinking we've been going about things the wrong way with the artillery bombardments and all the noise. We need to take the enemy by surprise.'

'What the hell do you think you're doing now, you worthless swine?' Simpson bellowed.

Marsh was practicing a silent attack drill with his squad. It had been going well and Simpson stood watching while Marsh manoeuvred a small group of tigers. They occupied a field the battalion used for training. The location was not the best re-creation of a battlefield, but it possessed shallow trenches with some wire obstacles. The tigers crept forward, almost human, but unnaturally silent in their movements as they crouched low. They offered the smallest of silhouettes for any defenders to spot. The accompanying live humans also moved from cover to cover, keeping very close to the tigers. Each of the living carried a club on their belt besides a primary weapon in their hands. Marsh brandished his shotgun, while the others did not even have bayonets fixed, for fear the shiny metal may give away their position to a watchful enemy. Stopping short of the enemy trench, the men slung their rifles across their backs, drew their clubs, or with Davies, his new machete. Three of them had thrown fake grenades, and as one, the tigers and humans had risen and charged into the simulated trench. At this moment, Simpson walked along the parapet of the practice trench, interrupting their efforts.

'We're just practising, Sarge.' Marsh said, hoping the obvious answer would satisfy the man. He could defuse the situation by treating Simpson's comment as a question rather than as a provocation. Marsh turned back to the tigers, shouting orders to them to ensure they did not wander off.

'Trench raiding, is that what you're doing? You think we're going to waste these tigers on trench raids? They're breakthrough weapons,' Simpson said, a patronising tone lacing his words. He was still disappointed at the use of zombies, but even more annoyed they may be further misused by the person in front of him. 'We will advance across the battlefield and seize the enemy trenches through overwhelming, and indestructible, numbers. You know the drill. We'll not deviate from the tactics devised by our betters.'

'These things aren't bulletproof, Sarge, nor are we. You saw that during the last attack. A machine gun will still bring down a line of tigers, and once the Germans get wise to their weaknesses, we'll never breakthrough.' Marsh knew his logic was on firm ground, enough to risk correcting the sergeant. He forgot for a moment that logic did not interest Simpson.

'Just because you're the Colonel's little pet, you think you bloody well know best, don't you?' Simpson said. A grimace of disgust theatrically passed over his face as he took the time to recognise the weapons he had been ignoring. 'Thugs with clubs. A bloody great big kitchen knife. Ah, also a shotgun. Are the King's bayonets and Enfield rifles beneath you? They're not too good for the rest of His Majesty's Army.'

'Bayonets ain't no use against machine guns. Nor is marching straight into a killing field,' Davies said, interrupting to defend his friend from Simpson's theatrics. 'Creeping up on them and smashing in their skulls is much better 'cause we might live to tell the tale.'

'It's cowardly and not the way we do things in the British Army.' Simpson's face grew red.

'Which British Army?' Davies asked, not holding back his contempt for the sergeant. He stabbed with his machete to punctuate his points. 'The army that got slaughtered at Mons? The one that just got slaughtered on the Somme? Or do you mean the one we've got left? It's time things changed a bit, because all we've done so far is get our own lads killed.'

'Watch your tone, you mutinous piece—'

'It seems the way we've been doing things so far hasn't worked out too well, Sarge.' Marsh said, before Simpson could take out his growing rage on the insolent private, or Davies could swing his machete any closer to the stubborn sergeant.

'You always were a sneaky, worthless bastard, Marsh. It's no surprise you'd stoop so low as to become a thug. After all, you can't do real soldiering. Barely passed out as a recruit, and then only because Wells was watching your back, just like he still does.' Simpson grew redder. 'You don't even have control over your mutinous gang. What about answering back to NCOs, running around with bloody swords and clubs? If it weren't for the Colonel, I'd break you down to private right here, right now. But I can see I'm going to have to be a bit cleverer. Mark my words, I'll have you out of this unit before long.' Simpson paused for breath, his voice having risen to just short of a shout. He checked Marsh up and down and, unable to think of anything else to say, he stomped away having had the last word.

'If he leads us, he'll soon get his wish. We won't be alive for long, let alone in this unit,' Davies muttered once the sergeant was out of earshot.

'Typical power crazed bloody hooligan,' Matthews said. 'If I had a bob for every one of his ilk I'd met in this army, I'd be filthy rich by now.'

11

ARRAS

'It is an overstatement to say things went to plan.
Right from the beginning we experienced problems.'
Interview with Samuel Earle-Thomas, 4th Australian
Division in Anderson, J, 'Oral History of the Aus-
tralian Imperial Forces of the Great War' (1984, Syd-
ney)

'Yes, Sir!' Marsh said, climbing out of the muddy hole in
no man's land. At least they were practicing on a simulated
battlefield, he thought. If it were real, a sniper would soon draw a bead
on him.

'So Corporal, tell us about these tactics you've come up with. How
do they work?' the recently promoted Field Marshal asked Marsh, his
grey whiskers damp in the misty air. Colonel Hudson nodded, having
already worked with Marsh in anticipation of this conversation.

'They work pretty much as you saw, Sir.' Marsh knew it was not every day you got to address a Field Marshal, so he did his best to stand to attention in his mud-caked uniform. He knew Simpson would be horrified by the state he was in, but the Field Marshal did not seem to be in the least bit bothered. The Field Marshal was still waiting for a detailed answer. 'We will not use a preparatory bombardment, Sir. Instead, we move close to the enemy as stealthily as we can before launching our assault. If we come across any enemy on the way, we deal with them quietly and quickly. We then seize their trench in a sudden strike, hurrying down the communications trenches to the second and reserve lines before the enemy realises they are under attack. The follow-up troops then cross no man's land as soon as we enter the first trench, so they are ready to take possession of the cleared positions as soon as we advance into the rear. Like us, they'll use the enemy communications trenches to move forward and if we're quick enough, we can force a breakthrough. This will mean fewer men exposed in the open, so there will be less opportunity for the enemy to inflict heavy casualties.'

'What happens if the enemy blocks the communication trenches?' Haig asked, interested in the idea and already thinking through potential issues.

'We send the tigers out into the open, around the back of the defenders, and assault from multiple directions. We'll bypass any heavily defended position and leave it to the infantry following on behind us. Constant forward movement will ensure maximum surprise and shock.'

'I like the spirit.' Haig patted Marsh's mud-covered arm. The Field Marshal's eyes lost focus, remembering a pleasant occasion. 'I used to hunt tigers in India. Challenging beasts, much more so than the foxes of the Bicester and Worcester Hunt. Mind those Indian tigers are not as fierce as your creatures here.' Haig moved closer to a tiger, scrutinising it. The one he examined was clad in a British Army uniform and wore a Brodie helmet. The creature snapped at him but otherwise stood still, following the instruction Marsh had quietly given. 'I say, they do smell awful. Are all your tigers in such poor condition?'

'Yes, Sir, and this is one of the better tigers. You've got to consider they are all dead and we rarely receive them in good condition. They're often damaged when infected by another zombie, or our lads have beaten them senseless when capturing them. Unless you have a handler nearby, they aren't easy to control, so getting fresh captures back to us is a massive challenge for frontline units. Also, tigers have a bad habit of accumulating damage in combat, even while it takes a great deal to slow them down.'

'The things scare me, and they're on my side. I should imagine Fritz will have nightmares for the rest of his life if he survives an encounter with one of these beasts. How many tigers do we have?'

'We have just short of one hundred, Sir. We've arranged them into ten combat groups along the lines that Corporal Marsh has developed and have deployed non-standard weapons to the soldiers in the teams,' Colonel Hudson answered, 'We're adding to the number of tigers, but as you know, the infection rarely breaks out in the wild, and when it does, our lads have an understandable tendency to destroy any new zombies they discover. If we could make use of volunteers—'

'I accept your point, but I will not be approving any plans requiring the deliberate infection of volunteers,' Haig said sternly. 'We have discussed this before, and I do not consider it an appropriate moral course.'

'You've made that clear, Sir,' Hudson said, disagreeing with the ethical judgement. 'Our challenge is we have too few tigers to make a decisive difference on the battlefield. It will take us time to enlarge the number of zombies available to us through combat alone.'

'Now, I've been pondering this conundrum since you first raised it with me and I have an idea where I can deploy your tigers, while growing your numbers via combat,' Field Marshal Haig said, pleased to possess a solution which may deflect Hudson from his obsession with infecting volunteers with zombie bacteria. 'We've been reviewing the lessons of the Somme and Verdun, and we will issue a new training pamphlet in which we will focus upon combat doctrine for small squads and platoons. Over time, this will change the whole combat approach of our army. It will be a little like the pre-war doctrine, and it seems your Corporal here, has come up with a perfect fire and movement tactic for your tigers, which will fit well with what we are soon going to have the entire army doing.'

'The Canadians have previewed the new tactics and are getting to grips with them. They are almost ready to deploy. The Australians, however, are struggling a little. I am not surprised, considering their discipline leaves something to be desired. However, I should not complain too much as their fighting spirit more than makes up for any deficiencies in discipline. We could use your combat groups to help strengthen the Australians and force a breakthrough in the new Australian sector of the front. You will need to get your men ready and worked up for an attack early in April,' Haig said, waiting until Hudson had comprehended the orders. 'Are there questions Colonel, ones we need to deal with now rather than at the Staff stage?'

'As you can deduce from Marsh's demonstration, we're using some unorthodox weapons to help us. We've only got a limited supply of these weapons. Can you arrange for more equipment of this nature to be issued to us as soon as possible, Sir?'

'Ah yes, the shotguns and those French machine guns. I had heard you gentlemen were playing at being cowboys, using shotguns and whatnot. However, I can recognise the point in using these weapons in trench warfare. There will be some political concerns about using shotguns, but I think I'll be able to quell those. I'll get some sent on to you as soon as possible, but the Chauchat, that will be a harder weapon to source. The French don't enjoy parting with them as there are not enough to equip their own troops yet. Now, I can see from the other unorthodox equipment the rest of your soldiers are using—' Haig said, examining the nearby men of the battalion. 'Well, they seem able to improvise the rest of the equipment they need.'

'Thank you, Corporal. Thank you for showing me what your men can do and giving us some alternative approaches to explore,' Haig said, dismissing Marsh. 'Now Colonel, there's a Military Medal and promotion for one of your men who has shown themselves to be brave in the face of the enemy. Shall we proceed?'

'Good God, Josh,' Marsh said, unhappy with Haig's news. 'Haig's gone and promoted Simpson. He said so in front of me.'

'Well, you know what they say. Shit floats to the top,' Wells said, pulling a face at the imaginary stink.

'Surely a medal would have been generous enough? Promotion as well? He got the medal for his work before he ended up with us. He barely knows what he's doing with the tigers and shouldn't be in charge of them. It's all spit and polish for him. That last time out, he almost got all his tigers wiped out and cost us the objective.'

'That's not the way the Brass see it. Lots of blood and death means success in their book. At least now he's commissioned it might keep him out of your way. Maybe the CO will put him on paperwork duties or give him a post somewhere out of our way.'

'But there aren't enough experienced officers to go around.' Marsh shook his head. 'They'll have to at least give him command of a platoon, or even a couple of combat groups.'

'Well, if Scott stays with us, we'll be safe away from that fool. I suppose the CO will have no choice but to put someone with a Military Medal in a combat position. Perhaps we'll get lucky and he'll get a Blighty, or perhaps the Hun'll get him? It's not like we're a regular unit and able to move our nuisances out to another unit. We're an experimental unit and we can't easily pick up new officers who understand what's going on, so we're almost always going to promote from within. Unless the Hun do us a favour, we're stuck with him.'

'Lieutenant Bloody Simpson,' Marsh said, spitting on the ground in disgust.

Several men nearby stopped working to call out their disgust in response to Marsh's loud announcement.

The battalion deployed to northern France, attached to the 4th Australian Division. Preparations for the joint action progressed as the date of the offensive drew closer with the battalion exercising alongside the 12th Brigade and, for the first time, some of the revolutionary new armoured vehicles christened as 'tanks'. The rhomboid-shape tracked vehicles were slow, noisy, and pretty much indestructible. Marsh at first marvelled at them until one of his tigers had almost been crushed by the tracks of a blundering vehicle. The crew of the tank had not even been aware of the near-miss.

The objective of the offensive was the village of Riencourt, between two German salients. To the left was the German-occupied town of Bullecourt, and to the right was a complex trench network known as the Balcony Trench. These German positions comprised part of the Hindenburg Line to which the Germans had retreated in late 1916, shortening their lines and improving their defensive positions. Two Australian brigades of the 4th Division were to advance into the salient, intent on smashing through all three defensive lines before proceeding two miles into the rear of the German position, to take Hendecourt. The tanks and tigers would act as key breakthrough weapons, the tanks on the left of the line, the tigers on the right, the whole spread across a two-mile front. The Australians would follow through on the attacks, securing the enemy trenches and then advancing to the final objectives, having broken out of the German trench system. Marsh hoped the element of surprise was being maintained. Coordination of such a force was impossible to keep secret from the enemy, but security around the tanks and the tigers remained high. The novelty of such weapons should disrupt the enemy's response.

The troops studied the maps, with the Experimental Battalion rehearsing the attack several times. B Company, with its four combat groups, practised Marsh's method of silent attack and rapid movement. Each combat group received a shotgun and Chauchat, with Field Marshal Haig exceeding on his promise by delivering the precious French weapons. The heads of the tigers were armoured with carefully secured Brodie helmets. Through trial and error, a method of securing the helmet had been achieved. Other attempts to armour the zombies were ineffective as the armour proved too weak or cumbersome, restricting movement or falling off. For every two combat groups, there was an officer and a non-commissioned officer, with Scott and Marsh taking these roles in the B Company combat groups they found themselves in. Lieutenant Simpson was, to Marsh's clear relief, in A Company. Simpson had engaged in a constant campaign to persuade his captain to continue with as many of the old infantry techniques and tactics as possible. He found a great deal of success, through a combination of mutual agreement and nagging. Simpson also resisted the issuing of shotguns. On this last measure, he was unsuccessful, having to back down to avoid creating discontent among his men.

What lacked in the battalion's preparations was coordination with other units. Although the tanks were to be deployed on the left of the assault, there had been minimal consideration of how the tanks would work alongside the tigers. The tigers were swift and deadly, while the tanks moved slowly and with great noise. The metal landships were lethal wherever they went, but vulnerable to the terrain and unable to wipe out the enemy from any one trench. They were also deaf and partially blind, only able to view the outside world through narrow slits in the armoured hulls. While the tank commanders experimented with communications methods such as semaphore, the units alongside them did not have access to the same approach. Similar problems existed with the coordination of the artillery, especially the Corps level artillery, which provided most of the artillery support on any battlefield. To further compound the challenges, minimal photo reconnaissance had been undertaken by the Royal Flying Corps, who had instead been busy providing the Canadians with photos for their sector of the attack at Vimy. The Canadians had built scale models of the terrain and rehearsed their attack. Marsh was envious. The Canadians were being far more thoughtful in their approach than the Australians and British before Riencourt.

Then, Marsh knew, there were the Australians. The Australians did not want British help, even specialised support from tanks and tigers. The Australians resented even a few British soldiers being present, and the men who met the tigers were amused by them, rather than fearful.

Marsh knew the Australians would fight hard. After all, they had already established a hard-won reputation during the war. Yet, he was concerned with the contrasting level of preparation the Canadians were showing elsewhere, and how similar efforts were not being made for the attack he was to take part in. He had even been given access to one of the tens of thousands of maps the Canadians had printed for the use of their troops, ensuring each individual soldier knew their role in the impeding offensive. Nothing like this was provided to him, or the Australians. The Australians he sought out made it clear the problem was with British leadership and higher-level coordination, not Australian reluctance to adopt forward-thinking ideas. It was obvious from the way the Australian troops worked together, they were experienced and eager to adopt fresh approaches which would help on the battlefield. Many of the men he spoke to referred to their previous campaign at Gallipoli.

Even the outcome of the initial Canadian assault on Vimy Ridge, to the north of Arras, failed to move along the preparations for the Australian assault. Marsh knew two days before, on 9th April as every artillery piece the Canadians had in Europe began firing to prepare for the attack. A heavy gun every twenty yards and a field gun every ten, was the rumour among the Australians he spoke to. Vast underground mines had been detonated underneath the enemy trenches and a new tactic, called the creeping barrage, had been tried for the first time. As the Canadians advanced over no man's land, field guns fired a volley just ahead of them, designed to stop the Germans from targeting the vulnerable Canadians. Every three minutes, the barrage shifted one hundred yards towards the objective. This kept the Germans from supporting their forward areas while the heavy Canadian artillery dealt with known German positions and countered the fire of the German artillery batteries. From what Marsh understood, the strategy was proving extraordinarily successful, and the Canadians soon overcame the Germans.

The success of the Canadian attack left Marsh ill at ease and inspired. The Canadian assault had taken place only a short distance away, on the other side of Arras, and the Germans in his own sector would not be alert for attacks. Whether the enemy would consider the Canadian attacks to be diversions, or not, the Germans would not want to give ground along the fortified Hindenburg Line. The lack of coordinated preparation was his primary concern, but Marsh was confident the tigers would achieve their objectives.

A further failure to coordinate was evident in the planned intention of launching the Australian attack one day after the Canadian offensive. The assault failed to launch as scheduled; the tanks could not get into position because of bad weather, and therefore the attack was postponed by another day. What was worse, one British regiment did not receive the postponement orders and unsuccessfully made their unsupported assault to the north of Bullecourt, further risking alerting the defenders.

'My God,' the Australian captain complained to Marsh. The Australians milled around the crowded trench with Marsh's men, ready to launch their own part in the Australian attack. 'We can't go ahead even after this delay. The Germans know we're coming and only eleven tanks are in position. There's also been a mess-up with the artillery barrage.'

'I thought there wouldn't be a preparatory barrage, Sir? We should have moved into position while it was still dark,' Marsh said, as a few friendly shells flew overhead. He hoped the gunners were careful. A few shells falling short would ruin the attack.

'That's almost right, Corporal. We were going to take them by surprise with a short barrage. Just enough to take out the wire,' The Captain said, leaning forward to peer through the trench periscope his men had attached to the parapet. 'But, what artillery there is — well, it's not enough to cut much wire. Here, have a look.'

The officer moved aside so Marsh could take a turn with the trench periscope. A British officer would not have offered the use of such equipment to a lowly soldier such as Marsh, but this Australian had a healthy respect for the specialist in his trench. Alfie had used a periscope before, but it still disorientated him, with his mind taking a few seconds to process what he could see. Much as he expected, he could make out the badly cratered mud of no man's land, occasional shells exploding amidst the still intact barbed wire. Splintered stumps of trees stood in small clusters which might once have been a small wood. The shell-churned muddy ground was saturated by the rain which had held up the tanks the previous day. Marsh knew the conditions were worse for the tanks. The Hirondelle stream drained through the battle lines there.

'I'm going to get on the telephone to headquarters to let them know the enemy wire isn't cut. I think the Staff should postpone the attack again until it's dealt with. General Gough will want us to attack, and that's pretty much all he wants us to do, but I saw this sort of thing at Gallipoli, and there's no way we can get through,' the officer said. He did not wait for a reply. Confident in his own expertise, he made his way to the dug-out containing the field telephone.

When the captain returned. His face was downcast, and he wasted no time calling his lieutenants for an impromptu meeting, along with Lieutenant Scott as the officer commanding the attached experimental B Company. Marsh held back at the edge of the gathering, tolerated by the gaggle of officers as the senior zombie expert. If he were not present, he suspected the captain would have summoned him, given their conversations so far.

'Battalion has passed our concerns up the chain of command. They know we're unhappy with the bombardment and the state of the enemy wire. Other companies have reported the same along their sectors of the line. However, General Gough still wants the attack to go ahead. No further delays are allowed. We'll just have to do our best with the wire,' the captain said, the surrounding officers greeted the news with moans or shaking of heads. 'Lieutenant Scott, are your tigers ready to go?'

'Yes Sir. The wire will affect us as well, since the tigers aren't great at untangling themselves. We'll have to stick to clear passages, and those are going to be covered by machine guns.'

'Fine. So, gentlemen, we'll be kicking off as scheduled in one hour. Scott, get your tigers out into no man's land and as close as possible for the assault, and then we'll follow you up as planned. Without the bombardment, we're relying on you to get us into the enemy trenches.'

'We'll do our best, Sir. Our artillery is still shelling no man's land, attempting to clear the wire. I can't get any of my teams out there until the shelling stops. It's bad enough the sun's up now. Without friendly artillery, our job will be much more difficult.' Scott caught Marsh's eye to check he agreed with the summary. Marsh did.

'Yes, I know the plan called for your boys to get into position under the cover of darkness, but with this mess up with the artillery, it's no longer possible. You'll just have to get them out there as soon as you can and hope our boys in the artillery don't drop any short rounds. General Gough was quite specific about that. We do what we can as soon as we can.' The captain could see Scott grimacing and shared his sentiments. 'Questions? No? Well, good luck, gentlemen. I'll see you in the German trenches.'

In the briefing's wake, Scott and Marsh soon found the other combat team leader, Tomkins.

'You heard what the Captain said, Marsh. We're going to get out there as soon as possible. Get as close as you can to the enemy trenches before launching the attack and don't attack until zero hour.'

'But Sir, it's daylight, and the artillery isn't dropping off yet. The Germans will spot us and pick us off as we get into position. We should have gone hours ago while it was still dark, and we may not even get into position in the time that's left.'

'As soon as it seems like the artillery is dropping off in front of your position, get out there into no man's land and get ready to assault,' Scott said, thinking for a moment, 'It could be we'll have to advance at the last minute, just ahead of the Australians. I don't want our lads out in the open while this shelling is going on. It's asking for trouble.'

'At least that'll keep Simpson happy over in A Company. He can pretend he's fighting alongside normal soldiers,' Tomkins said, his distaste for Simpson clear.

'Tomkins, I'll accompany your group. Wells will be with your team, Marsh. Remember, handlers are in command during combat, so don't let any of us with rank stand on your toes,' Scott said. They both nodded to acknowledge the arrangements. 'Any questions?'

12

ASSAULT

'These poor buggers charged past us — in fact, they was barely ahead of us as we advanced over no man's land. A motley bunch those tigers, and the lot soon got wiped out. We had a tough fight to shift the enemy. I heard elsewhere there was a bunch of tigers which smashed into the Hun trenches and our lads had nothing much to do. Wish I'd been on that end of the line, we took heavy casualties and I lost a few of my mates.'

Interview with James Elliot, 4th Australian Division in Anderson, J, 'Oral History of the Australian Imperial Forces of the Great War' (1984, Sydney)

THE SUPPORTING ARTILLERY FIRE, although sporadic, did not drop off until five minutes before the revised attack was due to begin. As a result, the tigers were still waiting in the forward trenches minutes before the attack, crammed in with impatient and enthusiastic Australians. Somehow, Marsh was preventing any accidents from happening with his tigers. Several of the Australians were enjoying teasing the snapping zombies, having recovered from the shocking discovery they were sharing the forward trench with tigers. Word of what to expect from the tigers spread among the Australians, who playfully engaged with the lethal creatures. Other than the Australian officers, the men had not known about the existence of these shock troops.

'Out we go, lads,' Marsh said, directing the living component of his combat group. 'Keep low, and I'll get the tigers to spread out. We'll get in close to the enemy lines, but if we can't, we go to ground and advance alongside the Australians.'

Marsh verbally and mentally ordered the tigers over the top. He gave them mental images of the wire and how to avoid it, ordering them to use the cover of nearby shell holes and to crawl as soon as they cleared the parapet. The protection squad pursued the tigers, all staying low as they rushed to the nearest craters. Marsh ended up in a crater with two tigers and Morgan. Within moments, a German machine gun position opened up on them, their exit into no man's land, drawing the defenders' attention.

'Great,' Morgan said, lying flat on the crater's inside as bullets cracked overhead. 'Pinned down and we've only just started.'

'So much for a stealthy attack then, Taff. It's looking like we'll have to charge down the gun position when the Aussies come out and join us. If we don't, they'll murder our boys.'

Marsh crawled up the shallow crater wall, taking a quick peek over the edge. Another machine gun opened fire, spotting his movement. He pulled his head back into cover, swearing as he did so. 'The wire's still solid ahead. There are a couple of gaps towards those MG posts, but I bet they'll have been set up as killing zones. We've no choice. We'll have to charge those guns and hope the tigers can stand up to the damage. I will not wait until the Aussies turn up. They'll get slaughtered.'

Marsh put his fingers to his mouth and whistled to get the attention of his spread-out protection squad. His first whistle was interrupted by a machine gun burst. 'I'm going to send them forward! Stay down and wait until the Aussies are ready!'

Without another word, Marsh mentally commanded the tigers to advance, staying low. Their objectives were the two machine gun posts at the top of the killing zone. The two zombies in his crater scrambled out and ran off, with both Marsh and Morgan risking a peek over the crater edge as they left. They watched the other animate dead rising to advance across their sector of the battlefield. As he lowered his head, Marsh glimpsed a smoking rhomboid shape to the north. The tank was ponderously crossing the front line.

'At least the tanks are moving up.' Marsh said.

'Those zombies really freak me out when they do that,' Morgan said. Marsh stared back at him, confused. 'You know, when they take off like hounds after a fox, anytime you give them a silent order.'

'Well, the tanks are moving to the north. The attack should begin any minute now,' Marsh said, ignoring Morgan's fears.

The two machine gun posts waited before opening fire on the new targets. They had paused, stunned at the number of enemy running toward them. When they opened fire, the lack of bullets flying over Marsh and Morgan suggested the enemy were targeting the tigers closing on their positions. Simultaneously, there arose a great roar from the Australian trench, and both Marsh and Morgan looked back at their own positions, seeing over the lower edge of the crater a bellowing khaki swarm emerge into the open. The mass of shouting Australians began the rush across the field towards the enemy and the gap in the wire currently assailed by the tigers.

'Christ!' Morgan said. 'They're scary bastards. They'll give Simpson kittens advancing at a run, too. Hell, they're even zigging and zagging.'

The Australians did not form up into orderly formations, but advanced in small groups. They were experienced soldiers who knew movement and speed were crucial for survival on the open battlefield. Needing to move on themselves, Marsh pulled Morgan up by the back of his webbing as the Australians drew level. The Englishman and the Welshman joined the advancing horde of Australians, struggling to keep up. Marsh did not want the Australians to get too far ahead of him for fear he could not protect them from his tigers. Neither did he want the Australians to have any cause to complain their allies were battle shy.

The tigers were almost upon the machine gun positions as Marsh left his crater. The enemy funnelling the animated dead into the narrow killing ground where the machine guns concentrated their rapid fire. Five of the zombies collapsed to the ground while approaching their objective, the machine guns chewing through flesh and bone to the extent the damaged tigers could only continue to progress by pulling themselves forward with their arms. A further two no longer moved, hit in the head by rapid machine-gun fire. The last three tigers, still upright and mobile, were almost on top of the two machine gun posts. Marsh watched as a lone tiger attacking the leftmost position was thrown backwards by the impact of multiple machine gun bullets. Yet it immediately rose, one arm dangling by strands of shredded muscle. Before he comprehended what happened to this tiger, the other two leapt head-first into the rightmost position. The gun fell silent. The constant chatter of the weapon was replaced by the sound of screaming and rifle fire from within the trench.

Rifle fire from the German positions picked up as the advancing Australians ran towards the enemy. The leftmost machine gun switched fire from the sole tiger to the rapidly moving Australians, scything many down before the gun fell silent, the tiger pouncing upon the gun crew. The crescendo of rifle fire from the German line also extracted a horrendous toll on the Australians as the unbroken wire filtered them into the narrow killing-zones. Despite the weight of the rifle bullets, the Australians continued to advance, the defenders' machine guns silent.

As the advancing men reached the crippled tigers, which were still crawling towards the enemy, Marsh's security squad put an end to each so no unfortunate new casualties would occur. Marsh also sent a mental order to the tigers occupying the machine gun posts. He did not know if the creatures still functioned, but he ordered them to head to a spot midway along the defended trenches between the two machine gun positions. Marsh also sent a caution to not attack anyone in Allied uniforms, hoping such an instruction would be followed. New zombies might have been created during the attack and these could also prove a threat to the living. He hoped these new creations would pick up on his orders and head in the same direction. Marsh had never tried to command new zombies without being able to see them. He was worried his skills did not extend so far. He needed to be closer to the action so he could take control of any reanimated corpses. In other sections of the line, such dangers were even greater since other handlers relied upon verbal commands.

The Australians stormed the German front-line trench, and fierce hand-to-hand fighting broke out, except for the section between the two machine gun posts. Instead of struggling, from this section came shouts of fear and disgust from the arriving Australians. As soon as Marsh got into the trench, he realised why. The fight was over and his three tigers stood at the meeting point half-way along the trench, their number swelled by a further eight zombies in German uniforms. The new tigers followed Marsh's commands, much to his relief. All bore hideous wounds, fatal to a human. To the widespread disgust of the living, the undead gorged on the remains of corpses which had not reanimated. The tigers had neutralised this entire section of the trench in the most bloody fashion, limbs, entrails and pieces of flesh scattered along the duckboards and up the parapet.

'Bloody hell,' an Australian voice exclaimed, his friend dry-retching at the charnel sights in the trench.

'Be glad they're on our side,' Wells said, slapping the Australian on the back.

'Poor buggers,' another Australian said, using his foot to tap a torn limp out of his way. 'I'm not sure what scares me more, a German machine gun or these things.'

'Marsh, call them off, will you!' Wells called to Marsh, amazed his friend had not already done so.

Marsh did as he was told and the tigers ceased their meal, hurrying away from the corpses and the frightened Australians.

Although the firing had slackened around their new position, the battle continued elsewhere along the line. Using a captured German trench periscope, Wells identified several broken down and smoking tanks to their north. Clearly, the tank attack was not penetrating the German line as planned. Where A Company's tigers attacked, there were large numbers of Australians lying immobile in no-man's-land, the volume of fire suggesting they were pinned down in the open.

Despite the localised success in their own part of the line, the wider attack was stalling.

'Marsh, can you get ready to move forward again?' the Australian infantry captain asked, having found the tiger handler.

'Yes, Sir.' Marsh needed only a few simple commands to ready his charges. 'We'll go as soon as you wish. I've just got to send the tigers a few instructions. The squad will take longer to get ready.'

'Good. We need to get into the German second line as soon as possible. We've got to disrupt the Hun as he's doing too well elsewhere. The rest of our brigade seem to be struggling to get their backsides moving. I've got a couple of squads moving down the trench to help break up the positions on our flanks, but we need to get forward with the rest of our strength. I want you to get your tigers into the next enemy trench, and we'll follow right on your heels. Then hopefully Hun will think about withdrawing.'

Several bullets cracked over their position, the Germans opened fire from their second line. The next step of the advance would be defended against. Marsh spread his tigers along the trench, ready for the next assault. The zombies moved quietly, taking up their new positions. Most of the Australians kept their distance, but more than one patted tigers on the back as they went by. Several wished the tigers good luck, getting a growl or a snapping of teeth in response. Near to Marsh, an Australian waved a bayonet he had just looted from a freshly created tiger wearing a German uniform.

'Ready to do this again then, Alfie?' Wells asked, intending to keep close by his friend during the next assault.

'Yes, but spread the word to the others. We need to get over there real quick, right with the tigers. I'm worried I might not control all the new tigers once they're out of sight,' Marsh said, concerned the moment was the wrong time to discover the limits of his skills. He did not want such a poorly timed discovery on his conscience.

'It all worked out well just now. None of our lads got bitten by the new zombies. It'll work out well again.'

'Yes, but I didn't know for certain it would work, and I don't want to risk any friendly casualties because I can't control the new tigers. We're really pushing the limits of my abilities. Anything might happen.'

'That's why I'm here.' Wells patted his unfired light machine gun. 'We've got your back when you need us.'

'Let's go then,' Marsh said, more reassured than he expected to be by his security squad. Should any disaster happen, the squad would deal with the breakdown in Marsh's ability to command the tigers. He knew the security squads elsewhere along the line had already put down tigers when their handlers fell in battle.

Marsh commanded his tigers out into the open again.

The heavily fortified land was not as wide as the previous stretch, and there was less distance to cover to reach the second German line. Within seconds of Marsh's combat group leaving the captured trench, the defending Germans spotted the movement and opened fire. The Australians manning the parapet, behind the advancing tigers, began cheering the deceased onwards. One of their number opened fire on the Germans to keep their heads down. The idea spread rapidly, the whole Australian line soon providing covering fire for the advancing tigers. Much of the Australian fire was aimed at the individual Germans, who gave away their positions with their defensive fire. Before Marsh even reached the first shell-hole, a major duel began between the Australians and the Germans. A couple of Australian

Lewis Guns opened fire, while several German machine gun positions joined in. Yet, the German fire slackened as their soldiers took cover from the incoming fire. Amid the exchange, less attention was paid to the advancing tigers. Such small numbers of men were deemed a lesser threat than the noisy Australians holding the German trench. Clearly, the defenders did not know who they were fighting. The element of surprise was paying off.

'Let's move quicker!' Marsh's voice was barely audible above the fusillade. 'The Aussies are keeping Fritz's head down.'

This time there was less wire to slow the advance. Where there had once been a great number of obstacles, few remained intact, the shelling having broken the wire. Instead of the tigers being funnelled into machine gun killing zones, they now advanced unimpeded. In this open space, the zombies rushed ahead of Marsh and his security squad, the living sprinting to keep up as the tigers leapt into the German second-line trench. Behind them, there came a fresh roar from the Australians, who took the disappearance of the tigers as their own signal to advance. The Australian fire slackened to almost nothing while the mayhem in the German trench grew, violence directed not at the advancing Australian troops but at the tigers amid the defenders.

Wells reached the top of the enemy parapet, pointing his Chauchat before firing a five-round burst. Marsh arrived just as a German rifleman crumple to the ground. Wells jumped down next to the lifeless corpse. This second trench line was the heavily manned main German line of defence. These could be the enemy soldiers readying to counter-attack. Marsh jumped down into the crowded trench before anybody could draw a bead on him. He headed in the opposite direction to Wells, firing his shotgun at a soldier who lunged towards him with a bayonet-tipped rifle. The shotgun blast caught the man in the face, his head disappearing in a spray of red. Marsh experienced an overwhelming urge to vomit as the sight tipped his fear into terror.

Marsh could not count all the enemy soldiers. There were too many. The vast majority were preoccupied with fighting the sole terrifying zombie which occupied their part of the trench. This tiger was among the number Marsh had begun the day with and now showed a great deal of wear from the hard fighting. Five of the enemy moved to corner it, seeking to pin the reanimated flesh to the parapet with their bayonets. Another group of soldiers were shooting the zombie, none aiming for the head. The zombie appeared unstoppable, but one lucky shot would be all it took. Marsh cycled his lever shotgun, firing into the group of soldiers pinning the zombie. As they fell, the tiger freed itself, grabbing at the assailants close enough to reach. Screams of terror and pain came from several mouths.

A soldier turned, and ignoring the threat of the zombie, aimed his rifle at Marsh. Both men knew Marsh would not get his shotgun ready in time. A scream from above marked the end of this shared understanding. Davies flew, machete in hand. His fall was broken by the German, the blade slashing through the man's arm before catching in the wooden rifle stock. Davies struggled to pull the blade free as the gun clattered to the trench floor, along with the severed arm. Frustrated, he stomped on the discarded rifle, the blade edge coming free. The German fell back, shocked, as he watched his own blood spurt from the stump of his arm. Davies turned, and in a frenzied scream, charged at the nearest unharmed German. The man readied his weapon. He would beat Davies in the race to attack. Marsh cycled his shotgun. The gun barked, ending the German. Consumed by battle-rage, Davies did not notice and still savagely fell upon the man as he slumped back against the trench wall.

The tiger quickly finished the remaining enemies who tormented it, rushing past Marsh and Davies, distracting the remaining Germans in the trench. A new zombie arose from the tormentors who had pinned the tiger. The man was missing much of his lower face, the bone of his jaw visible, yet he moved with the fluidity of the zombies as he rose. The new tiger pushed Marsh out of the way and fell upon the remaining defenders.

'Surrender!' A German soldier shouted, throwing down his rifle and raising his hands. Others did the same, overwhelmed by the terrifying attack.

'Stop,' Marsh said, his voice barely audible above the wider noise of the battle. The two tigers stopped on his command, hunched over their victims, but no longer attacking. Marsh wondered if all the tigers under his control were also frozen in mid-action, vulnerable to whatever occurred out of his sight. Marsh summoned the tigers he could reach to him so they would not become frozen targets for the enemy. This way, he could be certain they would also not cause friendly casualties.

The tigers had disrupted the sections of the trench they assaulted. The following Australians met no organised resistance. Marsh marvelled, knowing his ability to control, without words, made the tigers under his command even more deadly. How would other handlers control so many tigers if they could only send verbal orders at close range? He knew he would have to examine this further. This mental control seemed to give options for other approaches during combat.

'What are these demons you have sent at us?' the surrendering German asked. The man was shaken, but still spoke English.

'They're something which will win the war,' Marsh said. Two more tigers joined him along with a sweaty Sergeant Wells who had pursued the fast zombies along the trench, fearful something untoward was happening to Marsh. Morgan joined them slightly after, unable to keep up with Wells or the zombies.

'We are truly in hell. They are monsters. You have unleashed monsters to fight us in this war.'

Marsh did not have time to reply. A dozen screaming Australians leaping into the trench interrupted him. They were the first of the follow-up troops to arrive.

'You ain't left anything for us to do, you greedy buggers,' an Australian sergeant said as he prodded a corpse with his bayonet.

'There're only prisoners left here for you, lads,' Morgan said. His announcement was greeted by cheers from several of the Australians. Relieved at having avoided a brutal fight, the Australians insisted on patting the four tigers on their backs, before securing the prisoners and policing the trench.

13

UNDERMINED

'Early inconclusive attempts to employ zombies on the battlefield were let down by the general wider inability of the Allies to coordinate combined arms operations. At Arras, any successes were already un-dermined.'

Milton Davies, A History of Zombies and Warfare,
(London, 2016)

'MESSAGE FOR YOU, MATE, from the company captain,' a runner said, catching his breath after jumping into the trench. He gave Marsh a folded piece of paper. The man stood puffing, relieved to be back below ground level rather than amid the dangers of no man's land.

Marsh unfolded the piece of paper and read the pencilled writing, reading it aloud to himself, 'Marsh, hold your current position in the second trench while we arrange artillery support to take the final trench. Tigers are to assault the trench at 11 o'clock.' Marsh glanced at his watch. This gave him three-quarters of an hour. He returned to the note, 'Australians present are to advance at the same time. Pass orders to senior Australian present. Attack progressing successfully across the front.'

'What's it say?' Wells asked, having not been able to hear Marsh muttering, the sounds of battle drowning him out. Marsh passed him the note to read.

'Please acknowledge receipt,' Marsh said to the waiting runner. The man crossed himself, unslung his rifle, and climbed out of the trench to find the company commander. Wells set off to find the senior Australian present.

'What we doing now then, Corporal?' Davies asked.

'We're waiting for some artillery before attacking again. It'll be a while yet. Find Matthews, he won't be far away.'

Davies wandered off up the trench, hoping he had chosen the correct direction. He recoiled from the bend in the trench when he reached it, and Marsh wondered what was happening. Four tigers walked around the corner accompanied by more of the cheerful Australians.

'We found these making their way here. Thought we'd make sure they found you,' one escort cheerfully said, when he recognised Marsh.

'Send any more you find this way.' Marsh wondered if the Australian knew the zombies were homing in on Marsh's summons rather than cooperating with any Australian escort. Marsh had launched the attack on the second trench with eleven tigers. He wondered how many he would have gathered by the time they advanced again. This latest group was not moving with any urgency, perhaps a sign of his own state of mind. Any other zombies homing in on his command may also be moving slowly.

After a few minutes of waiting for Davies to return, Matthews appeared from the opposite direction, accompanied by ten tigers. The living human was happy but tired. The tigers were bloody and dead, although animated by whatever process kept their deceased remains moving.

'You and your bloody silent orders, Alfie,' Matthews said. 'We were in the middle of a scrap with at least a dozen Huns, and the bloody tigers froze solid. Before we knew what was going on, they walked along the trench, away from the enemy. I just stood there looking at the Germans, and they were staring back at me, all left on my own. Thank God they threw their weapons on the ground. Twelve of them surrendered to me on my own! I couldn't believe it. The tigers had them shitting themselves.'

'These tigers are mostly ones I gathered up when looking for you. To be fair, I just had to follow them to you. They knew where they were going,' Matthews said. 'Oh, there were more, but I put a couple down, too badly mangled by a grenade or something.'

'Where's Davies?' Matthews asked, having patted Wells on the back by way of greeting.

'Alfie sent him off to find you. He went the wrong bloody way,' Wells said, pointing to the bend Davies had gone around.

'Bloody typical. So how many tigers we got then?' Matthews sat down on an upturned crate and lit a cigarette.

'Eighteen at the moment.'

'Can you handle that many, Alfie?' Matthews was not concerned. Marsh was still in control of the zombies and appeared composed, considering he had just taken part in two assaults.

'I don't see why not. It's not like I've got to see the tigers. As long as they're in range, I think they'll do what I tell them. There might be a maximum number I can control, but I've not hit it yet,' Marsh said.

'What are the other handlers going to be doing? How are they going to cope with all the extra zombies? You're the only handler who can do that stuff in your head. The rest have to say their commands out loud,' Morgan said, worried other handlers would be struggling.

'I dunno? I suppose their security squads will deal with any zombies they can't control.'

'But what happens if things get out of control in those squads?' Morgan asked. 'Oh,' he said, as he recognised the mortal precariousness of their situation for the first time.

'We don't think it's likely to happen. But, if it does, you get every soldier on hand and put down every uncontrolled zombie you find until things are under control again. If there are too many zombies to control, reduce the number,' Marsh said. Morgan looked blankly at him, still not comprehending the consequences. 'Remember the village? We can't have that happen again.'

'We were nearly wiped out the first time we met those things,' Matthews said, recognising the point Marsh was reinforcing. Morgan went green at the memory.

'Remind me later, and we'll look into it,' Marsh said. How the other handlers functioned on the battlefield was going to be important in how the tactical use of zombies developed.

'Davies!' Matthews called as he greeted the returning soldier. 'Get over here, you lazy bugger. Where've you been?'

'I bumped into Lieutenant Scott up the line. He held me up. Loads of questions,' Davies said as he sat down on an upturned crate.

'Tell us. How's Scott?' Morgan asked.

'Furious.' Davies took out a silver hip flask, taking a long swig from it before offering it to the others.

'Don't just leave us hanging. Tell all,' Wells said when Davies did not speak again.

'While we did all right, Simpson's got his zombies well and truly bloody slaughtered. He held the tigers back and didn't let them out ahead of the Aussies. The Germans almost wiped them out. They strolled like they was out for a walk in the park. The attack only succeeded because the Aussies are nearly as tough as the zombies.' Davies took his helmet off and ran his hand through his greasy hair. 'There were heavy casualties both for the Aussies and our lot.'

Wells passed around a packet of cigarettes.

'Bloody idiot, that man,' Marsh said. 'He's stuck in the last century, not an original thought in his head.'

'It's not just him, though. Those new-fangled tanks also got bogged down in the mud. They were absolutely bloody useless. Again, the Aussies broke through there, but no thanks to the tanks.'

'Those tanks are a complete waste of time, didn't I tell you?' Matthews said. 'What business have they got driving across a battlefield in a great big clanging bell of metal? Mark my words, nothin' will ever come of them.'

'Scott is also annoyed with corps headquarters. The artillery they promised was a complete cock-up. He's probably also cross because the Aussies are really pissed off and chewing his ear off. They didn't think they'll be able to hold the gains from today without the artillery support. When I left, there were loads of messages being carried back and forth. I tell you what, I wouldn't like to be on the other end of one of them messages. Those Aussies really know how to let you know when they ain't happy, even their officers are in on the act.'

'Some things don't really change,' Matthews said. 'It doesn't matter where you are, or who you are fighting alongside. You wouldn't believe the number of times there's a cock-up behind the lines which stops a proper follow-up. Either the artillery shoots at the wrong target, the follow-on units get lost, or the cavalry forget to shine their bling. That's before someone misjudges the wind and the bloody gas gets blown back at our lads.'

'And on that cheerful note, it's time to get ready,' Wells said, ending the impromptu moaning session before their spirits were further sapped.

The combat team moved into position. With eighteen tigers present, the trench was crowded with zombies. As with the previous assaults, the large group of Australians made a big fuss of the tigers about to advance before them. They knew if the tigers were successful, their own advance would be much more bearable. To have a fearsome weapon on your side was entirely different from facing an unstoppable weapon in the hands of the enemy. Everyone would leave the trenches at the same time for this attack. The Australians had seen the tigers in action and knew Marsh would have them sprint ahead to distract the Germans from the advancing vulnerable ranks of living soldiers. Any Germans aware of what had already occurred this morning would prioritise targeting the tigers.

Eleven o'clock arrived without the fanfare announcement of artillery. Despite the planned use of heavy guns to support the next stage of the advance, there was silence, punctuated by the sporadic rifle fire of tense soldiers awaiting the next climax of the battle. Both sides knew the attack was inevitable, and on the hour, whistles sounded along the line. The final advance was announced.

'Up we go!' shouted Wells, more from a need to let off steam than a requirement to issue an order.

The Australians did not stand on ceremony and left the trenches as quickly as the tigers. As the tigers rushed ahead, the protection squad zig-zagged from cover to cover, the zombies drawing the German defensive fire. The Australians were also using the fire and manoeuvre tactics they had recently trained with. About half of them fired from cover while the other half advanced, the two halves reversing the practice, so each group leapfrogged the other. This kept the enemy under pressure while the Australians progressed. As before, the Germans trained their machine guns on the tigers. Most of the bullets were wasted, but lucky head-shots still took down three tigers. These zombies fell to the ground, no longer moving.

With the tigers advancing across such a broad front, the defenders had no chance of stopping them all. By the time the zombies arrived at the defensive positions, Marsh was barely half-way across the same ground. He watched another two tigers go down to what appeared to be aimed shots. One still moved, but Wells was heading in the right direction and would make sure the tiger did not become a threat to their own side.

The rest of the tigers launched themselves into the final assault with a gusto for flesh already displayed twice this morning. Screams and wild shots came from the enemy trench. The organised defence of the trench broke down in seconds with the immediate threat of the zombies outweighing the danger posed by the large number of advancing Australians. A series of minor explosions showed the defenders were using every available weapon in a last-ditch defence. As the advancing Allied soldiers arrived at the trench, the German defenders broke, some dropping their arms and seeking to surrender, while others climbed out of the opposite side of the trench to get away. Many of the runners were felled by Australians who knelt on the reverse parapet taking pot-shots. Yet, a few enemies continued to fight, mainly in a desperate defence against the personal attentions of the tigers.

Marsh realised the enemy was defeated, and the Australians were in place to take custody of the surviving Germans. He called off the tigers, regrouping them. The fight for the final trench in the defensive line had been short and fierce. Terrorised both by the fearsome tigers and the many Australians, the enemy were overwhelmed by the speed and ferocity of the assault. The German lines were broken, the rear of the German defences open to exploitation, the breakthrough was underway, and the tigers had proved themselves.

Again, the combat group came through the fight intact, with no significant injuries, although Matthews sported a couple of grazes to his face. He claimed these were caused by shell splinters, but Morgan, who had been with Matthews most of the assault, suggested the injuries resulted from a clumsy fall. The last attack had been so fast, no new tigers had been created. Marsh happily counted off thirteen functional tigers, a better number than he had begun the day with.

'Marsh!' Lieutenant Scott called as he strode along the trench, hands on hips, inspecting the last German line. The officer had spotted the tigers, but not yet found Marsh.

'Over here, Sir,' Marsh waved.

'Are you boys all right?' Scott grinned widely and patting each of them on the back, euphoric at the successes of the day.

'We're all fine, Sir,' Marsh said before running through the details of unit strength and injuries.

'You've fared better than most of us, although the rest of B Company hasn't done badly. It's time to pull back now.'

'Already, Sir? We will not continue the advance? Surely we've triggered a breakthrough?' Marsh was unhappy their success was to be thrown away. Now was the time to keep pressing. They should send the cavalry through the break forced in the German lines. Once the cavalry charged into the enemy rear, the whole German front would collapse and either the enemy would have to retreat further, or sue for peace.

'Orders from above. It sounds like the cavalry isn't ready to move. There'll be no more advance, and we'll just consolidate this position. The advance is over, so we're no longer needed this far forward. I want you to help the Aussies get these prisoners back, and your surviving tigers. We'll drop back to the assembly lines, as we'll be no use defending.' Scott was right. Nobody had yet worked out a successful tactic for using the tigers in defence. Zombies remained offensive weapons, pure and straightforward tools of shock and terror.

'So that's it, Sir?' Marsh asked. He felt deflated. After all the work to prepare for today, and the dangers of crossing no man's land multiple times, he was annoyed at the failure to grasp the opportunity.

'The Aussies don't have the strength to keep going forward. They may have fared well here, but elsewhere they've taken heavy casualties. We can't rely on any artillery support, and they've failed to do their job. The follow-on division and cavalry are also not yet in place because of the wet conditions. Orders have come down to hold the ground. We'll continue the advance when the rest of the troops are in position.'

'But, Sir, now is the best time. Now is the time to attack. We've got the enemy on the run. There's only their supply lines and artillery park ahead of us.'

'Yes, and we don't have the strength to take them,' Scott said. 'The Aussies are crippled and won't be going any further. Do you see any cavalry nearby? You can't take out the whole German army with a handful of tigers.'

'It's bloody typical,' Matthews said, interrupting. 'Every bleeding time we break through, there's a massive cock-up. The cavalry spend so much time sat on their fat arses, waiting for the breakthrough, you'd think they'd actually be ready when the time comes.'

'That's enough, Matthews,' Scott said. Having received his commission recently, he was prepared to take some challenge from men he respected, but he still needed to dismiss the negative comments, even though everyone present knew the sentiments were correct. 'It's our necks on the line, and if we advance without proper support, we'll all end up just as dead as your pets there.' Scott pointed to the zombies.

'Great, so we just pack up and go home,' Marsh said, defeated. He ducked as several German shells landed in a nearby cluster. The incoming artillery just missed the newly captured trench. Shrapnel whistled through the air, one sizeable chunk scything through the belly of a nearby Australian. The surprised man crumpled to the floor, wailing in agony as he tried shoving his intestines back into his belly.

'Let's get moving now! Their artillery has these trenches zeroed in and I bet they're pulling together enough men to mount a counter-attack.' Scott was energised by the return of danger, running off down the trench to give the rest of the company the news. He did not wait for a reply from the men he left behind.

It took minutes to organise the withdrawal. The enemy artillery barrage continued, growing in ferocity. Scott was correct. The Germans had already ranged their guns in on their old positions and would soon launch a counter-attack. When it happened, Marsh knew he, and his tigers, would simply be in the way of the Australian defence. Attaching themselves to a small group of Australian soldiers escorting German prisoners, the combat group quickly made their way out of the captured German trench into no man's land, rushing back towards their own lines, despite the danger from the German artillery.

The German barrage extended well beyond the trench they had just vacated. Timed fuses on the shells caused airborne explosions. Each of these sent out small balls of metal and torn shell casing across the battlefield. The fused shells exploded like harmless puffs in the air, but maimed soldiers moving in the open and those in uncovered trenches. Adding to the danger, shrapnel rounds were mixed in with high explosive shells. Each of these dug sizeable craters out of the already torn up ground. Chunks of rock, earth, and corpses were lifted high into the air. Blast and shrapnel from these explosions proved lethal to anyone caught within reach. Though the retreating soldiers and their prisoners crouched close to the ground, they could not negate all the risk. A near miss dropped several German prisoners and an Australian guard. These men were ahead of Marsh, and as he ran past them, there was hardly a mark on their bodies. He assumed they had been killed by the blast rather than high-speed splinters of metal.

While their journey seemed to take forever, within a minute, the survivors leapt into the second German trench, looking for better cover from the artillery.

'Bloody hell, they got me,' Morgan said, blood pouring from a cut in his sleeve.

'Here, let me see,' Wells said, grabbing at Morgan's flapping right arm. A shell went off nearby, and clods of mud fell from above as Wells pulled up Morgan's sleeve. 'You daft bastard, it's just a scratch. Look at it.'

'It bloody hurts.' Morgan swore as he prodded the small hole in his forearm and the tiny exit wound around the back. His face went white as a sheet and his facial tic started up for the first time today.

'I'll get a tourniquet on your arm. We can't have you bleeding to death. We'll never hear the bloody end of it.' Wells pulled out his dressing kit. Someone handed him a belt, which he tightened around Morgan's arm, above the wound. 'You're got some small bits of shrapnel stuck in your arm, although it looks like a sizeable chunk went straight through. Hold this.' Wells gave one end of the bandage to Morgan to hold while tightening off the bandage before tying a knot.

'Sarge! Sarge! Bandage me next,' Matthews said in a child-like voice.

'Shut up, you stupid git,' Morgan said, forcing the words between gritted teeth. He drained his hip flask in one gulp. 'It bloody hurts.'

'Everyone else here?' Wells asked.

'The Aussies and their prisoners took a hit too,' Davies said, taking out his machete to sharpen the edge again. He was shaken by the experience of the last few hours, a few nicks on the edge of his blade, proving he had been in the thick of the fighting.

'We lost a tiger to a direct hit,' Morgan said before clenching his teeth again.

'Which one?' Marsh asked. 'I didn't see it happen.'

'It was one of the ones we began the day with. One second he was there, then the next, there was mud and chunks of zombie flying through the air. I finished off the bit of him that didn't want to die. It may well have been the German guns which got me, but I don't know which is bloody worse, zombies or artillery?'

'You can have a cuddle with a zombie and then tell us if it's worse than kissing the Hun artillery,' Matthews said, laughing.

'Ha, bloody ha.'

'Someone give Morgan a cigarette. It'll keep him quiet,' Marsh said. Wells followed up by lighting a fresh cigarette and sticking it in Morgan's mouth. Morgan drew deeply, nearly choking himself.

An increase in rifle fire came from the forward trenches as the German artillery barrage ceased. During the bombardment, the Australians had been too busy focusing on survival to be bothered with firing back. A significant counter-attack was now developing, and the Australians fought hard. Shouts came for the forward trench, revealing the battle was being fought hand-to-hand. More Australians advanced across no man's land to reinforce their foremost units as the combat group resumed their withdrawal from the field. Marsh was annoyed they could not offer much support in the defensive battle. He would have to think about the situation when he was not so exhausted.

For the tigers, the battle was over.

PART 3 - GAS! GAS! GAS!

14

A NEW ALLY

'Large numbers of men from Ireland volunteered to fight in the British Army during the Great War despite the ongoing issue of Home Rule. Even when a conscription law was passed in 1918, it was not enforced, adding to the growing pressure for political separatism. Despite the tense situation within the country, the men of Ireland fought hard, with casualties in line with other nations within the British Empire. It is unlikely that the brutal experiences of the trenches were a direct cause of the creation of the Irish Free State, but it may have been one of many complicated contributory factors.'

Extract from an A Level revision website, (2009)

'MARSH! GET HERE.'

'Yes, Sir,' Marsh entered the tent, saluting while standing to attention. The trip to the stores could wait until later. Simpson would monopolise his time for now.

Following the failure of the recent advance, the Experimental Battalion remained in the Arras area. The tigers, effective in their own assault, could not carry the day. The experience of battle across the battalion had varied, with some tigers, specifically those under the control of Marsh, being key to the advance. Yet, the brave Australians they supported had been forced back to the start lines, suffering heavy casualties. The lack of supporting artillery, and the failure of the follow-on units, were among the deciding factors. The tigers, withdrawn from battle once the advance stalled, were of little use while on the defensive. Marsh was already working on the defensive use of tigers, playing with a few ideas.

'While Lieutenant Scott is off preparing the new positions, I will be in command of B Company,' Simpson said, letting the news sink in. He watched for a reaction from Marsh, letting the time drag out, eager to identify evidence of his rival's unhappiness. Simpson believed Scott mollycoddled the men, something which wouldn't happen while he was in charge. Still, there was no reaction from Marsh. 'Because of our recent losses, the two companies will be merged and we'll reorganise with four combat groups. You'll continue to run one group, but I'll be putting a second handler with you, considering the problems we've experienced.'

Simpson made it clear he would have preferred to remove Marsh from any responsibility for a combat group. The option was not open to him, not while handlers were so few. Simpson intended the second handler to be some sort of stooge. The two men had a long history and Simpson considered Marsh a shambles. If he showed Marsh was incompetent, Simpson might remove him from the combat strength of the battalion. For now, the officer was constrained by the fact Marsh was the most effective handler of tigers in the British Army. The re-animated soldiers, pressed into service with the experimental British unit, had first been brought under control by Marsh, and although there were now other handers, none were yet his equal.

Simpson's idea of a second handler possessed some merit. He assigned an extra handler to each combat group because of an incident in his own company when a handler was killed during the assault at Bullecourt. The tigers were controlled by voice, although Marsh's own control of the zombies functioned on a mental, even telepathic, level. During the combat, when Simpson's handler fell, the tigers turned upon the mass of supporting Australians. Each combat group was accompanied by a security squad, tasked with putting down any out-of-control zombies in a situation such as this. The chief fear, and one which had so far proved academic, was a zombie outbreak would occur with no handler to take control of the new zombies. It had been close-run. German defensive fire had helped retrieve the situation, thinning out the assaulting Australians ranks to the point the zombies could not infect many of the soldiers. In the chaos, the security squad had performed their role, wrestling control of the situation, but there had been no margin for error during the crisis.

'Things were close-run. We cannot have tigers running around causing chaos. We just kept them under control. It would be unforgivable if we were to cause an outbreak among our own ranks,' Simpson said, still angry about the chaos following the death of his handler. Rumour had it, Simpson was in the thick of the fight against the rogue zombies.

'Perhaps if the tigers were used as planned, then they wouldn't have been mixed up among the Australians. The zombies should have been out in front, with their handler and protection squad easing forward using cover.' He knew he risked Simpson's wrath by criticising the officer's alteration of the tactical plan. The tigers were for use out ahead of the supporting infantry to maximise the shock the enemy experienced, while minimising the risk of friendly casualties.

'It's essential for good morale that our boys can see our tigers fighting alongside them.' Simpson's belief in his own assessment of modern tactics was unshakeable. 'From this point onward, each combat group will have a second handler and we will double the size of the security squads to ensure we have sufficient numbers to control any situation.'

'Has the Colonel agreed this, Sir?' Marsh knew he was pushing his luck with Simpson, but was surprised Colonel Hudson would allow such a change in tactics without discussing it with himself. After all, Marsh had led on most of the tactical developments in using zombies.

'He has little choice. It's a numbers game. We have so few functioning tigers, we cannot deploy again on the same scale. The Colonel also cannot risk upsetting our infantry any further. So, while you may have made lots of new friends among the ANZACs, their commanding officer has complained to the General Staff about how his soldiers were attacked by the tigers,' Simpson said, missing that his own tactical flaws were at the root of the failure. He also overlooked Marsh's re-cruitment of tigers during the combat.

'Tigers need to be used apart from the normal soldiers, Sir. We've established that now, but I agree with having extra hands to help keep them under control.'

'No, we need to rebuild the soldier's confidence in the tigers. We need the tigers to work close by, and alongside, not creeping into the German trenches. If using zombies on the battlefield works, it will be as a mass formation,' Simpson said, unwilling to go any further with his justification. 'I'm not prepared to discuss this with you any further,

Corporal. It's tough if you don't like how we deploy the tigers. You will do your duty like the rest of us.'

'Now, Marsh, your new handler will be Corporal Mullen. You'll work with him and the two of you will control your tigers. The rest of the security squad will be confirmed later. Be sure you don't slip up.'

Simpson returned to the paperwork on his makeshift desk. The situation was crystal clear. Still standing at attention, Marsh recognised the interview was over. Marsh saluted and left the tent, frustrated at Simpson's insistence on defunct tactics. Hopefully, Lieutenant Scott would return soon and overrule the foolish man. Marsh also made a mental note to seek out the Colonel on the issue.

'Hallo lad.' Mullen offered his hand, which Marsh shook. Marsh knew Mullen was a decent choice. If he had chosen a handler to be paired with, Mullen would have been in contention. Marsh could have been saddled with someone far worse. Mullen could run a combat group on his own, so perhaps Simpson had a hidden agenda here, intending to replace Marsh at the earliest viable opportunity? Yet on reflection, Marsh thought it was more likely Simpson had no clue about how good the pairing was. Marsh had seen Mullen possessed an instinct for working with tigers, far more than most handlers.

Mullen was new to the unit, having arrived from an infantry depot in Belgium, awaiting redeployment after a time away from the frontline. He had been there recovering from an injury which had separated him from his original unit. Like many of the handlers, while in the depot, he had shown an aptitude for working with tigers during the recruitment tour Marsh had led. Given the unexpected opportunity, Mullen had stepped into the role of handler, able to manage fifteen tigers with ease during his early training sessions. Although he did not obviously possess telepathic control of his tigers, Marsh spotted something unexpected. The zombies showed some indications of a response to Mullen's non-vocal commands. Marsh was optimistic he could develop Mullen's skills in this area.

'We'll be working together then,' Marsh said, shaking the offered hand. 'How'd you get on at Bullecourt?' Mullen had been under Simpson's command.

'T'was awful. We advanced at the same time as the Aussies, straight into the German fire. Didn't even have any supporting artillery, absolute carnage. I heard you did well, though.'

'We didn't get the artillery support either, but we advanced as we'd planned and practiced before,' Marsh said. 'At least at first that's what we did.'

'Lieutenant Simpson wouldn't let us move out as planned. He called the plan cowardly and sneaky, changing it at the last minute. The daft git insisted we advance alongside the Australians, everyone out in the open.' Mullen scratched his nose and Marsh decided the man had a very low opinion of Simpson, seeming to hold his breath as he sought to control his anger. 'Our advance went horrifically wrong. The tigers went out of control after a couple of handlers were killed. They just turned on the Australians. We were all packed in so close together, the protection squads couldn't get a handle on the situation. Loads of Aussies were injured or killed, our own lads too, a complete blood-bath. Not all of it was done by the tigers, either. The Germans took a share in the killing.'

'You did fine though, didn't you?' Marsh asked, curious to discover how Mullen got on.

'Well, there's only so much one bloke can do when you've been ordered to keep the formation together and everything's going to shit around you. Tigers aren't meant to walk across a battlefield towards the enemy. They're meant to fly at the enemy, ripping 'em to shreds. Sure, they'll take more damage, but why walk them in the open and give the enemy an extra chance to harm them? I lost most of my tigers, so I said, stuff it, and sent them forwards at speed. Once the beasts got ahead, they did some damage, but there's only so much they can do in small numbers.'

'Well, get used to giving the enemy the time to do damage. Somehow Simpson has convinced Hudson to introduce mass attacks,' Marsh said, his face making it clear what he thought about the idea. However, he was glad Mullen shared his assessment of how best to use the tigers.

'You knew Simpson before he got commissioned, didn't you? Was he always a bastard?'

'Absolutely awful, a spit and polish regular without an original thought in his head.' Marsh knew he was glossing over how Simpson, as an instructor, had bullied him throughout training for being a misfit.

'You know, I volunteered at the start of the war and there were plenty like him, regular army men who, by design, had missed the last boat to Belgium. They particularly liked the Irish, like myself,' Mullen said, sarcasm in his voice. 'They ruled over us just like bloody feudal Lords. "Get back to the bog, you Fenian bastard!" they'd shout, forgetting we're just as British as they are. We're not bloody colonials. If it weren't for this damn war, we'd already have got Home Rule. We got the damn law through the Lords and then this bloody war stopped it from happening.'

'Looks like Home Rule is on hold for the duration, especially after the Easter Rising,' Marsh said. He did not know an awful lot about the situation in Ireland, but the attempted revolution of 1916 had been significant news, and even he possessed an awareness of some of the surrounding issues.

'Maybe, but there were a lot of martyrs created when they put that one down. What happened changed the minds of many people, you know. People are prepared to put up with a lot of crap. Hell, look at the years since the Famine, but things are changing.' It sounded like his mind might have been one of those changed.

'What do you think should happen, then?' Marsh asked, curious as to Mullen's opinion. It could matter if the Irishman was not prepared to risk his neck on the battlefield.

'Let's sort out this war first. We need to put an end to the Kaiser and his ambitions. Besides, from the rumbles I've heard, the Frenchies are getting even more mutinous and don't forget the Russians have already overthrown their Tsar and brought in a government. What's happening in Ireland will have to wait for a less dangerous time.'

'The Tsar? Yes, but even creating a new government has not stopped the Russians from losing every fight they've had with the Germans. Still, the Russians are tying up the Germans. If the Germans could concentrate their forces in the West, the French would have lost Verdun last year, and where would we be now?' Marsh asked. The brutal attritional battle around Verdun had bled both the French and German armies throughout 1916. 'I'm worried about what I hear about the French as well. Their latest offensive isn't going to plan. Our attacks around Arras supported them, but there's still been no breakthrough.'

'Well, the Brass are sure to return us to the line at some point. When they do, how do you want to play it? Should we follow Simpson's lead?' Mullen's voice suggested he had no desire to remain in the role Simpson had cast for them.

'Tell me, have you ever had your tigers respond in ways you've not told them to?'

'What do you mean?'

'Have they ever acted on your thoughts rather than your vocal commands?'

Ah, Corporal Marsh. What can I do for you?' Colonel Hudson asked, looking up from his desk. He waved away the adjutant who had escorted Marsh into the tent.

'Lieutenant Simpson has informed us we'll be following new tactics, Sir. Well, Sir,' Marsh said, hesitating as he was going behind the back of an officer. 'I would have mentioned nothing to you, but I've worked with you on our tactical approach. I'm concerned his plans are moving in the wrong direction, considering the work we've already done.' Marsh stood to attention as he raised the criticism, knowing he would need to make the best possible impression.

'Relax, Marsh, take a seat.'

Marsh sat across the desk from the Colonel. Instead of relaxing, he sat as smartly as he could.

'I know corporals do not usually get to develop tactics, but your contributions have been crucial. Officers do not always know better than experts,' Hudson said. Having met Marsh just after the infantryman had encountered his first zombie, Hudson quickly spotted the potential hidden in Marsh. Circumstances led them to plan many of the tiger tactics between them, and Hudson had been delighted to confirm Marsh's ability as a thinker and leader. In traditional parts of the army, a corporal questioning an officer would prove scandalous, but the use of zombies was far from traditional, and Marsh was the most skilled man available to the British. In Hudson's opinion, Marsh had earned the right to ask such questions. 'Now, we are limited by our shortage of tigers, just as much as by the fear they'll cause more damage to our own side than the enemy, as demonstrated in our last action. We, therefore, need to make the best use of the resources available to us. We're not going back upon the excellent work you've already done, but we are restricted by the realities of our current situation.'

'But massed attacks, Sir? While having a second handler present is excellent and something I can recommend, the strength of the tigers is their speed and shock value. Our key strength is small and flexible groups, not massed formations.'

'It seems the enemy is already adapting. During the last attack, they used a tactic known as elastic defence. Did you notice how their front line was lightly manned?' Hudson waited until Marsh nodded his agreement. 'Their second and third lines were better manned, with most of their forces in these or even further behind the initial trenches, ready to assault our gains while we were still in the process of consolidation. They even pre-registered their artillery, ready to bombard their own positions whenever they fell to our advance. They played a sophisticated trap upon us, allowing us to exhaust ourselves during our assault, then sending in fresh troops just when our lads were exhausted.'

'But Sir, this response would suggest our tactics are working. We've got the Germans responding to us for once. We just need to push the elements which work and ensure the follow-up troops move forward quickly enough. Enemy artillery needs to be suppressed until we've finished our consolidations. We need better counter-battery support and targeted fire to break up counter-attacks before they happen. If we'd had effective artillery support on my section of the line, we would have been able to hold the position as the Australians secured the trenches.'

'Unfortunately, we cannot rely on the follow-up forces moving quickly enough, even though they did where you were at. This new elastic defence seems to be flexible enough to absorb our tiger assaults before ejecting our follow-on troops from our gains. If we move to massed attacks, we will seize control of an entire area while retaining full control of our tigers, so the follow-on troops move into the objectives alongside us. It is critical we can hold the trenches we take.'

'If we walk across no man's land, Sir, we will be decimated by the enemy machine guns. Surely the difference in tactics, as used by Lieutenant Simpson, demonstrated this won't work. His tigers were far less effective than mine,' Marsh said, pointing out the obvious flaw in the Colonel's argument. 'It's the movement and resilience of the tigers that gets us into the enemy trenches. If we walk across the battlefield, we'll just be sitting ducks and the enemy will pick us off before our tigers can achieve anything.'

'It's the movement which is the problem. We're too fast for the rest of our forces to keep up. Yes, in your section, the Australians knew what they were doing and could advance quickly across the battlefield, but few units are as experienced and well-trained. The General Staff are concerned the follow-up support cannot keep pace with our advances. They're even blaming your successes for the failure of the artillery support. Your section so outstripped expectations, the artillery could not work out which lines you held. Rather than risk placing you under friendly fire, they held back.'

'Sir, that's nonsense. The artillery failed to fire at their prearranged targets at the appointed times. They weren't holding fire because we were in the way, they simply failed to turn up. That we advanced so well without artillery support shows how effective the tigers are.'

'Whether you are right or wrong, current technology and doctrine are struggling to adjust to the potential offered by the zombies. The Canadians used a new tactic called the walking barrage to great effect at Vimy Ridge. The Brass want us to adopt this. In future, the artillery will fire slightly ahead of our troops, switching to the next target at timed intervals while the infantry follows behind the barrage. This tactic works at a fast-walking pace and the artillery officers doubt it will be effective at the faster pace used by our tigers. There's also a widespread belief in the tank as the way forward, as they operate at walking pace, allowing the infantry to keep up.'

'All the tanks failed at Bullecourt, Sir.' Marsh knew no further argument was needed, having seen several bogged down tanks abandoned by their crews.

'I'm aware of what happened, but there are great hopes for them from the top levels of Government. Whatever the merit of your points, and there is much to commend what you say, we do not have the strength to continue to operate in our present form. We must concentrate our forces to remain effective. We still have the confidence of General Haig, despite the mixed reports given by the Australians during our last experimental deployment.'

'Your job, Corporal Marsh, is to make sure we keep the best elements of our previous tactical experiments. In your combat group, you are to marry them to the new requirements as well as you are able. However, try not to flout the new tactical approaches,' the Colonel said, knowing how Marsh would follow the orders if the last caveat was not added. 'I've also thought about your idea of head armour for the tigers. Unfortunately, we cannot develop something for our zombies with the limited resources we have on hand, but we have improvised something.'

The Colonel stood up and stepped over to a large wooden travel chest. He released a clasp and raised the lid, leaning into the depths to remove a helmet. At first, it looked like a standard Stahlhelm coal scuttle helmet, just like the Germans had introduced the previous year. The design provided additional splinter protection lower down the back and sides of the head, a vast improvement on earlier German designs, and far in advance of those used by the British. This specific helmet was further modified by the addition of a short chain mail skirt hanging off the back and sides, extending the shell splinter protection.

'It won't stop a bullet.' The Colonel handed the helmet to Marsh. 'But it will stop a glancing splinter. With what we have on hand, this will provide more protection around the heads of our tigers than our existing battle bowlers do.'

'What about our lads mistaking the tigers for Germans when they're wearing this?'

'They may do so, so it'll keep them on their toes a bit more and remind them not to get too comfortable around our tigers. If our boys think they're shooting at Germans, they'll not aim at the head, and we know our tigers can soak up a lot of damage elsewhere,' Hudson explained. He reached back into the chest and withdrew another heavy object. This one looked like a helmet which had been cut in half. He offered it to Marsh. 'Here, attach this to the front of the helmet using the lugs. Now run the belt around the back of the helmet. The Germans call this piece of kit *stirnpanzer*. It's an armoured plate for the front of the helmet.'

'It weights a lot,' Marsh said, attaching the armour plate to the front and then tying the leather strap around the rear of the helmet to hold the heavy armour in place.

'That's why you don't see it a lot. It is not only heavy but also unbalances the helmet. Therefore, the average Fritz loses his as soon as possible to avoid carrying the extra weight.'

'Will it stop a bullet? It feels thick enough.'

'Perhaps, but it's still much better than a normal helmet,' Hudson said. 'We have scavenged plenty of examples, so we'll be issuing the kit to all our tigers later today.'

'That's progress, Sir. At least we'll increase the survival chances of the tigers. Their vulnerability to head damage is their key weakness.'

15

A STROLL IN NO MAN'S LAND

'You'd think after all the training we'd got, they wouldn't have had us walking in the open towards the Hun's guns. Every time we went into action, we tried the same stuff again. It never worked.

Then we tried something different.'
Interview with William Murphy in Duncan, F, 'A Soldier's War: Accounts from the trenches' (1931, London)

T HE NEW HELMETS WERE issued during the afternoon. Marsh also set about equipping his enlarged combat group with the afternoon spent fitting the new helmets to the ten tigers. Several problems existed with the helmet straps, which needed to be resolved because of the combat speed and movement of the tigers. Improvisation would have to do for now. The task was also an opportunity to introduce Mullen, and the other recent additions, to the rest of the security squad.

'Corp, how're we going to stop 'em if things go wrong?' one of the new riflemen asked. He had just been assigned from the remains of A Company. 'That armour plate'll stop any bullet I fire to put a tiger down.'

'We do the same as before, chop their bloody heads off,' Davies said before Marsh could reply. Davies placed his hand on the hilt of his sheathed machete to show he knew what he was talking about.

'You know, I don't like these new tactics, Alfie,' Matthews said. He had hardly said anything since Marsh went over the new tactical approach with his enlarged team. 'It all smacks of the stupidity which went on in the months before I met up with you lads. I know I was in the depot at Eat Apples for a while, but before I got injured, I saw quite a bit of combat. As all the experienced and well-trained lads disappeared, the Brass dumbed-down the tactics for the new boys.' Matthews used the slang name for Étaples. He coughed before putting on a posh voice to represent the officer class. 'Walk slowly towards the enemy, men! Our fighting spirit will beat the evil Hun.'

Several of the men laughed.

'Well, the General Staff don't want us to outpace the follow-up troops,' Marsh said. 'Nor do they want us to run into our own artillery barrage. They think we move far too quickly.'

'Then the follow-ups should bloody well run faster, and the artillery shoot further,' Matthews said, offering his simple solution. 'The whole point is to smash through the enemy lines. We've tried everything but speed and none of it's worked. The enemy collapsed when we turned up with zombies. We've seen it for ourselves.'

'Maybe, but think about the trouble we had with the artillery in the last attack. That'll be fixed by us going slower. There is the silver lining of not getting shot up by our own artillery.'

'I've heard that excuse before. How hard can it be to drop a few shells in the right place? But, you know, we're carrying quite some firepower all by ourselves now. Perhaps we can operate independently of the rest of the infantry? Maybe we don't need too much artillery either?'

'We've got a couple of them Chauchats, and each handler has a shotgun. The rest of us have our rifles and toothpicks, and we've got enough other blades to open a butcher's shop,' Davis said. 'Do we really need anything to replace the artillery? If we're moving fast enough, maybe taking the other lot by surprise, we might do without the whizz-bangs.'

'Ha, you and your bloody knives. I don't know which you like more, your toothpick of a bayonet or your machete? But maybe we should think about moving in closer with the tigers?' Matthews suggested. 'With the firepower of us living alongside the tigers, we've got the strength to seize the German trenches. The follow-up guys can just turn up and make us a brew.'

'It'll depend on how we're meant to advance,' Marsh said. He grinned at his friends, wanting a cup of tea as they took a break from their work. 'When we first looked at these tactics, we were thinking about sneaking across no man's land like a trench raid, but we've been advancing from our trenches directly at the enemy. We're giving him the chance to turn his machine guns on us.'

'And that will not change soon. We need to get back to what we were intending to do. We could seize a trench in seconds if we sneak up on it, close in with the tigers. It's a perfect idea for night-fighting.'

'I know, Tom, but for now we have explicit orders on how we're to fight.' Marsh was uncertain how he would marry the new orders to the Colonel's guidance to blend in the best of the existing tactics. To find an effective way forward would require some thought.

'Great, we'll keep moving at snail's pace across open ground then, making sure the Hun gets lots of opportunities to shoot at us,' Matthews muttered to himself. He gave up on persuading Marsh to a different approach. Everyone knew Simpson was behind the change in tactics, and all knew his obsession with traditional formations and formal military conventions. Simpson remained stuck in the last century. Everyone knew it. He possessed no desire to apply the lessons learnt, and relearnt, every day in the trenches. The man consistently showed a desire to have neatly arranged files of parade-ready soldiers march towards the enemy. They were facing an enemy armed with machine guns, rather than breech loading muskets, but such considerations did not feature in Simpson's thinking.

'Aye,' Mullens said. 'And don't anyone cross Lieutenant Simpson or you'll be peeling potatoes for a week.'

'Or feeding the worms more like,' Davies said, almost sounding cheerful.

'Lads,' a freshly arrived Sergeant Wells said. He had just arrived from the Commanding Officer's tent. 'We're moving out tonight. Just us, none of the rest of our lads.' Several surprised looks greeted the news.

'Just us Sarge?' Davis asked. 'With our tigers as well?'

'Yes. There's a blockhouse causing problems for the British division north of Bullecourt. The battalion has been asked to take it out. Colonel Hudson wants to try out our new tactics and Simpson suggested our team. It's a limited objective, so they don't need the entire battalion, even though there's few of his remaining. We'll be going over the top in the morning, so get your kit stowed.'

A business-like bustle developed around the camp as the enlarged combat group got to work preparing for movement and the upcoming action. Personal effects were stowed and tigers were readied for action. The latter task took the most time with the handlers paying careful attention to their work, ensuring there were no accidental injuries either to the living or the dead. The tigers would be moved up to the frontline in covered wagons before moving to the start point via trenches, on foot. Their efforts were less of an attempt to conceal the movement from prying enemy eyes than an attempt to keep friendly troops safe from the zombies. Final checks of weapons were also completed, and many men took spare minutes to compose last letters they hoped would never be read. Going over the top remained a brutal experience and there were no illusions about the chances of survival, even for Marsh's tiger combat groups, which possessed an excellent combat record. Other tiger combat groups had suffered grievously in combat.

The preparations proceeded without major issue. As a handler, Marsh attended the briefing with Colonel Hudson and returned to his combat group, ensuring each man possessed the full details of the operation. Marsh had long ago recognised every person in his team played a part, and they would do so with greater effect if they knew how their task fitted into the big picture. Well-informed men would also be more able to improvise if casualties led to problems with the plan. Lieutenant Simpson would also accompany the force, as Lieutenant Scott was at General Headquarters working with a new liaison team.

As usual, Marsh, as the senior handler, would be in command during the assault, but for all other purposes, Lieutenant Simpson would command. This situation was not ideal in Marsh's mind, as Simpson had such a strong dislike of him and a track record of interfering with the use of tigers in the field. However, Simpson's combat record showed him to be a brave and capable soldier, having achieved recognition for his abilities in battle before he joined the battalion.

Simpson took Marsh aside as they left the briefing in the Colonel's tent. 'Remember, Marsh, we'll be using my tactics. I expect you to keep to them.'

'Of course, Sir,' Marsh replied, uncertain he was effective in his use of the innocent tone favoured by the lower ranks when patronising their officers. He did not want to cause any problems prior to combat under Simpson's leadership, but he knew what he would do once on the battlefield.

'I'll be watching you closely,' Simpson said, a growl in his voice. He expected trouble. 'Don't mess up. Just follow my orders and we'll do well. I expect you to lead by example. It's important we do this correctly as the Brass are watching from afar.'

'Yes, Sir.' Marsh knew all would go well so long as Simpson did not overrule his control on the battlefield. It would be typical behaviour from Simpson to insist on complete control, even when it was necessary for the handlers to be in charge.

'Oh, and Marsh?'

'Yes, Sir?'

'Get your kit cleaned up before we move out. You can't be an effective example to the men under your command with filth on your boots and trousers.'

Simpson walked off before Marsh could respond. The officer always liked to have the last word.

Moving into position took most of the night. Few in the combat group caught little more than a brief nap prior to sunrise. As dawn broke, the men of the Experimental Battalion again found themselves in a forward trench, ready to go over the top once more.

The stench of unwashed bodies overwhelmed the trench. The earth was muddy and slippery following a night of constant rain. While the men remained silent, the crash of artillery made for a noisy start. Visibility was improving, but a slight mist remained despite the churn of exploding shells. The objective, the enemy blockhouse, was only just visible to the men peering over the parapet during the dawn stand-to. Few of their heads were raised far above the sandbags for fear an errant shell would land nearby. The artillery barrage continued, having begun during the night to provide cover for the combat group and the supporting infantry battalion. Under the constant bombardment, the enemy would not have heard the hundreds of soldiers moving into their initial assault positions. The barrage grew in intensity as the sun rose; the shells falling in significant numbers right up to the start time. Marsh could not help but think the bombardment optimistic. The main intention was to dig the Germans out of their bunkers, a strategy which had failed to work so far during this war.

The British troops from the supporting battalion kept well away from the tigers, many of them no doubt aware of the problems the Australians had faced fighting alongside such unnatural allies. Their enthusiasm was further tempered by previous experience of the trenches and the dampness in the air. The infantry muttered, but no-one stopped Marsh. The reputation and unnatural perception of the zombies was rubbing off on his approachability.

For the attack, Marsh assigned five tigers to Mullen, who was to take the left flank, while Marsh would go to the right. Neither group was to advance directly on the bullet-pitted concrete blockhouse. They would seize the trenches either side and then advance on the fortification, hoping it did not have any gun-slits along the sides, drawing a bead on the trenches they intended to advance along. Lieutenant Simpson intended to advance with Marsh's group, while Sergeant Wells would accompany Mullen.

Throughout the waiting time in the trench, Simpson interfered in minor matters, while keeping Wells at a distance. Ever since their arrival in the start positions, Simpson was at pains to establish his dominance, not wanting the supporting infantry to suspect a mere corporal, not the senior officer, would lead the tigers during the assault. While Simpson agreed to Marsh's initial dispositions, he continued to insist that the tigers would advance at a slow pace, just ahead of the bulk of the British infantry. Simpson was adamant the mistakes of Bullecourt would not be repeated because there was an extra handler and a larger security squad present. He ignored the key mistake of slowly advancing across the battlefield in the open sights of the German defenders. Marsh knew even if the full range of mistakes were not repeated, Simpson's limited measures would not protect them from the German defensive fire. Only surprise would help, but as the assault was not being launched from no man's land, the intended set-piece battle would exchange the element of surprise for a long advance from the starting trenches. The extended artillery barrage served as a further beacon, alerting the enemy to the upcoming assault.

'We'll be going over the top in two minutes,' a British infantry captain called to his assembled men. These would be the soldiers who would advance alongside the zombie forces.

'I'm ready, Alfie,' Davies said, even though Marsh had not asked him a question. Davies sheathed his machete, putting away the sharpening block he had been using on his blade.

'How can you look so calm, Colin?' Morgan asked Davies. A slight tick flicked around his mouth and his knuckles were white from gripping his rifle.

'I'm not calm, but I'm ready.' Davies was satisfied his pre-battle routine of preparing a blade was helpful.

'Right lads, stay at a steady pace. Keep low and don't rush ahead of the infantry,' Marsh said, reminding them of the plan, just as Simpson came around the corner of the trench.

'Ah, there you are, Corporal. Are we ready?' Simpson asked.

'Yes, sir.' Marsh moved to his position next to the trench ladder. He held a tiger at the bottom. As soon as the whistle blew, he would launch the creature up the ladder and then out into no man's land. With the tigers spread out along the length of the trench, it made more sense to get them to exit via ladders. Only the most mobile zombies were taking part in the assault. Any significant pre-existing damage to limbs would have prevented the use of the ladders. All five ladders near Marsh were assigned a waiting tiger. The zombies would leave the trench at the same time.

'Good. Keep the tigers close to our lads.' Simpson was hard to hear over a sudden crescendo in the barrage. 'We want to make it hard for the Germans to spot our tigers among the rest of our lads. Hold the creatures back among our ranks and then unleash them at the last moment.'

Marsh did not have time to reply as the noise of the artillery dropped, the targeting shifting to the enemy's second line. The creeping barrage moved right on time, and they needed to get up close behind it before the enemy recovered. Whistles sounded along the British trench, signalling the advance.

'Up and out,' Marsh commanded his tigers. He clarified the instructions in his head, adding detail of how to use the ladders. Alfie knew the mental commands would unsettle Morgan and many other soldiers present, hence the unnecessary verbal command, but mental orders were the easiest way to control the creatures without using a detailed stream of words. If they survived this attack, he would have to work with Mullen to see if the Irishman could develop the same ability.

The tigers leapt up the trench wall with inhuman speed, and Marsh reminded them to slow as they reached the top of the short ladders. In his excitement and anxiety, he had forgotten his emotions might leak into the mental commands. Marsh followed a tiger up a nearby ladder and emerged onto no man's land, taking up a brisk walk. He hunched forward, anticipating the impact of a bullet in his fragile body. A sense of total exposure almost drove him to the ground, but he recognised the sensation before he acted upon it. The terror of battle descended upon him. Looking to both sides, the assaulting infantry were just behind his tigers. To the artillery-dazed Germans they would appear like a single advancing line, the deadly tigers concealed among the massed bodies of the advancing men.

No defensive fire came from the German lines, not even the blockhouse. Marsh worried the fortification was barely affected by the preparatory artillery barrage, the concrete having protected the men inside, the occupants waiting for the British to walk into their killing zone. The enemy parapet utilised a slight rise, the thin line of sandbags and bare earth heaped with churned mud from the recent shelling. A short distance behind the German line, the continuing maelstrom of the creeping barrage targeted the German support lines, preventing them from offering any help to their forward troops.

One of Marsh's feet slipped out from underneath, his ankle twisting as he fell onto his knees, the butt of his shotgun preventing him from going right over. He looked down, he was kneeling in the remains of a soldier, flesh oozing a putrid fluid in the misty light. He almost vomited as the scent of corruption overwhelmed his nose, all the terror of the dangerous advance forgotten because of the horror beneath him.

'Get up you coward,' Simpson snarled, the officer suddenly beside him, chiding him on, while offering no physical help.

Marsh gritted his teeth at the pain as he rose. He swallowed the few choice words he would like to have spat at the officer. He brushed off the muddy end of his shotgun and took a step forward, the pain and horror of the present still overwhelming the terror of the advance in the open. Pain shot from his damaged ankle and he struggled to maintain his balance. He hoped nothing was broken; it may be a bad sprain. Yet with the unsympathetic Simpson present, he would just have to walk it off, moving forward with a limp.

Within seconds of Marsh recovering his feet, the blockhouse opened fire on the assaulting troops. A fusillade spread along the German line as the defenders left their shelters to hold off the British. Marsh bit his lip, tasting blood as he leant forward into the hail of lead. He resisted the urge to send the tigers on ahead, the horror and pain of the last few moments disappearing under the terror of being shot at in the open. Simpson had been clear, the tigers must stay with the rest of the troops until they were close enough for a sudden last assault.

Screams came from near Mullen's team. The advancing infantry were scythed down by machine gun fire from the front of the blockhouse. Marsh traced the fire back to the low concrete building. He identified a second gun firing from a slit on his side of the building. The bullets flew over the heads of the troops as they advanced, but he knew the aim would soon be corrected. By the time the British launched their last assault, the machine gun would enfilade the rank he was in. Marsh suspected a similar gun position existed on the other side of the blockhouse. These guns were going to wreak havoc with the planned attack.

Over the noise of the machine guns, Marsh heard the shout of 'Zombie!' from the German lines. Within seconds, a tiger on his right was hit by several aimed rifle rounds, one of which created a spark. As the helmet was hit, the tiger fell backwards from the impact. However, the creature rose to its feet, the heavy helmet armour having deflected the rifle round from the vulnerable areas of the brain. The advantage of surprise was being lost. The enemy recognised they were under assault by tigers, and Marsh was concerned his slowly advancing zombies would not last against an organised defence.

Marsh paused at the edge of a shell crater as his ankle flared with pain. He knew he was pushing his injury too hard, but hanging around in no man's land was an even worse idea. The sheer volume of British troops was greater than the Germans could cut down. Struggling to keep up, the number of corpses and injured men was greater than Marsh had ever seen. Even compared to the slaughter at Bullecourt, the number of casualties was horrific. Rows of men lay where they fell as the machine guns worked death along the ranks of advancing soldiers. The injured screamed and moaned. The fallen rows a riving mass of maimed flesh.

'Marsh, send them forward now!' Simpson bellowed at the top of his voice. Years of work on the parade ground ensured his voice cut through the noise of battle. Marsh was stunned. His rival stood in the open next to a smoking crater, untouched by the abattoir of battle.

A crack of exploding grenades brought Marsh back to his senses. The Germans were throwing the explosives over the parapet in a last-ditch attempt to keep the attackers out of their lines. Marsh urged his five tigers forward at full speed. He tried to keep up with the zombies with the best limping run he could manage, catching and overtaking the main body of the advance. His ankle held up better than he expected, and the rest of the protection squad spotted the surge forward, joining him, shouting as they went. Unable to miss the sudden change in pace, the British troops broke into a roar as they joined in the sprint, relieved to hurry across the remains of the dangerous ground.

Simpson fell behind. He watched Marsh, searching for signs of cowardice. The man did not even bother to shout out the orders to his charges. Simpson's rage disappeared, stunned by the change which came over the handler. He had never seen Marsh in action, neither had he seen so expert a handler ordering the tigers in the unnaturally silent fashion Marsh had perfected. In common with many men, an icy finger of fear ran down Simpson's back as he watched the corporal unleash the terrifying power of the tigers. Such power was not right. Such horrific, even supernatural violence, had no place on the battlefield. Simpson knew, in his bones, this man was to be feared. He should be crushed as soon as possible.

16

GAS! GAS! GAS!

'Great big bloody clouds of the stuff! It was all you
could do to keep from soiling yourself when you saw
that muck creeping across no man's land toward you.'
Interview with William Murphy in Duncan, F, 'A Soldier's War: Accounts from the trenches' (1931, London)

THE GERMAN DEFENDERS STOOD no chance in their assailed trenches, overwhelmed by terrifying creatures attacking with teeth and hands, clawing and biting at exposed flesh, ripping and tearing, rendering men down to bloody chunks of meat. Where organised resistance persisted, booming shotgun blasts and the rattling, repeating fire of the Chauchat broke down any stubborn defence. A sight straight from hell, covered in blood and waving a giant blade, shrieked off in pursuit of two retreating Germans. Marsh barely noticed his squad-mate pass as he worked his way toward the blockhouse.

The ranks of British soldiers poured into the trench, but they were caught by the enfilading fire of the blockhouse, much as Marsh had expected. Scores fell wounded, or dead, within yards of their objective. Most times, the men fell in rows, like freshly harvested corn. The slaughter was unbelievable, and beyond anything in Marsh's experience, akin to the rumours about the Somme offensive almost a year before. He had to do something about the blockhouse. Marsh mentally summoned his tigers, sending them off ahead, advancing along the zig-zagging trench line towards the defensive structure. At the last bend Marsh caught up with a blood-soaked Davies, puffing and leaning against the parapet, somewhere between hysteria and exhaustion. Given his location, Davies was fortunate, just shielded from gunfire from around the bend.

Marsh took in the fearsome appearance of his friend, his huge eyes, uniform and machete drenched in blood. 'You look like hell, Davies.'

'Can't — I can't go any further,' Davies puffed. 'The blockhouse has got the last bit of trench covered with a bloody machine gun.'

Marsh risked a peak around the corner. He glimpsed the machine gun slit, dark against the concrete at the far end of the trench. Before the blockhouse sat jumbles of boxes and assorted pieces of wood fashioned into an improvised barricade. The barrier just exceeded the distance Marsh could toss a grenade. He doubted Davies could throw one further, given his current state. In the nick of time, Marsh pulled his head back, knowing the defenders would line up an accurate shot on him. Despite his speed, several rifle bullets slammed into the exposed length of the trench beyond him. Clearly, there were German infantry behind the barricade, alongside the machine gun defending the building.

'It's tight. We'll have to rush it. I can't see a way into the blockhouse, so the entrance has to be around the back, or maybe on the other side,'

Marsh said, thinking out loud rather than expecting Davies to think anything through in his condition.

'We rush it and we're dead,' Davies said with a better grasp than expected.

'That's what our tigers are for. They can charge in and take out the barricade.'

'And what will they do about the blockhouse? They're can't chew through concrete, can they?' Davies pointed at a zombie strolling up the trench toward them. Behind the reanimated corpse, a wary Simpson advanced in the company of a small group of soldiers.

'Why have you stopped here? Shouldn't you be seizing the block-house, Marsh?' Simpson asked in his most patronising tone. He thought the answer to his question was cowardice, or incompetence, and such a conclusion was clear to all.

'The trench ahead is blocked, Sir. There's no way we can get up to the blockhouse. They've set up barricades. I was considering sending the tigers up and out of the trench to outflank the position.'

'That's not an option. We can't have your beasts running around outside the trench. The German second line will pick them off one by one.' Simpson glanced around the corner, pulling his head back just before a volley of bullets, fired from the barricade, smashed into the trench wall.

'Are you sure, Sir? The barrage should keep rear-line heads down,' Marsh said, unconvinced by Simpson's logic.

'Don't bank on it. I want you to send the tigers directly to that barri-cade. Once it's fallen, we'll then rush the blockhouse.'

'You realise there's a machine gun covering this trench, they've got it holed up inside the blockhouse? They caught us in the flank before we got into the trench, Sir.' Marsh was not convinced Simpson had a full grasp on the situation.

'Well, it's a good job your tigers aren't easily stopped by a machine gun then. The gun might be a problem when we follow up. I doubt your tigers will soak up all the bullets. Can you give your beasts an order to force their way into the blockhouse?' Simpson asked. He knew he would have to rely on Marsh's expertise and the special abilities of the zombies.

'They can use a door handle if I tell them what to do, and they can definitely batter down a door. But, I bet there'll be some sort of heavy duty door they won't easily be able to shift. It'll also be locked.'

'Can they use explosives? Perhaps we can give them a Mills bomb to pop through the gun slit?' Simpson speculated, fishing for a solution.

'We should give them a live grenade, but then they'd have to cover the ground and pop it through, Sir. I doubt I could get them to do something as delicate as pulling a pin on a grenade, at least not under fire. It's not something I've tried with them before.' Marsh shook his head, dismissing the idea.

'Well, we've got most of the protection squad here, plus the infantry. Get the tigers moving directly at the barricade and then at the bunker. It'll have to be enough to overwhelm them.'

Marsh did not like the idea of sending the tigers directly into point-blank machine gun fire, but Simpson was correct. The zombies could take a lot more punishment than the humans. Getting them close enough would open up opportunities, especially if the door to the blockhouse could be forced. The barricade needed taking out before assaulting the blockhouse and the tigers were perfect for this job. He would keep them in the trench to begin with, but if necessary, he would risk them out in the open to flank the defences.

'Go!' Marsh shouted, simultaneously sending a complicated mental command to each of his zombies.

The tigers roared around the corner, eager to assail the humans behind the barricade. The machine gun opened fire, no longer using controlled short bursts, but a panicked and sustained fire, hoping to halt the fearsome tigers. Opposite Marsh, the exposed wall was hit by dozens of bullets within the first few seconds, mud flying into the air. Loud splattering sounds communicated flesh being rendered by bullets. A tiger was thrown back into Marsh's line of sight, pinned against the wall by the impact of a stream of bullets. The tiger did not stop for long, regaining its footing and again running toward the objective. Screams came from further along the trench and the sporadic rifle fire ceased.

The machine gun switched target to an area nearer the barricade, allowing Marsh a cautious glimpse of the action. The tigers were indeed at the barricade, tearing apart the defenders. Two zombies lay on the ground, no longer moving. While his view was obstructed, Marsh knew the two tigers must have received head wounds, the heavy machine gun bullets penetrating the armoured helmets at such close range.

'They've stalled at the barricade,' Marsh shouted to Simpson above the noise. He described the scene to the officer stood next to him. 'They seem to be out of sight of the gun at the moment, but if they move forward, they'll be targeted again.'

'Send them forward. Get them to the blockhouse.' Simpson was willing to spend the tigers in a futile assault rather than living men.

Marsh peered around the corner again, silently issuing the instructions to his tigers. He knew he did not need line of sight, but wanted to monitor the outcome of his orders. He handled these tigers, formerly human beings, soldiers who had already paid the ultimate sacrifice. If he kept these reanimated corpses in the fight, the lives of other British soldiers might not be needlessly spent. The zombies stood upright, turning as one towards the blockhouse before snarling and running. The machine gunner was ready, opening fire once again. One tiger was smashed by a steady stream of bullets, the heavily damaged creature still climbing back to its feet to continue the advance.

While the defenders were distracted by the tigers, Simpson seized the opportunity to lead a squad of riflemen to the barricade. Half a dozen men rushed by Marsh, almost reaching the barricade when, at the last moment, the machine gun turned its attention to these new targets. The tigers, having disappeared behind the blockhouse, seeking a way in, were no longer an effective diversion. The first soldiers, including Simpson, made it to the barricade, but the last two men fell to the ground, riddled by the bullets.

Marsh ducked back behind the bend to avoid becoming the next target. The fists of his tigers were banging on the iron door of the building, unable to break in. Panicked German voices came from the blockhouse and the machine gun fire ceased as the occupants focused on the impending threat. The voices became calmer at the realisation they were safe from the ineffective assault by the tigers.

'Simpson! What's going on? Can't you get any closer?' There was no immediate reply, the silence again punctuated by a brief burst from the machine gun.

'No! We're pinned down,' Simpson replied in the silence following the burst. 'Can the tigers get in?'

'No. I'm going to move them back in case there's a counter-attack from up the trench.'

A few minutes passed with no change to the stalemate. Whenever Marsh or Simpson sneaked a glance at the blockhouse, they were met with a rapid burst of machine gun fire. Time ticked away, the trench not yet secure. Every second brought the inevitable counterattack closer. If the Germans made their move soon, Marsh knew they would be successful.

A tremendous crash came from the rear, as the back of the blockhouse exploded as if hit by a shell. Within seconds Simpson took advantage of the surprise, getting his soldiers up and running, before the defenders recovered. Marsh and his team followed. Marsh did not even think to order his tigers into the building. Everything was so fast. The attackers entered the blockhouse through a narrow gap torn in the rear, soon establishing the defenders were dead or too injured to offer any further resistance. Marsh crawled out while the riflemen stayed behind to give first aid to the surviving Germans.

'We've done it,' Marsh said to no-one, slumping down into a crouch, back leant against the trench wall. He was exhausted. Simpson, close enough to hear, nodded his head in agreement.

'A lucky artillery strike, that's all it took,' the officer said. His grin faltered as he looked along the trench.

'What do you think, lads?' an Irish voice called out. Mullen swaggered down the trench, shotgun casually propped atop his shoulder, a massive grin plastered on his face.

'Bloody hell. You did this?' Marsh asked, returning the grin as he got up, brushing dust and mud from his uniform.

'Indeed, it was I. You was taking your time about things, so I thought I'd hurry everything along a bit,' Mullen said, enjoying their surprise.

'What about the machine gun over on your side of the blockhouse? Was there one? We were pinned down,' Simpson asked.

'There was a bloody great big gun, Sir. We were stuck as well. Then I saw this great big trench mortar the Germans left us as a present. I got one of my tigers and tied a big mortar round to him, at least thirty pounds of explosives. I'm surprised he didn't slow down much. Then I charged him at the blockhouse, kaboom!' Mullen mimed the expanding explosion with his hands.

'You got a tiger to set a bomb?' Simpson asked.

'No, Sir. The tiger was the bomb,' Mullen said, a broad smile showing how pleased he was with his ingenuity. 'I positioned the fuse where he just had to hit it at the right time, and off it went.'

'You told the tiger to hit a fuse?' Marsh asked, impressed. 'That's quite some skill you have there, and a damn smart way to take out a fortification.'

'Think this through, this may be an excellent way of using the tigers to take out—' Simpson said, his thought incomplete as events overtook their discussion.

'Gas, gas, gas!' the call ran up and down the captured length of German trench.

All activity ceased aside from panicked struggles with gas masks. The masks, despite regular drills, were not the easiest equipment to use. They had to be removed from storage pouches, usually attached to the webbing at waist height. Each soldier then needed to remove their helmet, pulling the box respirator over their head, hanging the box from their neck with the mask pulled over their head and the helmet finally replaced. Terror coursed through Marsh as he put his mask on. It stank of rubber and the chemicals used to neutralise the gas. The air in the mask warmed as he breathed in and out, the hose from the mask pulling in air from the respirator mounted on his chest. He could barely see out of the small eyepieces, so he adjusted the balance of the mask. His bile rose as claustrophobia made itself known to him. This was the first time Marsh had used a mask in combat. The fear of the unknown pushing him to the very edge. He was panting. Noticing this, Marsh slowed himself down, clawing his way back to full control.

As soon as Marsh was ready, he checked on Mullen before moving on to the rest of his squad. During training, every soldier was drilled to protect themselves first, before checking on their buddies. Every person he checked wore their mask correctly, and Marsh remembered the gas itself was not very dangerous. However, the use of gas was a prelude to a fierce counter-attack by the Germans. Listening to the muffled voices around him, Marsh could work out the direction of the impending threat. He looked toward the German second line trenches and a large greenish cloud floating toward them. Chlorine, if he remembered his training correctly. He knew his mask could cope with the gas and the tigers would be fine since they did not breathe, chlorine being a gas which asphyxiated the victim. The cloud was still a terrifying and unnatural sight, made worse by the claustrophobically restricted vision of the mask. He knew it would be hard to fight in these conditions.

The cloud drifted across the landscape, blown by the gentle breeze. Clearly, the Germans had been ready with gas cylinders, prepared to release the gas in the event of a British assault in the area. The green cloud hung in the air and Marsh had time to wonder if the Germans had mixed phosgene in with the chlorine, as was their reported practice. Phosgene was a far more dangerous gas, but again, it killed by affecting the lungs, so there would be no impact on the tigers or anyone with a functioning mask. However, anyone suffering a mask failure would receive a lethal dose.

'Marsh!' Marsh recognised Simpson by his size and uniform rather than by his voice. Everyone was stripped of their identities by the masks, and it was hard to understand what was being communicated. 'Get the tigers ready. If the Germans advance behind the cloud, we'll need to be ready to repel them. They may even come through the cloud and the tigers might give us the edge if we end up fighting hand-to-hand. I know you've not trained to use them defensively, but it looks like we've no choice.'

'I'll spread the word, Sir.' Marsh used the opportunity as an excuse to check the masks of the surrounding soldiers again. For once, Simpson made sense, and Marsh wanted his men ready.

As the cloud reached the parapet, the first tendrils poured into the trench, much like a liquid. The soldiers grew nervous. If a counter-attack were underway, contact would shortly be made. Davies had his machete out; Marsh readied his shotgun; Matthews had his sharpened trench shovel ready in one hand, a bayonet grasped in the other, his rifle propped against the trench wall.

'Can you smell the chlorine? There's something like hay too?' a rifleman asked. The man began coughing.

'Shit, your mask's not working,' a neighbouring soldier said. He threw down his rifle and turned towards his companion, hands scrabbling as he checked the hose connection on the box respirator. 'It's shredded!' He waved the loose end, hit by shell or bullet, possibly damaged in the hand-to-hand fighting.

The exposed soldier struggled to stay standing. The coughing became something awful. Most of the surrounding soldiers turned to watch with morbid fascination. Several checked their own packs for something to help repair the hose. Others checked their own mask and respirator again, terrified they would be the next victims of the gas.

'Put this over his mouth and tell him to close his eyes.' Matthews said, his own voice muffled by his mask. He handed over a thick cloth he had just poured water over. 'It'll stop the chlorine for now, but the phosgene will still get through. You'll need to hold it in place the way he's coughing while we'll get him evacuated. Can you handle him on your own?'

'I can get him back,' the soldier said, tending to his hacking companion.

'Where'd you learn to do that?' Davies asked Matthews.

'Back in the days when both sides first used gas, we had to improvise masks. The chlorine'll still bugger up his eyes, but a damp cloth will stop it getting into his lungs. Phosgene, though,' Matthews said, shrugging. 'Who knows? It'll take hours to show unless he's had a huge dose.'

'What was that about his eyes?' Marsh asked.

'It's with the Gods. Chlorine damages the eyes. He'll be lucky to avoid at least temporary blindness. It may be permanent,' Matthews replied.

'Shit! What about the tigers? Will it affect their eyes?' Marsh asked. He had only considered how chlorine disabled living lungs, how it would not harm his zombies. He had not considered their eyes.

'I've not thought about that. The tigers are dead, aren't they? It shouldn't be a problem for them.'

'But they use their eyes to see what they're doing. I'm sure they'll keep functioning without them, but then they'll just depend on sound and smell. They won't be as much use then.' Marsh knew the zombies possessed keen senses, and he had seen many occasions when a tiger had picked up the scent of a distant battlefield, carried across the miles by the wind.

Marsh called his remaining tigers over, checking each pair of eyes, looking for any damage. All three had irritated eyes. Even without pain to contend with, the damage to the visual sense would degrade the zombie's combat effectiveness. The moisture in their eyes was already reacting with the chlorine in the air to form an acid which burned the tissue.

'Here they come!' a nearby shout alerted Marsh before he had time to think through the actions he would need to take to save the sight of the zombies.

The German troops closed from their second line trench, emerging from the green tinged cloud only a few yards from the trench they had lost to the British assault. Marsh could not tell how many assailants there were, just countless men continuing to emerge from the mist. With their masks, the enemy resembled creatures from another world. Marsh saw it was not just the defenders who were hindered by the gas. Several of the Germans tripped and fell as they charged. The living, on either side, could not make out obstacles in front of them. The restricted vision of the gas masks was a problem. As the first of the Germans fell to close-range defensive fire, Marsh decided he was facing experienced troops. The counter-attackers used the limited cover well, but it was clear the effort of advancing while wearing a gas mask was tiring them out.

In the few remaining precious seconds during which more defenders managed a final aimed shot, few had time to react further. The first Germans were soon on top of their old position. The assaulting troops jumped into the trench, bayonets leading their assault. A British rifleman was driven through by a German bayonet as an attacker leapt into the trench. The British soldier was thrown off his feet by the momentum of the charging enemy. Another masked horror knelt on the parapet, emptying his rifle into the clustered defenders. Elsewhere, a corporal parried a bayonet thrust, a second and then a third, before he was stabbed through the leg by another assailant who leapt into the trench behind him.

Marsh considered the surrounding violence. Matthews was on the ground, wrestling with a German soldier, both possessing drawn blades. Matthews had no intention of fighting fairly and used his stiletto to cut the hose on the German's gas mask. Elsewhere, Davies beat off the attentions of another attacker, his machete biting deeply into the wooden butt of a German rifle. Morgan and Simpson stood back-to-back, defending themselves from all around. Simpson used a bayonet-tipped rifle he had snatched from a fallen soldier.

A masked shape leapt over the parapet, intending to break his fall by landing on Marsh. There was no time to aim the shotgun. The weapon discharged with a crash, shredding the right arm of the attacking soldier, who spun to one side as his remaining momentum landed him on Marsh. The man screamed in agony, unable to continue the fight, as both attacker and defender collapsed to the bottom of the trench.

'Kill the Germans!' Marsh shouted at his tigers as he lay working the reload lever on his shotgun. He was pinned to the ground by the weight of the thrashing German soldier. Yet around him, the zombies surged along the trench with a fury he had never seen. Their strength was superhuman at the best of times, but this violence was unprecedented. The first German in their way had his throat shredded, while another pulled off the victim's arm with a sickening tear. The man fell to the ground with a disbelief showing on his wrecked face, the sudden brutality of the attack overwhelming him. Still, the tigers did not stop to gorge on the victims, instead they launched themselves forward, seeking new prey. The three tigers fought fiercely. This was the first time Marsh had seen the tigers fight when the urge to hunt and eat was not at the forefront. They seem to kill for the sake of killing, efficiently and quickly. One German even got his rifle up in time to protect himself with the bayonet. The attacking zombie did not even check its pace to avoid the blade, impaling itself on the tip then pulling itself up the weapon, the bayonet and much of the rifle barrel soon protruding from its back. Within an instant, the tiger was close enough to seize hold of the soldier and maul him.

The tigers were moving at least twice as fast as a normal human, and the German counter-attackers stood no chance. When the zombies had obliterated all their prey, they stopped to sniff the air. The trench was empty of prey and the hunt was on for more flesh to render. The shocked and bewildered British soldiers looked around at the fallen Germans, men who, a few seconds before, were threatening to overwhelm them. Several of the defenders picked themselves up from the ground, having been knocked off their feet as the tigers cleared the trench. Many of the British soldiers now drew back from the creatures as they returned to their handler. The horror of the unnatural defence was compounded by the sight of a zombie with a rifle and bayonet still stuck through the stomach. For any living human, the injury would have been agony and soon fatal. The tiger was not in the least bit bothered.

'What the hell was that, mate?' a masked man asked Marsh, his voice shaking as he noticed an arriving tiger.

'That's our secret weapon,' another voice announced. Marsh recognised the Welsh accent, it was Taff Morgan.

'That's a secret weapon?' the soldier asked. 'Why don't we have more of them? They're incredible.'

No one answered as the defenders busied themselves checking and treating injuries. Several soldiers readied themselves along the parapet expecting a follow-up German counter-attack. The green tinged mist still hung around the trench, pooling in pockets while continuing to restrict vision outside the trench. There would be minimal notice of another attack.

Marsh checked over his tigers. They had taken quite a beating, fighting off the German assault. Alfie pulled the rifle from the stomach of the impaled tiger, leaving a gaping hole from front to back, soon filling with the internal workings of the creature. Several soldiers tried peeking through, one making tutting noises on noticing the damaged tiger. The post-combat bravado of the victors displayed their relief at surviving the counter-attack. Other men kept away, not just suffering the trauma of combat, but fearful of their terrifying new secret weapon. All three zombies showed slash injuries from bayonets. One was even missing the fingers of its left hand. The third tiger was beaten around the jaw, flesh hanging loosely from the side of the mouth, teeth missing and bone showing through the pulped mess. Yet these tigers were not deterred by their injuries. A different type of injury concerned Marsh. As he checked each of his zombies, he noticed the eyes becoming whiter, as if a film were forming over the surface of each pupil. He could already tell the zombies were compensating for their reduced vision with a greater focus upon their senses of smell and hearing. He was unsure how he would withdraw them to the British trenches in this condition, barely able to spot the obstacles in front of them, yet able the sense every living thing across the battlefield.

'That was close,' Lieutenant Simpson said, his voice muffled by his mask. 'Are you ready for another attack?' Simpson reloaded his pistol, ready to continue the fight.

'You don't mean we're going to attack the Germans again, do you, Sir?' Marsh asked incredulously.

'No, no. Of course not.' Simpson shook his head, but Marsh could barely make out the gesture through his own tiny lenses. 'Will you be ready if the Germans attack us again?'

'I'm not sure, Sir,' Marsh said, scratching at his neck. The seal of his mask irritated his skin. 'Look at their eyes. They can't see very well now, and the longer they're exposed to this gas, the more damage will be done.'

'You want to pull back?' The words were loaded with obvious implication. The officer's tone gave away what he thought of the idea.

'These tigers won't be as much use to us if the enemy attacks again. If they can't see, they'll not be able to move around effectively,' Marsh said, not knowing how true this was. Their other senses would compensate for losing sight, to a degree, but he was unsure how to communicate the general idea to Simpson. 'I may move them around if I work closely with them, but the slightest obstacle on the ground could have them fall over.'

'So your pets are not so indestructible then, are they?'

'Hey, Sir,' Mullen interrupted. He had worked his way back from the other blockhouse, having checked on his own charges. 'Fought 'em off at the other end, Sir, but we've taken some casualties. Are we pulling back? I reckon it'd be a good idea.'

'How are your tigers?' Simpson asked.

'Not good, Sir. There's few of them left and those, well, they're bloody blind,' Mullen said, waving his hands in front of his gas mask lenses in an exaggerated mime, knowing Simpson would not respond to words alone.

'Like mine then. We might get them back to our trenches, but they're no use now,' Marsh said.

'We won't be able to stand another German assault, Sir, not a chance. I think Marsh is right. We need to lead the tigers back behind the lines while we can.' Mullen knew he still needed to prompt the officer. 'So what are your orders, Sir? Shall we get them back?'

Simpson thought for a few seconds before replying. They had taken their objective: casualties were high, and not just for the tigers, but also for the supporting infantry. He was not one to run away from a fight, but he could not allow a withdrawal without checking the infantry would not be left behind.

'I need to check with the infantry CO,' Simpson said, postponing the decision. He walked off to find the officer without another word.

'What the bloody hell does that mean?' Mullen asked to the officer's back, disgusted by the indecision. 'We haven't got all day, you know. Fucking spineless.'

The whistle of incoming shells caused everyone to dive for cover. The rounds turned out to be a mixture of high explosive and airburst shrapnel, with the open trench offering only minimal protection.

'There's your answer, Mullen,' Marsh said. 'We won't be able to take much more of this. If the Germans follow this up with another counter-attack, it'll be a slaughter, and we won't be on the winning side.'

'That's right. Let's get out of here the moment Simpson says we can.' Mullen ran off, crouching low down.

As far as Marsh could tell, their costly attack was disintegrating. First the casualties, then the gas, and now the Germans preparing a second counter-attack to seize back their positions. As the artillery barrage grew in volume, Marsh made preparations to get his tigers and protection squad back to friendly lines.

Simpson did not delay once the decision to withdraw was made for him by the infantry officer. In fact, the infantry commander, grossly overwhelmed by the casualties his men had suffered, the man wanted to know why Simpson was not already withdrawing. The infantry seemed to have been ready to withdraw all along. Within minutes of Simpson's return to his men, the surviving British troops abandoned the captured German trench, risking the barrage while disappearing into the gas-laced mist.

17

VOLUNTEERS

'When I was at Wipers I learned not to volunteer. I'd
been wanting to go out on a trench raid and I spent
days working up the guts to do it. My mates had told
me not to waste my time, but what did I know? I was
only fifteen. Bill asked me, 'Why'd you bloody go and
do that?' He thought I was right stupid, and I suppose
I was. Bill caught a packet the next day. Of course, I
didn't find out until later as I broke my leg during the
raid and was evacuated across no man's land. Last time
I ever bloody volunteered for anything.'
Transcript from an unbroadcast radio interview with
Philip Saunders. Published in Graham, D 'A study of
    child soldiers of the Great War.' (2016, New York)

'SIR?' MARSH STOOD AT attention inside Colonel Hudson's
tent. 'You can see from the last attack, charging directly at the
enemy alongside our own troops leaves us open to defensive fire for

far too long. They whittled down our numbers so much that by the time we made it to the German trenches, we had already lost too many tigers.'

'Ah, I appreciate your concern for the well-being of your tigers, Marsh. But we seized the objective,' Colonel Hudson said, putting down the pen he was using to sign a pile of documents.

'Yes sir, but the initial success came at the expense of our offensive capability. We lost every single tiger in the attack, either to enemy action, or due to them no longer being combat effective because of blindness caused by the chlorine gas.' Marsh paused before risking reminding the Colonel what he thought should have happened. 'Sir, we should have sneaked close to the German trenches, then launched a lightning assault. That way we keep our own casualties down while quickly seizing the objectives, the same tactics used in successful trench raids and tactics we were deploying ourselves.'

'And how will you secure the enemy trench? Is it not still the case we will need to move large numbers of troops across no man's land so we can support you and consolidate your position?'

'Yes Sir, indeed. If we assume the success of our assault, we should coordinate the support troops exiting our trenches at exactly the same moment we launch the final stage of our assault. By the time we have the enemy trench secured, the infantry will be ready to take possession and hold the territory,' Marsh said. He had worked out the best tactical approaches based upon his experiences and the capability of the tigers. The Colonel had always been interested, encouraging even, of his tactical insight. However, Marsh knew Simpson's influence and a shortage of tigers were pushing Hudson in a different direction.

'And what of the gas?' Hudson asked, curious to hear Marsh's solution for the unexpected problem posed by the chemical weapon.

'Goggles, Sir. We'll use driving goggles, just like with those makeshift gas masks used back in '14 and '15. It's a simple way to protect the zombies' eyes from chlorine. The other effects of the gas aren't a problem for them.'

'Goggles, you say? They do sound like they would do the job. I must also say, I was very impressed by Mullen's initiative in taking out the blockhouse. What a stroke of genius to attach a bomb to a tiger and then send it to the target.' Hudson offered Marsh a cigar before leaning back in his chair, lighting his own cigar while contemplating the most recent action. 'Mullen's idea, well, if it saves lives, we can afford to trade tigers like that. It's another way we can use these zombies, and it's certainly going to strike terror into the hearts of the enemy.'

'I'm looking to work with Mullen and his abilities. I suspect, like me, he will instruct the tigers by thinking, with a little work,' Marsh said. He was already forming a deep respect for the Irishman's skills and quick thinking.

'Ah, that's interesting, Marsh. I had been wondering when we would turn up someone else who would possess the advanced abilities you display,' Hudson said. He placed the cigar on an ashtray, steepling his fingers while he examined Marsh. 'While you gentlemen have been working hard on the battlefield, I've had Lieutenant Scott travelling around searching for other potential handlers. He's had little success, as you will be unsurprised to discover. You, and your skills, are still something of a mystery. Why do you have this unique ability to control the zombies by thinking alone?'

'I don't know, Sir, but like I've already said, I think Mullen may be like me. I wish I knew why I've got these skills, as then we could find more people like me and make better use of the few tigers we have.'

'What do you need? How can you work out if you can develop and use Mullen's skills?' the Colonel asked. He picked up his pen and a pad of paper, ready to note down any requests.

'Time and opportunity, Sir. That's what I need,' Marsh said, thinking about his requirements. 'I could do some basic work with him and a couple of tigers, but once we're beyond that, we'll need to try things out on a larger scale with a full combat group. Then, after we've worked out what we're doing, we'll need to use those tactics against the enemy. Maybe some small-scale raids would help at that stage, Sir.'

'And naturally, you'll be testing out your ideas for wider combat use as well?' Hudson asked, looking up from the notes he was taking. His cigar burned untended, forgotten in the ashtray.

'Of course, Sir. One of the main reasons for changing our tactics was because of tigers getting out of control. If I can develop Mullen's skills, there will be a lot less chance of that, as my tigers never seem to move beyond the range of my thoughts. If Mullen's ability works in the same way as mine, it'll reduce the battlefield risk.'

'And how long is that range?' The Colonel had undertaken a few basic experiments, but not got very far towards the establishment of any clear rules.

'The tigers I've worked with have never gone too far away. I've tried half a mile and can still control them.' Marsh thought for a moment, watching the smoke curling from the barely smoked cigar he held. 'I'll look into it when I'm working with Mullen.'

'You know, Lieutenant Simpson is still not very keen on your approach to combat. Why is that?' Hudson asked, aware of the ongoing problems between the two men. He knew the answer, but he still wanted to know what Marsh had to say about the situation.

'The Lieutenant still believes in traditional tactics, Sir. He's part of the old regular army and his thinking's still very much grounded in those ideas,' Marsh said, careful not to expand more. He was taking a risk criticising an officer as an enlisted man, even to a senior officer who was enquiring about a situation. Simpson disliked the use of tigers, so he wondered if he should point it out. He could have been blunt, but he knew the Colonel could read between the lines.

'I understand the two of you have clashed?'

'He trained me back before he was commissioned, Sir. I didn't fit his idea of an effective soldier and I still don't.'

'It is a common problem when promoting from the ranks, in that the man does not always fully adjust to his new life or leave the old behind. However, with the sheer number of casualties we have suffered, it is necessary to promote experienced soldiers to the officer corps. Despite what you may have understood, the casualty rate among junior officers is worse than any other section of the Services. We have an enormous officer vacuum which can only be filled with battle-hardened junior ranks. As an experimental unit, we are limited in whom we can re-cruit and promote. Someone like Simpson, or your friend Scott, are immensely valuable to me as they get to the cusp of the issue and get things done.' Hudson considered his man, seeing through to the unsaid opinions and hoping his rebuke was gentle enough. 'Are you still able to work with Lieutenant Simpson?'

'I don't see why it should be a problem, Sir.' Marsh said. He could think of several reasons the dysfunctional relationship would not im-prove, not least the extra duties Simpson liked to give him, but these were not matters which concerned the Colonel.

'Then you will continue working under Lieutenant Simpson while Lieutenant Scott pursues other important duties elsewhere. You are to train Mullen, and when ready, trial your combat approach in both practice and combat conditions. In the meantime, you may, as may the entire battalion, be deployed should the General Staff require it. So be ready for sudden changes.'

The most interesting opportunity over the next fortnight was an investigation into the distance at which tigers could be controlled. Experiments were undertaken. On one occasion, Marsh maintained line-of-sight to the tigers. Another time, buildings, ground and trees blocked the view. The tigers were left with Wells, and another handler was ready on standby, while Marsh walked off to issue his commands. Every hundred yards, Marsh would stop and mentally instruct his tigers to change their behaviour. The time of the command was logged by Marsh, with Wells at the other end logging the times different behaviours were observed. To their great surprise, Marsh could instantaneously control the tigers at a distance of a mile just by using his thoughts, with obstructions having no effect. In a follow-up experiment, it was shown that the zombies always stayed in range of their handler, if they had freedom of movement. Other handlers in the experiments showed a far shorter range of operation based on voice commands. Finally, it was discovered that tigers with restricted movement would be removed from the handler's control should the handler move out of range.

The same experiments were duplicated by Mullen, who discovered he had a control range of three-quarters of a mile. Under Marsh's tutelage, Mullen progressed in his mental handling of the tigers, becoming able to match Marsh's sophisticated instructions. Between them, they experimented with the different commands they could issue and found the tigers could follow almost any instruction which did not require advanced comprehension or dexterity skills. This led to a great deal of thinking on the use of tigers for specific battlefield tasks, such as the bomb delivery Mullen had already improvised.

Another area of experimentation for Marsh and Mullen covered the emotional element of their mental orders. During the attack on the blockhouse, Marsh had noticed a particular speed and savagery stitched into the behaviour of his tigers. This had emerged at the time of the closely fought German counterattack. The more he thought about it, the more Marsh was convinced his own fears drove the zombies to a heightened state of aggressiveness. This was a complex area to experiment with, as they soon established tigers did not respond to fake emotions. In this respect, Lieutenant Simpson proved his worth.

Throughout the research and training opportunities, Simpson had continued his bullying campaign of Marsh. The Lieutenant would seize upon any minor fault in Marsh's uniform, publicly berating him like the drill instructor he used to be. This occurred frequently as Colonel Hudson had allowed Marsh to continue combat experiments, which meant Marsh would get dirty in the field. As if Simpson's attention was not enough, the officer also complained about the unsporting use of zombies in combat and placed obstacles in the way of the experiments. Mullen was not bothered by Simpson's behaviour, unleashing his own tension with a stream of insults and curses, frequently within earshot of the officer. Marsh, however, was cut deeply by the behaviour. The weight of his own drive to be an effective soldier, borne from his brother's death, undermined his confidence alongside Simpson's criticisms. Marsh still knew he could not be the effective soldier Simpson, and the army, required. Yet, he was a key handler of tigers, the most effective.

Due to the additional stress, Marsh's frustration and anger frequently bled into his commands to the tigers. A pattern emerged in the aggressiveness and speed of tiger reactions linked with occasions when

Marsh was emotionally charged. Under pressure, Marsh moved the tigers far faster than the average human, or even the average zombie. The parallels were obvious to the situation outside of the blockhouse. At these times, the zombies were more aggressive, with heightened senses, able to detect humans at a greater distance. However, the tigers remained compliant to Marsh's will.

Another area Marsh and Mullen investigated was who controlled the tigers when there were multiple handlers operating. Handlers issuing verbal commands controlled any tigers within earshot, but with the mental commands, there was the potential for controlling tigers at a greater distance. Marsh had previously seized control of tigers, and at a distance, but had never attempted to take control of zombies operated by other handlers. Mullen also established that he could issue mental commands to tigers that were under the control of Marsh. It turned out that Marsh could do likewise with tigers under Mullen's command. To push the boundaries, both of them tried issuing a single tiger with contradictory orders. The tiger simply ignored both commands. As the next stage of the experiment, Mullen discovered you could bind the zombies to an individual handler by issuing a simple mental command instructing the tiger to ignore all commands from other handlers while under mental control. A series of exercises followed, whereby the two handlers took turns in seeking to break the control of the other handler. All these attempts to seize control were failures.

Elsewhere among the Allied forces, there was significant development of a variety of fast moving tactics during this time. Sergeant Wells had been keeping track of these developments and was busy constructing a mock trench system for general training, inspired by the stories of the relentless practices the Canadians had undertaken before their successful attack at Vimy Ridge. Making use of this practice area, the two handlers extended their range of tactics for combat, implementing the hard-won experiences of the Canadians. By late July, Marsh was ready to deploy a few of these new tactics in a combat environment. The living elements of the combat group were relieved when these relentless exercises and experiments finished. They had been run ragged by all the activity, and while each person knew they were about to face the enemy again, they recognised they had reached an unprecedented peak of training.

Marsh approached the Colonel to volunteer the combat group for a trial under combat conditions.

18

EVOLUTION

'The evolution of the combat tiger was stimulated by a
pronounced clash between the new ways of thinking,
and the old.'

Regimental History of the Royal Zombie Corps
(1969, London)

A FTER EXHAUSTIVE TRAINING AND preparation, Colonel
Hudson arranged a combat trial of Marsh's tigers against a
German position on the edge of some woodland. Several members of
the General Staff intended to observe the attack. The ground featured
a slight rise, and at this point of the front, no man's land stretched
two hundred yards. Marsh was to be given full reign, using the tactics
he and Mullen were developing. Should either Marsh or Mullen be
incapacitated, other handlers would be available to ensure a zombie
outbreak did not occur. Elsewhere along the line, several spontaneous
zombie outbreaks had occurred during recent weeks. Each had been
put down with significant bloodshed and there were fears the ene-

my had triggered the outbreaks to disrupt the Allied lines. A general heightened awareness of the inherent risks of using tigers now existed.

To prepare for this assault, Wells worked hard to source the means necessary to plan the attack. Making use of aerial photographic reconnaissance, as well as maps and visits to the forward trenches, Wells constructed a full-size replica of the ground to be attacked. He had been successful in this task, and the combat group spent several days practicing their tactics on a replica of the battlefield, every man coming to recognise their role. Below the wood, at the bottom of a gentle slope, ran a small stream. This feature was covered by three machine gun posts, mounted in blockhouses in the German forward line. By the stream, there were a couple of forward listening posts, no doubt aimed at detecting trench raids and obtaining intelligence by listening to the daily noises of the British front line. The actual front zigged and zagged along the high ground, the brow of the hill, with the three machine gun posts as the central features. When the Germans pulled back to the Hindenburg line, they chose the best defensive territory, and in this sector, they had chosen the wooded heights. This gave the defenders the advantage in stationary warfare, forcing the advancing Allies to dig trenches on lower land which would be exposed to the fire from the elevated German defences. It also gave them the advantage should the Allies attack, as they would have to fight uphill, exposed to dangerous German crossfire.

Two communications trenches linked the forward positions to the German second line, a further two hundred yards to the rear of what remained of the shell-battered woodland. This secondary position featured indeterminate locations, perhaps machine gun emplacements, yet the positions did not possess a clear field of fire as the maps showed their location was on the back of the hill and not fully able to support the primary trench. The final German line was a further three hundred yards back, again following the contours of the land. This was positioned after the start of the next shallow hill, again ensuring the advantage of height. In the gap between the two supporting lines were the most interesting features, several gun positions for mortars and light artillery, as well as supply dumps and locations hosting other supporting functions.

With supporting infantry, the British goal was to take and hold the front two German lines, capturing the hilltop and exposing the support functions, and the third line to direct fire. If the opportunity arose, Marsh had planned a contingency in which the tigers would lead an assault on the third line. If the defenders appeared overwhelmed, he wanted the option to press them further. The essence of his intention was a rapid advance, with close infantry support. This would be a surprise attack, with no artillery preparation to give warning of the impending assault. The lack of artillery would mean German reinforcements remained unhindered, but the expected shock value of the zombies should reduce the combat effectiveness of any enemy reserves which joined the fight.

Intelligence confirmed widespread consternation about the tigers among the German infantry, who only possessed countermeasures such as machine guns and headshots. While it was suspected the enemy possessed their own tiger program, especially considering the recent frontline zombie outbreaks, no other progress was clear on the battlefield. However, interrogations revealed the deployment of small numbers of flamethrowers for use as an anti-tiger weapon. Marsh hoped this countermeasure would be ineffective, not quick enough to protect the defenders from the rage of a burning zombie. An absence of reports implied the enemy did not suspect the deployment of gas might degrade the effectiveness of the tigers. Marsh experienced relief. The enemy had not yet identified the vulnerability of tigers to chlorine damage.

For the first time in his military career, Marsh faced the unusual challenge of giving his initial briefing to the officers commanding the supporting infantry. As a corporal, he was unused to speaking to so many officers at once, and while Colonel Hudson delivered the main points of the briefing, Marsh was present to answer questions and expand on the specific details of the tactics. The Colonel would oversee the entire operation, but the effective command of the advance would be in the hands of a mere corporal, admittedly a corporal with a rather unique set of skills. It would be Alfie Marsh who would judge the conditions on the spot.

One of the infantry officers had complained vociferously about this irregularity, but Hudson pointed out conventional tactics had not worked for the last three years and with this method, it was essential for the lead handler of the combat group to set the pace of the assault. Speed and shock were essential and the complainant should treat any request coming from Marsh as an order from the Colonel himself. Colonel Hudson made clear the corporal possessed his full support and confidence; Corporal Marsh being one of the few specialist tacticians, and one of only two advanced handlers in the entire British Army. The rank of the soldier was irrelevant, and Hudson suggested the officer should take it up with a tiger if he thought he could do a better job. The officer had gone pale.

'Hey Alfie, how'd it go?' Morgan asked Marsh as he returned from the final pre-attack briefing.

'It's all go.' The final briefing had gone much better than the earlier briefing with the non-compliant officer. Only hours remained until the attack, and this time the officers were focused by the imminence of combat, aware that if Marsh's plan was successful, there would be far fewer casualties than would normally be the case for such an assault.

'Where's Simpson?' Wells asked. Wells had assigned himself to Marsh's combat group, not wanting to miss the opportunity to explore tactics he possessed great faith in.

'The Colonel has assigned Mr Simpson to act as a liaison to the infantry commander. It'll make it a little more palatable for them if any instructions I send are delivered by an officer.'

'That's good news, Alfie. It gets that idiot out of our way.'

'Bet that's been arranged because the Colonel didn't want Simpson buggering up our tactics,' Morgan said, articulating what everyone knew to be true.

'Maybe, but the man is still good in a fight,' Marsh said, remembering his rival's bravery on the battlefield.

'Don't defend him Alfie, he hates your guts,' Wells said, challenging Marsh's good-natured interpretation.

As soon as darkness fell, the combat group moved into position. Marsh commanded twenty tigers, having convinced the Colonel of the need. This comprised almost the entire complement of zombies available to the battalion. Tiger recruitment was not progressing well. Other than the outbreaks in combat zones, which had been put down, few cases occurred in the wild and even fewer zombies were being created in, and surviving, combat. Marsh fretted about what would happen if they ran out of fresh zombies. Would the Colonel again pursue the deliberate infection of volunteers?

The tigers were split between Marsh and Mullen. Each zombie wore head armour, and a quarter of them carried mortar rounds for use as demolition charges, should the need arise.

'Do you know your timings?' Marsh asked Mullen just before they parted ways in the forward trench, ready to complete their final preparations before emerging into no man's land.

'Aye. Race you there. First one in the Hun trench gets one of Wells' bottles of grog. But I'll race you silently. Wouldn't want to give Hun any warning.' Both sections of the unit would co-ordinate, with Mullen leading the left wing and Marsh the right, silently advancing towards the enemy line.

As they crawled out into no man's land, Marsh knew again the rising terror he always experienced whenever he first exposed himself to danger. Every noise he made seemed to be magnified in the quiet, despite distant booms from an artillery exchange elsewhere. The night was dark and while a new moon attempted to glow, the cloud cover was more than sufficient to ensure the darkness was adequate for their needs. Spread out on either side of him were his tigers, trailed by the protection squad. The living remained almost silent, having practiced this careful movement. Still, Marsh worried German listening posts would be alerted as they crawled past, bypassing the lookout positions.

As expected, it took over an hour to cross no man's land and arrive at their assault positions. The deployment was successful. No signs announced the Germans were alert to their presence, and Marsh waited as the hands on his luminous trench watch moved round to the assault time. Positioned just short of the German first trench, they heard the enemy soldiers talking, relaxed, and joking. Alfie thought about how similar the noises were to those he made with his own friends. Only the language was unfamiliar. He dwelt on the irony of this war being fought against people so similar to himself. Yet these thoughts did not relieve his concern, they increased it. He was so close to the enemy they would notice him make the slightest sound, and he was fearful an enemy patrol of no man's land might lead to the accidental discovery of his assault team. The lack of artillery support had been regarded as a significant weakness in the plan, at least according to the infantry. Its absence meant any noises he made were not masked by the noise of a barrage. However, Marsh was convinced the use of artillery would have alerted the defenders to an impending attack. This way, the Germans would be unprepared.

'Forward,' Marsh thought at the appointed time. He gave his tigers a mental shove and a reminder to move quietly, attack quickly and with violence. His own fearful emotions would give an edge to the thoughts, which would drive the zombies to a higher pace.

The tigers rose, responding to the silent command. They kept low and leapt into the trench, some on top of the defenders, the heightened zombie senses able to identify the warm humans without a direct line of sight. Within seconds, the tigers had torn the life from their targets with the use of clawed hands, teeth and sheer superhuman strength. The zombies did not eat their prey. Instead, following their orders to hurry, they sought to kill every single target in the trench. The defenders were stunned by the sudden appearance of the fast-moving, flesh-tearing monsters. Several seconds went by before any Germans sounded the alarm and opened fire.

The humans in the combat group rose as fast as their slow human reactions allowed. By the time the first Germans defended themselves, the human assailants had arrived in the trench, setting about targeting any defenders who had been omitted by the assaulting zombies. The attackers were armed with clubs, knives and machetes, and an assortment of other improvised weapons. Firearms would be used as a last resort, ensuring the enemy experienced the maximum terror and surprise. The attack would be overwhelming, silent and fast. The only noises were the sounds of screams and shouts in German, alongside a sporadic and decreasing volume of gunfire. These noises would alert the second line and the listening posts, but Marsh hoped the silent assault would terrify any nearby Germans while preventing them from recognising the scale of the assault.

Marsh advanced along a stretch of trench towards one of the machine gun blockhouses, exactly as he had planned. A tiger moved ahead of him, despatching any defenders who dared to reveal themselves. To his right was one of the deep bunkers the Germans built to shelter their men from artillery bombardments, down which he sent another tiger. Muffled screams sounded as the tiger killed every person in the bunker before returning to the surface covered from head to foot in blood. Already Marsh could sense additional tigers responding to his commands, as some of the first Germans to die reanimated under his control.

The concrete blockhouse was not locked when Marsh arrived. He turned the handle, pushing the steel door inwards.

'Klaus?' asked a man terrified by the commotion outside.

'No,' Marsh replied, ordering a tiger into the blockhouse.

Scuffled noises, pleading cries and screams came from the building as the occupants fought against the overwhelming strength of the zombie. A field telephone in the blockhouse rang. Germans elsewhere in the defensive system were noticing something unusual was occurring in this sector.

Marsh checked his watch. He had reached the objective two minutes early. They had seized their goals and the infantry would move up to secure the gains. There had been no significant noise from Mullen's flank, and Marsh assumed the two blockhouses Mullen was tasked with assaulting had fallen just as fast as his own objectives. Marsh used the remaining time to send orders to his tigers, readying them for the next phase of the attack.

'Alfie,' Wells said, bulky machine gun slung across his back, bloodied bayonet in hand. 'We're ready to go.' Wells had the role of policing this section of trench for damaged zombies with no further usefulness.

'How many new tigers did you count?' Marsh asked.

'I counted at least five. There'll be more in the section Matthews is policing up.'

Marsh was still unclear how many tigers he could control. He had never been stretched. As always, too few zombies were available. This could change tonight, he thought. From the work with Mullen, he knew he could control many more tigers when using mental control. Voice control was just too simple; crude commands expressed with words rather than thoughts and emotions. Mullen controlled a respectable fifteen tigers before training with Marsh. Now the Irishman's upper limit was also unknown.

'We'll move on in another minute. Have we any casualties?'

'Not that I'm aware of. A few scrapes here and there among the boys. Mind you, some of the new tigers look rough.' Wells thought of one new zombie missing an arm. The limb perhaps torn away, rather than gnawed off, simply because of the pace with which the assaulting tigers had inflicted the injury on the doomed German soldier.

For the next phase of the advance, stealth was a lesser consideration. The second German line was at least alerted by the screams, shouts, and occasional shots from the frontline trench. Speed was again critical, and Marsh sent the tigers ahead while the human element of the combat group followed on as quickly as possible. The continued advance meant vacating the German forward trench before the infantry arrived to take possession, but Marsh knew the follow-up troops were leaving their trenches to seize control of the listening posts already, and would soon be in the empty, forward trench. No survivors remained to cause any problems. The tiger's senses had seen to that. The follow-up troops would then hasten on to the German second line so they would arrive just after the tigers had secured it; assuming the infantry stuck to the plan and did not suffer an unforeseen delay. Marsh had wanted a similar approach for the first line, but the need to bypass the listening posts meant the support troops delayed their own advance.

Silence could not be maintained at the speed the tigers now advanced, especially as they passed through the tortured woodland, broken trees sticking up out of the ground. Some tigers moved along a communications trench, but found no opposition. At any time the enemy could fire a flare and light up the battlefield, risking the exposure of the tigers and the supporting humans. Marsh almost bit his tongue as the concern ran through his mind while he ran from tree stump to tree stump, trying hard not to fall behind the tigers ahead of him. He knew Mullen was mirroring his advance on the left wing. Clearing the brow of the hill, the second line loomed on the rear of the hill. As he advanced, the leading tigers leapt into the second trench. Shouting, screaming, and the occasional gunshot again revealed how unprepared the enemy were for the surprise attack. The defenders had not recognised the noise generated by the first assault for what it was.

A green flare flew high into the dark sky, fired by the defenders. On seeing the green-tinged light, Marsh threw himself to the ground just short of the German line. He experienced overwhelming terror at being caught in the open. The flare had been fired at the worst possible moment. Shots sounded from his right, and he was unsure if these came from the defenders or his own protection squad. A snarl was audible from the German positions, convincing him a tiger was already clearing the trench to his front. Marsh rose, rushing forward the final yards before throwing himself into the dubious safety of the cleared enemy trench. He lay exposed in the dying light of the flare as it fell to the earth. Visible in the fading light, were several dead defenders, and a tiger hunched over a corpse, gorging on the flesh.

Marsh readied his shotgun and made his way up the trench, where he expected to find Matthews and Davies. He sent the tiger on ahead, interrupting its impromptu meal. It ran off around a bend in the trench, ready to meet any enemy threats. Marsh's caution was wise. A fusillade of rifles sounded, and the tiger was flung back round the corner, falling motionless, its head smashed by a rifle bullet.

Marsh peaked around the corner. He knew the risk he was taking, given the numerous Germans spread along the next stretch of trench, ready to resist an assault from his direction. A defender noticed him, but was too slow to fire an aimed shot. Marsh checked his webbing for a Mills bomb. He was unsure he could throw the grenade far enough with any accuracy. As he considered the angles, Wells arrived next to him, his arrival in the trench unannounced.

'Josh, there's a bunch of them up ahead, just around the bend,' Marsh said.

'Chuck a grenade, and then we charge? I see you've got no tigers nearby.' Wells grimaced at the dead zombie.

'Tigers?' Marsh asked. He had forgotten an alternative way to deliver his Mills bomb.

Marsh reached out with his mind. He summoned several tigers, which were busy gorging on the far side of the block in the trench. He could solve this problem without using a grenade. Marsh ordered the zombies to head towards the rear of the German blocking position. The tigers responded. Several screams of 'Zombie!' marking the progress of the creatures through the defender's position.

Alfie reattached the grenade to his webbing and nodded his readiness to Wells. There would be no need for the bomb. The enemy was already distracted by the attack on their rear. The two British soldiers both ran around the corner, guns firing unaimed into the surrounded defenders. He knew if he did not aim high, he would be unlikely to harm his own tigers in any important way.

The Germans did not stand a chance, overwhelmed by the ferocious attack from behind. Two tigers ripped their way through the rearguard. Several of the Germans dropped their rifles and ran away from the horrific monsters, straight into the fire from the two British soldiers emerging around the corner. The rest of the defenders fell to the claws and teeth of the undead. Within seconds, the remaining terrified and pained screams were cut off as throats were torn out and stomachs ripped asunder. Calm descended on the trench, the noise of the wider battle reasserting itself.

'Thought I'd find you here,' Davies said as he strode through the carnage. He came from the same direction as the tigers. 'I knew when my tigers took off, it must have been you that summoned them. Don't look like you needed my help, either.'

'It's all sorted now, Colin. Is everything secure up the trench?' Marsh asked.

'Yes, and we're ready to go again.'

The follow-up infantry arrived right on cue to take ownership of the trench. The Tommies jumped, or lowered themselves, from the parapet.

'This is easy,' a sergeant of the infantry said. 'Keep going and we'll be in Berlin soon!'

19

BARRAGE

'One thing was certain during this war: artillery. Small, medium and heavy guns dominated every battlefield in Europe, extending the pattern of the previous century.'

Milton Davies, A History of Zombies and Warfare,

(London, 2016)

A T THE AGREED TIME, Marsh sent the tigers forward, knowing the infantry following on would be ready to support them again within minutes. The defenders in the final German line were now alert, unable to ignore the noise of the previous assaults. Sporadic rifle fire came from some positions. However, the defenders were hampered by the location of their forward artillery and supply posts, now between the new front lines, having previously been between their second and third defence lines. Where possible, the defenders spiked their guns and destroyed supplies, but a general sense of panic had already taken hold and chaos spread. As the tigers rushed forward, they overran the isolated gun posts and supply dumps. Marsh allowed each zombie the brief delay of clearing positions they encountered.

Alfie stumbled over some netting he had not seen. He dropped through the camouflage, which had hidden a supply dump from him. Winded, he picked himself up from the ground of the cutting, thankful he had not landed awkwardly. His head had just missed a solid-looking crate. Marsh knew a moment of terror. The enemy would soon be upon him, but the position was deserted. Alfie got up, several parts of his body smarting with what would become a significant collection of bruises. He checked his shotgun and was pleased to identify no obvious problems, wiping away a small clump of mud. In seconds, he advanced again, now lagging some way behind the tigers.

A tiger jumped into a gun pit. Three Germans were attempting to dismantle a trench mortar to prevent the weapon from falling into British hands. The busy soldiers survived for mere seconds. The tiger, finished with its rendering of flesh, jumped out of the pit to continue the advance. As Marsh watched, a defender re-animated, falling under the handler's control and joining the assault. Looking across the width of the battlefield, most of the tigers in the advance wore German uniforms, freshly reanimated this very evening. Dozens of these new zombies arose as he watched. He had never seen so many tigers in one place.

Marsh knew these new tactics were creating significant numbers of new zombies, solving the problem of the shortage of tigers. There had been an ongoing problem of how to create new zombies, despite the unreasonable demands of wartime. The principal source so far was naturally occurring zombies. These were captured around the front lines. The other major source was those created from among the enemy during attacks. However, the nature of the attacks, to date, also ensured a good many zombies were spent, therefore the Experimental

Battalion had never grown the number of tigers available to them, at least not enough to keep up with combat expenditure. The attrition at Bullecourt had been a good example of this, where most of the attacking tigers were wiped out and too few replacements recruited.

The tigers were slower to advance this time, no longer driven by the fear Marsh had channelled into them during the earlier phase of the attack. Now they were in the enemy's rear, the edge had been taken off Marsh's trepidation. The tigers picked up on this and spent more time gorging on human flesh and less time advancing. Marsh ran past several abandoned field guns, their crews nowhere to be seen. The defenders had made their escape upon hearing rumours of the presence of tigers. If not, they would have fled when they spotted the zombies bounding across the battlefield.

The defensive fire from the final German line increased in intensity, but remained sporadic despite a further flare lighting up the battle-field for the defenders. Temporarily illuminating the field, the flare burst as Marsh reached the bottom of the last hill, allowing him to hide in the shadows and observe the surrounding battlefield. At his back, the supporting infantry advanced, keeping low to the ground and using the cover available to them, especially the hollows of the now deserted German gun positions. To his flanks were the members of his protection squad moving from shadow to shadow, avoiding a dangerous charge directly at the enemy, while attempting to keep pace with the tigers. Ahead of Marsh, the tigers streamed into the enemy trench, the sheer number of them overwhelming the defenders. Marsh rushed forward, certain there would be no further opposition. He leapt into the final enemy trench, finding several tigers gorging themselves on the flesh of the fallen. Only a few of the deceased were given the opportunity to reanimate.

The final stage of the attack was a complete success. As dawn broke, the support troops secured the last trench in enough numbers to ensure any counter-attack by the enemy was doomed to failure. Marsh knew if they had the means, the British would have continued to push forward into the vulnerable rear areas of the enemy, the areas containing all the support functions. Such a breakthrough would cause widespread panic across the enemy front and the German defensive line would have collapsed for miles in either direction. However, there were no mobile reserves to exploit the opportunity. The aim of the attack had been to show such an assault was possible using tigers. The General Staff would be impressed, certain to move forward with the experimental unit.

'How many Tigers did you make?' Mullen asked once he had found Marsh. Mullen wiped his face, tired but elated.

'Dunno? I ended up with at least a couple of dozen more than I started with, but I've not done a count,' Marsh said. He was too busy securing the tigers, preventing any unfortunate accidents. He had not got around to counting them. Alfie had never handled this many zombies before.

'I took forty-two new ones. Also, I reckon I can control quote a few more than that.'

'It's new ground. We've never been this far before,' Marsh said, grinning before he got back to counting his tigers.

'Where the hell did he come from?' Morgan asked, his disgust clear as Lieutenant Simpson strode along the captured trench. There were no prizes for guessing who the officer was searching for.

'Where's Marsh, man?' Simpson demanded of Morgan. The soldier shrugged his shoulders in response. Exhausted from battle, Morgan held his dislike in check.

'Over here, Sir.' Marsh waved his hand. He sat at the bottom of the trench, leaning on some supply crates with Mullen. Their backs were to the arriving officer, and they had been enjoying a well-earned rest after the hard work of the night. Marsh wondered what the Lieutenant wanted this time. No doubt to discuss some fault, imaginary or real.

'We're to push on,' Simpson ordered. 'Get your tigers ready to advance again in ten minutes.'

'But Sir, we've achieved the objective. No follow-up troops are ready, and the sun's up now.' The goal was to capture the three German lines, a limited plan. The use of tigers as the primary assault means was proven effective.

'Orders from above, Marsh, don't argue about it,' Simpson said, looking hard at Marsh. The challenge was obvious. Simpson desired an argument with Marsh. The officer was almost willing it. 'A decision has been taken to follow through on our successful assault. The infantry are still fresh, so we push on. You're to lead the advance again.'

'But Sir, we're trained to assault trenches, not advance across open ground in broad daylight,' Marsh complained. 'That's what all our tactical planning has been about. Right now, any fool with a machine gun can stop us in our tracks.'

'Exactly. That is what you trained for and why I'll be taking over and directing the movement. I have the training and the experience, so you won't need to worry about such matters. Just do as I tell you.'

'Bloody hell,' a disguised voice behind Simpson complained far too loudly. The anonymous voice was not the only unsolicited comment. The volume of complaint grew among the protection squad.

'Keep your troops in line, Marsh,' Simpson glared at Wells, Morgan and Davies. 'Wells, you too, get some order established here.'

Wells made a show of lingering among the rest of the protection squad, checking their kit and readying them for the next assault. He would not allow the officer to push him around. The lieutenant ignored Wells, turning his attention back to Marsh and Mullen.

'There are some farm buildings east of here. We suspect these are being used as a command post. We'll advance, take them, and then move on from there. Are you able to do that, Marsh, or should I give the task to someone else like Mullen?' Mullen waited until Simpson's gaze returned to Marsh before unleashing a glaring at the Lieutenant. 'You'll advance in open order, ahead of the infantry and if you come across any resistance, you're to stamp it out. The infantry will provide fire support and hold any ground you take. Questions?'

'There's hardly any cover, Sir, we'll be in the open. We're not trained for that. Our tigers will be sitting ducks,' Marsh complained.

'Those are not questions, Marsh. Now get your men ready,' Simpson snapped.

Simpson stood watching the flurry of activity he had unleashed. Marsh began by calling out orders to the combat group, sending Mullen back to control his flank. The Irishman unleashed a stream of curses at the idea of the additional advance, and audible groans travelled up and down the combat group. They had been expecting to stand down and thought they deserved a well-earned rest. The supporting infantry were also unhappy at the news. Having survived a successful assault with minimal casualties, they were only expecting a simple job of securing the defences rather than moving into the open.

'How're we going to do it, Marsh?' Wells asked in a pause between passing on the orders.

'Spread out like the Lieutenant wants, and we use whatever cover we can to move forward quickly and quietly.' Marsh wondered if he sounded convincing. The chances of this working were minimal.

'They'll see us coming and we'll be in the open. We'll be massacred.'

'Well, let's hope they aren't ready for us then. We've broken through their lines. We'll only be attacking cooks and pen-pushers, otherwise we may have a problem. Make sure you keep the security squad close by. We may need their firepower if we end up in a firefight.'

'Ready the advance!' Simpson shouted, moving back up the line, intent on positioning himself by Marsh to ensure his orders were followed to the letter. An infantry officer echoed the call, with the riflemen hastening to ready themselves. Several of the men swore aloud at the apparent injustice of the turn in events. None were happy to further expose themselves to danger even though they may, at last, be taking part in the long-awaited great mythological 'break-through'. The German lines had remained intact through the three years of the war, and this success should have cheered the Tommies, but it was clear advancing in daylight would be far more dangerous than the experimental night attack.

'Tigers forward!' Simpson shouted for show. Stood next to Marsh, he need only have spoken the order to the handler.

'Forward!' Marsh echoed, yet the simultaneous mental command did the work. He need not have commanded out loud, but his squad appreciated being aware of the order. Mullen shouted the same command further up the line and Alfie wondered if the vocal command was just as redundant there. The advance reminded Marsh of the skirmishing tactics of the Napoleonic period. He had read about these when formulating his own tactical ideas. Yet, Simpson was intent on repeating the unsuccessful tactics of the preceding three years of the war.

The tigers advanced in large numbers, so dense from the front they would have appeared to be an animated shield of flesh and bone which the infantry could hide behind. Marsh had not taken in quite how many new zombies had been recruited during the assaults, far more than either he or Mullen had counted. He was not prepared to risk their number, sending mental instructions to spread out and move quickly, using any cover they could find. The protection squad climbed out of the trench next, and with the tigers ahead of them, they moved from cover to cover, as carefully and quickly as they could given the limited options available. The infantry advanced, unsure of themselves. Some soldiers copied the movement of the tigers and protection squad, the rest advanced in the open order they had been trained to use.

'Why are your tigers using cover, Marsh? I want them out in the open, driving fear into the hearts of the enemy,' Simpson called. He was staying close to Marsh, although not making use of the cover.

'We need to keep low, Sir,' Marsh said. He prepared to sprint to a shell crater just ahead. 'We'll move quickly, we'll surprise whoever we find, and with luck, they'll not hit us.'

'I said I want them up and advancing correctly, not hiding like cowards in the shadows.' Simpson strutted in the open. 'We will use the correct form of attack.'

'But Sir, we're an experimental unit, and this is how we work.' Marsh stopped and turned to look up at the officer standing over him in the open. The situation was unbelievable. They were having an argument during the middle of an assault on a possible enemy position.

'And I'm the commanding officer and I say do it my way. Or are you refusing a direct order?' Simpson said, sneering. His hand moved to the handle of his pistol. Despite the move, the pistol remained in his holster.

'No, Sir.' Marsh knew he was taking a risk by arguing with the officer, but if he did not stand his ground, men might die. 'But, the Colonel put me in tactical command.'

'Is the Colonel here? You were in tactical command for the assault and now we're now moving on. I'm in tactical command now,' Simpson shouted, spittle flying from his reddened face. He kicked at Marsh. With Simpson on the higher ground, it caught Marsh on the shoulder. 'Now get up and do what you're bloody well told!'

Marsh got up, stung rather than hurt by the unexpected kick. Stood next to the Lieutenant and looking around the rear areas of the enemy line, he considered shooting Simpson. No enemy was in sight and there was no shooting, the only noise and movement was coming from the British troops. He knew Wells would approve, and Mullen would shoot Simpson in the back the first opportunity he got. He could pursue revenge for the kick, but he felt exposed, stood in the open.

'See, it's safe, isn't it?' Simpson asked in a tone close to an accusation of cowardice. 'Now get your tigers moving in open order.' Spotting Wells ahead of their position, Simpson repeated the same order at full parade volume for the protection squad. Several men ignored the order and Simpson hurried off to berate them. Others also suffered contact with Simpson's boots.

Marsh grudgingly sent the order and his tigers rose from their cover, slowed their pace, and continued to advance towards the new objective. Mullen's tigers rose soon after, with Mullen having spotted what Marsh was doing. The Irishman would have understood the reason and wished to avoid his own confrontation with Simpson. The three lines of the British advance were soon in the open, the tigers, followed by the protection squad, preceding the main British force of infantry. Simpson made a noise which could have been interpreted as satisfaction as he moved back to his position near Marsh.

'Marsh, get those beasts on the right to close up,' Simpson snapped when he noticed a defect in his orderly advance. The farm buildings were almost in reach and Simpson ordered Marsh to coordinate the tigers in a manner which would allow them to outflank the building on both sides. The ground grew firmer, having not been turned over by the constant shelling which bedevilled the front lines. Marsh even noticed some crops growing, suggesting the farm was inhabited.

Several cracks sounded as bullets passed overhead. The gunfire came from a small gun-pit, or dugout, hidden behind a bush, to the front left of the farmhouse. Mullen surged some of his tigers forward, the cries of the defenders announcing the success of the assault. In front of Marsh, a concealed machine gun position opened fire, chopping through several of the closely packed tigers. Some zombies did not rise again, having taken hits to their heads. Most of the tigers were recently reanimated and therefore not wearing the improved head armour provided the night before. Even if they wore head armour, Marsh doubted it would have offered much protection from a machine gun at this range.

The revealing of the machine gun seemed to be the signal for a renewed German defence, with several rifles firing from the windows of the farmhouse while mortar rounds dropped among the advancing

British forces. The Germans had organised a hasty but effective defence. In the distance, on Marsh's flank, a large formation of German infantry was moving out of the cover provided by a small wood. They were being flanked by a German counter-attack. Screams from behind revealed it was not just the tigers who were targeted by the defensive fire, but the advancing infantry as well. If he could get his tigers moving, perhaps the farmhouse could be taken quickly, allowing the British infantry a building to base their impending efforts to fight off the German counter-attack.

'Keep them steady, Marsh,' Simpson said, having noticed Marsh was about to rush his tigers at the farmhouse. 'We'll close the ground at a steady pace and then follow up with a quick charge. I want both the machine guns and the farmhouse taken. Don't launch the assault too soon.'

Mullen followed Marsh as the British continued their advance under fire. The defenders were targeting the tiger's heads, with a steady stream of the creatures falling and not getting up again. The panic rose. They could not sustain this tremendous bloodshed. Several of the protection squad were also hit. The enemy was prioritising them, having identified their function in controlling the tigers. Shortly after this realisation Wells was hit, a bullet smashing into his machine gun before travelling through his right arm. Wells shouted at Marsh to continuing advancing as he lay down, waiting to receive aid from one of the supporting infantry. Another soldier in the protection squad, Francis, disappeared when hit by a mortar round. Just body parts remained where he had stood. Marsh was uncertain of Francis' first name. He had not yet got to know the recently arrived replacement. Through all the mayhem, Simpson strode, invulnerable to the bullets and shrapnel.

'Charge!' Simpson shouted when he deemed them close enough to launch the assault. Marsh would rather have charged much sooner. At least now he could unleash his forces rather than stay in the open as plodding targets.

The tigers rushed the machine gun post, several of them falling, and staying down, as the stuttering chatter of the machine gun became a constant and desperate rattle. A zombie rushing in from the flank evaded the gunfire, the gun falling silent, replaced by the screams of the defenders and the groans of the wounded attackers.

The farmhouse was soon surrounded by scrabbling zombies, the defenders firing as rapidly as possible through the windows and doorways, hoping to hold the attackers at bay. Marsh had never seen zombies swarm a building like this and wondered if a mortar-laden zombie was needed to demolish a side of the building. He realised this would not be necessary as first one tiger, then another, leapt through open windows. The gunfire retreated within the ground floor of the building before falling silent. A moment later, the firing from the upper floor turned inward, screams tracking the progress of the tigers through the building. It ended when the final enemy defender fell from an upstairs window accompanied by a tiger tearing at his neck. Both landed with a thud on the hard ground outside, but only one continued to move, feeding on the fresh flesh.

The German mortar fire increased in volume, joined by heavier artillery, as the rest of the combat group took shelter in and around the farmhouse. Only a few hundred yards away, the German infantry dug in, no longer prepared to advance, having seen the brutal attack by the tigers. Several of the enemy set up machine guns, opening fire on the advancing British infantry, who now had to find any cover they could.

Marsh took cover. 'The attack's stalled!' Marsh shouted to Mullen, who had just joined him behind a wall next to the farmhouse. 'We were too slow. It's given them time to organise.'

'We've got to get out of here.' Mullen ducked as a shell flew overhead. It exploded a short distance away and shrapnel whistled through the air. 'The artillery is zeroed in on the farmhouse. We need to get away from here. Where's Simpson?'

'He's in the house, upstairs, trying to spot what the Hun are up to,' Marsh explained.

'He better get out of there soon, because it'll not be standing for much longer.'

A voice carried from a short distance away, 'Dig in!' The infantry were a hundred yards behind Marsh and Mullen and the shout had come from them. They were desperately digging shallow scrapes and expanding any craters they found themselves in.

'They're pinned down by those machine guns and the artillery,' Marsh said after another near miss shook the wall he sheltered behind.

A loud whistle grew in volume. A blast of hot air and a shock travelled through Marsh's body. The vibration of the ground threw him into the air and he was showered by chunks of the destroyed stone wall. He hit the ground, winded, ears ringing and body unresponsive. Everything went dark.

Mullen was there, muttering. Marsh's arms were in agony, he was being dragged across the ground by them. Darkness descended again.

20

BLIGHTY

'A Blighty wound was a popular term describing a wound which would put a soldier out of action, requiring him to return to England for recuperation. The word Blighty came into common use among British soldiers during the Boer War, as a term for home, introduced by those who served in India. During the Great War, the usage expanded to refer to injuries. Wounds of a short-term nature were considered far more favourably by the average soldier. Wounds to extremities of the body, the hands or the feet, were treated by the authorities with increasing suspicion as the war progressed. This was often the case when the circumstances of the injury were less than clear.'

Historymain.com 'The experience of the trenches' (2014)

T HE DAYS AFTER THE attack were barely measured by points of pain and boredom, as Marsh moved through the medical system. Early during his ordeal, he recovered consciousness, but remembered nothing. At least, this was what the medical orderlies and nurses had later told him. His first memory of the time after the attack was waking up in a canvas tent. He later recalled there were a dozen beds full of injured soldiers in the tent.

Joshua Wells sat on the bed next to him, grinning from ear to ear as Alfie woke again. Marsh could not make sense of anything. The words were just noises without meaning. He fell asleep.

'Alfie, Alfie, wake up.' The voice was insistent, and Marsh forced open his eyes. He lay in the warm bed, wishing he had not been disturbed. 'You're awake, good. Have some more water,' said Wells, offering a mug of water to Alfie's parched lips. Marsh was surprised he understood the words his friend spoke.

'What happened?' he asked, pushing the mug away. His throat was sore, and the left side of his body ached as he pushed himself upright.

'You caught a Blighty.' Wells handed Alfie the mug now he was upright. 'Congratulations.'

'What do you mean?' Marsh asked, his mind still muddled. 'I hurt.'

'It's not surprising you hurt. You stopped a stone with that hard old head of yours and got yourself peppered with shrapnel.'

'Stopped a stone?' Marsh could not recall the events.

'At the farmhouse. A shell landed by the wall you sheltered behind. Mullen says the stonework saved you from the blast, but a chunk of it smashed into your helmet and knocked you out. Apparently, the rock came off far worse than you from the encounter. Then, as Mullen got you out of there, you took a bunch of splinters from another near miss. You were bloody unlucky from what Mullen says. He was next to you both times and was untouched. I don't think you were unlucky, I think he had the bloody luck of the Irish. He didn't pick up a scratch. The surgeons operated on you and pulled out all the shell splinters using some new-fangled thing called a Death-Ray, or X-Ray, or some such.'

'So that's why my head hurts,' Marsh said. A jumble of memories came back. He looked down at his left arm and side of his chest, seeing clean bandages covering significant amounts of flesh. 'My side hurts like hell.'

'The Medical Officer wants you shipped back to Blighty for recovery, so it seems like we'll be getting out of here soon,' the cheeriness in Wells' voice was unmistakable.

'We? So that's why you're here as well? You got hit too?'

'That's right. A Hun bullet smashed my gun,' Wells said. He breathed heavily, disappointed at his loss, despite the appalling reputation of the Chauchat. Wells loved the weapon. 'Then the bullet punched through my arm, clean through. It missed everything important, a nice clean wound. I spotted you at the casualty station and I've stayed with you since.' Wells put his hand on his upper right arm, but Marsh could see nothing unusual beyond the sling cradling his friend's injured arm.

'A blighty as well?' Marsh managed a grin, despite the extra pain which rolled across his face.

'So, you're not going home without me? You wouldn't know how to enjoy yourself without me about to show you.'

Marsh smiled at his friend. Despite his good mood, Wells looked awful, the grime of the battlefield still engrained around the edges of his face, even though he had washed several times since being injured. Josh was pale and his free hand held an unlit cigarette. Marsh wondered if he looked just as bad. He suspected he did. He checked off his own wounds. The back of his head was a dull ache, like a terrible hangover he had suffered after drinking too much cider on the farm. Constant pain streamed down his left side, especially his leg, but it was not overwhelming. He must have been dosed up with effective painkillers. He hoped the pain would not be too bad once they wore off.

'What about everyone else? How are the rest of the boys? What about the attack? Did we succeed?' Marsh asked, concerned for his friends, impatiently waiting for Wells to answer.

'Mullen did well. He went back out into the open and pulled back as many tigers as he could after getting you back, but we lost many of the zombies around the farmhouse. We'd all been worrying the tigers were going to go out of control, but they seemed locked into your last command until he somehow overrode it. Later on, Mullen found me in the clearing station and filled me in on everything he knew. He said he saw Davies and Morgan and they were as fine as you'd expected with those two. He'd not heard about Matthews then, but I've since found out he got pinned down at the farmhouse and snuck back much later. Bloody Simpson was fine though, and crowing about a brilliant victory, despite most of our casualties coming from when he pushed us at the farmhouse.' His face showed his opinion of the officer's claim. 'Jones and Flannery are dead, and Francis is missing.'

'Francis is dead,' Marsh said quietly. 'I saw him hit by a shell. Nothing was left of him. You know, I didn't even know his first name?'

'Neither did I, poor sod. But it was the attack on the farmhouse, which was the problem. Everything before went smoothly,' Wells said, repeating his opinion as if the repetition would ensure it was true.

'What happened after we left? Did we keep the ground?'

'Mullen said we had to pull back from the farmhouse, back to the last trench we captured. The Germans dug in and got organised to such a degree our lads couldn't stay, even though they were digging in as fast as they could.'

'Useless. We should have stuck to the plan. We weren't meant to follow through on any breakthroughs. There wasn't any support for such a foolish advance.' Marsh shook his head and immediately regretted it. 'Have you heard anything from the Colonel yet?'

'No, not yet, although I shouldn't think he'll be too happy with Simpson for screwing up at the farmhouse. The fool should just let you move the tigers the way you wanted, rather than falling back on his bloody textbook approach.'

'Well, we know what it takes, but Simpson's ideas haven't moved on since General Gordon and Khartoum,' Marsh laughed as he made the comparison, instantly regretting it as he felt a fresh stab of pain.

'More like Harold, at Hastings, if you ask me. But it'll not be our problem for a while as we'll be off home to recover. Just think of those women, the pubs, and the peace and quiet. Oh, and don't forget the women. It's not like we've had much leave. If we were in any other part of the army, we'd have had more time at home.'

'The joys of being in such demand,' Marsh complained, knowing they were well overdue a spot of leave. 'It'll be nice to be away from Simpson for a while. I don't envy Mullen, or the other handlers, who'll stay here and deal with him.'

'They'll not let the other handlers do anything more than herd the tigers. Other than Mullen, they don't possess your skill. It'll be too risky,' Wells said. 'You two are in a different league, not limited by voice or small numbers. I've not seen any other handlers control by thinking alone. The Colonel will keep the unit out of action until you're ready for it or he finds more talent.'

'Well, we'll be out of it for a while,' Marsh said. He was relieved he would not need to face the terror of combat for a while, especially the sharp end of combat. 'It's not like I'm much of a soldier, and without the tigers, I'll just be useless again.'

'Polishing your boots in the trenches is not what good soldiering is about, whatever Simpson thinks. You're a damn good soldier from what I've seen and wasted as a mere corporal. I'd say you've proved that with your work on the tigers.' Wells plastered a great big smile on his face. 'Now, let me tell you about the nurses we've got here looking after us.'

'Sit down, gentlemen. You need not stand, given the condition you're both in,' Colonel Hudson said, waving to the two unused chairs in the wooden hut. He waited for them to take a seat. Marsh was slow, uncomfortable because of the amount of exercise he had already undertaken. He was working hard to get his fitness back. While his injuries were not serious, they pulled and ached whenever he exerted himself.

'You may wonder why I'm here,' Hudson began. 'Well, you two chaps are pretty indispensable, and I've had to intervene to stop your trip back to good old Blighty.'

Marsh grimaced, and Wells examined his shoes as they listened to the news.

'I can tell you're both disappointed. I will arrange some leave for you, possibly in Paris. You have more than earned the break. I know you deserve a trip back home, however, you are indispensable to the war effort. We need you to continue your work with the tigers, even if this means you are desk-bound for some time. We do not possess the capacity or the skills on hand to lose either of you, despite that fool Simpson doing his best to further thin out our numbers.' Hudson said. An officer criticising another officer in front of enlisted men was highly irregular, but the Colonel was unimpressed with Simpson's intervention during the recent combat. He needed Marsh and Wells to understand they were not being held responsible for the near disaster at the culmination of the demonstration attack. Their tactics were sound. Simpson was the one at fault.

'Now Marsh, your new tactics worked brilliantly, and it was pure foolishness by the Major in charge of the infantry along with Lieutenant Simpson. There should not have been any advance beyond the agreed objectives. The General Staff were impressed with the pace of your advance and therefore instructed us to prepare to lead a future offensive. The offensive will include a force ready to exploit any breakthrough you create.' Hudson stopped talking. Marsh and Wells beamed at each other, much cheered by the positive evaluation of their performance. 'I even overheard comments about how Field Marshal Haig was correct in putting great store in our work.'

'Now you, Marsh, along with Mullen, possess a unique understanding of the zombies and will be the centrepiece of our future work. We also have quite a few handlers who could be made greater use of, even though they are far more limited in their abilities. Once you return from your short leave, we will ready ourselves for the next "Big Push". How does that sound, Marsh?'

'Ideal, Sir,' Marsh said, unable to think of any other response to the praise which washed away his disappointment at not going home.

'Sergeant Wells, we need to talk about changing your role a little, especially if Marsh agrees. So far, you have provided close protection to the handlers and have been available to step in should they lose control of their tigers. This has brought you into contact with the enemy, as the tigers have stormed the trenches. The General Staff would like to expand your number and equip you with more trench fighting weapons so you will become assault troops alongside the tigers. They were so impressed with the pace of the attacks, they want to ensure we will not outrun our support. Therefore, we will attack with a greater number of live, and specially trained, soldiers. The follow-on troops will also be brought under our command during attacks. So, Wells, your challenge is to make this work. Of course, your resourcefulness will be a great asset in achieving this, but I must ask you to not liberate any more of my personal effects and supplies,' the Colonel said, winking at the last part of his request.

Wells was left wondering which of the many liberated supplies the Colonel referred to.

'We are to be formalised into a separate branch of the army. Like the Royal Flying Corps, we will form our own corps. The Heavy Branch of the Machine Gun Corps will become the Tank Corps and we will be known as the Tiger Corps because we have proved ourselves an effective offensive weapon. I would have much preferred Royal Zombie Corps, but some wag at General Headquarters decided that the civilians back home would struggle too much with the pronunciation of corps and corpse, leading to obvious jokes,' Hudson said, almost hugging himself with delight as he finished delivering the good news.

'Sir, that news calls for a drink,' Wells said, extracting a bottle of late 19th Century cognac from his kit and three enamelled mugs. 'Sorry about the mugs, Sir, but I'm sure the quality of the cognac will be more than good enough.' Wells poured the amber spirit.

'I hope that's not one of my bottles?' Hudson asked.

'Of course not, Sir.' Wells laughed as he passed around the mugs. 'It was donated by a French officer.'

'The Royal Tiger Corps,' Hudson said, raising his mug.

'No, to the Royal Zombie Corps, Sir,' Marsh said. 'The civilians might not cope, but to us out here in the field, that's who we really are.'

'The Royal Zombie Corps.' The three men made the toast. Marsh coughed as the drink burnt his throat.

'I'll see what I can do to persuade the Brass to change the name,' Hudson said.

'Sorry, Sir, I'm not used to this kind of medicine at the moment,' Marsh said after his coughing fit finished.

'Well, you'll have to get used to little drinks like this, as you've got a little more celebrating ahead,' Hudson said. Marsh looked quizzically at the Colonel, suspecting the surgeon had held back on some of the good news. 'We're expanding, so I'll need to make you up to sergeant. I can't have a mere corporal strutting around giving the orders anymore.

It's too humbling for most officers. At least they're used to sergeants knowing better than them. Congratulations, Sergeant Marsh. You'll still be running our tactics and leading us on the field.'

Grasping the officer's proffered hand, Marsh was stunned by the news, unable to speak. Never in his wildest dreams had he thought he would end up as a sergeant. He was too often the butt of complaints about his ineffectiveness as a soldier, especially from Simpson, and would have been content to remain a corporal for the rest of the war. Now he would have a far greater responsibility than before as the battalion, no corps, expanded and became one of the principal spearheads of the British Army as it sought to break the deadlock of the trenches. He would have to be a good soldier, but not the traditional variety Simpson seemed to favour. Instead, he would be the person who got things done in the real world, the world of the trenches. His family would be proud, a warrior to match his dead brother.

'Cat got your tongue?' Hudson teased. 'Nothing to say?'

'Thank you, Sir,' Marsh squeaked, unsure if it was the powerful spirits, or the shock, which had stolen his voice.

PART 4 - TIGERS AT CAMBRAI

21

OUT WITH THE OLD, IN WITH THE NEW

'A rare, but not unknown phenomenon saw unpopular officers and NCOs experience "accidents" while on the battlefield. A certain British company commander I knew, was shot in the back by his own men while advancing across no man's land. His crime had been ordering the carrying out of Field Punishment Number One on a popular, and probably innocent, private.'

General Haddox, 'A Doughboy in the Great War'
(1936, New York)

'HOW ON EARTH AM I meant to lead a group of men?' Marsh asked, refilling his glass of wine.

The small bar was crowded with a wide range of different soldiers, drawn from a multitude of nationalities. One thing most of the soldiers had in common was they were drunker than Marsh and Wells.

The opportunity for leave was being enjoyed to the maximum, and neither man was too disappointed they had not been sent back to Britain, as would often happen to men wounded in the same way as themselves.

'You lead them the same way you lead a group of tigers. You tell them what to do,' Wells replied.

'But you're a natural leader. People follow you and you're a damn good soldier. I'm not?' Marsh swallowed a rather large mouthful of wine. The waitresses were quite nice in this establishment, better than the place they had visited the previous day. Clearly, the wine was not only dulling the pain from his recent wounds.

'No, I'm a good talker. I get what I want with charm and deals, not battlefield skill. My shooting is so bad, I still can't hit anything, even with my Chauchat. It spits out loads of bullets and I still miss everything I aim at,' Wells said. He lit a cigarette using his uninjured arm and looked at the men in the room. 'These soldiers here would follow me, but not because I'm a good soldier. They'd follow because I've got three stripes on my arm and even then I'd talk them into it. If that didn't work, I'd just keep them supplied with booze and then they'd follow me to the ends of the earth, or until the drink ran out. With you, though, they'd follow you because you know what you're doing on the battlefield. If it wasn't for you, we'd never have worked out how to employ those tigers. They'd just be another nuisance of the trenches. Besides, there's always the option they'd follow you for fear you'd feed them to a tiger.'

Since their arrival on the Western Front, over a year before, both men had been intrinsically linked to the effort to employ zombies on the battlefield. Codenamed 'tigers', Marsh had first stumbled across the little understood creatures when he brought one back from no man's land during a failed assault. When they later suppressed an outbreak of the creatures behind the lines, Marsh had discovered he possessed a measure of control over the beasts, something they had been exploiting ever since in their experimental unit. Their recent injuries, bad enough to send them home for recuperative leave, were received during a successful proving of the zombies as a weapon capable of breaking the deadlock of the trenches. As men central to the tiger project, the needs of the war prevented them from returning to England.

'So, why do I get such grief off Simpson all the time? If I'm such a good soldier, why doesn't he leave me alone?' Marsh refilled his glass. The wine was full-bodied and a pleasant change from tea and the treated water of the trenches. Yet, his relationship with Lieutenant Simpson was not good. They had first met in a training depot in 1916. Marsh had just been conscripted. Simpson, then a mere drill corporal, had taken an instant dislike to the first tranche of conscripts, singling out Marsh for his ire.

'Look, Alfie, the man's a bully. He may be a war hero and all that, but he needs someone to pick on and he doesn't like change. This war's a big change for someone like him, trench warfare, conscript armies, new weapons, and you represent that change for him. You're a soldier who doesn't fit into his nice old world. But you fit the new world, both with the tigers and your understanding of how a battlefield works.'

'Bloody hell, Professor Wells. Where'd you get all that from?' Alfie replied, stunned at the lucidity his friend possessed, despite the wine they had consumed.

'I told you, I've the gift of the gab. Oh, and much of my charm comes from observing and working things out. If you watch something for long enough, you'll understand it,' Wells said. His smile was half-hearted as he thought of their prospects tonight. 'And on the subject of observing, there's no chance of charming the waitresses here tonight. We either go somewhere else or drink ourselves stupid.'

'Keep drinking.' Marsh emptied the bottle into his glass before calling over a waitress and ordering another bottle.

'So how do I deal with Simpson? He's an officer. I can't just tell him to sod off.'

'Yes, you can,' Wells replied. 'He's threatened by you and thinks he'll get away with mistreating you, as you'll do nothing about it. Tell him to swing his hook, and he'll leave you be.'

'But there's nothing I can do. I can't tell him to get lost,' Marsh said before pouring from the newly arrived bottle of wine.

'You know, there are quite a few things you can do. Start by telling him to bugger off. If that doesn't work, just ignore him, simply walk away. You might have to punch his lights out if he doesn't take the subtle hints.'

'If I hit him, I'll be court-marshalled, and what'll happen then?' Marsh was mortified by the idea, aware both the French and British armies took a very strict line on mutiny.

'He knows you would never take him aside. That's why he pushes you so far.' Wells leaned forward. 'Of course, there's always the possibility of an accident on the battlefield. It happens to all the most deserving officers.'

'I could never—'

'And that's why he'll get away with it. Do us all a favour and feed him to a tiger. It's better than he deserves and it may even shorten the war with all the meddling he's got up to.'

The silence grew between them, only ending when an engineer played a popular song on an out of tune piano. The room soon erupted into drunken song. Neither Marsh nor Wells resisted.

The summer of 1917 was spent training and expanding the Tiger Corps. Colonel Hudson found time to lobby for a change of name. He expected he would be successful and they would soon be known as the Royal Zombie Corps. The small battalion expanded out to eight companies, each capable of cooperative or independent action. Each company was built around a small nucleus of a couple of handlers and up to twenty tigers. The reality was less impressive. Only two handlers in the entire corps possessed instinctive control of the tigers. Lesser skilled handlers made up the rest of the number, and even these skilled men were rare. The rest of each company was arranged like a standard infantry company, but trained to protect the handlers; providing last-ditch control of the tigers; and launching close assaults on the enemy. They were equipped for fast and stealthy assaults, attacks focused on the punching of a hole through enemy lines. As assault troops, the Corps would not exploit the gaps they created. This would be left to the traditional manoeuvre sections of the army, especially the cavalry.

The first full-scale combat use of the tigers at Arras, in the spring, had proven the concept. The idea had been developed further over the summer, resulting in tactics designed to penetrate the enemy lines. Their weaponry was a mixture of the improvised and newer automatic weapons, or close-quarter weapons like the American trench shotgun. Very few of the soldiers were raw recruits, the majority having rotated through the trenches at least once. Their skill levels were high and applications were continuously received from experienced fighters, far outweighing the number of posts available. Applications from among the tough men of the ANZACs had been high, following their experience of fighting alongside the tigers in the fierce fighting of the Battle of Arras. The Royal Tiger Corps was achieving a similar cachet to the Royal Flying Corps and the Tank Corps. The only reason the Corps did not expand further was the low number of handlers available.

Marsh and Wells were the key components of A Company, with a far wider function of developing the fighting strategies of the entire corps. This was not just because they had been the first to work with the zombies, but also because of the skills Marsh showed with the creatures. They were doing the jobs of warrant officers. Just as across the rest of the army, a great number of troops fulfilled temporary roles, needed because of expansion, or to replace casualties. Lieutenant Scott was the company commanding officer, a role normally fulfilled by a captain, with Scott himself having been promoted from alongside them in the ranks. However, in this new unit, officers did not have effective control over the battlefield. Instead, the tiger handlers controlled combat, men who all ranked as corporals or sergeants. This meant a higher level of reliance on non-commissioned officers than was usual in the British Army. Simply put, the men controlling the tigers were the best people to hold tactical control in combat, with the obligatory officer liaising with accompanying units and managing overall strategic control.

B Company was the only other flexible company in the corps, led by Lieutenant Simpson, but handled by Mullen. While Simpson was a burden for Mullen, Marsh knew the Irishman was a near equal to himself in his control over the tigers. Therefore, there was great confidence B Company would perform well on the battlefield. The other companies were a mixed bag comprising experienced handlers who could command by voice alone, lacking the sophisticated mental controls both Mullen and Marsh possessed. Recruitment had recently identified several more handlers, including a small number who seemed to have the potential for mental control, but it was still early in their training and deployment. For now, only two companies would deploy advanced handlers. Marsh's assistant handler in A Company had significant potential and the setup in B Company was the same, where the mentorship of Marsh and Mullen would transform such potential into ability. However, the remaining companies would remain less flexible until these promising new handlers were trained.

The other limiting factor was the sheer number of tigers needed to bring the Corps up to a full compliment. Accidents happened during training, both to humans and zombies, and while the zombies were unlikely to be badly harmed, there was a noticeable attrition rate. Replacements were always in demand. Colonel Hudson ran a poster campaign in reserve areas and it proved successful. He aimed it at Tommy Atkins with slogans such as 'Catch a Zombie' and 'Send Kaiser Bill a Tiger'. The words were accompanied by various images of zombies and precise advice on how to capture the reanimated dead. A reward for soldiers capturing a zombie also helped. As a result, the flow of captured zombies from the frontline increased within a matter of weeks. In fact, the flow became so significant the General Staff worried there may be the beginnings of a plague of zombies breaking out along the entire front. In consequence, Colonel Hudson made contingency plans in case such an eventuality occurred. Orders had been drafted for the urgent liquidation of all identified zombie outbreaks, although these orders were not issued.

The creation of tigers was becoming an area of intense scientific scrutiny, no longer just in the hands of Colonel Hudson. As originally discovered, there was a bacterial element and transmission usually appeared to occur when bitten. The bacteria could survive outside of the reanimated corpse for a significant period and could enter a living human by other means, by routes not yet established. It seemed not everyone was susceptible to the bacteria. Some people seemed to resist reanimation, however much they had been infected. Compared to other living research subjects, the bacterial link with the handlers seemed stronger. The latest thinking suggested infection by the bacteria, but instead of dying and then reanimating, some form of change occurred within their brains, possibly reawakening some ancient and enhanced part of the mind. The key problem here was handlers could not be created by exposing soldiers to the bacteria, as the same bacteria could cause some of those said soldiers to die and then reanimate as zombies.

Marsh enjoyed this extended time of preparation, contributing to the development of new tactical uses of the tigers. However, Lieutenant Simpson remained a problem, despite commanding a different company. There should have been far less contact between them, but Marsh's critical role in the development of tactics brought them into regular contact. At every opportunity, Simpson would criticise Marsh's uniform or appearance, even his tactics. Simpson would direct Mullen, his chief handler, to stick to approved forms of assault. Fortunately, Mullen recognised the tactical incompetence of his commanding officer and would circumvent this in ways the officer could not spot. The men of B Company recognised Mullen as the man in charge. Alongside Marsh, Mullen helped to develop the new tactics, ignoring his commanding officer as often as he could get away with. Simpson did not relent and took every possible opportunity to obstruct the development of unconventional tactics, continuing to hark back to the pre-war days of massed infantry movement.

'What do you think you're doing?' Wells had cornered Simpson in an empty supply shed one afternoon. A sharp glare sent all the supply clerks scurrying. While the clerks were familiar with Wells, having had many dealings official, and otherwise, with him, they knew he should not be crossed. He wanted a quiet word with the Lieutenant, so they gave him privacy.

'To what are you referring, Sergeant?' Simpson asked, adding the rank as a reminder of how to address officers.

'Marsh,' Wells said, grabbing Simpson by the collar and slamming him against a stack of packing cases.

'So, manhandling a senior officer, is it?' Simpson said, his voice calm. He did not react to the hand clasping his collar, appearing in control of the situation. He grinned, 'I could have you up on a charge for this. Or would you prefer we settled this the old-fashioned way? I'll put my rank to one side if you wish.'

'You'll settle it by leaving Marsh alone. He's the key to the success of this entire unit. We fight smart and we'll break through and win this war,' Wells said, ignoring Simpson's offer.

'Marsh is everything that is wrong with this unit. He's a slovenly, useless soldier,' the bile was clear in Simpson's voice. 'Now, are we going to resolve this the old-fashioned way, or are you going to hold on to me forever?'

Simpson did not wait. He did not even give Wells time to respond. Instead, he punched the sergeant hard in the kidneys. Simpson had learnt his craft in the ranks of the pre-war army and had taken more than his fair share of knocks. He had allowed Wells to get close, knowing it gave him the advantage when he struck. Although Simpson was now an officer, he could still use his fists. The men respected such physicality. Wells crumpled to the floor in agony. It took Wells several painful seconds to notice Simpson was strutting around the room, talking, rather than continuing his assault.

'Given the state of the Army today. They let anyone in, useless civilians like your friends. Hell, even Jews like you, parents fresh off the boat from Russia. There's no respect for how things should be done any more. If we'd stuck to our traditions, we would have been in Berlin by the Christmas of '14. But no, the lousy French didn't keep their side up and we ended up stuck in the trenches. Only ten years ago, we were getting ready to fight those French bastards. The mutinous scum are no better now than they were then.'

Wells took time to recover some composure while Simpson continued his rant. 'Then they stick me behind the lines nurse-maid to useless children like yourself while good men are out dying on the Front. When they got desperate enough to let me back into the action, they were so short-handed I ended up as an officer before I could blink. No wonder we're not winning this war with useless cannon-fodder like you and your chums. What's more, it's all these bloody amateurs, gentlemen, officers straight out of school who have never—'

Wells cut Simpson off, tripping the officer as he strode by. Simpson fell with a crash. Yet he was almost as quick as Wells as they both rose to their feet. Wells leapt at the officer, punching him in the face. The Lieutenant clattered to his knees after a savage blow to the jaw.

'It's bastards like me who are going to win this bloody war,' Wells spat, each word punctuated with a punch.

'Stop,' Simpson said in a weak voice. He raised his hands to protect himself before falling to the ground.

'You'll keep out of Marsh's way and fall into line with what we're doing here,' Wells demanded, pulling up the officer by his tie. Simpson had no choice but to stand, somehow rising without being throttled. Their faces were close together again. 'Is that clear?'

'Yes,' Simpson said when Wells moved to hit him again.

'By the way, you tripped and knocked over some boxes. I'm sure you know the drill better than I do for this sort of thing. Now get yourself cleaned up and get out of here,' Wells said, moving aside so Simpson could leave.

'You'll be hearing more about this.' The threat was undermined as he wiped his bleeding lip with a sleeve.

'Then the tigers will hear your name the next time you turn your back,' Wells said. It warmed his heart as what little colour remained in Simpson's face drain at the threat.

'What the hell happened to Simpson?' Morgan dealt out the cards. 'He looks like he's gone ten rounds with someone bigger than him. He's been looking that way since yesterday.'

'He said he got knocked over by some packing cases in the supplies shed? At least that's what I heard.' Matthews picked up his hand. 'I don't believe a word of it, of course.'

'He's got one hell of a shiner and some nice bruises. I'm surprised the boxes didn't break his nose as well. He had it coming, of course. He should have gone easier on those boxes, especially as they seemed to have fists,' Morgan said. They all knew it was no accident. As the banker, Morgan was having a run of good luck, and making a tidy profit from their game of pontoon.

'Hopefully he'll learn his lesson,' Marsh said, grimacing as he looked at his hand. He threw in a farthing, the minimum stake they were playing for. He knew Wells had taken the officer aside. After it happened, Josh had sought him out. Wells faced a challenge convincing him it was for the best, but Marsh was pleased he would no longer have to deal with Simpson and the officer's constant bullying. Simpson had been a thorn in his side since they first met, impossible to please with his insistence on the correct way to be a soldier.

'He got much better than what I thought was going to happen to him. With all the zombies around here, it's a wonder none of the beasts have eaten him.' Matthews pulled a face. 'There was this guy in my last unit who said his mates bumped off a Regimental Sergeant Major. A right bastard apparently, that RSM. It happened early in the war, back before everyone dug bloody enormous holes in the ground. They advanced towards a wood with some German cavalry hidden in it. Hun opened fire and before they knew it, his own men shot the RSM in the back. Thing is, whoever shot him didn't do a good job of it. The man was lying there turning the air blue for a good ten minutes before he croaked.'

'And let that be a lesson to us all,' Davies said. 'Aim true and kill the bastard, good and proper, with one shot.'

'I'm sure things won't need to go that far. Lieutenant Simpson is certain to be nice to his packing cases from now on,' Morgan said with a chuckle.

'Good job. I've never seen a packing case carrying a rifle,' Matthews laughed.

'Let's get ready, then. We'll be going into action soon and this time we're going to smash the enemy.' Marsh had already grown in confidence in the hours since Wells had intervened. He knew he had the support of his men. Simpson would no longer be standing in judgement.

'Sarge,' Matthews asked Marsh, 'can we finish the game first? I think you'll be parting with some more money before we go.'

22

CAMBRAI

'The Battle of Cambrai is consider to be the first modern combined arms battle. For the first time in history, the British managed to co-ordinate all the arms available to them. Drawing on the hard-won experience of three years in the trenches, the British advanced quickly and effectively. The nightmarish experiences of 1916, of men walking to their slaughter, became distant memories. Yet the battle was not one-sided. The defenders fought hard and there was a widespread introduction of storm-trooper tactics. The German storm-troopers rivalled the Royal Zombie Corps for impact, with the latter operating on a much smaller scale than the conventionally manned, and numerous, German units.'

'The battle became the template for the advances of the Allied offensive at the end of the war. British and Imperial forces demonstrated they had become the most effective, and industrialised, army of the war.'

Translated from Emilia Busch, 'Überdenken - Der
Erste Weltkrieg' (1969, Munich)

T HE NEW OFFENSIVE HAD taken months to prepare and was
the most sophisticated and forward-thinking project Marsh
had been involved with. Tanks, tigers and assault troops were to be
deployed, all intent on punching through the German lines. These
combined forces would create a breakthrough which would end the
war. Alfie knew a great deal of hope was being placed on the attack.

Earlier in the month, devastating news had come from Russia. A
second revolution was spreading across the country like wildfire, led
by a small faction known as Bolsheviks. Nothing was clear-cut, and
many competing factions tore the country apart in the first stages of a
civil war. The Bolsheviks were against the continuation of the Russian
war effort against Germany. The British General Staff, and most of
the British Army, feared an imminent Russian collapse would lead
to the redeployment of experienced German armies from the East.
Such reinforcements would force the Western Front Allies onto the
defensive. Besides the developments in Russia, there were growing
concerns these revolutionary ideas would spread to the French and
British trenches, reigniting the mutinies of the past year. Therefore,
this new assault at Cambrai needed to succeed. Too much was riding
on the outcome, far more than had been intended.

Through the patronage of Colonel Hudson, Marsh noticed the full
intricacies of the battle and the overall strategic concerns resting upon
the outcome. Marsh worked out both the tactical approaches for the
tigers, and how their piece of the puzzle would fit into the overall

plan of battle. From somewhere unspecified, perhaps loose talk over a bottle of Scotch, Hudson discovered the Royal Artillery and the Tank Corps were also seeking to deploy some promising new tactics. Hudson followed up on these rumours and the Royal Zombie Corps was soon integrated into their plans.

The origin of the plan for an attack at Cambrai started with General Byng, of the Third Army. Byng wished to seize the key German supply point in the town of Cambrai. From this town, an entire section of the Hindenburg line was supplied. Byng had visited Haig and requested the Royal Zombie Corps deploy as an element of the attack. The Royal Flying Corps were assigned to fly close air support, another first in this battle. It transpired the attack would be a set-piece based on the large-scale use of these new ideas and tactics. The new concepts, combined, would hopefully break the three-year deadlock of the trenches. This was the battle that Hudson had been hoping for to use the new tactics Marsh was developing with the zombies. Their demonstration attack, before the General Staff, had been an overwhelming success. Only the last-minute decision to exploit the breakthrough failed. The tigers had smashed through three defended German lines before floundering, unsupported, in the open to a well-organised German counter-attack.

As part of the co-ordinated plan for Cambrai, Major General Tudor of the Royal Artillery met with Hudson. Their respective staffs plotted the details of the attack while the two leaders discussed strategy over after-dinner cigars. It became clear the artillery had developed several new tactics to deploy, moving away from the fruitless and endless bombardments aimed at digging out the enemy. Such approaches had failed against well-built German defences. Instead, the artillery planned to use new fuses so their high explosive ordinance would explode before burrowing too deep into the ground, reducing the creation of deep craters and the problems this caused to troops advancing across a smashed battlefield. A fresh approach to the pre-aiming of guns before the battle would also help. Precise use of maps and mathematics would mean every shot was aimed, giving the enemy no warning. This would make the creeping barrages far more accurate and less likely to fall short, killing friendly soldiers. This was an important feature the Royal Zombie Corps could exploit. The greatest change facing the artillery was the long phase of artillery preparatory bombardment. Instead of days of bombardment, there would instead be a very intense and short bombardment to shock the defenders and hinder their support lines. Additional improvements were being made in the location, and silencing, of enemy artillery through the use of sound ranging and counter-battery targeting. As a result, the artillery was again being deployed as an offensive weapon and Tudor planned to sneak over a thousand guns forward to support the attack.

Marsh knew the attack would be unstoppable if the artillery could deliver. Their new ideas would help his tigers as they moved forward. The expanded size of the tiger company would make quick work of any defenders who survived the artillery assault. Well armed, both as a security against zombie outbreaks and as assault troops, the Royal Zombie Corps was a force to be reckoned with. Following support troops would then clean up any resistance left behind by the tigers before garrisoning the captured positions.

The work of the Tank Corps impressed Marsh. Although the tigers would not be assigned to work alongside the tanks, the sheer scale of the planned tank usage was overwhelming. Marsh had not been impressed by the tanks in combat at Arras. Most had broken down, even though a few smashed through the German positions. Yet, he understood the potential and knew this new technology was experiencing rapid development. For Cambrai, almost five hundred tanks were to be deployed, unthinkable numbers when considering the resources which would be used. These would lead the infantry forward, smashing barbed wire and tackling tough German positions. Apparently, the Tank Corps were only looking for an opportunity to use their numbers for raiding, but General Byng identified an opportunity to use the monsters as an armoured fist at the front of the assault. Co-ordinated with the artillery, tigers, and aircraft, an unprecedented battle was about to begin.

To Marsh, the fantastic bravery of the Royal Flying Corps was as impressive as the powerful metal land-battleships of the Tank Corps. Marsh could still not fathom why a person would strap himself to an enormous engine, staying airborne through flimsy pieces of wood and flammable fabric. Yet, the ground-attacking contribution of the aircraft would be new to him, having only seen aircraft dogfighting or making routine flights. He was as fascinated as the next man by flight and had followed the rapid evolution of the plane with great interest. In the attack, the aircraft would be another form of artillery, precise and responsive to changing circumstances. The aces of the air would hunt ground targets worthy of their bombs while strafing trenches with their machine guns. Marsh had not yet been on the receiving end of a strafing aircraft, but he had heard stories of how unpleasant and personal it all was.

Learning from their own experiences, Marsh had Wells create a vast model of the battlefield to help prepare their own contribution to the attack. Wells had taken this idea from the Canadians after Arras, and it worked well during the demonstration attack. By using a full-scale model, the Royal Zombie Corps prepared for the assault. Every soldier would know their role and how they were expected to advance. If their leaders fell, they could continue the attack. In this sense, the handlers were still the weak spot. If a handler fell, then their tigers could end up out of control, turning upon the nearest living people. This could lead to a zombie outbreak, with the zombies reverting to uncontrolled violence. However, with the sheer number of infantry now in the unit, there should not be any real problem with dealing with a few out-of-control zombies. The creatures were less dangerous when not controlled, because they lacked purpose and a directing mind. Certainly, when Marsh had been knocked unconscious in their last assault, there had been no problem with rampant tigers. They had stayed locked to his last order. Certainly, with the advanced handlers who used mental commands to control the zombies, this held true, but there had been less successful experiences with handlers who used vocal commands for control.

The most telling thing about the preparation for the attack at Cambrai was how experienced, and skilled, soldiers of all types had become at advancing across open ground. They made use of every piece of cover to creep toward the enemy. They fought as small combat groups, heavily armed and able to protect themselves. Marsh had worried the scale of the operations would prevent his soldiers from moving into position quietly enough to surprise the enemy, but exercises on Wells' replica battlefield confirmed surprise could be achieved.

The greatest shock of Marsh's preparations was Simpson's absence. Despite Wells' denial of all the rumours, Alfie knew his friend had spoken to Lieutenant Simpson in a very effective and personal way. Not only was Simpson conspicuous in his absence, he had not materialised to argue about the use of non-conventional tactics. For the first time, the officer had deferred to Marsh's expertise.

Mullen had also contributed to the tactics the Zombie Corps would use, especially the decision to bypass strongpoints or attack them. Marsh did not know how he managed before the Irishman joined the unit. His ideas proved insightful, and whenever Marsh pondered a problem, he could rely on Mullen to argue the competing factors through to a successful conclusion. For example, because of Mullen's input, one company in the battalion was tasked with demolition tasks.

Any strongpoints would be bypassed by the assaulting companies, with the support company moving in later to use exploding tigers to remove any chokepoints. This would ensure the shock value of the fast moving tigers was maintained as they took the enemy by surprise, but further reduced the risk to the follow-up infantry.

All that remained was for the units to move into their start positions, ready to launch the attack.

'Flipping heck!' Marsh shouted, as the horizon behind them lit up with the flashes from one thousand artillery pieces. Some of the larger guns were firing from right behind the front, close enough to keep up with the expected advance without needing to move. While he knew what was about to happen, seeing it was something else all together.

'Wouldn't want to be the Hun when that lot hits him.' Wells was lying on his back, staring at the sky. He was spotting fuses and the trails they left as the artillery rounds flew overhead.

'Bloody hell!' Morgan exclaimed. He looked over the parapet at the instant the barrage fell upon the German line. His voice was lost as the continuous crump of explosions reached them. The bombardment was short and fierce, focused on key points over the five miles of the front on which the attack would take place. The very ground shook, with loose earth rising to form a faint cloud of dust around them.

'Poor blighters,' Matthews said, sympathising with the defenders on the receiving end of the artillery. Alongside the company commander, Lieutenant Scott, Matthews was the most experienced soldier among Marsh's friends. Having served several tours of the trenches before joining the Royal Zombie Corps, he had been on the receiving end of many barrages.

'They'd do the same to us,' Wells said, giving up on his aerial spotting and getting up to view the battlefield from the parapet. Everyone knew he was right.

'Doesn't mean it's fun for them either,' Matthews said, the voice of experience.

Alfie looked around the trench to monitor how his men were coping with the pressure before the advance. Davies was less than happy and had his machete out, sharpening the vast blade, as was his habit before going into action. Lieutenant Scott stuck his head out of the dugout in response to the noise of the shelling. Noticing no-one was concerned by the noise, Scott returned to his work. Behind him, he drew the blackout curtain across the entrance cut into the wall of the trench. The flimsy material just stopped light and would make no difference to the noise. Bill Rose pushed aside the curtain, leaving the dugout. He nodded to Marsh. Rose was the first handler Marsh recruited at Étaples. He had turned into an effective handler, but lacked the advanced mental control ability which marked out the most powerful handlers. As a result, Rose was assigned to the demolition company where his steady competence would be best used. Marsh took in the rest of the scene in the trench. Morgan and Wells looked over the parapet, consumed by the view. Marsh got up to join them. He knew the sight would be spectacular.

All along the horizon, the German front had disappeared beneath the dust thrown high into the air by the bombardment. The cloud was expanding, fuelled by a mixture of earth and smoke, despite the fuses designed to prevent the shells from penetrating too far into the ground before exploding. This innovation was only a partial success, but with luck, the ground would still be easier to cross than the usual churn of the battlefield. As they watched, the cloud grew thicker, the whole miasma stoked by the rapid fire of the artillery to their rear.

Somewhere behind them, a roar of engines sounded against the booming barrage as the tanks readied themselves. Several armoured vehicles were supporting this sector of the attack. The noise of the moving monsters was just audible above the artillery as they took up their start positions. Even if the enemy heard the tanks, the furious barrage kept German heads down.

Alfie knew the fearsome Hindenburg Line was almost unbreakable. Unlike the attack at Arras, this attack would be on the toughest part of the German line. Two lines of solid fortifications needed to be overcome, along with a third, which was well under construction. Each line was accompanied by belts of barbed wire, yards deep. The tanks were essential to clear a way through the wire. Marsh knew there were concrete emplacements and bunkers buried far under the ground, full of defenders who would survive the barrage. His tigers would have the job of clearing the living obstacles.

'Here come the tanks,' Wells said, pointing out several lumbering vehicles heading towards their position. 'I hope they get across our trenches without getting stuck.' Several bridges had been built over the wider sections of trench, so the tanks would not have to slow their progress. The rhomboid shape of the tank meant it should be able to cross smaller trenches, but it did so at a significant cost to the pace of an advance. The tanks risked overstraining their engines, with tank breakdowns as effective as enemy fire at putting a tank out of action.

'They'll clear the wire,' Marsh said loudly enough for the assault troops around him to hear. He hoped he was right. 'We'll follow them straight through the gaps they create and then take out the first line. The supporting infantry will follow on after.' These plans were known to everyone present, but a reminder did not hurt. The tigers had been assigned to support the 20th (Light) Division, and as with the other five divisions in the attack, the aim was to push the enemy back to the

St Quentin Canal, and beyond. The advance would push toward the key town of Cambrai, around six miles from the starting position.

'I'll buy the first man into Cambrai a crate of wine!' Scott shouted as he emerged from the dugout. Cheers sounded as the news of Lieutenant Scott's prize passed up the line. As the head of A Company today, Scott would lead the assault troops while Marsh focused on his usual role of handling the tigers and the local tactical situation.

'Here it comes,' Morgan said, as a tank clanked its way over a trench crossing. 'They should be called land-whales, not land-tanks. They're so bleedin' big and slow.' This tank carried the name 'Red Devil' with a colourful cartoon motif of an imp-like devil painted on the side.

'Tigers forward,' Scott said as the tank lumbered ahead. He checked his watch. The time was 0610, the exact time for the advance. The artillery shifted to a rolling barrage three hundred yards ahead of the advancing forces, firing a mixture of high explosive, to keep the Germans under cover, and large quantities of concealing smoke.

23

RED DEVIL

'I wasn't at Cambrai, but I did work with the tanks later on. When they didn't get stuck or broken down, they passed through the enemy lines like a hot knife through butter. The problem was keeping them moving. Between the mechanical problems and the Hun getting wise, many tanks broke down.'
Interview with William Murphy in Duncan, F, 'A Soldier's War: Accounts from the trenches' (1931, London)

MARSH SENT OUT HIS tigers. They swarmed out into the open, behind the six tanks advancing through his section of the line. He followed on behind, keeping up with them, along with the rest of the company. Everywhere he looked, men placed the armoured bulk of the tanks between their own fragile bodies and the enemy positions, wearing the tanks like a cumbersome form of armour. The enemy had not opened fire yet, but being above ground again was terrifying and the advancing men acted to preserve themselves. A tank, a short distance ahead, tore through the first tangles of barbed wire.

The ground had not been scarred by the bombardment, and previous fighting in the area had been light. Marsh was surprised by all the greenery, despite it being late November. As the sun rose, visibility got better. The previous few days were misty, allowing the preparations for the attack to be hidden from the prying eyes of German aerial reconnaissance. Now, Marsh noted with concern, the absent mist left him exposed. He hoped this would mean good things as far as friendly air support went, but advancing across no man's land behind a slow, clanking metal monster was not where he wanted to be, especially in good visibility. Marsh felt exposed, and only training and experience held the terror at bay.

Heading toward the village of La Vacquerie, on the right of the vast attack, were the combined formations of the 20th (Light) Division, Royal Zombie Corps and Tank Corps, expecting to meet heavy resistance. The advancing troops had half a mile to cover to the village and a similar distance beyond to the first part of the Hindenburg Line. Most of no man's land was covered with barbed wire and listening posts, from which the enemy fell back upon spotting the advance. They did not put up a fight, either stunned by the bombardment or ill-equipped to deal with the armoured vehicles in the spearhead. However, the defenders had fortified La Vacquerie and it would have to be taken first. The creeping barrage hindered the enemy's withdrawal while keeping the advancing British hidden.

The first belt of wire was over ten yards deep, coil upon coil of wire. With 'Red Devil' ahead of them, the advance did not pause. The vehicle destroyed the obstacle, some of the wire catching on the body of the tank. More wire was torn apart by the strength of the tank, with a narrow stretch crushed into the ground by the weight of the passing vehicle. Within a minute, the first belt of wire was torn open, while each neighbouring tank likewise punched through the defences. Marsh recognised how useful these tanks would have been earlier in the war, saving the countless lives of men who had been caught on wire or funnelled into killing grounds. The tanks ground on, ready to assail the next wire belt.

'It doesn't feel right being out here in the open,' Marsh said to Wells, his voice raised despite his friend being close by, in the tank's lee. Not only was the vehicle noisy, it was easy for the troops to keep up as the tank moved at a walking pace with the tigers following behind 'Red Devil'. The lack of German fire, and the slow pace of advance, gave them time for an unexpected chat.

'I'm glad we've got the tanks with us, Alfie. I'd hate to attack this place with just artillery to break the wire. It's such a distance to the Hun lines.' Wells waved his trusty Chauchat at the rear of the tank. Despite the problems with mud getting into the open magazine and jamming the weapon, Wells still preferred the French light machine gun to the popular Lewis Gun. Of course, he had broken several of the delicate Chauchats. His last weapon was smashed by the impact of a bullet, which while slowed, had still put Wells in hospital.

'I thought that. It would take days to cut through this wire and clear it for an attack. It's not a job I'd want.' Marsh looked ahead of the tank as it mounted the next belt of wire.

'See that rubble ahead, over there? You can just make it out through the barrage.' Wells slowed his pace and pointed, waiting until Marsh made an affirmative noise. 'That's the remains of La Vacquerie. There's not much standing.' The village had been demolished by the artillery of both sides during intense fighting earlier in the year. When retreating to the Hindenburg Line, the Germans fortified it to cover their retreat. The flat land leading up to the village also forced assailants to approach in the open.

'We're that far already? We're about halfway to their lines,' Marsh said, surprised at the pace of the advance. All the assault troops had rehearsed the plan on maps and models prior to the attack. Opposing trenches were almost always positioned closer together, but when the Germans had withdrawn to the Hindenburg Line, they took the best positions and the British positioned their own trenches in poor ground before the well-chosen enemy positions. Forty tanks converged on the fortified village, many of them in Marsh's line of sight. Between the tigers and the tanks, the village should fall. The accompanying infantry of the King's Royal Rifle Corps were also visible in large numbers.

'Looks like it's time for action,' Marsh said, as the barrage shifted beyond the village. Only one more belt of wire remained between them and the village.

'Will you let the tigers go on ahead as soon as we cross the last wire?' Wells asked. The wire ended just short of the edge of the village. Trenches and fortified buildings were just beyond.

'Yes, that's the plan.' The front of the tank ploughed into the last, very thick belt of wire. 'It won't be long until Fritz is out of his dugouts. We need to catch him on the hop.'

Rifle rounds clanged off the tank. Fortunately, it was a newer Mark IV, and it shrugged off the impacts. If the vehicle were an older tank, armoured-piercing rounds from a rifle were a threat, piercing the armour or sending splashes of molten metal around the inside of the vehicle. A thump sounded as an artillery piece fired from the edge of the village. A tank several hundred yards away screeched to a stop, smoke pouring from the viewing slits as the crew threw open their doors to bail out. Not all escaped.

'They're using artillery on the tanks!' Marsh could not believe the enemy had moved their heavy weapons so close to the trenches. The crews of artillery pieces were vulnerable and their weapons too valuable to risk so far forward. Yet, he was already admiring the German ingenuity. They had discovered a way to defend against the tanks. 'Bloody hell, they're firing over open sights rather than pulling back.'

Machine guns opened fire from several buildings, winking from the fortified positions as the defenders emerged from their dugouts, having weathered the British artillery barrage. The Germans intended to defend the village. A tap-tap-tap came from the front of the tank Marsh sheltered behind. Several rounds glanced off the side, sparks flying. The German machine-gunners sought the soft and fragile infantry walking behind the armoured vehicle. Everyone crouched lower as a fresh storm of bullets flew past. The artillery gun in the village selected a new target on the flank of the attack. Despite the gunner's initial good fortune, the gun barked, and the shot missed.

'Red Devil' cleared the last of the wire, allowing Marsh to order his tigers forward. The trenches were visible, the brown earth parapets scorched by the recent artillery barrage. 'Red Devil' made straight toward the nearest one, a machine gun futilely winking from a sandbagged emplacement, unable to slow the metal monster. The thirty tigers under Marsh's control surged from around the tank, leaving the protection of the lee of the vast vehicle. They ran at the enemy positions, followed by the assault troops of the company. The defensive fire rose in pitch and frequency with the added crump of grenades being used in a last-ditch defence. Before he had time to think, Marsh threw himself into the trench, fighting hand-to-hand with one defender, far too close to use his shotgun to fell the man. The German did not last long. A tiger tore into his throat, distracting him just long enough for Marsh to move the shotgun around and fire point-blank into the man's belly.

The gunfire within the trench soon became sporadic, replaced with the cries of terrified and dying men. Once again, the tigers had been decisive in the bloody hand-to-hand fighting, the assault troops more than sufficient to overwhelm any remaining enemy. The machine gun nest continued to fire, bullets ringing as they struck 'Red Devil'. The tank closed in on the gun position. Mounting the parapet with one of its tracks, the vast land-ship crushed the gun and crew in place, not even pausing as it drove on.

Marsh, however, stopped to take in his surroundings, winded by the sudden action. The attack was progressing, building up an unstoppable momentum. He knew he could not dwell on the horrors he had already seen. He needed to move forward, keeping up with the attack. Marsh ordered the tigers forward into the buildings of the village. Several zombies fell to headshots from the ruins. The close range prevented their armoured helmets from offering protection. More freshly created zombies rose from the trench, gore pouring from them as Marsh seized control, these new tigers rushing to attack their former countrymen. Several tigers were blown into the air by mines the defenders had laid around their positions, yet the maimed tigers still dragged themselves forward, their ruined legs trailing behind, reanimated corpses which would have to be policed up as the company advanced. The risks of a general zombie outbreak meant no damaged zombie could be left to the mercies of chance.

A whooshing noise overwhelmed the sounds of the battlefield. Marsh glimpsed a mushroom-shaped cloud as it rose above a tank, a fierce fire burning through a jagged tear on top of the vehicle. Ammunition continued to pop in the heat. The Germans had scored a hit on the magazine. The crew would have stood no chance, and while Marsh pitied them, he knew their end was quick. Marsh had already seen there were many ways a tank could breakdown or be knocked out, and most options featured the prolonged suffering and agony of the crew. As he watched, the troops behind the vehicle, who had all been blown off their feet, tried to rise. Several of their number dived back to the ground, this time avoiding intense machine gun fire. These men found themselves pinned down, their advance having not yet even reached the German defences.

'Machine gun nests ahead,' Wells shouted to Marsh over the noise. 'They've got us covered. There's no way we'll get close to them without using a tiger charge. 'Red Devil' is too busy to help.'

'It's too open. We'll lose too many tigers. I'm not sure we've got enough to get both nests,' Marsh replied.

'Who the hell is that?' Davies pointed his machete at a rifleman from the King's Rifles. The supporting infantry had caught up as the assault wave fought in the trench. They watched in stunned silence as a lone rifleman rushed towards one of the machine gun nests, immune to the bullets, even as the gunners spotted him. When the man reached throwing distance, he lobbed a Mills bomb before throwing himself to the ground. The machine gun position fell silent as the grenade exploded.

'Bloody hell, he got them,' Wells said, whistling. 'Get the tigers forward into the other gun position, quick while they're distracted by what's going on.'

The tigers rushed the other machine gun position, several falling, hit in the head by the desperate fire of the defenders. Their gun was in a ruined barn, firing through a hole hacked in the wall. A tiger threw itself at the hole, blocking the gap as its torso was riddled with bullets.

Marsh sent in a second tiger, one in possession of a demolition charge. The creature, while limited in its ability to operate anything complex, was more than capable of setting off the charge. It detonated itself behind the first tiger, blowing a larger opening in the wall through which the remaining tigers swarmed. The machine gun fell silent amidst the screams of the defenders.

'Up!' Wells shouted at the assault troops. 'And watch out for mines.'

The British continued their advance into the edge of the village, staying low using any cover available. They had advanced a dozen yards when bullets streamed in from the side, tracer rounds zipping past Marsh.

'They've got us enfiladed!' Wells shouted, pointing to where he thought the gunfire had originated from. A ground-floor window beyond a small open area of land was the source. No tigers were nearby to attack. Marsh would have to move some more into position, which would take time.

Pinned down, the men of the Zombie Corps watched as the riflemen following close behind fell to the ground, also pinned down by the gun position and unable to help. Several of the riflemen no longer moved. A soldier, Marsh thought it was the same one who had just attacked the machine gun post with a grenade, ran around getting the men into cover. The man then ran over to 'Red Devil', streams of bullets chasing him but all failing to hit. He banged on the door and conversed with a crewmember, who cracked the door ajar. Once the tank crew understood what was needed, the vehicle changed direction, heading towards the machine gun nest in the building. 'Red Devil', guns blazing, charged the basement at the best speed it could make. Right down to the last second, Marsh could not credit what appeared to be happening, but the tank continued full ahead, bullets ricocheting off the front armour in a shower of sparks. The vehicle smashed into the building, demolishing a wall and continuing through the building as the roof fell forward onto the street, landing across the body of the tank. Grinding to a halt, the tank went into reverse, spewing out black fumes from the exhausts and further shaking the unstable building. The machine gun crew was crushed in the wreckage.

'Bloody hell,' Wells said, rubbing his eyes, disbelieving the sight of the tank extracting itself from the ruin. 'That thing's still going. I'm glad it's on our side. It's unstoppable.'

'Seems we're not the only people who know how to demolish a building,' Marsh said, his eyes wide.

'The infantry took heavy casualties,' Davies said, having wandered over to talk to his two friends, oblivious to the ongoing battle around him. Marsh could have sworn Davies was humming to himself as he stood in the open, watching the tank reverse out of a cloud of dust. The infantry advanced, even though several gawped at the behaviour of the metal monster. Just as many of the infantry did not get up from the ground upon which they had fallen when the machine gun position revealed itself.

'Let's get moving again,' Marsh said, knowing he could not let the supporting infantry get ahead of his assault force. Minimal gunfire came from the next buildings, so Marsh sent forward the tigers to check they were empty. The zombies were soon followed by the assault troops of the Zombie Corps.

Three tigers entered a stone facade building through the door, intent on hunting down the people they sensed inside. A gush of flame came from the doorway and the three tigers were engulfed. Despite burning, the zombies did not stop their advance, screams announcing the moment they found their prey. As Marsh closed in on the building, one tiger came back out of the door, still burning. The others did not reappear, overwhelmed by the fire which they had taken into the building. Marsh made a choking nose as he smelt the unpleasant smoke. The assault troops joined him in avoiding the odorous cloud. The enemy was using flamethrowers. Marsh and Colonel Hudson suspected the Germans may deploy these weapons as an anti-zombie defence. It seemed the enemy had been of the same mind. While the defenders had not survived, two tigers had been destroyed and the zombie torch moving down the street would not last much longer as it was consumed by the hungry flames.

The last buildings in the village were just as well defended as the first. Several spewed flaming liquid across the open ground whenever tigers or tanks advanced. The tigers were more vulnerable, but tanks were also being knocked out by the flames. 'Red Devil' had caught up with Marsh again, drawing the attention of the defenders. Grenades bounced off the mesh on the roof whenever the vehicle passed too close to a defended building. On both flanks, other tanks charged the enemy defences. Marsh sent his tigers to attack various objectives, as did other handlers who assaulted the village. Yet, it was only when the assault troops were used, the defenders broke. A few defenders surrendered, most could not.

'A nasty business,' Lieutenant Scott said when he joined Marsh and Wells after they stormed the last building. They had all followed the tigers in, helping to clear the defenders. Scott's uniform was covered in mud and dust, his face scratched from shrapnel and debris. He had fought in the trenches as a soldier, and even as an officer, he was not afraid to throw himself into the thick of the combat, and it showed.

'A nasty business indeed, Sir,' Wells replied, brushing imaginary and real dirt off the mechanism of his Chauchat.

'How bad are your casualties?'

'Twenty-three men missing, Sir.' Wells had already conducted a head-count the moment the village was cleared. 'Some of them will turn up as we advance, some we'll never see again.' While fighting, men were often split from their units, rejoining when they got an opportunity. Many were also lost without trace, victims of explosives.

'And you Marsh? How many tigers have you got?'

'I'm not sure, Sir,' Marsh replied. He took his helmet off and scratched his head, unhappy at being less efficient than Wells. He had tried counting, but several zombies were too badly damaged for further use. 'We lost quite a few in the attack. You saw the flamethrowers?' Marsh sucked his teeth. 'Then there are a few tigers which will need policing up, but we also created a few new ones.'

'The tanks took a battering as well,' Scott said. 'I counted ten which were broken down or knocked out. The Germans were ready for them as well as for us.'

'The infantry were bloody well murdered as well. They were well and truly ready for us here.' Wells spat on the ground in disgust. 'The place was fortified, like we expected, but they knew how to deal with tanks and tigers. It's a wonder we've taken the place.'

'Intelligence said it was an experienced unit here. Men who had fought against French tanks,' Marsh said, remembering one of the many briefing documents he had seen.

'Well, we've got the first objective. Get your men, and the tigers, ready to move on.' Reloading his revolver, Scott gave the order. 'We'll move out in five minutes and head straight for our next objective, as planned.

The barrage is just about ready to shift beyond the village and we need to be ready to keep up if we're to stand a chance.'

Scott looked around for someone to act as a runner. 'Davies, let the tankers know we're almost ready.' He examined the man. 'And put away that bloody ridiculous blade of yours before you scare them to death.'

24

THE ROAD TO MASNIERE

'Cambrai was the first emergence of combined arms
warfare and the modern British Army. By the end of
the war, no other army matched the resources, skills
and experience the British fielded. This was the first
glimpse of an unstoppable war machine.'

Milton Davies, A History of Zombies and Warfare,
(London, 2016)

T HE SECOND GOAL OF the day was the breaching of the main
German defensive line. This began just under half a mile beyond the village. The rest of the Royal Zombie Corps had taken
heavy casualties in the assault on La Vacquerie, with the supporting
infantry suffering worse, but the advance still had momentum. Large
numbers of British troops moved forward on the German trenches,
with reinforcements not far behind, and everywhere freshly created
tigers joined the force. From what Marsh could tell, only a dozen accompanying tanks moved forward with the attacking waves of British

troops. The rest remained in and around La Vacquerie, broken down or destroyed in the fierce fighting over the village.

No defensive fire came from the main German lines, smothered as they were by a smoke-laced barrage. Less wire also obstructed the British as they advanced, although the remaining tanks were still essential for clearing paths through what remained. Abandoned German artillery pieces were scattered across the terrain, some spiked to prevent their capture intact; many more showed signs they had fallen victim to the new British tactic of counter-battery fire. The remains of their crews evidenced the fierce British return fire. Little resistance was encountered, the occasional sniper or machine gun post, each dealt with by either tank or tiger.

'We've got to be ready for the flamethrowers,' Marsh said to Scott as they advanced. The creeping barrage shifted from the German front line. As they closed on their next objective, he worried about this new defensive innovation. 'The tigers are far too vulnerable to them. They might not knock out a zombie straight away, but a flamethrower does enough damage to knock them out, eventually.'

'Wells, pass the word to the assault troops. Prioritise anyone who looks like they're carrying a flamethrower,' Scott ordered. Wells shouted out the command and it was passed down the line.

'I'm sending the tigers forward. We're close enough now.' Marsh did not wait for a response, knowing he had the tactical command in this situation. He launched his tigers at the still silent German line. The defenders would only now be exiting their deep dugouts, the creeping barrage having moved on. They would be in a hurry, knowing a British assault was incoming. It would be a race between shell-shocked veterans leaving the safety of their dugout and the racing zombies who would soon leap into the artillery-wrecked trench, followed by the assault troops.

A roar of flame caught his attention as the tigers disappeared into the enemy lines. The flame poured along the trench from right in front of Marsh. His worries about fire were more timely than he would have liked. One of the assault team to his right got a clear shot at the German carrying the flamethrower, aiming before firing his rifle. The round hit the fuel tank the German carried and there was a sudden thumping noise as a column of flame roared out of the trench. Marsh was so close the heat burned his eyebrows and for a moment he wondered at the bravery of a man who would strap on an explosive fuel tank in the seconds after a creeping bombardment moved on. Marsh leapt into the trench, to the side of the burning mass that could only have been the soldier who had carried the flamethrower. Next to the remains were two other defenders who had not escaped the blast.

'Look out,' Wells shouted a warning as he leapt into the trench. He tried to train his machine gun onto a target Marsh could not see.

Marsh cursed at his own inattention, turning to find the entrance to a dugout behind him. The deep dugout was cut into the parapet, and full of Germans, protected from the most powerful of artillery barrages. Several defenders emerged, ready to man the parapets and shoot down the advancing British. In an instant, horror registered on their faces, the enemy had already arrived. Marsh lowered his shotgun, firing and working the lever furiously, hitting the emerging men in face and chest, while more men behind them tried to push their falling comrades out of the way. From out of nowhere, Matthews arrived. He threw first one Mills bomb, then another, in through the crowded entrance. Shrieks of terror emerged from the men inside as the bombs flew deep inside. Marsh did not think to get out of the way, but

Matthews pushed his friend to one side of the entrance, following at the same time.

A crump was followed by a piercing scream. This ceased with a second explosion. The shock of the blasts travelled through the earthen wall, where Marsh had fallen when Matthews pushed him clear. Iñ an instant, Matthews was on his feet, charging into the dugout. He held a bowie knife in his hand, intent on clearing the position. Marsh followed, shotgun at the ready, but expecting any survivors to surrender. Through the smoke from the explosives, Marsh could make out the scent of open sewers. His eyes adjusted to the gloom, and it became apparent there were no survivors. The enclosed concrete space had ensured the bomb fragments and blast tore apart the occupants. As Marsh clawed his way back into the daylight, his stomach turned. No matter the number of unpleasant experiences he suffered, he always discovered a new way to be horrified by the brutality and bloodshed.

Once out of the dugout and back in the trench, the two men advanced along its length, soon establishing the defence had collapsed under the vicious onslaught of tigers and assault troops of the Royal Zombie Corps. Tigers fed on their victims, exploiting the lack of orders from Marsh. Yet the defence had again been fierce, another successful, but costly, assault. Many corpses lay where they fell, including a great number of charred tigers. There had been widespread use of flamethrowers along this defensive line.

'We've got to keep pushing forward,' Lieutenant Scott said. Marsh spotted him waving at the next bend in the trench. 'Keep them unbalanced. Get ready to move on again in five minutes. We've got to keep up with the barrage.'

'I'll gather up all I can, Sir, but things are a bit confused and I'm not sure we'll have many tigers to move forward.' Marsh had seen more than a dozen tigers, and suspected quite a few more would be within range of his commands, but he had seen many more incapacitated or destroyed by the fierce fight. Occasional gunshots told him the assault squad was working hard, policing up the less mobile zombies.

'Do what you can. We've got enough of the company to keep pushing forward. The enemy is collapsing. One more line and we'll be through,' Scott said, close enough to grab and hold on to Marsh's arm. The officer was convinced the breakthrough was imminent.

'Where are the Hun?' Matthews asked Wells as they finished their capture of the lightly held final defensive line.

'This was meant to be their last line. They fought bloody hard for the other two. There should have been more of them here.' Wells pursed his lips and tilted his head to the side. The resistance in the last line had been very weak. Only a dozen defenders held the stretch of trench.

'Most of the bunkers were unmanned, not just the trenches.' Marsh had sent several tigers to assault the concrete fortifications, but they found no defenders, even though equipment had been put in place.

'The wire was out there. What were they up to?' Wells thought out loud, referring to the bank of barbed wire before the final trench system. 'It's almost as if they've only just finished this line and haven't manned it yet.'

They did not have to wait long before Lieutenant Scott arrived to confirm the theory. 'It looks like Hun didn't get around to deploying troops to this bit of the line yet. We knew they were short of men but didn't suspect they were this pushed for bodies. One of our infantry officers has interrogated a prisoner. The lad confirmed his unit was taking over this position, and he'd been sent out in advance. The rest were to arrive today.'

'Should we still be expecting them then, Sir? We can give them a warm welcome,' Wells said, clapping his hands together in a show of mock bravado. He knew the surrounding men would look to him for a lead. They would be concerned about hundreds of fresh and heavily armed German soldiers turning up.

'No, we'll be moving on. The advance is proving to be such a success that the enemy will march to our tune for a while. We'll be pushing forward as planned. It's open country now, no prepared defences. We've broken through.' Scott's face was serious for a few moments as he checked his watch. 'We'll move again soon, as scheduled. We'll bump into the men who were headed here, so make sure you have pickets out ready to report back if they make contact.'

'Will do, Sir,' Wells replied, lifting his chin. This time they would be ready to advance across open country. Between Wells and Marsh, they had worked up a tactic which would keep the tigers moving. At least it would be a better approach than the debacle Simpson had foisted upon them the last time they smashed through the enemy lines and advanced into open country.

The soldiers moved over the open and undamaged countryside. They all noticed the strangeness compared to advancing through the unreal terrain of no man's land. At any second, a machine gun could begin the chatter of death. To be outside the enfolding protection of earthen walls was unnatural to the men as they advanced towards the distant horizon. In territory mostly unscarred by the fighting, there was a distinct absence of shell-holes to provide cover. Some men felt naked, taught by both their training and bitter experience, to keep below ground level if they wanted to survive. Concealment could still be had in this undamaged countryside, a bush here, a small wood there. This cover could also work for the enemy. Every shadow could hide a machine gun ready to fire upon their vulnerable bodies.

As the British advanced, they once again encountered small groups of the enemy, the vast majority of whom were so surprised to be caught up during a British advance, they promptly surrendered. A few enemies fought back, each group soon extinguished by the armed pickets and the tigers Marsh maintained at the forward edge of the advance. While the advancing men might have been aware of their vulnerabilities, the tigers were not. Good pace was maintained as the Allied troops advanced in a series of broad columns, piercing deep into the heart of German-occupied territory. The panicked defenders found themselves pinned between tank and zombie, pushed back against the river far to the rear of their positions.

Approaching Masnieres, a village several kilometres southwest of Cambrai, Marsh and his advancing tigers linked up with another advancing column from the 29th Division. The elation of such a rapid advance was infectious, and there was a great deal of back-patting as the two groups of troops merged. Together they headed to the final objective of the day, the canal crossings at Masnieres. With the crossings at hand, the most optimistic goal for the first day was achievable. The men were ecstatic. A challenging goal was about to be achieved, in stark contrast to the constant failures of the preceding years of war. A victorious mood spread among the troops and the horrors of the fierce battles of the day were draining away.

'We're nearly there, Sarge,' Matthews said, walking along next to Marsh. He had relaxed into a comfortable stroll, the terror of the advance across the open ground wearing thin as the miles passed with no sustained threat. His rifle slung on his shoulder, he kicked a stone along before him. For all intents and purposes, he could have been going for a walk back home in Bedfordshire.

'It seems that way,' Marsh replied. He checked his zombies were keeping pace on the flanks of the column. He did not want to be caught out by a sudden attack, not so close to their goal.

'We'll get a nice beer in Masnieres. I bet the Germans have left loads there.' Matthews licked his lips. The advance had already brought them through various German supply dumps, overrun by the rapidity of the attack. He pulled a bottle of wine out of his satchel, one of many liberated by Wells from a cache a few miles back.

'When we get to Masnieres, we can have several beers, I should think.' Marsh took a swig from the bottle when Matthews offered it to him.

'We'll get across the canal and then we'll be able to help ourselves to the very best the German Army can offer. What with all their supply routes going through Cambrai, I should imagine they'll have everything there. You know, I once heard Germans make excellent beer. I even tried a Dortmunder, a pale beer, one time on a trip to London. It tasted good.'

'Yes, with a bit of luck, we'll have their supplies and their booze. Their supplies will be on one side of the canal with us, and their army will be stuck on the other.' Marsh passed the bottle back. 'Mind you, don't let Scott or Simpson see that bottle, or you'll be up on a charge.'

'Scott'll ask for a bottle all for himself, and who cares what Simpson says or does?' Matthews almost shouted the last words, comfortable in the illusion of a peacetime stroll.

'Speak of the devil, here comes Scott.'

'He can smell the booze, Sarge,' Matthews tucked the bottle back into his first aid satchel. 'How goes things, Sir?' Matthews asked Scott. The officer ignored Matthews' suspicious behaviour.

'Masnieres is just over the next rise, we'll be there within the hour. Then we'll secure the bridge over the canal. After that, we'll get some rest with the cavalry passing through to take over the advance,' Scott said. He stopped and placed a hand on Matthew's arm, ending his stroll. 'Give me some of that bottle, you greedy bastard.'

Matthews groaned at being caught out, handing over the half-drunk bottle. Scott pulled out the cork and took a long swig. 'Ah, that's good. Wasn't so long ago I was one of you. Remember, I know all the tricks.'

'It's not fair, Sir. How's a dishonest soldier meant to get away with anything when there's an officer like you in charge?' Matthews whined, but his grin made it clear the complaint was a sign of friendly respect.

'You'll get away with things the same way we always have, any time no-one's looking.'

Scott fell to the floor as a bullet cracked past, an arc of red flying from his back. Everyone froze for a fraction of a second before diving to the ground, hoping whoever had fired the shot would not seek them out. Even the tigers mimicked Marsh's movements, seeking cover, his preservation urge surging through his mental link to the zombies.

'Sniper!' An unnecessary call came from the lead troops.

'Dan, Dan!' Matthews was already leaning over his fellow veteran, blood spreading across the mud beneath the officer. Scott gasped for air.

Oblivious to the danger, Matthews tried to staunch the flow of blood from the entry hole in the officer's battledress. Marsh scrabbled around in Matthews' first-aid bag, pulling out a field dressing which Matthews let him press on the wound.

'His back, as well,' Matthews said, lifting Scott's upper body off the ground. Marsh got another dressing and attended to it.

'Shit, that hurts,' Scott complained in a weak voice. 'Hurts worse than the bloody shits.' He coughed, blood speckling his lips. A bubbling wheeze sounded from his mouth.

'It's gonna be fine, Dan. We'll get you back to the aid station,' Matthews said, comforting his friend, but knowing the situation was futile.

'Stretcher-bearers!' Marsh called. Scott was consumed by a fit of coughing. 'Stretcher-bearers!' It was not looking good. The bullet had punched straight through a lung, possibly worse.

The two men giving aid ducked as another bullet cracked by, but otherwise they ignored the risk to themselves.

'I see him!' Came a nearby shout, 'Up in that thicket.' Several shots rang out as the rest of the company swamped the threat with a storm of lead.

'Stay with me, Dan,' Matthews said, the panic in his voice rising. He and Scott had been in the army since the beginning of the war, Scott a regular and Matthews an early volunteer. They had not known each other before joining the Corps, but as veterans, they had been drawn to each other.

Scott stopped coughing, his eyes glazing and his body relaxing.

'Don't die, you bastard!' Matthews pressed harder on the dressing as if he could force the life back into his friend.

'Sergeant Marsh, get over here!' Simpson shouted in his best parade ground voice.

Marsh took his time, picking his way through the rubble which was once the outskirts of Masnieres, wondering what the bloody idiot wanted now?

'Get your slovenly backside here now. Stop taking your bloody time. The war will have ended before you get your act together,' Simpson growled as Marsh strolled over. 'Tell me, what the hell have you done to my tigers, you worthless sack of shit?'

'I've done exactly what should have been done.' Marsh did not rise to the abuse. He did not respect Simpson, but he held back out of respect for his rank.

'What's that supposed to mean?' Simpson's nostrils flared.

'I didn't stick my head in the ground like you. So I finished it, Sir,' Marsh did not care how much he offended Simpson. Scott was gone, an outstanding officer and a friend. Simpson was useless in the role.

'What!' the guttural roar came from Simpson. 'I'll have you on a charge, I'll—.'

'You were making a frontal assault again,' Marsh interrupted, his voice firmed by his tactical competence. 'It doesn't matter how many times I tell you, you just don't get it. You can't take out a bunch of fortified houses by just running tigers at them. That's not what tigers are for. Hell, you just don't understand, do you?'

'You blew up my tigers,' Simpson complained, not quite losing the power of speech as he spluttered.

'Yes, I blew up a couple of your tigers. That's what they're for. Both of them carried demolition charges. I had them take out the buildings. And what were you doing? You pointlessly threw them away. Your own men took casualties as well.'

'But you overrode my handers. You took control of my tigers without my permission. You wait until I tell Lieutenant Scott about this. I'll have you on a field punishment.'

'Lieutenant Scott's dead, so he won't give a damn. And your stupid handlers blindly followed your idiotic orders. You'd all be dead now if I'd not intervened.'

On clearing the rise concealing Scott's killer, Masnieres had come into view. It had turned out their objective was already under attack from another British column, led by Lieutenant Simpson. The assailants were grinding themselves down against a series of fortified houses on the edge of the village, the cowed handlers of Simpson's company having sent their tigers into action rather than using the tactics developed for such a situation. Marsh had taken in the scene's futility. Perhaps it was the rawness of Scott's death, but instead of showing his usual restraint around Simpson, Marsh intervened. He identified two tigers with satchel charges, seized control and sent the walking bombs to end the German resistance. It had been a minor challenge for Marsh to take control of Simpson's tigers. The handlers only verbally controlled the zombies, so their control had been over-ridden by Marsh's mental commands. Mullen was not present. As Simpson's most capable handler, the Irishman's presence might have prevented Marsh from wrestling control. But then, Marsh knew Mullen would also have kept Simpson away from the tactical side of things.

'Where's Mullen? He'd have used the tigers the right way?' Marsh asked, worried at Mullen's absence.

'Mullen caught some shrapnel a way back, walking wounded. Now, I'm in charge and you have no right to interfere,' Simpson complained. 'I'll speak to the Colonel about—'

'On the battlefield, I'm in charge. I'm the handler, not you.' Marsh's temper snapped. He sent a command to a nearby tiger.

'I'm the officer and you're just a worthless piece of shit who would never have even been given a rifle if we weren't so desperate.'

'Look to your left, Sir, and you'll see why I'm in charge,' Marsh said almost in a whisper. He was icy calm.

'Don't do it,' someone muttered. Maybe it was Matthews, or perhaps Davies.

Simpson held his breath and turned his head. He stared at a tiger less than three feet away. The creature had crept up upon the officer, unnoticed. The colour drained from Simpson's face as he recognised his precarious situation.

'Now I'll thank you to keep yourself away from the front, Sir.' Steel entered Marsh's voice. Simpson had never before detected such strength in his rival. 'Let the real soldiers get on with the soldiering.'

25

FLYING FOX

'Haig through the Hindenburg Line'
  Headline in the Daily Mail, 23rd November 1917.

'There was a bloody great big tank on the bridge. I dunno which damn idiot decided they could just trot one of those bloody monsters across. Well, the first one drove onto the bridge, which was only just wide enough to fit it. I was about to cross using the path along the side of the roadway when there was this creaking and screeching. Everyone scarpered and before we knew it, the whole bridge had collapsed under the weight of the tank.

You should have seen the sight. The canal isn't deep, and the tank was almost entirely above water. The whole bridge had collapsed, folded around this tank. All these Royal Engineers were running around having fits while the crew of "Flying Fox" bailed out and climbed up the remains of the bridge. It was sheer bloody chaos. I remember this cavalry officer, great big bushy moustache he had. Well, he was screaming blue murder at one of the tankies. Of course, it didn't matter how much he screamed, no-one was going to fix the bridge in a hurry. Bushy moustache had missed his glorious opportunity to charge into the enemy's rear.

Thing is, this was the only decent bridge for miles and by the time we'd got something else ready, well, the Germans had counter-attacked.'

Interview with Private Gavin Johnson, published in Barnes, S 'The Great War Remembered' (1978, Oxford)

'WE'VE GOT BOTH COMBAT companies across the canal. The Colonel says we need to hold on while the engineers get a bridge into place,' Wells said. He shook his head. 'He can't get the rest of the battalion across as the infantry are monopolising all the other crossings. They're desperate to get across to build a bridgehead.'

'Stuff the bridgehead. What about continuing the breakthrough? The Germans'll set up defensive positions over there if we let up the pressure.' Marsh pointed a finger at a wood a little to the east.

'Our orders are to hold until the cavalry passes through. How they'll get the cavalry across the canal, I don't know. It'll be them, not us, that'll lead the breakthrough.'

'Well, everything was going too well,' Marsh said, taking off his helmet and running his fingers through his sweaty hair.

'There's a silver lining.' Wells patted his new toy. 'Seeing the boys in the tanks are out of the fight, they've lent me this.' He held a Lewis Gun, complete with the distinct round magazine on top. 'It's got a faster rate of fire and easier reload. It's also much less likely to jam than my old Chauchat. Besides, a spring broke in the old girl, so I needed a replacement.'

'I'm surprised the tankers swapped with you.' Marsh was also surprised Wells had changed his choice of weapon. He had always seemed wedded to the French gun and not interested in getting a Lewis.

'You could say that they didn't notice they'd swapped it,' Wells said, shuffling his feet.

'And what other ill-got gains have you for us, Josh?' Marsh recognised what his friend had been up to.

'I got a bag of stuff.' He pulled the bag closer and removed the items, one by one. 'There's a few Hun potato-masher grenades. I picked them up in one of their supply dumps. They might come in useful. Oh, and a few bottles of their beer as well.' The bottles clinked together as he laid them on the ground. 'There was some food, but believe me, what they feed their troops makes our bullied beef appear amazing in comparison.' Wells wrinkled his nose, remembering his bite of the sawdust tainted bread. 'How they expect their lads to fight on what they feed them, I don't know.'

'Perhaps the blockade is biting?' Marsh asked, referring to the long-running and famous blockade of Germany. It was one of the few things the Royal Navy obviously contributed.

'Also, I got you this,' Wells said, revealing a sword he had been concealing. 'You might find it useful, considering some of the close scrapes you seem to get into.'

'Thanks Josh. Where the hell did you get it?' Marsh drew the blade from the scabbard.

'I traded it with some of the King's Rifles. A corporal said he'd found it in a bunker. He swapped it for some of the wine I had.'

'You shouldn't have.' Marsh admired the gift, a straight-bladed infantry sword with a Prussian eagle-shaped guard and the cipher of Kaiser Wilhelm stamped on the blade.

'Well, I had more wine than I could carry anyhow.' Wells watched as Marsh swished the blade around. 'You be careful with that. You'll have someone's eye out.'

'That's the idea,' Marsh chuckled, trying a fencing style jab before examining the weapon again. 'Could come in very useful.'

'Aye, but be careful. It's not a Scot's claymore. Stab with it, no slashing and smashing.'

'Where's mine?' Davies asked. He was slumped next to them with his back to the stone wall.

'Don't you already have a machete, Colin?' Marsh asked. 'I'm pretty sure I've seen you sharpening it a time or two?'

'Ha, bloody ha,' Davies replied. 'I'll swap you two tins of corned beef for that there sword.'

'Not likely. Anyway, who do you think you are, Jack the Ripper? Fixated on blades you are.'

'I wasn't even born back then. I'm not an old fossil like you.'

'Hardly. I'm not that old,' Marsh complained, nevertheless feeling old because of the aches of accumulated combat experience.

'Josh, can I have the next blade you find?' Davies asked.

'We'll see,' Josh replied. He mimed taking out a waiter's notebook and pencil. 'I think I'm taking orders, Sir. Would you like the blade gold inlaid or not? Perhaps a general's blade, or are your tastes simpler, a mere lieutenant's?'

Davies snorted, waving a dismissive hand. He reached into his breast pocket and withdrew a packet of cigarettes, sharing them around.

'I can't believe Dan's gone,' Marsh said as he studied the burning end of his cigarette. Lieutenant Scott had been with them since they had arrived in France, an experienced soldier who had first deployed with them from the replacement depot. Scott was promoted to officer as the use of zombies gained traction. The Corps were eager to advance capable men already known to them, rather than drawing from the much diminished pool of the traditional officer class.

'I can't believe it either,' Davies said. 'One minute he's here, then the next he's gone. It makes no bloody sense.'

'Here.' Wells offered an uncapped hip-flask.

'I thought I'd bought it earlier. That advance to the first line was bloody awful, especially when those riflemen got pinned down. But when we got into the village and the Germans started using flamethrowers. That was when Hun nearly got me.' His hand shook as he took a long drag on his cigarette.

Marsh and Wells waited patiently, passing the flask, while he exhaled. Davies was not one to get things off his chest by talking, preferring to conceal his upsets and nerves by sharpening his blade. If he was telling them what happened, he needed to share his burdens.

'Thing was, the Hun, he was only a child. He must've been barely old enough to fight. It's not right, he shouldn't have been out here with us.'

'Well, we've got our fair share of lads like that. They lie about their age when they join up. It's not like the recruiting sergeants are going to turn them away,' Wells explained.

'I understand Josh, but that still doesn't make it right. I should be dead. He had me cold. I froze. He looked just like my little brother, Sam. Like I saw a ghost, my own brother in a German uniform. Hell, my brother isn't even old enough yet, and neither was this kid,' Davies said, shaking his head. 'Well, he will be old enough soon.'

'It's tough. We all find it hard. We're not doing a normal job and it'll mess with your head given half a chance,' Marsh said, hoping Davies would find some comfort in the words. A memory of his own brother flashed into his mind before he suppressed the next image.

'I shouldn't have frozen, but you see, he froze too.' Davies carried on as if he had not heard Marsh. 'He had me in his sights. He couldn't miss, but he just froze.'

'There's nothing wrong with that. Heat of the battle. Everyone freezes at some point,' Wells considered. 'You freeze sometimes, and at other times you don't. Sounds like you got lucky.'

'Yes, but he should have nailed me. Him freezing. Well, that gave me my chance. Before I knew it, I was on him. My blade took him down. The look on Sam's face,' Davies sobbed. The stress of the moment made him conflate the German and his own brother.

'He wasn't your brother, mate,' Wells said. He moved along the wall to hug Davies. 'Sam's safe at home in Blighty.'

'But his look.... It was just like him....'

The first sign of the German counter-attack arrived when a lookout spotted an advance on the British positions. Only a few hundred of the British had got across the canal, many of them already exhausted from the rapid advance. Preparation of defensive positions had been going on since the first crossing, but in a few brief hours, little progress had been made. The next stage of the advance was still expected, and the men were reluctant to spend much effort on preparing positions they would soon vacate. The Royal Zombie Corps remained in the spearhead, their assault troops made up half the force across the canal. They were ready for the next stage of the advance. However, the collapse of the bridge over the canal had slowed the reinforcements to a trickle. The whole advance was now delayed.

During the intervening period, Wells and Marsh scouted the surrounding land. They were just as exhausted as the infantry, and snatched brief sleeps, fragmented by the echoes of their experiences during the rapid advance. Matthews used the time organising a reluctant group of assault troops, making them dig foxholes along a stone wall. While he worked on this, Morgan sipped at his hip-flask, not the only soldier anaesthetising themselves with alcohol while they awaited the next phase of the battle. Morgan kept Davies company, while Davies wrote a letter to his younger brother, hoping to excise his own personal demons.

Marsh considered his earlier liberation of several loaves of freshly baked bread from a house ahead of their position, something the group of friends enjoyed together. At least, it had been baked earlier that day, left in haste when the Germans evacuated the village as the danger from the British advance became clear. Often Wells provided the treats, but Wells was distracted by the number of buildings which could provide cover for an advancing enemy. Once they finished the bread, the two sergeants had gone exploring to allay Wells' fears.

Marsh and Wells jumped at the first crack of gunfire and a shouted alert. The commotion came from further round the bridgehead, but everyone was on their guard. Crouching down, close to the ground, they made their way to the wall of a nearby barn, sneaking glances around the corner. It should give them a good view of what was happening.

'Shit! Here they come,' Wells said as he spotted movement.

'Where? I can't see them.' Marsh expected predictable ranks of advancing field grey soldiers.

'The yellow farmhouse,' Wells pointed off to their own flank. 'I just saw a bunch sprint into cover behind it.'

Marsh watched for a minute. Just when he thought Wells was seeing things, he spotted movement. Two soldiers sprinted from behind a bush to an outbuilding. The Germans were not attacking dumbly; they were using their own Storm-trooper tactics. It would be a tough fight, as these were experienced troops who knew their job and were armed for the task. Their tactics were like those used by the Royal Zombie Corps, and Marsh knew that even without fielding tigers, the enemy would be well-armed and ferocious in their assault. German artillery dropped on the British bridgehead.

'We need to get back,' Wells said, already leaving along the quickest route back to their position. Marsh carried his shotgun, but Wells had left his machine gun with Matthews so they could move unencumbered. 'Straight across the road, by the trees. That'll get us there quick.'

'What about the shelling?' Marsh asked as the artillery fire picked up, some of it smoke, some air-burst shrapnel.

'We'll have to take our chances. We stay here, we'll be captured in no time.' With that, Wells was off.

26

BRIDGEHEAD

'A general breakthrough is on the cards. Our forward
elements have crossed the St Quentin Canal at Masnieres.'

Extract from a communique sent to the Field Mar-
shal Haig by Major-General Henry de Beauvoir de
Lisle, commanding 29th Division during the Battle of
Cambrai. Published by On the Conduct of the War
Committee, House of Lords Select Committee, 1919.

T HE BRIEF JOURNEY BACK to the stone wall was eventful. The
two men dived behind cover several times, each occasion barely
protecting themselves from nearby shell bursts. Shell splinters had always zipped harmlessly past. Marsh doubted they would have survived
if the artillery were firing more shrapnel and less smoke. Visibility
dropped to a few feet where the smoke was thickest, and still the
artillery fed the growing smoke screen.

'Get down, will yer!' Morgan shouted over the noise as they regained their positions. The Welshman lay in a shallow scrape he had dug behind the wall. He was furiously digging, trying to get deeper underground to avoid the shelling.

'I can't see bugger all, through this damn smoke,' Matthews said, as Marsh and Wells collapsed next to him in the shallow foxhole he had dug. They were busy getting their breath back, having sprinted flat out before vaulting the stone wall.

'Did you get the lads ready?' Wells asked through his gasps.

'They're all ready.' Matthews' voice was calm and professional against the noise of battle. 'We saw some Huns moving towards us when the barrage began. They looked like they meant business.'

'They'll be here soon enough.' Wells took his Lewis Gun when Matthews offered it back. 'Alfie, have you got your tigers ready?'

'What?' Marsh had forgotten his role. 'Oh yes. In a group like we planned, not spread out.' Rather than spread the tigers out piecemeal along the line, Marsh intended to hold his tigers back, ready to counter-attack in force at a decisive moment. Simpson remained with this reserve, along with several other handlers who would lead the tigers should Marsh be incapacitated. Unfortunately, as Mullen was out of action, the remaining handlers were limited in their skills. Marsh worried Simpson would not have any competent minds to hold him back from rash, ill-judged decisions.

'Over there! There they are!' A shout came from the far end of the wall. In front, there were a few buildings, walls, shrubs, and trees. Most obscured by the shifting smoke.

'Where? I can't see a thing.' Wells called back.

'The pink house. Someone looked around the side.'

They looked again for the elusive enemy. The pink house could just be seen through the smoke, with no signs of life.

'By the trees!' The shadowy figures moved through the smoke before taking cover. Several smoke rounds fell across the front of the British positions, reducing visibility.

'Bugger, they're moving in and we can't see them,' Wells complained. 'Can't you use the tigers to sniff them out or something?'

'I could do, but don't forget, the Germans aren't advancing through the smoke yet. They're sitting just behind. If I put the tigers out there, the Germans'll pick them off at leisure.' Marsh thought through the idea. It might work once the enemy advanced, but it would mean the tigers operating unsupported by infantry. 'Besides, we concentrated the tigers so we could counter-attack. If we want to go hunting in the smoke, we'll need to split them up again. It'll take time to get them into position.'

'Stick with the original plan, then?'

'Too right,' Marsh replied.

A sudden shift in the shelling announced the next stage. To harass any reinforcements, the focus of the bombardment moved back to the canal crossing and far bank. The few shells still landing close by stoked the smoke screen.

'Here they come, lads!' Wells positioned the bipod of his Lewis on the wall, cocking the gun, ready to open fire on anything emerging from the smoke. Along the improvised line, the British readied themselves. 'Give 'em hell!'

The first shadowy figures emerged from the smoke, mere yards away from the defenders. The German tactics had brought the storm-troopers in close, ready for their assault. These storm-troopers were good, Marsh acknowledged. They knew what to do and were trained for this type of assault. None of the advancing Germans ran in straight lines at the British positions. The enemy zigged and zagged in and out of the drifting smoke, almost impossible targets for the defenders. Even at close range, the lack of visibility made the attackers harder to hit, and few fell to the initial volleys of defensive fire.

Wells opened fire with a series of short bursts from his machine gun, seeking targets appearing from, and disappearing in, the smoke. Marsh fired his shotgun at a silhouette running at him. He missed as the figure changed direction, disappearing into a drift of smoke, no longer a direct threat. Marsh was concerned what the situation would be like elsewhere on the bridgehead, where regular infantry held the line, not the well-armed assault troops of the Royal Zombie Corps. Although the infantry were better equipped to fight close quarters battles than earlier in the war, they still did not possess the close-range fire-power of the Zombie assault troops.

That was the last conscious thought Marsh had. The storm-troopers fell upon his position, and a desperate battle ensued. Grenades flew as the enemy sprinted the remaining yards. Heavy fire from the defenders took a toll on the attackers as they left the concealing smoke, but their momentum was too great to halt. Well trained, and heavily armed, the German storm-troopers overran the British position, hand-to-hand fighting taking place along the length of the line.

Wells turned his Lewis Gun to their flank, enfilading the enemy along one length of the wall, even as the assailants leapt over the barrier to close with their prey. Marsh shot at a screaming grey uniform charging at his busy friend, the impact of the shotgun round lifting the man into the air. Time became sluggish as the attackers swamped the position. Brutal hand-to-hand fighting took place. Both sides were well-armed for the close-quarter combat. An uncountable number of clubs, knives, and bats appeared. The weapons of ancient warfare were in the ascendent in the middle of a modern industrialised battlefield. Wells discarded his Lewis Gun when it ran out of ammunition, drawing his stiletto knife to deal with a nearby attacker who had vaulted over the wall. At the same moment, Marsh's shotgun emptied. He discarded it, drawing his new sword, using the hilt as a knuckle-duster to smash down an attacker.

'They just keep coming! There's too many of them!' Marsh shouted, a note of panic entering his voice.

'Call in the tigers!' Wells snarled, leaping at another attacker.

Through the smoke, Marsh glimpsed the battle. The men of the Royal Zombie Corps were holding their own, but the sheer number of attackers would soon tell. He knew if the infantry elsewhere in the bridgehead were suffering from as ferocious an assault, they would be on the verge of collapse. The time had arrived. Now was the moment. Without the tigers, the position was lost. Ducking behind the wall, Marsh issued the detailed mental commands to the tigers held in reserve. He would spread them in groups across the bridgehead, supporting the vulnerable conventional infantry. He just hoped he had the numbers to make a difference.

'Achtung Zombie!' cried a German masked from Marsh by the drifting smoke.

Marsh watched as a pair of tigers emerged from the same direction, running towards him. Snarling, the zombies tore into the attackers with abandon. The assault troops of the Royal Zombie Corps cheered as their zombies arrived, although the cheers were short-lived as the soldiers returned to the defence of their position.

The German storm-troopers were forced back, the ferocity of the defence trumping their own substantial martial prowess. As the attack faltered, the first victims of the tigers reanimated, adding to the number of zombies under Marsh's command. While some tigers had been defeated by luck, or calculated German shots, the number of zombies was swelled by the reanimations. The balance was tipping and Marsh noticed it as he sheathed his sword and retrieved his shotgun.

The remaining enemy retreated into the smoke, a few zombies using their senses to hunt down the withdrawing targets. Marsh watched as a tiger advanced into the smoke some way off. It had picked up the scent of a man, speeding up to make an attack. A shriek from the smoke confirmed his assessment just before the smoke flared. A roaring noise was repeated through much of the smoke the enemy had retreated into, the flame lighting up the clouds as the tigers chased their prey. It took Marsh a few seconds to understand what the signs meant.

'Wells, get everyone ready!' Marsh called, hoping Wells could hear. 'I'm pulling the tigers off the chase. They'll be coming back through our lines. The Hun have moved up flamethrowers ready for us.'

'Flamethrowers?' Wells asked, not connecting the events of the last minute with the weapon.

'Yes, flamethrowers. These Germans know what they're doing and they know we've concentrated all our zombies here. The tigers can't chase down retreating troops if they've got flamethrowers in position ready to take out the advancing tigers.'

'Friendlies coming back! Hold your fire!' Wells shouted. The cry was taken up along the line just before the first returning tigers emerged from the clearing smoke screen. Some tigers had got too close to the flamethrowers and were aflame.

'We've lost quite a few to the flamethrowers,' Marsh said to Wells, who had joined him to consult on their next course of action.

'But didn't we pick up a lot of new tigers when we fought off the attack?' Wells changed the pan magazine of the Lewis Gun he had just retrieved.

'That's true, we did.' Marsh suspected there were still many more zombies than had been the case at the commencement of the German counter-attack. 'I'm going to send them back to Simpson. He can do any other policing which needs attending to. Few are still in combat condition.'

The damaged zombies, which were still mobile, had to be destroyed, not just the seriously burnt ones the assault troops had already dealt with. Battlefield hygiene was essential to ensure the syndrome did not spread out of control, even if it would be temporarily advantageous. There had been several zombie outbreaks in the trenches since the discovery of the reanimated corpses. Both sides had used combat troops to put down outbreaks, and it was one of those policing actions which had led to the formation of the Corps. During that action, Marsh had uniquely taken control of several zombies. Neither the French, nor the Germans, experienced much fortune with the zombies and so far only the British Empire employed the creatures in combat. A rumour of a major outbreak behind the German lines had led to the redeployment of thousands of troops to deal with it. The French suffered the loss of several regiments in one outbreak, amounting to thousands of men. During the French outbreak, only the scale of the military build-up in the area had allowed them to regain control of the situation. No-one knew what would happen if there was a widespread outbreak, everyone feared the consequences.

'Alfie, have you ever wondered what would happen if some feral zombies got loose in a city?' Morgan asked. Morgan, Davies and Matthews had found their two sergeants, the squad turning to the business of readying their position for the next enemy attack. 'I don't much like how you keep them under control. It's creepy, but it bloody well works. Wouldn't it be sheer bloody slaughter if there were no handlers? I mean, we'd be the ones slaughtered, not the zombies.'

'Bloody hell, Taff, isn't this enough bloodshed for you?' Wells asked. 'What do you think would happen in a city?'

'He has a point.' Marsh put his hand out for the hip flask Morgan sipped from. 'What the hell is this?' He coughed as the harsh liquor burnt his throat.

'Some liberated brandy. Lovely stuff.' Morgan wiped his bloody bayonet clean on the grass.

'I should think zombies would spread like wildfire if there was no-one around to keep them under control. They'd scare the living daylights out of everyone and you'd only be safe behind locked and barred windows and doors,' Marsh said, once he had caught his breath.

'That's what I thought. All it would take would be one zombie. It bites a few folks and then you've got a few more zombies. Before you know it, you're overrun by the buggers.'

'What's stopping that happening, then?' Wells wondered.

'God, you lot are cheerful,' Matthews complained under his breath. 'We've just fought back a major counter-attack; there's another one likely any minute; and you're all debating the end of the world.'

'There's not a lot stopping an outbreak happening, from what I can see,' Marsh said, making a mental note to raise the issue with the Colonel.

'Couldn't we just drop a few zombies into some German cities and let them end the war for us?' Morgan suggested.

'Taff, that just wouldn't be right. We don't fight civilians. We're soldiers,' Wells said.

'But the Hun have used their battleships to shell our towns and Zeppelins to bomb our cities,' Morgan persisted. 'And we're blockading their ports, trying to starve them out. All of that is fighting civilians, isn't it?'

'I suppose so. And I bet that if you're devious enough to suggest it, then the other side has already thought it up as well,' Wells conceded. 'Alfie, you be sure to have a chat with the Colonel about this the next time you meet him.'

'Aren't you forgetting something while you're chatting grand strategy? Come on, we need to get dug in. We barely got started earlier and how long do you think it will be before they attack again?' Matthews did not wait for them to respond. He was already scratching at his foxhole with his trench shovel, not in the mood for speculation.

'Yes Sir, no Sir, three bags full Sir!' Sergeant Wells squawked at the Corporal like a music hall act. He reached for his entrenching tool to improve the position.

27

COUNTERATTACK

'Cambrai showed what the Corps could achieve. It
also highlighted our weaknesses.'

Hudson, O, 'One Hell of a War: The Memoirs of
Brigadier Oliver Hudson' (1934, London)

'**G**AS! GAS! GAS!' THE cry spread along the line. Despite having been on the receiving end of gas attacks, the experience
was still far from routine for the men of the Royal Zombie Corps.
Barely controlled terror was the experience of the British defenders as
they struggled into their protective gear.

The Germans dispensed with the artillery. Instead, gas cylinders created a cloud of gas which would drift over the British bridgehead.
The defenders checked their masks, knowing the approaching cloud
signalled another attack. Any doubt ceased as a mixture of smoke and
gas shells started landing on the British positions.

'We can't risk bringing the tigers forward until we need them,' Wells said to Marsh through his respirator. 'If that's chlorine, we'll get one use out of them.' He recognised how vulnerable the tigers were to certain gases. Depending upon the gas used, it may deteriorate the effectiveness of the zombies to a state where they would have to be disposed of following combat. While zombies did not breathe, gases such as chlorine would damage the soft tissues, especially the eyes. Zombies could function without working eyes, using a range of senses, but damaged, they became much less effective as weapons.

'I doubt that anywhere around here will be safe from the gas,' Marsh replied. 'They're going to gas the whole bridgehead, and I'm worried. These Germans seem to understand what they're doing, they've got flamethrowers and gas. They were ready to deal with our tigers. I hope Simpson's got the goggles ready for the tigers, because if this is chlorine gas, the tiger's eyes are going to go first.' After their previous experience with gas, goggles had been issued to help protect the zombies. Putting a pair on a zombie was not the easiest task, especially for soldiers who were not handlers.

'Let's just hope it's only chlorine gas, because if it's Yperite, or something else, we're in trouble.' Wells said, scratching at his exposed neck. Everyone knew he was referring to the yellowish gas which stank of onions and mustard. It had first been used by the Germans at Ypres earlier in the year. Yperite was not quick acting, but the gas masks provided little protection, with the gas creating horrific blisters on the skin, soaking through the clothes. Contact would not likely kill, but it could cause painful injuries to develop over the course of the next day.

'Well, the cloud's a sort of greenish-yellow,' Marsh observed. 'So it could be Yperite, or chlorine, or White Star? Hell, who knows what else they'll have mixed?' At least the soldiers would be protected from the mixture of chlorine and phosgene, known as White Star. Their masks were more than capable of handling the concoction, but the tigers would still be damaged by the chlorine.

A runner dived into their cover behind the wall. 'Sergeant, message from Lieutenant Simpson,' he said, his voice muffled by the mask having sprinted through the embryonic gas clouds wearing his respirator.

'What does he want?' Marsh asked, aware for the first time of his own respirator muffling his voice.

'He has eighty tigers on hand after the last attack. He orders you to hold until relieved.'

Eighty tigers were many more that they had begun with, a phenomenal number for Marsh to coordinate in their defence, a greater gathering than he had managed on any previous occasion. He wished Mullen was available to help him, worrying about how badly injured the man was. The unit did not carry enough goggles for so many tigers, and many tigers would be degraded when they encountered the gas.

'Hang on, hold until relieved? Doesn't the Lieutenant know about the gas?' Marsh asked, worried another German onslaught, one which took advantage of the reduced the effectiveness of the tigers, might be one assault too many. Even a vast number of tigers could be overcome by a clever enemy, and Marsh suspected they faced an exceedingly clever enemy.

'There was no gas when I left the Lieutenant. Of course, it's everywhere now, so I'm sure he knows about it.'

'Alfie, you're in charge out here. You're the handler. If you're not happy, you need to let Simpson know. Anything that's going on here will affect both companies and you'll need Simpson on board,' Wells said, reminding Marsh the whole of the Corps' combat resources were committed in the bridgehead.

'You're right Josh.' Marsh turned to face the runner again. 'Let the Lieutenant know I think the gas changes the situation. Unless we get more support from the infantry, we won't be able to hold off another determined German assault. They know exactly how to deal with our tigers. We're neutralised and need to be replaced on the front line.'

'You sure about that Sarge? We can't give up the bridgehead,' the runner said, his disappointment not masked by his respirator.

'Make it clear to him, we need more men or we'll be pulling back,' Wells interrupted, explaining the decision he knew Marsh would have to face. 'Now get going before it's too late. If we're not replaced, the bridgehead will collapse.'

Without another word, the runner sprinted off into the growing cloud of smoke and gas.

'Matthews, go right and check everyone's ready. Stay there and keep a handle on the situation,' Wells ordered. 'I'll go left.'

'Wait!' Marsh shouted through his respirator as the two men moved. 'Keep a close watch on what's going on. If the tigers lose effectiveness, we'll have to pull back.'

'Will do.' Matthews replied. 'We'll hold on.'

'Oh, and get my message along the line so everyone knows the plan.'

After Matthews and Wells disappeared into the smoke, the first signs of enemy movement were reported.

'Alfie, a lad, swears he saw something moving in the smoke,' Morgan said, having passed the message on. 'He says the smoke lifted for a fraction of a second and he saw waves of German infantry advancing.'

'So, no storm-troopers then?' Marsh asked.

'A fraction of a second Alfie, that's all he glimpsed. He had no chance to take in any details, but he was clear there were a hell of a lot of Germans.'

'They're going to wear us down with sheer numbers.' Marsh knew the fight would be bloody. Regular German infantry, in vast numbers, would stand little chance against his tigers in a normal battle. However, they would get close because of the smoke, and the gas would degrade the tigers. Something niggled at him. Why the change in tactics? The enemy had already shown they were ready for the tigers with their storm-troopers and widespread use of flamethrowers. What were they up to?

'Enemy to the front!' A rifle went off, pulling Marsh out of his reverie and back to the real world.

Once again, the Germans closed in on the British bridgehead, this time outnumbering the few hundred defenders. Weapons sounded along the line, the rate of fire much slower as the defenders struggled with the encumbrance of their gas masks. The flow of the battle tilted in favour of the attackers in the areas visible to Marsh. A crescendo of desperate rifle fire, from further along the line, informed him the attackers were almost among the defenders again. He sent the command to the tigers to advance, knowing Simpson would not have been able to find enough pairs of goggles to protect the vulnerable eyes of the zombies and the gas would have already degraded the effectiveness of many of his tigers.

An open line of grey-coated attackers emerged from the cloud in front of Marsh's position, and all thoughts of the bigger picture fled his mind. The attackers appeared other-worldly, their faces replaced by huge masks with vast glinting eye-pieces. Each soldier advanced several paces away from his neighbour, not bunched together shoulder to shoulder, as would have been the case earlier in the war. A shiver of fear ran down Alfie's spine, and at the back of his mind, he knew the emotion would drive the tigers on to more ferocious behaviour.

All around, the men of the Royal Zombie Corps opened fire, a cacophony of noise from a wide range of different weapons. The enemy was already close enough for Marsh to use his shotgun. He opened fire, hearing others equipped like him making use of their shotguns. Troops tasked as bombardiers bowled their grenades at the enemy, desperate to stop the overwhelming tide of advancing grey soldiers, further ranks emerging from the smoke. The Germans took horrific casualties facing the close-combat firepower of the defenders, but still they advanced at a steady trot, the front ranks breaking into their final sprint.

Quick as a flash, several among the German ranks were thrown backward as they were impacted not by bullets, but by darting zombies. Marsh paused, his mouth falling open in shock at the brutal speed of the zombie attack. He watched a sprinting tiger leap through the air, crashing into a German. Both fell to the ground and the frenzied tiger tore into the man before selecting another target. The tiger jumped frog-like from an almost prone position, straight onto the back of a nearby German.

Cheers emerged along the British line. The tigers attacked with the same overwhelming violence elsewhere. Certainly, in front of Marsh, the German advance faltered as panicked men focused on the terrifying attack of the zombies. Clusters of Germans formed, using their numbers to protect themselves against the tigers. The groups were almost like the infantry squares of the musket era, designed to protect against the ravages of cavalry. The attack stalled, the enemy no longer advancing.

'Keep firing!' The shout spread in response to the slackening of fire as the defenders watched the spectacle. The clumps of Germans were vulnerable to the sustained firepower of the defenders.

Already, new tigers reanimated and joined the fight. Marsh knew those still wearing gas masks would not be as effective in their violence. Although tigers used their hands and nails, their teeth were their most effective weapons. These new tigers would not yet be degraded by the gas. Once the Germans withdrew, there may even be a few effective tigers still available.

A bright flare of red off to his right caught Marsh's attention. A zombie staggered, burning brightly, out of a concealing cloud of gas. To the left of Marsh's position, more flares glared in the drifting clouds of smoke and gas. A jet of liquid flame flew across the battlefield right in front of him, turning a zombie into a burning torch. Marsh watched horrified as another jet of flame hit a knot of German soldiers who were doing battle with a tiger. All burned. On some level, he understood the Germans were already doomed. The zombies would have overwhelmed them. Yet, it was horrifying to observe the enemy's desperate calculation in action.

Another wave of attackers passed through the stalled German formation. As they closed on the British position, the tigers were being destroyed along the entire German line by the efforts of the flamethrowers, storm-troopers also closing in to deal with individual tigers while the regular German infantry returned to the advance. Before he had time to call out that the flamethrowers should be targeted, the Germans broke again upon his position.

Marsh parried a bayonet thrust with his shotgun. A sliver of wood was hacked out of the butt, close to his hand, but he deflected the blade from his body. Stepping back and twisting his weapon, Marsh fired off a shot at point blank range. The German in front of him flew backwards with the impact, much of his torso shredded. Reloading, Marsh did not have time to select another target. The next assailant fell upon him, thrusting with a long bayonet. Again, Marsh fired his shotgun into his attacker, this time the round smashed the man's rifle as the fragments peppered the German's chest. The attacker dropped to the ground in agony, but more enemies filled the space he vacated.

Marsh threw his shotgun to the ground, unable to keep up with the pace of the enemy attack. He gave ground to keep out of reach of a probing bayonet. Drawing his new sword, he remembered he did not have any real training in how to use it, but the blade would give him a defence against the bayonets which kept thrusting toward him. All around, the surviving British gave ground, many of them bloodied, several falling. The Germans pushed them back, and with the canal behind, there was nowhere to go, nor any way to escape contact with the enemy.

Marsh stumbled on something that caught on his heel. He fell to the ground, twisting his ankle on the way. The impact of the hard ground made him lose his grip on his sword. Disarmed, he watched, terrified, as a German drew himself up to smash the butt end of his rifle into his face. The man was pale, his face drawn out as if from a poor diet. A long moustache stuck to his face with the sweat of his exertions, his gas mask long lost. Marsh noticed all of this as time seemed to slow to a halt. He reached out with his mind but could sense no tigers nearby. He noticed an absence. Few tigers were left functioning on the bridgehead. Yet he could sense they were away from the combat areas, probably with Simpson. The enemy anti-tiger countermeasures were effective.

Stars appeared across Marsh's vision as the rifle butt slammed down on his head, a glancing blow. Anything else would have killed him. The pain stunned and paralysed him. He had no clarity of thought, neither calling for his tigers or moving his hands to protect his head from the German. His assailant, seeing his prey still, raised the rifle to strike again. Marsh closed his eyes, waiting for the impact, knowing there was nothing stopping it. He had reached the end. This was it. He would die on a foreign battlefield, not a brave hero, just hurt and empty, suffering pointless pain.

The blow did not fall, instead there was a snarl. Marsh opened one eye. The German was no longer there. He raised himself onto an elbow. A solitary tiger savaged the man who had attempted to kill him. Marsh could not sense the creature, stunned as he was. He opened his other eye, but the sickening double vision made him close it tight.

The German fought fiercely with the tiger, holding the snapping jaws back with the barrel of his rifle. The man had already been bitten on the cheek. A flap of skin hung free. Marsh rolled over, pulling off his gas mask as he vomited, his head spinning from the fight. In the background, he noticed British voices and the snarls of more tigers. He breathed deeply, the air clear of gas.

'Nein!' The German shouted, pushing the tiger away.

No longer interested in the man it had been attacking, the zombie ran off to attack another target. Something was not quite right. Through his daze, Marsh could not put his finger on it. The terrified German looked him in the eye before scrambling to his feet and fleeing from the fight, hand held to his wounded cheek.

Someone grabbed Marsh by the shoulders, dragging him across the uneven ground. He did not know how much time had passed. His head was fuzzy, and he had a nagging doubt he was missing something important, something about the German with the bitten cheek.

'Come on lads, let's get him back across the canal before Hun starts tossing more gas at us or realises we've legged it.' Marsh recognised the voice but could not place it. Exhausted, he slipped out of consciousness again.

Marsh came to his senses in an aid station on the British side of the canal. It took him a while to establish this, fading in and out of consciousness. Every time he floated back to consciousness, he was lulled by the warmth of the blanket and the comfort his body took from the low-slung stretcher. Despite this, the noisy bustle of the place helped him to focus his senses. The moans, sometimes screams, of the other injured, helped him to reconnect, as did a familiar and unpleasant reminder of latrines. The stench wafted past him in waves, driven by passing bodies. He soon established the surrounding voices were speaking English. Yet, some accents were unfamiliar. When he opened his eyes, braving what he feared would be a painful experience, a medical orderly tended to him. The orderly explained he had suffered a concussion from a blow to his head. A little rest was required, and he would soon be back with his unit.

The forecasted rest turned out to be far shorter than Marsh expected. He was not sure how he felt about this. His guilt towards others standing in the way of danger in his stead fought against the relief of being out of mortal peril. As he had been pondering this dilemma, members of the military police passed through the aid station. They were on the lookout for any member of the Royal Zombie Corps.

Their orders were to gather the walking wounded and get them back into the care of the Corps at the earliest possible moment. The MPs had been efficient in their work, overwhelming the protests of the medical staff, deflecting the inquiries of doctors, and rounding up the walking wounded before them. Every challenge from the medical staff was met with signed orders from a higher power. Besides this, the MPs noted down the names of those too badly injured to police up, not wanting the valuable men of the Royal Zombie Corps to disappear into the vast casualty clearing system which supported the British armies in France.

The ragged procession set off, many injured men leaning upon one another for support, friends and acquaintances catching up with each other when opportunities arose. The ground was firm, the road mostly intact, the odd crater the only evidence of fighting as they moved away from the front line. Many of the buildings remained in good condition, spared by the rapid British advance. Yet all expected this to change now the advance had stalled. The British had pushed the frontline from the distant churned up battlefield to new positions along the route of the canal.

Behind a farm building, a couple of lorries awaited passengers. 'Load up lads!' An MP shouted. 'We've advanced so far, it's going to take you a while to get back to your camp.'

'Where's that then? Have we moved it forward already?' a private asked. The man was Hanson, Marsh remembered, his mind still fragile from the concussion.

'You're going back to where you started,' the MP replied.

'You're pulling us out of the line, then?' Hanson asked, unable to hide the optimism in his voice.

'Well, you ain't bloody good for anything else right now. Have you seen yourself?' The MP grimaced. He did not need an answer from the private. 'We're just going to hold the ground. Hun has got it into his head that he wants it back. I heard it from Lloyd George's barber himself.' There were a few titters at the joke.

'As if he's ever seen a haircut,' someone muttered.

The rest of the journey was uneventful and uncomfortable. With minimal suspension, the lorries bumped along the road. The backs of the vehicles were open to the elements and, from their vantage point, the men noticed the passing evidence of the war. This damage was clear as they crossed the old front line, the launch point of the assault. All the way back, pioneers policed the battlefield, repairing roads and barricades, and recovering corpses. Engineers from the Royal Tank Corps swarmed over the many broken down tanks lining the route. Some vehicles would be salvaged and repaired for future use. The sheer number of damaged vehicles was astounding. Marsh understood the British had deployed vast numbers of tanks, but it was impressive seeing this many of the metal monsters, even if these were the vehicles which had fallen out of the advance.

For a while, Marsh was anxious about a German plane, or a confused friendly one, attacking the vulnerable vehicles as they travelled along the road. Several times, low-flying aircraft drew the attention of the passengers. Fortunately, these were all friendly. At least, they were presumably friendly, as the passing aircraft did not strafe the slow-moving column the lorries were ensnared in. Yet Marsh's worries faded into an uneasy sleep as his exhausted body made the bumpy ride seem like a comfortable bed.

His dreams were fractured, the stresses of the battle bleeding out in his sub-conscious mind. The unsteady movement of the lorry threatened to throw him from his sleep. The image of a pale German soldier cycled through his dreams. He sought to process the danger he had been in, the blow to his head vividly recalled and repeated. It did not matter how he raised his arms to protect his head, the German still rained down repeated blows, each connecting. His arms did not move fast enough to provide protection. The hungry German developed in his mind, the tear on his cheek growing as if the zombie bit at him from the inside. The man grew ever more enraged, taking on the characteristics of a zombie, the rage less focused as he snapped at Marsh, biting deep into the flesh of the raised protective arms.

Marsh awoke with a start as the lorry exited a metalled road onto a bumpier track. The slumbering men were hardly disturbed. Little was visible from the back of the vehicle, just empty ploughed fields and a solitary building in the distance. The lorry struggled up the track, the incline of the hill forcing it to slow. It picked up speed again, having cleared the brow of the hill. The camp came into sight. The guards waved them through a series of sturdy fences, military police providing the security. They travelled on to the inner compound, where the men of the Royal Zombie Corps were based along with their charges.

'Bloody hell, Alfie,' Wells exclaimed as they were reunited. 'You're rough. Matthews said you'd taken a knock to the head.'

'I'm still a bit out of sorts.' Marsh unpacked his kit. They were in a roughly finished wooden barrack block which had been built for them. The room was adequate and far better than a tent, with beds for four men ranked as sergeants. The building was much more spacious than the open plan barrack block crowded full of the lower ranks. A lit stove in the centre of the room gave out just enough heat to offset the draft from the poorly fitted window. It also gave off enough smoky fumes to make the room smell, despite the chimney.

'I knew you'd be back soon enough, so I saved you a bunk.'

'What happened then?' Alfie sat down and lit the cigarette Wells offered him. He coughed, an occasional smoker, but Wells gave him the whole packet. 'Last thing I remember, there were Germans everywhere. I ended up in a fight with one. He beat me down to the ground before running off. Then there's a blank before I remember being dragged off. Everything after is a complete blank until I woke up with medical orderlies all around me.'

'Matthews found you,' Wells explained. 'He stumbled over you as we pulled back. You were sprawled across the ground and Tom dragged you back by your webbing. He said you were in and out of consciousness, rambling about how some German had shouted at a tiger. Anyhow, he got you back to the bridge, the lads got you across it, and then it was off to an aid station. That was the last we saw of you.'

'A German shouted at a tiger?' Marsh asked, a thought tickling the back of his mind.

'What?' Wells was puzzled. 'Oh, yes. You'll have to check with Tom, but he said it was something about a German getting bitten. You kept saying he shouted "No!" at a tiger and then the beast ran off. I've been thinking it through since Matthews told me. Do you think the German was a handler?'

'I'm not sure.' The memory played through Marsh's mind. The pieces made sense. 'I don't think he was a handler. The Germans would never have let him close to our lines without guards if he was. But perhaps something happened during their assault. Perhaps when he was bitten, he was infected. I didn't think it worked that quickly, but the tiger responded to him. It happened right as I lost control of the zombies. A hit to the head seems to be a pretty effective way to break my link with them.'

'So, if they've got handlers now, we're going to have problems?' Wells asked.

'I'm pretty certain the man didn't have a clue what was happening. He'll not work it out. At least I hope he won't,' Marsh replied before they both fell silent.

'How many of us got away? Did we stop the counterattack?' Marsh asked, interrupting the thoughtful silence which hung between them while they considered the possibility of German handlers.

'The unit's intact. We've still got stragglers, like yourself, making their way back. The Rifles had it far worse. It would have been a disaster if Simpson hadn't been there.' Wells raised an eyebrow to underscore his words. 'You've got to hand it to the bastard. When it mattered, he came up with the goods. He's a useless bastard most of the time, but after you lost control of the tigers, he got the other handlers to rally the beasts long enough for us to withdraw. He'll probably get another medal for it.'

'Good God! He'll be insufferable.'

'He's already insufferable. But we knew he had a gong, and no fluke; the man has guts. Just a shame he doesn't have the brains to go with them.'

'How many of the tigers came back with us?'

'Not enough. We'll be up against it, rebuilding with what we have. They're still bringing in fresh infections from the battlefield and there should be enough to pull the unit back together, but it'll take a while.

We'll also need a few living replacements as well for the men we lost from among the assault troops.' Wells scratched the tip of his nose, thinking through the death of Scott and the probabilities for the future. 'I'd say that's us done for this campaigning season.'

'I thought we'd end the war this year,' Marsh thought out loud. 'We should have smashed through at Cambrai.'

'Maybe, but we've shown it can be done, especially with what we've achieved with the tigers. One more good attack in the spring should be enough to make the Germans crumble. The Americans will be here by then as well. The Hun won't stand a chance.'

AFTERWORD

T HE INITIAL IDEA FOR this story came in 2015, when I experimented with some dictation software. The BBC History Magazine had published transcriptions of oral history interviews with veterans of the Great War to commemorate the centenary. I was intrigued and wondered if I could dictate something similar. After half an hour with the microphone, I had a thousand words and the start of a counterfactual history story.

By the end of 2015 I started writing, influenced by a recent re-reading of 'The Third World War' by General Sir John Hackett, a classic piece of counterfactual historical writing. Without realising, I was also influenced by 'World War Z' by Max Brooks, itself influenced by Hackett's work. Other influences included the Harry Turtledove series 'The Great War' and 'American Empire', and 'The Bloody Red Baron', part of the 'Anno Dracula' series by Kim Newman.

Initially, I split this story into four separate episodes, but it works better as a story. These instalments were published separately but are recombined into this single edition.

Although not explained in the story, the Spanish Flu runs parallel with the zombie infection. This was drawn down from several pieces of research which suggest the Spanish Flu was present in Europe for a while before the famous 1918 outbreak. Some theories suggest it may even have been circulating among the armies in the trenches. Given the recent global experience of Coronavirus, I'm happy with how I've treated this aspect of the story.

Many of the locations in this book are based on actual sites. Bringing them to life, in a fictional sense, has been a challenge. Sometimes, this is because of the lack of source material to illustrate them. In Blood, Mud and Corpses, the Richborough site is a particular case. The importance of the port and later reincarnations in the 1930s and 1940s are largely forgotten, even in local memory. Likewise, the troop staging camp at Étaples is also fictionally recreated, with only the mutiny by Australian troops based upon actual events. Notably, Étaples has become central in some interpretations of the origin of the Spanish Flu.

The Battle of Arras is the primary historical setting for Tigers On The Western Front. This battle took place between 9th April and 4th May 1917 as a series of eight battles. Arras saw some limited successes for the British. The Canadians and Australians were notable in their contributions, especially the systematic Canadian attack on Vimy Ridge. The first attack at Bullecourt took place on the 10th and 11th of April. This is the setting of my fictionalised assault alongside the ANZACs. Casualties were high during the historic battle, and supporting British tanks soon bogged down, suffered mechanical failure, or were defeated by enemy action. A lack of planning, because of the last minute orders to attack, may have contributed. I have written the tigers into this battle, with the outcome little changed.

During this phase of the war, the Allied tactics on the Western Front experienced rapid development. The raw volunteer armies of the British Empire gained hard-won experience in the trenches. In February 1917, tactical movement on the battlefield was reintroduced as more flexible combat formations were created based around light machine guns and fast movement. The slow 'walking' advances of 1916, which were not as widespread as popular belief suggests, were consigned to history. To a degree, my characters reflected this evolution, some with much less flexibility and willingness than others.

While Gas! Gas! Gas! continues the story at Arras, Tigers At Cambrai sees the deployment of an effective new weapon in the form of the tiger. With the Battle of Cambrai, I have largely kept to the historical details. As the men advanced, Albert Shepherd, a corporal in the King's Royal Rifle Corps, rushed a machine gun holding up the attack. He later took command of his fellows, getting a tank to support them. For these acts of gallantry, he was awarded the Victoria Cross. These events are played out in the story I have written.

Tanks were of critical importance at Cambrai, not so much to the outcome of the battle, but to the future of warfare and the successful British tactics of late 1918. Massed use of co-ordinated artillery and air support were also key features. Cambrai was the first large-scale combined arms battle where the British got their timings tolerably correct. The tank 'Red Devil' is fictional. However, 'Flying Fox' was a real tank, and did indeed collapse the bridge at Masnieres, preventing the British from expanding a very precarious bridgehead over the canal. This bridgehead was eventually liquidated, and I have sped up these events for my story. In the last weeks of the battle, not covered here, the British lost many of their gains. However, they proved combined arms assaults worked.

While writing a counterfactual history story, it has never been my intention to write an accurate description of the conditions faced by the men fighting in the trenches of the Western Front. My teacher's love of detail has shone through at times, but the story has been the driving force, not accuracy. My aim was to introduce a 'wild card' to the narrative, which would be played out against the actual events of the war. Taking the model of the British secret weapon, the 'tank', I explored the zombie as a new war-winning weapon. The twist on the usual zombie story is that a few people have a mysterious link to the creatures, able to control and manipulate them.

Foremost, this is a fictional story. Therefore, any errors and deviations from the historical events are deliberate or because of the failings of the author. Even with fictional zombies, this story cannot bring to light the genuine horror of the trenches. Several excellent eyewitness and historical accounts exist, and the reader may wish to pursue these for a more accurate reading of the history.

Walton-on-the-Hill, August 2022.

REVIEW REQUEST

I F YOU HAVE ENJOYED this book, I would be very grateful if you would leave a quick review on the book's Amazon page. You can scan the QR code below to find the Amazon page.

MAILING LIST & WEBSITE

Join C M Harald's mailing list for the latest information and offers. This includes a free copy of 'On Discovering A Zombie' and 'Point Zero'. These short stories are only available to subscribers.

In 'On Discovering A Zombie', Dr Hudson studies a patient who is suffering from far more than a controversial diagnosis of shell shock. This is a prequel to the RZC series.

'Point Zero' sees the culmination of the Zombie Eradication Programme reach its conclusion during the 1980s.

www.cmharald.net

ABOUT THE AUTHOR

C.M. Harald is a writer and high school history teacher. He lives in a small village just outside of London. He writes a range of historical, counterfactual and fantasy fiction.

C.M. Harald can be followed on his blog, Linktree, Facebook, TikTok, or on his mailing list.

f   facebook.com/CMHarald

♪   tiktok.com/@cmharald_author

Also By

Have you read them all?

In the Royal Zombie Corps Series

Blood, Mud and Corpses (RZC 1)

During the maelstrom of World War, an unknown threat arises. In a war which has already killed millions, a conscript discovers some of the dead are no longer staying dead.

Outbreak London (RZC 2)

1918, London. The zombies which have plagued the fighting of the Western Front find their way to the capital city of the British Empire. Caught up in the greatest zombie outbreak so far, can Alfie Marsh save himself and the British war effort?

Dead Handler (RZC 3)

Amidst the chaos of the Great War, the Germans have a new weapon. With Britain reeling following the zombie outbreak in London, the Central Powers launch their Spring Offensive. For the first time, Germany uses zombie soldiers in a last desperate attack to knock Britain and France out of the war before the vast resources of the USA are brought into play. To end the new zombie threat, the British despatch their leading zombie expert to duel with the notorious Dead Handler.

See the linktree for this author at linktr.ee/cmharald for

The Sands of War (RZC 4)

Accused of murder, Britain's leading zombie expert must choose between his conscience and the hangman's noose. Germany is spent, but undefeated. The Allies gather their strength to unleash a last offensive to end the war. To bring about a quicker conclusion, the British unleash the full horror of their zombie armies.